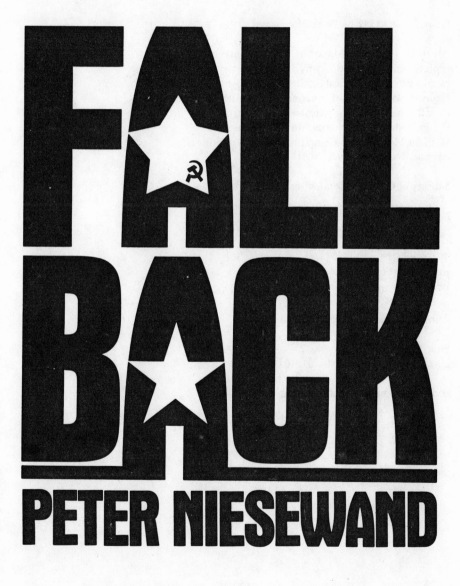

FALL BACK

PETER NIESEWAND

WILLIAM MORROW AND COMPANY, INC.

New York   *1982*

Library of Congress Cataloging in Publication Data

Niesewand, Peter.
    Fallback.

    I. Title.
PR6064. I33F3 1982   823'.914   81–11252
ISBN 0–688–00819–4   AACR2

Printed in the United States of America

First Edition
1 2 3 4 5 6 7 8 9 10

BOOK DESIGN BY MICHAEL MAUCERI

To Nonie

NOTHING DISTINGUISHED NUMBER 5/6 from other drab brown doorways along Pushkin Street. The stairs leading to it were worn and dusty. They had been swept, along with everything else on the sidewalk, by squat old women with birch-stick brooms, but nothing except rain and snow can really keep down Moscow dust.

Filipp Ivanovich Levin walked quickly, muffled against the after-noon frost in a shabby black coat and a gray woolen scarf. His eyes glanced toward the doorway as he drew level with it, but his head did not move.

A man, dressed in the same dark colors and shabby cut of clothes, had been in the crowd filing out of the Metro station and had walked fifty yards behind along the same route. Levin noticed him because he was apprehensive about being followed. He turned right and so, thirty seconds later, did the man.

Levin crossed the road at the traffic lights and turned right again. The man stayed behind him, casual, apparently indifferent. Levin became aware of his own heartbeat, and he felt automatically in the pocket of his coat for the small package, lumpy against his gloved hands. His breath misted into vapor, and the touch of the air chilled his skin.

He walked on, uncertain. The man might be KGB—probably was. Levin's mouth became dry at the prospect. He swore this would be his last drop: If he could complete this one safely, he would never take the risk again. Just this one time.

It was natural that because of his position in the Chief Artillery Directorate, Levin would be subject to periodic security checks. The man behind him could be part of such routine surveillance. If that was so, he should do nothing to alert suspicion. Levin walked on, willing his feet to keep an even pace, forcing himself not to look around again. He was a man taking the early winter air, nothing more.

He passed a *pivnoyzal*, a working-class beer parlor, and on impulse went in, slipping the small package into his trouser pocket as he checked his overcoat and hat at the counter. It was hot inside and not yet full. He drank standing at the communal table, and through the window he watched the mist blurring the darkening street. The man, if he was still following, did not enter.

Levin felt his heartbeat gradually subside and decided he was becoming too jumpy. The KGB would never wait in the cold street. They would want to know if he was meeting anyone in the *pivnoyzal*, to whom he spoke, what he did.

When he had finished, he collected his coat and hat and headed for Pushkin Street. The temperature was dropping. The wind felt like ice against his face and down his neck, where his scarf had been carelessly wrapped. Levin shrugged the scarf into place as he glanced casually up and down the street. Those hurrying along did not notice him.

The man was nowhere in sight.

Levin wanted to make the drop quickly now, but, even so, he deliberately overshot 5/6 Pushkin Street before making a final check, peering back between the trucks and two Volchyas for a sign of the KGB presence.

Satisfied, he retraced his steps and opened the door of the apartment block. It was gloomy inside but warm. A single naked bulb hung in the center, unlit. Levin glanced to his right and saw the dark shape of the radiator where he expected to find it. He waited a few seconds unmoving while his eyes adjusted properly and his ears strained for evidence of others. The building was silent, as if deserted.

Levin quietly crossed to the radiator, warming himself as he peered cautiously behind it.

The radiator was fastened to the wall with special hooks, which left a gap of about three inches. Farther down, and to the side, was another hook.

Levin stripped a glove off one hand and pulled the package from his pocket: a matchbox, wrapped in brown paper and bound with tape and thin wire. He noticed his hand trembled slightly as he leaned forward to attach the package to the hook, making him fumble his first attempt, and for a sickening moment he thought he might drop it, unreachable, down the back. Then it caught and held.

His breath came out in a rush. Thank God. Next time, he would make sure he used a magnet.

There would be a next time, of course, he knew that. The game of roulette would go on until the day he succeeded in defecting, or was caught, or betrayed. But never again would he go to 5/6 Pushkin Street. He had made his cache, and it would be collected later when he gave the signal.

He hurried back into the cold, toward the Metro and a public telephone.

In the crowded concourse, Levin dialed a number and let it ring three times. He hung up and dialed again. It rang twice before he replaced the receiver and turned away.

The voice was friendly but with a hint of authority. "Something the matter, comrade? The telephone is not working?"

Levin felt himself start and fought for composure. The same man? Hard to tell. So many people were dressed alike, looked alike.

Levin gave a thin smile. "Busy," he muttered as if it was his own fault. "I'll try some other time."

DAVID CANE WAITED CASUALLY BY the elevator doors, drumming the fingers of his right hand unconsciously against his thigh, and watched the lights flicker from floor to floor.

Cane yawned. He needed sleep. His son had picked up a virus and had run a fever which peaked at 103 degrees sometime around 2 A.M. the previous night when, drenched with sweat, he began mumbling the incoherent nightmares of a six-year-old. It was the first time the boy had seemed seriously ill, and Dr. Spock, hauled from the bookshelves after years, counseled quick medical advice.

Maryann phoned the family doctor and, as usual, got the answering service. She left a message, asked him urgently to come. After an hour Cane was on the verge of telephoning his office for help. The Defense Intelligence Agency looked after their men pretty well— and, by extension, their families—and could be relied on in emergencies to send one of the DIA doctors around. Cane decided to give it another five minutes before bothering them, and he was glad he did because the boy's fever broke suddenly and he fell into a deep sleep. After that, there was nothing for him and Maryann to do but change the sweat-soaked sheets and go to bed themselves.

At five-thirty Cane was awakened by the far-off shrilling of the doorbell, and, feeling punch-drunk, he stumbled over to the spare-room window where he could see the front door. He flicked a specially installed switch controlling the hall light two rooms away, also serving to distract whoever had come while he got the chance to look them over. It was a routine precaution for unexpected night visits.

Cane groaned and closed his eyes for a moment: the doctor. Then he pulled on a bathrobe and went to answer the door.

Considering both men had spent most of the night awake, they were surprisingly civil to one another. The doctor took ten minutes checking the boy but decided not to wake him. He said he'd return around noon for tests but thought the worst was over. Then he accepted a glass of whiskey, as Cane had been afraid he would when he tentatively offered one.

The sky was lightening and birds were brawling in the trees when Cane finally crawled back into bed. The sheets on his side were cold. So was his skin, and his wife instinctively rolled away, leaving him a warm patch to sleep on.

It seemed his eyes had been closed no longer than five minutes when the alarm shrilled in his ear, and Cane, gritting his teeth, mumbled, "Goddam, goddam."

He felt slightly better after a hot shower, and worse after negotiating the Washington morning traffic to get to the DIA parking lot.

Now, when he was expected to have his wits about him, he found it hard to stop yawning.

The elevator had paused a couple of floors below but was finally moving again. Cane tensed as many muscles of his big body as he could locate at short notice and took several deep breaths. He guessed he was as ready now as he would be at any point this side of eight hours' rack time.

The doors slid open and he held out his hand.

"Professor Ross? I'm David Cane. Come this way, sir."

Martin Ross stopped himself from wincing at the strength of Cane's grip and in turn squeezed harder.

"Good to meet you, Mr. Cane."

They fell into step along the hall leading to the heavy security door. Cane flipped a metal plate at the side and punched the entry code on numbered buttons out of Ross's sight. The lock clicked open, and when they had passed through, the door slammed shut solidly behind them.

The corridor leading to the DIA Director's suite was long and thickly carpeted, and there was no sign of anyone else. Ross noticed closed-circuit TV cameras fixed at intervals to the ceiling. The doors they passed were closed and somehow gave the impression of being locked, with empty offices beyond.

As a member of the Institute for Defense Analyses, Ross had been called to the National Security Agency complex at Fort Meade, Maryland, on many occasions during the last dozen years, but the atmosphere there was busier, more businesslike somehow. Security was certainly strict, but there were people moving about, walking, talking. You could hear typewriters as you were escorted to the offices of the NSA director. You could go down to the shopping center and see people dropping off clothes at the dry cleaner's, all within a remarkable eighty-two-acre complex, guarded by two circles of barbed-wire-topped fencing and one five-strand electrified wire.

The contrast between Maryland and the Defense Intelligence Agency—or the small part of it he had seen so far—could hardly have been greater. The silence, the feeling of being watched—Ross glanced up as they passed another ceiling-mounted camera, hell—the *fact* of being watched, not only here but even in the elevator coming up, a camera lens glimpsed through the ventilation grids, made him uncomfortable.

"How do you survive in a place like this?" Ross asked his escort. "Can they pick up our voices too?"

Cane glanced over and grinned. "You'll get used to it," he said.

Ross shook his head. "No, sir," he said slowly. "You're used to it. You're a young man. I'm fifty-eight years old, and I'm used to my own office and to Princeton University. I'm even used to that damn corridor at the NSA."

"The thousand-footer?"

"Nine hundred and eighty feet, Mr. Cane. It threw me for a long time, but now I don't mind when I take a few minutes walking down it. At least I don't feel George Orwell was right."

"It nearly is 1984, sir. George Orwell was wrong."

"Smile for the camera." They passed under another closed-circuit lens.

"We're almost there," Cane said.

"Do they have these things in the john?"

"Yes, sir." Cane grinned again. "Especially in the john. The Director gets to see those videos himself."

Professor Ross smiled back. "Now I know they're not listening in. Makes me feel happier."

They stopped at a door with a brass nameplate: Lt. Gen. Lyndon Yardley. Cane pushed it open.

A secretary, who Ross guessed was perhaps five years younger than himself, and who was wearing a bright shade of red lipstick suitable for a woman decades younger, looked up from her electric typewriter and smiled expansively.

"Good morning, Professor Ross. The Director will see you right away. Can I get you some coffee?" Her accent was pure Brooklynese.

"Good morning," Ross replied. "That would be fine. Black please, no sugar."

"David?" Ross noticed the slightly arch tone with which she addressed the young man behind him. So there were favorites in 1984.

"Thanks, Lucy."

The secretary crossed from her desk and opened a pair of double doors. "Go right in," she said.

General Lyndon Yardley was sitting behind an enormous desk at the far end of a large office. Ross noticed both the desk and the room itself were about half the size again of those occupied by the Director of the National Security Agency—a sign of relative importance. He knew how bureaucracies operated and he was impressed.

As he walked slowly across, Yardley rose and came to meet him, his face wreathed in a broad smile of greeting that made Ross think he was expected to remember him from somewhere. As far as he knew, and he had an excellent memory, he had never seen Yardley before. A large hand came from behind and rested on his shoulder. Cane. Reassurance? Or did he think he was going to run?

Yardley's hand when Ross shook it was hard and cold.

"Good of you to come at short notice, Professor," General Yardley said. "Fort Meade keeps you pretty busy, of course, and your own business. How's everything going?"

"Pretty well." Ross settled into a leather armchair at the side of the office, with Yardley on a sofa facing him. Cane chose an easy chair and offered a pack of cigarettes.

Ross shook his head no. "I've given up," he said. "Good for my lungs, but bad for my weight."

Yardley looked at him in an assessing way, as if he were considering a purchase. "You are a bit overweight," the general agreed. "One hundred and eighty-three pounds at your medical last month. For your height and build, you have to lose thirty pounds."

Ross felt a stillness come over him. "Aren't you somewhat too important a man to worry about my weight, General?" he asked affably.

"We worry about many things, Professor." Yardley seemed to be choosing his words deliberately. "I worry because David over there smokes too much, although it doesn't seem to have affected his health. Not yet. I care about all our men."

"I am not one of your men, General."

"No." There was a silence while Yardley stared at him. "No," he said again, "you are an NSA man."

There was a trace of asperity in Martin Ross's voice. "I am my own man, General. I work essentially for myself. As you're no doubt aware because you are informed even about my present weight, I have a successful business as a computer design consultant. Partly because of this, I am also a member of the Pentagon's think tank at Princeton. And because the Institute for Defense Analyses serves the NSA, I do my best for them as I do my best for any client who comes to me. But I repeat, I am my own man." He finished, feeling he had been too vehement.

David Cane stared at a spot somewhere on the ceiling. General Yardley studied his large, square fingernails, which Ross noticed irrelevantly had been manicured. After a while Yardley said, a little distantly: "I'm glad to hear it."

At that moment the secretary brought in the coffee. She served Ross first, then Yardley, and finally—with a smile and leaning close to him—Cane, who winked at her. Thank God for Cane, Ross thought. A human being, at least. Yardley was hard to take, even for a few minutes. There was something about the man's attitude, an arrogance and a possessiveness that disturbed Ross. He was a man you didn't altogether like or trust, but one who was probably aware of your secrets, however big or small, while you knew almost nothing about him except that he paid someone to look after his fingernails.

Ross sipped his coffee and found it very hot. He placed the cup on a glass table beside him.

"How much time have you got, Professor Ross?" Yardley asked.

Ross shrugged. "I'm in Washington for the day. How long do you want?"

"I thought we might have lunch." Ross felt a twinge of irritation. "A working lunch, with David sitting in, of course, after we've had a preliminary discussion and, I hope, reached an agreement."

"Very well." It was not a particularly gracious acceptance, Ross realized, but it was the best he could do. Perhaps he was getting cantankerous in his old, and overweight, age.

Yardley rose abruptly and went to his desk, where he unlocked a drawer and took out a manila folder. It looked incongruous, bureaucratic, and ordinary against the mahogany desk, the thick pile carpet, and the leather chairs.

As he crossed back, Yardley extracted a sheet of paper and held it out to Ross. "You'll remember this," he said. "It's the secrecy pledge you signed when you started work for the NSA. And that's your signature at the bottom."

Ross did not take the paper, but looked up at him calmly. "Are you accusing me of breaking my pledge, General?"

"Good heavens, no."

"Then forgive me if I find your drawing it to my attention in this manner a little—let's say—insulting."

Yardley did not seem disturbed. "I hope it will become clear to you later," he said. "Meanwhile, I want to remind you of the pledge and"—he held up a placating hand as Ross seemed about to pull himself out of his chair—"to say that what we are about to discuss is undoubtedly the most sensitive and vital national matter you have ever dealt with. Whatever happens, whether you accept our proposition or not, you are never to discuss it, write about it, or allude to it even in the most general terms, ever, unless specifically authorized by myself or David. Not to anyone. Not to your wife, for example. Is that understood?"

Ross paused, uncertain whether he wanted to hear more. In thirty-five years of marriage, he couldn't remember keeping any professional matter totally secret from his wife. Elaine had the same security clearance he did and worked on many of the same projects. But he nodded slowly.

"Good," Yardley said. "Whether you agree to go further with this proposal or not, David will give you a cover story before you leave this afternoon. Now let's get down to business. What do you know about Soviet computers?"

Ross was caught off-balance. "*Soviet* computers?" he repeated. "Not very much. No one, as far as I know, knows much. Except that they're pretty far behind us."

"Why?"

Ross shrugged. "Marxist-Leninist theory. They started later. Stalin insisted on pure dogma, and that held everything back. Just as the Soviets weren't able to build an atomic or a hydrogen bomb until they'd accepted the theories of relativity and quantum mechanics, they couldn't develop computer technology either until they came to grips with the principle of cybernetics. It was a big ideological jump for them, and they didn't make it until Stalin died. But I'm sure you know that. Khrushchev started the movement. He realized Russia was far behind the world in technology because their scientists weren't being given freedom of research. So he ditched some of the dogma. That's how it happened."

"But they've made strides." Cane was talking this time, lighting up his second cigarette.

"Great strides," Ross agreed. "Mostly thanks to us."

"Copying." Cane again. General Yardley was sitting back on the leather sofa, relaxed, listening, the folder beside him. Ross had the impression it was now between himself and the young man. He felt better not having to deal with Yardley and turned to face Cane more directly.

"Exactly. They trade on the fact that the United States is an open society. We publish an extraordinary amount of information in specialists' journals, and we're happy to give demonstrations, lectures, slide shows, and anything else you care to name about the latest advances, because we're in the business of selling most of our discoveries. The Russians have almost certainly bought computers from us —using some foreign companies as a front, I suppose, and then shipping them off to Moscow. I don't know that for a fact, but I can't imagine they'd be without every American specimen worth having."

"That's true," David Cane said. "We've confirmed that."

"Well, there you are. We also meet Russians at international conferences from time to time. We share information."

"No, we don't."

Professor Ross smiled wryly back at Cane. "Well," he admitted, "*we* share with them. They don't share with us. Except sometimes they drop hints about big advances made in the Soviet Union, or enormous projects they've started but can't discuss yet. Occasionally we hear a rumor from some academician who seems to have had too much to drink that they're working on something amazing."

"Do you believe these stories?"

"It's not impossible. I guess it's improbable, though. We spend a good part of our time analyzing the leads they give us, but I think they're just stringing us along."

"*That is true.*" Ross looked sharply at Cane. He had slipped without warning into Russian.

Ross replied in the same language: "*You have talents I wasn't aware of, comrade.*"

"*It is a small thing,*" Cane said. "*My specialty is the Soviet Union.*"

"*Your accent seems excellent. You look like a White Russian too. I think in Moscow if you were to join me in a bottle of Starka at a restaurant, no one would think we were foreign. Except for our clothes.*"

"*I am afraid that half a bottle of Starka is too much for me to drink and still be sure of my tongue,*" Cane said.

"*You know the proverb. The sober man thinks what the drunkard says.*"

"*I think about keeping away from Dzerzhinskiy Square.*"

"*Everyone does. The KGB have long ears. Have you traveled much in Russia?*"

Cane shrugged. "*I have done some work there. Perhaps we will return together.*"

"I don't think so," said Ross, reverting to English. "When I go to Moscow again, it's going to be with an Intourist group."

Cane smiled faintly. General Yardley cleared his throat. "Now that you two are better acquainted," he said, "you ought to know that David here has been over to the other side on several occasions, working undercover, and he's unknown to the KGB."

"Can you be sure of that?"

"Pretty sure. He's been involved with a network of agents—well, the details don't concern us now, but there have been no brushes with the KGB. The agents remain in place, and David has gotten in and out without trouble."

"I'd like to know how," Ross observed. "They keep a pretty close scrutiny, as you know better than I."

"Let's leave that for later, shall we?" Yardley said.

Cane stubbed out his cigarette in an onyx ashtray and leaned forward. "I think we might let the professor have a look at our problem," he said.

General Yardley picked up the file and leafed through it. He extracted two typewritten sheets, stapled at the top left-hand corner, and handed them over without comment. Ross accepted the document and settled back against the brown leather, feeling the eyes of the man upon him: Yardley's gaze hard, appraising, remote; Cane's professionally interested, perhaps a little anxious, but basically friendly.

Ross knew this was his moment: He was now in charge. The reason for calling him to the DIA was contained here.

It was an extract from an intelligence report, apparently originating inside the Soviet Union. It was immediately clear that this was not the original but a sanitized, retyped version, although if the KGB laid their hands on it, they could probably track it back to its home department, perhaps to within ten or twenty people.

"Is this a digest?" Ross asked, glancing at Cane.

"It's verbatim for the parts you need to know," the agent said. "The rest was for another department."

Ross nodded and began to read carefully, taking his time. Cane reached automatically for another cigarette, avoiding Yardley's disapproving stare, and lit up.

He studied the professor without embarrassment.

He knew Ross's dossier, of course. Probably knew more about him than did his wife, Elaine, after three and a half decades of marriage. Cane doubted she was aware of two brief postmarital affairs. Ross had taken care to be discreet, and now thirty years had passed since the first, fifteen years since the second. There probably wouldn't be a third. His crisis had passed.

The Professor was sterile. Cane also knew that from the file. The computer had printed out the 1953 medical report, complete with Ross's sperm count at the age of twenty-seven—just three years younger than Cane. He and Elaine had obviously been trying for a child because there were doctors' reports on both of them. The result must have been a hard blow for Ross. He had his first affair shortly afterward with one of his students. Cane summoned up her photograph in his mind. Ross couldn't have chosen a more different woman. Blond where his wife was dark, gregarious where Elaine was private and studious. It lasted four months before the girl took up with a jock from the college football team and was soon pregnant.

The second affair came when Ross was forty-three, a more civilized one too, Cane recalled. Not hurried afternoons in a tiny studio apartment near a university campus, but weekends, even weeks at a time, in hotels in Los Angeles, San Francisco, and Washington, while Ross was supposed to be lecturing on computer technology and his wife continued her own research at home in a suburb a couple of miles from the Princeton University campus.

The computer had no record of Elaine Ross meeting either of the two women, and there was no reason to suspect she knew about them. For the last fifteen years, Ross had been faithful.

Now he was in late middle age, his once-black hair was gray and thinning, and his belly bulged over the belt of his trousers as he scrutinized the document. Cane noticed he read without glasses, and he was perfectly relaxed and in command of himself intellectually if not physically. It was clear he didn't like Yardley very much—the general tended to specialize in unfortunate first impressions—but Ross was not intimidated and could not easily be bullied. If things got difficult and Yardley wanted to use biographical leverage on him, Cane knew he would advise against it. Instinct told him Ross would laugh in their faces.

Ross finished reading and grunted. He returned the papers to Yardley, and Cane knew Ross would not have to ask for them again. They were committed to an extraordinary and voluminous memory.

Yardley replaced the document in the file and glanced over at his agent.

"What do you think?" said Cane.

"It makes sense," Ross said. "As I understand it, that's pretty much the way we operate our missile projects. What are *porokhovyye konfety* by the way?"

"Powder candies—the slang term for missiles."

"Hmmm. Well, I don't see anything immediately wrong there. But as I say, I'm not an expert in that field."

"We're rather excited about that report, Professor. The reason isn't obvious to you because we're talking about the state of *our* art —our knowledge of the Soviet missile program—and that's been top secret and out of your own areas of work for the NSA," Cane said. "But let me take you through it and see if I can make you as enthusiastic as I am. The code name, Special Collection, is a Soviet military doctrine to strike first, at any cost. You're aware of our own Cruise missile program, of course. A Cruise is computer-controlled, designed to fly in low, hugging the contours of the land, keeping close to hills and mountains, and so sneak in under Soviet radar. We *were* ahead on that one. We aren't now. We've also got a new shield for missiles which you probably haven't heard about. It doesn't deflect a radio signal in the ordinary way so that it bounces back and comes up as a blip on a radar screen; it absorbs it—a little like an acoustic tile. So in effect, our missiles will be invisible to everyone, including us."

"And our aircraft too, I suppose," Ross said, nodding appreciatively. "That's good."

"It is. Unfortunately, the Russians are on to that too. Add it together with the Special Collection doctrine of striking first, and the answer is we won't even know World War Three has started until our cities are in ruins and a lot of our missile bases have been taken out."

Ross looked at him speculatively. "I see why you smoke," he said. "It's not a happy thought."

"Exactly. And if this becomes public knowledge, there'll be an uproar. As it is, the President's a very worried man, and he demands that we do something about it."

"Why should Reagan lose sleep? If ever America produced a man who'd strike first, he's up there in the Oval Office right now."

Cane grinned. "Spoken like a true Democrat. Unfortunately, Moscow believes that too, so they're likely to be even faster on the draw than an ex-movie cowboy."

Yardley shifted uncomfortably and shot a disapproving look at his agent, but Ross noticed he did not intervene. This really was Cane's show.

"So that's the picture," Cane said. "We have to stop them. The question is, how? We feel the answer might be contained in the report you've just read."

Professor Ross frowned. "I don't see why. It's just a basic rundown of a missile computer setup."

"It's more than that. It tells us a lot of things we only suspected. For example, the computers at Soviet missile bases can be overridden by a central computer, five hundred feet underground in the Urals."

"Vologda base, near Sverdlovsk."

Cane nodded. "That's the one. The report makes it clear that the underground complex is so large that the entire Politburo *and* the Central Committee, their families, and a whole lot of hangers-on could hole up there in comfort for the duration. Of course, if Special Collection works, that wouldn't be longer than a day or two. We've got to make sure that Special Collection doesn't work. That's where you come in."

Ross pursed his lips. "I'm not an expert in the field, Mr. Cane," he said. "But it seems to me you need someone to invent a radar that gets around the problem of the absorbent shield. Then you'll see them coming."

"That wouldn't solve the problem, even if we were making prog-ress on such a thing and we aren't. There's still the problem of nukes getting in under the radar. It seems to us that the solution is some-where there, in the central computer. Let me give you a scenario. Feel free to shoot it down as hard as you like. Let's imagine we can get access to that central computer. Now in turn it's connected to all the other computers in every missile station in the Soviet Union—Kasputin Yar, Novaya Zemlya, Norilsk in Franz Josef Island, the whole bunch—right?"

"If you say so."

"Right. Take our word for it. And every missile has its own mini-computer on board, keeping it on course, at the right height, and guiding it to target. Okay?"

"The master computer is the one underground. The others at the stations would really be peripherals," Ross observed.

"And the onboard computer just accepts instructions and carries them out. That's right, isn't it? Good. Now the rationale for having continuous computer connections is to give the military a chance to reprogram any missile, or bank of missiles, at short notice and send them somewhere else. Get them to take out Los Angeles instead of San Francisco. Or destroy them in midair if the Politburo change their minds about a strike. So our problem is this: If we had access to the central computer, could we alter the program?"

"For all the Soviet Union's missiles?" Ross raised his eyebrows in astonishment.

"All of them."

"Good God." He paused in thought. "In theory, yes. But they'd probably notice and change them all back. It would be a waste of time."

"We'd have to make sure they didn't notice."

"Mr. Cane, a computer program is there for all authorized personnel to see. They can make it come up on a screen. And the problems are enormous. Let's assume for the sake of argument—and it's a big assumption—that you do get access to the master computer terminal. Let's say you know the passwords into the computer system. Let's even imagine you know the language."

Cane blew out a cloud of smoke. "Language?"

"Every computer system has its own programming language. There are enough of them, God knows. In the United States alone you can choose from ALGOL-60, ALGOL-68, COBOL, FORTRAN, LISP, SIMULA, SNOBOL . . . need I go on?"

"No."

"Perhaps the Russians have borrowed one of our languages. Perhaps they've invented their own. You'd have to know it, intimately and exactly. There's no room for error. Then you'd have to reorganize their basic program for every one of thousands of missiles in such a way that they wouldn't notice it."

"An impossible task?" Cane was looking quiet and guarded, disappointed. Yardley examined his nails in a distant way, as if they belonged to someone else and were objects of suspicion.

Ross stared at the ceiling. Finally, he said: "No. Not impossible. Terribly difficult, though. You would have to know the language and the original program. And all the other things I mentioned earlier. Then maybe you could alter it in a way the Russians wouldn't notice. Add something on, perhaps."

"For example?" Ross looked over at Cane and saw the reborn, almost boyish, enthusiasm.

"A new set of instructions," he said, shrugging. "Something that would be programmed into all the missiles, and which would take effect only after firing. This means the launch sequence would remain untouched."

"Wouldn't they notice it?"

"Not if it was accessible only by keying in a new password."

"Which they wouldn't know."

"Precisely."

Cane laughed triumphantly. "That's it!" he said. "We'll have them! And they wouldn't have a clue what was going on until those birds were in the air and not responding to commands!"

Yardley seemed to pull himself out of some reverie, but Ross was sure he hadn't missed a thing. "Just what would you propose keying into the missile computers?" he asked mildly.

"A new fail-safe code, perhaps. A further instruction necessary to keep them on course. If they didn't get that, they would abort: blow themselves up, crash into the sea. Whatever you want."

"And something to tell us they were on their way?" Yardley prompted.

"I suppose that could be arranged. I'd have to think about it."

"That's great!" Cane said.

"I'll let you have my ideas in writing."

"We need more than that," Yardley said. There was a stillness in the room again. The general stared at him in a peculiar way. Cane hunched forward in his chair, face serious, his big hands gripped together so the veins stood out clearly.

He spoke in Russian again, softly. *"You are a very special man, Martin,"* he said. *"You have talents shared by no one else in this country. A brilliance of mind. A command of the mother tongue. Computers are your life. No one else has all this. We want you to go with me to Vologda base and do this thing."*

Ross stared at him as if struck. He opened his mouth to refuse, but no words came. He felt short of breath.

"Go with me, Martin," Cane urged. *"I will look after you with my life, get you in to the master computer. We will train together, you and I, and you will grow to trust me as you would your own son. And I will care for you as if you were my father. We will not go until we are ready. Think of the stakes, Martin. We will save the world from war."*

"We will not save the world from war. We'll only save ourselves," Ross said at last, in English.

"We'll save our world, Martin. America . . . Europe. We will have time to retaliate. To destroy those who want to destroy us. To rid the world of communism."

"And Reagan will press the button."

"Him. Or the next president. Don't forget there's an election soon. Or the one after. It makes no difference. Our task is to prevent an aggression. The means for responding are already at hand. We will save our own families, our own countrymen. The war is not something we will start."

"I am an old man." At last, Ross was speaking to him in Russian, and Cane felt a wave of relief. A breakthrough. *"This is the work of the young. I am, as your friend there points out, fifty-eight years old and thirty pounds overweight. I have never killed another human being, and I'm frightened that this task of yours will involve killing."*

"No!" Cane said vehemently. *"No one will die. This must be carried out quietly and without anybody ever realizing we were there. If they even suspected American agents had been at their master computer, they would check everything a hundred times—perhaps erase the master program and start again. No killing. It must be done by stealth."*

Ross nodded slowly. *"That much is true,"* he said.

"Well? Will you go with me? I promise I will make it as easy as I can."

"I have to think."

"You can think. Do you want to discuss anything more?"

In English again, looking at Yardley: "And I want to tell my wife."

The general exhaled ponderously. "I don't know about that . . ." he said.

"Or I'll refuse now," Ross said firmly. "I'm not going into a thing like this without her knowledge and agreement. I can't live a lie for as long as it takes us to get the plan operational. And Mr. Cane here spoke about training."

"The name's David," Cane said. "We'll keep it as simple as we can. We just have to get you into some sort of condition. Not an Olympic athlete or anything."

"It's too late for that," Ross said ruefully.

"Just some basics. A little running, not much. Some unarmed combat in case you ever need it. If you're going to hang around Washington anyway, it's useful against muggers."

"But my wife must know." Ross's tone was final.

Yardley sighed. "Well, her security clearance is as high as yours. So long as she realizes the serious implications of even the smallest slip . . . I guess you'd better speak to her then."

"Thank you." To his surprise, Ross did feel grateful. "What about the NSA?"

"Oh Jesus," said Yardley dismissively. "Not a word to them. This is a Defense show. We don't have any contact with the NSA or the CIA, or any of the other operators flatfooting it around town. We keep them all at arm's length. We report direct to the Pentagon, and the Pentagon reports to the President. At the moment only half a dozen men know what's going on, and that's the way we want to keep it. Half a dozen men, and . . ." he paused for emphasis, " . . . your wife. That's the limit."

"Okay," said Ross. "I'll talk it over with Elaine and let you know."

"I'll visit you at your house tomorrow," Cane said.

"Come for dinner. About eight."

"That'll be fine. You ready for some lunch? Or a drink?"

Ross shook his head. "No, I've had enough of you both for the time being," he said. "I have to do some serious thinking, and I don't want David here impressing me with what a great guy he is, and how big a man he's going to turn me into, so I'll say yes for some absurd macho reason and end up being shot through the neck by the KGB. All I want is to be shown the way out."

Ross felt the pressure from Cane's hand on his shoulder as they walked to the door.

DR. ELAINE ROSS SAT AT HER DESK,
writing in a neat, precise hand. Her workroom was similar to her
husband's next door: shelves of technical books reaching almost to
the ceiling, covering more than half the wall space, much of the rest
taken up with wood-framed photographs of graduations, professional
colleagues over a couple of decades, and diplomas. There was a bowl
of flowers on the large desk, where Martin kept a rack of pipes which
he no longer smoked but wouldn't get rid of.

A long-haired gray cat, curled on an easy chair in front of the desk,
had not stirred for at least an hour, and the low rumble of a purr
began to come from it.

Elaine Ross glanced up fondly for a moment, then resumed her
work, referring occasionally to notes. She was completing a report for
a large corporation which had changed over to a new generation of
computers and had adopted the MESA system implementation language developed by Xerox, with disappointing results. All the
reports and deliberations leading to a multimillion dollar investment
had ended in producing exactly the problems they were designed to
avoid. There was nothing wrong with the computer hardware, and
MESA was theoretically fine for their purposes, but the programs

were full of syntax errors—violations of the computer language rules —or when these were avoided, the running program suddenly encountered execution errors, illogicalities, or impossibilities that brought everything to a halt.

Xerox experts were themselves ironing out the programming difficulties, and Elaine Ross had been brought in to identify the staff problems which had caused them in the first place and to recommend retraining.

Elaine Ross was fifty-six, two years younger than her husband. Her hair was, with help, as dark as it had always been, but this was her only vanity. While some of her contemporaries disappeared for a few weeks and returned with their wrinkles gone, she rejected the idea of acquiring a younger face and having it betrayed by the same old hands and neck. She was determined to age gracefully. The lines around her eyes and on her forehead gave her a kind, humorous air, which she supplemented with a laconic wit, often at her own expense.

The cat stopped purring and fell asleep in the chair. In the hallway an antique grandfather clock struck the half hour with low, resonant chimes. Elaine Ross lit a cigarette and inhaled deeply as she reflected on the precise phrasing of a recommendation. She hated trade jargon, which, although it seemed impressive and knowledgeable, usually hid a minefield of alternative interpretations and served to create new problems.

She did not hear the key turn in the front door, or her husband's footsteps through the carpeted hall. She had not expected him back until the following day, and she gave a start when he rapped quietly on her door and pushed it open.

"Hello, Martin," she said, looking up from her work in surprise. "Why so early?" She turned her face up, and Ross kissed her affectionately on the forehead.

"How's the report going?" he asked.

"Almost finished. How were the DIA?"

He picked the cat out of the chair and put it on his lap, where it began to purr again as he stroked it abstractedly. "They had a proposition for me. I have to talk it over with you."

She leaned back in her chair. "So talk.'"

"Finish that first. It'll take a bit of time."

She hesitated a fraction. "Okay, give me fifteen minutes," she said. "Is it too early for a drink?"

"Martini?"

"Very, very dry."

Ross took his time mixing the drinks and carried them to her office. Elaine was shuffling through her papers, collating them for the typist. He put the martini in front of her and went back to close the door.

"Remind me," he said. "When was this room swept last?"

She shrugged. "The NSA were in three weeks ago," she said. "All clear."

"Let's have some music anyway."

Elaine stared at him briefly, then crossed to a small stereo system on the bookshelf. "Brahms?" she asked.

"Sounds fine."

They waited until the first notes of the Second Piano Concerto were filling the room and she had settled back behind her desk with a cigarette. Ross began to talk, taking his time, recalling the scene, sketching the characters of Cane and Yardley and the obsessive concern with secrecy.

"I hadn't realized how powerful the DIA were," Ross said. "I didn't even know they ran operations of their own, for example, and that everyone else was kept out. The CIA, the NSA—they just ignore them. The more I think of it now, the more extraordinary it is. The DIA's an intelligence structure *within* an intelligence structure, if you see what I mean."

"McNamara started it, if I remember correctly," Elaine said. "In 1961 or thereabouts. I've got a rundown of its statutory functions somewhere on the shelves. We'll have a look at them later."

"I don't know what it says on paper, but they seem to operate far beyond the statutes," Ross observed. "Successfully too, or we'd have heard about them before. It's not easy to keep failure secret."

Elaine furrowed her brow. "Strange," she said. "Let's find out right now." She crossed to her bookshelves, selected an official volume, and leafed efficiently through it.

"Here it is. They're responsible for—quote—the organization, direction, management, and control of all Department of Defense intelligence resources assigned to or included within the DIA—unquote. They also provide military intelligence to the Secretary of Defense, his staff assistants, the joint chiefs of staff, and specified commands." She paused. "The operative words seem to be the ones which talk about intelligence resources, '. . . included within the

DIA.' Since it doesn't say exactly what resources are 'included within' them, it could mean anything. So for all we know, they do have a free hand."

"They want to send me into Russia." Ross came out with it as a flat statement, instead of after the careful buildup he had been rehearsing on the way home.

She stared at him, uncomprehending. Then she said: "I think you'd better give it to me slowly, step by step, just as you planned."

He smiled suddenly and lifted his glass, frosted with condensation. "You know me too well," he said, and she gave him a fleeting smile in exchange.

Ross spoke at length, and she heard him out in silence. "Cane is coming around for dinner tomorrow night," he said. "I told him he'd have his answer then. You'll like him."

"Will I?" Elaine replied vaguely. "I wonder. *You* like him."

"Yes, I do."

"And trust him?"

Ross hesitated. "I think so—yes," he said. "He looks as if he can take care of himself. And me."

"You've already decided to accept. You want my blessing." It was a statement, not a question, and Ross denied it immediately.

"It's got to be a joint decision," he insisted. "If you're against it because it's too dangerous, or you don't think it'll work, then I won't go."

"But if I think it's a good idea, you'll go?"

He was being backed into a corner, something he knew from experience she was skillful at doing. "Well, maybe."

"Only maybe?"

"Okay, probably. But I don't know enough yet," Ross said carefully, sipping his martini. He noticed hers remained untouched on her desk, but she was smoking continuously, the only sign of tension. "I don't know what the training will involve, for example, or precisely what sort of plan Cane's going to come up with to get us into the central computer building. But he seems a resourceful young man, and his Russian is really extremely good."

"So you said."

"If we decided later during training that the plan was too risky, or its chances of success too slim, I could always refuse to go through with it."

Elaine lifted her martini and took a long sip. She half-turned away from him, and in the gathering gloom of the study, he watched her profile. Age spots were beginning to show on her face, just as they already had on his, and he thought how incongruous it was for two people, in their late middle years, to find themselves involved in this kind of life-and-death decision. The world was suddenly a jungle in which they were invited to stop being tourists and become either the hunter or the hunted. Perhaps even both.

Cane lived permanently in that world. He had made his choice early in the game, when the prospect of death, although accepted theoretically no doubt, would seem in fact remote and fantastic. Even serious injury would be something that happened to others.

Ross remembered this time from his own young manhood and how gradually the perceptions altered. How real death seemed as one grew old and realized how much there was still to do. What time remained seemed to him infinitely precious.

Why then was he preparing to risk it? He wondered if he would ever really know the answer.

The silence grew and he let it. At last, Elaine said: "You're all I've got, you know. You and Luther. I don't particularly want to be left with just a cat." There was a rough edge to her voice as if she were, for the first time, standing on a precipice and seeing loneliness beyond.

Ross didn't reply. The room was getting dark now, and the piano poured out from the stereo in a magnificent crescendo of notes.

"Why can't they just leave us alone?" She spoke quietly, without inflection or bitterness, and Ross had to strain to hear her voice. "We've done our bit. Our duty, so-called. World War Two. Projects for the NSA. We're almost senior citizens, Martin. If we were on their full-time payroll, they'd be getting ready to retire us, rather than sending you out to be cannon fodder." Then she said: "I think I need another martini. Would you mind?"

He took her glass and went through to the kitchen. There was no point in him speaking now. Elaine had the facts and would have to make her own decision. But he felt uneasy and, he had to admit, already a little cheated by her initial reaction. She was right: Left to himself, he would go, and he could not totally explain why.

Her room was dark when he returned, and he stood uncertainly in the doorway. "Shall I turn on a light?" he asked.

"No," she said. "I think better in the dark."

He waited until his eyes had adjusted, and then moved cautiously over to her desk with the drink. The tape cassette had clicked off, and he turned it over. The cat had gone from his chair.

"I want to see this David Cane, Martin," she said suddenly. "I want to see if *I* trust him."

"Tomorrow night at eight."

"I want to hear his Russian."

"It's very good. You'll approve."

"What accent?"

"Muscovite. We can talk Russian the whole evening if you like. Give him a few drinks: hear what he sounds like."

"Can he do Cossack dancing?" The lightness was back in her voice but he knew it was a mask.

"He looks as if he can."

"A useful man in a fight?"

"Very, I'd say. He's offered to teach me unarmed combat. Helpful against Washington muggers."

"He's right, you know," Elaine said. "You are the man for the job. I've been doing a mental inventory of every computer expert I can think of—particularly the whiz kids. But none of them know the language: not to the same degree as you. And if you're going to blend in with the Soviet landscape, you can't pretend to be deaf and dumb, can you? *And* you've got the element of surprise. Who'd expect the United States to send in a geriatric agent?" She paused. "I'm sorry. That was unkind."

"Near enough to be true." She could tell by his voice he was wounded.

"And it *is* important," she said earnestly. "God, how important. Remember Hiroshima? Nagasaki? Multiply the suffering and the devastation by ten thousand and that'll be the United States if Special Collection ever succeeds. There'll be almost nothing left, Martin. Lord knows there are things wrong with our society, but it's nothing compared with what's wrong with *their* society. How can we stand by and let the barbarians inherit the earth?"

"I thought you voted Democrat?" he accused.

"I lied." She chuckled and, for an instant, a match flared and illuminated her face as she drew on a cigarette. "I don't think we have a choice, Martin," she said. "Not really. Not a choice we could live with in our remaining years. What if there was a nuclear strike and we survived to walk through the ruins and see the death which we— you, my dear—might have been able to prevent? Still, I don't think you should underestimate the personal risk. Whatever kind of superman this David Cane is, it's going to be dangerous. Who knows—the Russians might have a store of kryptonite down there in the Urals.

Then you'll be on your own. I don't think the KGB allow food packets. But that's up to you."

She had finished, and they sat in the darkness, listening to the Brahms.

"I don't think it will come to food packets," Ross replied, only half-convinced.

Ross AWOKE THE FOLLOWING morning feeling fresher and more alert than he could remember in years, and realized immediately his body was pumping extra adrenaline, triggered by the prospect of danger.

He bathed and toweled himself dry, then studied his body critically in the mirror and was depressed by what he saw. He didn't *feel* that old, that out of condition. But he could see his muscle and skin tone were going, and, in places, his flesh was beginning to hang in folds. His waist bulged into a paunch that did not disappear even when he sucked it in with all his strength. It was undeniable. He was turning into an old man. His body, this machine he would be relying on in Russia, was preparing itself for death. Could Cane and his training arrest the slide? Ross thought he'd make a damn good try.

At least his mind hadn't deteriorated. His brain was as sharp as ever. There were no memory gaps, no searching for names or trying to recall problems. If his body, and Cane, could get him to the computer terminal underground at Vologda, his brain would be in peak condition to deal with any reprogramming problem. No guarantees of success, but, as Elaine said, he was the best they had.

His thoughts turned to failure: to capture and death. Probably torture. Of never again seeing his home, or Princeton, or anything loved and familiar, and he felt the tension that would live with him from now until the mission ended in quiet success or strident disaster. He turned away from the mirror.

Elaine was still asleep. Her door was closed and Ross could hear no sounds when he paused outside. They had slept in different bedrooms for years, a fact he regretted, but he was a restless and, she claimed, a sometimes noisy sleeper, and they had grown comfortable with the separation. Occasionally, less often than Ross would have liked, he made the late-night journey to her room and was back in his own within the hour.

Ross fixed himself toast and coffee, and settled down to read the papers in the warmth of the morning sun that streamed through the window. He finished the crossword in eight minutes, a somewhat better time than usual, and wondered idly if adrenaline was responsible for the improved performance.

The doorbell chime interrupted his reverie, and he glanced at his watch. Eight-thirty: early for callers. Ross kept the door on the chain and peered through the crack. He could see two—no, three—men on the step.

"Professor Ross?" The voice was neutral, professional.

"Yes. Who is it?"

"DIA, sir."

An identity card was pushed through the crack, and Ross studied it. Defense Intelligence Agency: Peter Childers. He slipped the chain off its hook and swung open the door.

The men were in business suits and carried black suitcases, but their bearing was military.

"Come in, gentlemen," Ross said. "What can I do for you?"

"We've been asked to check over your house if you don't mind, sir. General Yardley's orders."

Yardley. Ross felt a wave of hostility. Typical of Yardley not to ask first. Still, if David Cane was coming by in the evening, it made sense. He stood aside.

"Be my guest," he invited.

The men moved into the entrance hall and glanced around.

"I suggest you begin with the living room-kitchen area," Ross said. "My wife is still asleep, so we can leave the bedrooms until last. I should tell you that the NSA swept the place a few weeks back."

"Yes, sir," Childers said noncommittally. "We're aware of that. On the seventeenth, I think. General Yardley thought it ought to be done again."

Ross led them to the living room and watched as they unlocked their suitcases and lifted out the electronic devices. Ross had seen the procedure many times before.

"I'll leave you alone, if I may," he said. "I'm just finishing breakfast. Would you like some coffee, by the way?"

Childers answered for them all. "No, thank you, sir. We've had breakfast."

The men took until lunchtime to cover the house. Elaine emerged from her room thirty minutes after they'd begun, but she was equally familiar with the routine and paid them little attention, beyond renewing the offer of coffee.

When they had gone, she started cooking dinner, taking, Ross noticed, unusual care in the preparation of the food. She even drove into Princeton to buy specific wines.

Neither of them spoke again about the DIA proposal or mentioned Cane, but there was an acceptance that their lives had changed radically and that the evening would officially mark this.

Ross tried to concentrate on some of his outstanding projects, with little success. His preoccupation with Cane, and the problems that would confront them, dominated his mind. He searched through his extensive library for references to Soviet advances in computer design, finding, as he expected, that there was almost nothing of value. He would have to depend on the DIA's own files, which he had no doubt would be much fuller.

Cane himself spent the morning at the DIA headquarters in Washington reviewing what was known about Soviet computer techniques, culled from the reports of agents run by every United States intelligence agency. His own office was a small, impersonal space with a laminated-top desk, two telephones, a square of carpet, a gray filing cabinet, and wall signs reminding him to empty his wastebasket and lock away anything sensitive before leaving—and locking—the room. He didn't care much about his surroundings and made no effort to imprint his own personality on them.

He chain-smoked as he read, his forehead furrowed with concentration.

There was a ban on the hoarding of information by any agency, so Cane was reasonably sure he was looking at all available documents.

More sure, for example, than he would be if he was a CIA man and had asked for information from Defense sources. The DIA regarded itself as a special case and kept some of its cards close to its chest.

Cane found he was getting a clear overall view of Russian computer technology, but very little specific information was available. There were Minox photographs of some computer printouts, and Ross might be able to deduce from these the language being used. That was, however, a long way from being certain of the system used in the underground citadel at Vologda.

Cane sighed, packed the documents back into a manila folder, and returned them to the DIA registry, then went to tell Yardley he was on his way to Princeton.

"Take a seat, David," the general said, indicating an upright chair in front of his desk that Lucy used when taking dictation. Cane relaxed into it and stared inquiringly at the Director.

"Any pointers on the professor taking the job?" he asked.

"A couple," Yardley said, pressing the tips of his fingers together and regarding Cane in a slightly detached way over the steeple they formed. "Nothing confirmed, but it's looking good. At least his wife seems to be fixing you a good dinner."

"What am I eating?"

"I'm not sure. She shopped for wine, not food. Léoville-Barton 1961."

"Not bad. It's a decent Bordeaux.'"

"It's better than decent. And Dom Perignon."

"Champagne. Christ—it looks like we've got a winner. How much are we offering Ross for the job?"

Yardley leaned back against the leather. "His usual retainer: twenty thousand a month."

Cane frowned. "Can't we do better than that? It might keep them in Dom Perignon, but it doesn't really cover the risk, does it?"

"That's only for the training months. Once you go operational, there's half a million in it for him: win or lose."

Cane considered this. "Can you explain the 'or lose' part, sir?" he asked.

"I mean, David, that if the professor is captured or killed, we pay his wife five hundred thousand dollars."

"And if we abort?"

"Then we'll negotiate a washout fee. But tell him it will be generous and will take the risks into account."

Cane shrugged. "Sounds fair. Nothing's come out of the house so far?"

Yardley shook his head. "No," he said. "Reception is good, but the Rosses haven't been talking about the plan at all. I suppose they thrashed it out last night and that's it. They're a strange couple. The house was clean, by the way."

"Fine. Well, I'd better get on over there. It'll take me a while to drive up, and I have to go home and change first."

"How's your boy?"

"Good as new. God knows what was wrong. A twenty-four-hour virus, the doctor said, whatever that is. You know what kids are like. Dying one minute, beating you at basketball the next."

Cane started to get to his feet, but paused when he caught Yardley staring at him in a peculiar way. He sat down again. "Something on your mind, sir?"

Yardley chose his words. "Yes, David, there is," he said. "In the future I'd appreciate it if you'd cut the jokes about me watching videos of people crapping. I know we allow you a lot of latitude, but sometimes you go too far. A little more discipline, please."

Cane felt the color rise in his face. Christ, there really was no privacy anymore. "Yes, *sir*," he said softly.

When he drove his Chevy out into the afternoon traffic and headed for home, Cane began to laugh.

He dressed carefully: dark wool suit, white silk shirt, conservatively striped tie. Respectable and responsible, that was the image in case the Rosses were still wavering. Trust me with your lives, folks.

Maryann watched him dress. "Got a date?" she asked lightly.

"I only go on dates with you." He smiled at her. "Business, I'm afraid."

"Will you be late?"

"Yes. Long after midnight, I guess."

"Will you wake me?"

"Don't I always?"

She put her arms around his waist, her head against his chest. Cane kissed her gently. "You always do," she said.

On the way Cane stopped at a florist, bought a bouquet of flowers for Elaine Ross, then turned onto the Turnpike toward Princeton, ignoring speed restrictions and timing himself to arrive just after eight.

The Rosses' house was expensive suburbia, set well back from the road in a carefully tended garden of shrubs and well-established trees. He drove past it once and around the block to see if he could spot either of the two DIA men on duty, and was satisfied when he could not.

He pulled into the driveway and parked. The front door opened almost as soon as he pressed the bell, and both Ross and his wife were waiting in the hall.

Cane was half-hidden in shadow, so Elaine Ross's first impression was of the size and height of the man who was to take her husband clandestinely into the depths of Russia, and perhaps even bring him out again. He was taller than she had imagined. Six two? But big.

"David, come in, come in," Ross said, and when Cane stepped into the hall and the light, she stared at him, almost mesmerized. He seemed young for the job and his face was wrong: too good-looking and humorous. He was not one of the short-haired CIA brigade whose trousers needed to be an inch longer to cover their socks. A different specimen altogether.

The bouquet of flowers was being presented to her, and she reached for it automatically. Roses—at this time of year.

"You are welcome to our home, David Cane," she said in Russian. *"I hope the journey was not too long."*

"The journey was a pleasure, as tonight will be." Cane smiled at the woman, who reminded him strongly of an aunt from his childhood.

His hand enclosed hers, and she was conscious again of size. Gentleness, but strength too. Martin was right. A useful man to have in a fight, to have on one's side. She had to admit Cane made a good first impression.

"I thought we would speak our common adopted language this evening," Elaine said. *"We get too few opportunities to practice."*

She led the way to the living room. Ross had lit a fire, and the evening chill was replaced by a warm glow.

"These roses are beautiful," she said, admiring them in their wrapping. *"Please excuse me while I arrange them in a vase. Martin will fix the drinks."*

"What'll you have?" Ross said in English when she had gone.

"Scotch, please. On the rocks." Cane looked around the room with admiration. It was impeccable: understated good taste, hand-knotted silk carpets, original paintings, and some excellent limited-edition prints on the walls. Muted colors, warm lighting.

"This is such a nice room," Cane said. "Your wife?"

Ross nodded. "She's a lady of many talents," he said. "This is one of them."

Ross poured a generous measure of Glenlivet into a glass and handed it to Cane. They toasted each other in silence.

"One of the world's fine malts," Cane said appreciatively.

"Glad you like it. Do you know Scotland?"

"I took my wife there on our honeymoon. We love the Highlands."

Elaine returned with a vase of water. *"I did not realize you were married, David Cane,"* she said. *"Surely yours is a job which does not lend itself to such ties. Your wife must be a very special woman."*

"She is."

"I meant long-suffering."

"She does not seem so," Cane replied with a grin. *"She knew she was going to be an army wife when she agreed to marry me. This is just an extension of that. She trusts me to take reasonable care and to look after myself."*

"I am sure you can do that very well."

"Yes, I can," said Cane frankly. *"I am one of the best there is."*

"Although not too modest," Elaine said with a small laugh.

"There is no point in being modest," Cane replied. *"It is an objective fact. If it were not so, I would not be here tonight. I would be dead. But I am not, and others are."*

Ross and his wife stared at Cane in fascination.

"I am not especially proud of killing," Cane said. *"But I am not ashamed either. It is what I have been trained for, and I do it when I must."*

Elaine arranged the roses in an automatic, preoccupied way. *"Do you have children?"* she asked.

"One," Cane said. *"A son, aged six."*

She considered the information. "I really didn't expect a family man," she said, reverting to English.

"Oh," said Cane lightly, "I'm pretty conventional really. Or a lot of my life is. I have a mortgage, friends who think I'm something boring in the government, a pretty wife, a fantastic kid, a company car. I mow the lawn on weekends and play bridge on Tuesday nights when I'm not working. I smoke too much."

"But no one tries to sell you life insurance," Elaine said, finishing the roses.

He grinned. "Oh, they try. I tell them I'm fully insured."

"Are you?"

"Sure. If anything happens to me, the DIA will take care of Maryann and Timmy. They look after their people really well. But I
expect to live long enough to pick up my pension checks. I'm looking
forward to playing baseball with my grandchildren, reading, smoking, and hardening my arteries with excellent malt whiskey like this."

"Another one?" Ross offered.

"No thanks. I'm doing fine."

"Will the DIA look after Martin and me?" Elaine returned to the
subject.

"Of course. If you decide to join, you'll have the same protection
that I and my family have." Cane spelled out the financial terms
authorized by Yardley. There was no reaction. He looked directly at
Elaine Ross. "Well? Are you going to join?"

She ignored the question, settled in a cream upholstered chair, and
reached for her martini. "Tell me about yourself, Mr. Cane."

Cane sat at ease, not discomfited by the questioning. "For starters,
most people call me David. I like it better that way. I'm thirty. My
folks lived in Indianapolis, where I was born, but I grew up in LA.
My dad was an accountant. My mother wrote poetry, not all of it
bad, she got some published too."

"They're still in Los Angeles?" Elaine asked.

"They died last year in a car crash."

"I'm sorry to hear that."

"Yeah, it was tough. They were crazy about their grandson. I was
an only child, and Timmy's an only child, so there's a family tradition. The folks wanted us to have more, but Maryann—my wife—
isn't keen on the idea. I'd have a dozen if I could."

"Where did you meet your wife?"

"When I was in high school. She was a blind date. That's true,
actually. We just hit it off. Then I was accepted at West Point, and
we got married in 1973 at the end of Plebe Year. I was recruited into
the DIA when I was twenty-three, mostly because of my languages."

"Russian and what else?" Elaine held out her glass for a refill.

"French, of course. German, a little Dutch, a little Spanish. I
always found languages easy, but I loved Russian. A friend of my
dad's was a professor at Moscow University who cut and ran while on
a visit to Finland. He did it on impulse, I think. Of course, once he
was committed, that was it. There was no going back. His wife and
kids were left to face the music at home. A very sad man. He wrote
letters to them every week, but never got a reply. He adopted us as

his family, I suppose. I could speak Russian fluently by the time I was ten. I think that's how I learned to love the people and hate the system. That families could be separated, totally cut off, with no chance of contact—well, I found it hard to take. And that's before we even consider the killings and the tortures and the brutality. I was a DIA natural."

"I understand you've been into Russia before," Elaine said.

Cane finished the whiskey in his glass. Ross, who had obviously made a conscious decision to leave the running of the conversation to his wife, hurried to get him a refill.

"I've been in and out five times now," Cane said.

"Legally or undercover?"

"A combination," Cane said vaguely. "The details are a bit complicated, but it works well enough. The professor and I will go in the same way."

"And how will you get him into Vologda? Assuming he goes?"

"At this point," Cane admitted, "I've no idea at all. We don't have nearly enough information to mount an operation yet. We have to sign Martin up first, then we'll be in a position to isolate the questions and get the answers from our guys inside the Soviet Union. That'll take months, no doubt about it. Meanwhile, we've got to get Martin into some sort of physical shape. But I give you this guarantee, Mrs. Ross, I won't take him in unless I'm reasonably certain of success. As I'm sure he's explained to you, the essence of this operation is secrecy. We have to get in and out without being noticed, and unless we can do that, there's no point in going. There are men inside the Soviet military—senior men—who'll help us on our way. We've got resources there we haven't tapped yet, and we'll use every one of them if we have to. You know what's at stake. We're not the CIA. We're not going to blunder into this and blow our chances. It's my job to see that this is a professional operation, and that we both get out alive. And that's what I'll do."

He lit a cigarette. Elaine Ross was staring at him, and he met her gaze frankly. He had the advantage of knowing her from her files, and he thought he understood what was going on in her mind. The intellectual decision had already been made. She was now coping with the emotional one—whether to trust an unknown man, young enough to be her son, with the life of her husband.

"I really am the best there is," he said softly. "And I'll prove it to you."

Her eyes dropped first, and she sipped her martini in silence. Ross was sitting in what looked like his favorite chair, watching but making no effort to intervene. *He* had certainly made his decision, intellectually and emotionally. It just remained to prompt his wife over the last few steps.

"Tell me, Mrs. Ross, how do you feel in principle about this proposal? Do you think it's worth doing?" Cane asked casually.

She nodded slowly. "If there's a way of aborting Special Collection, then it must be found," she said. "A nuclear war here would be unthinkable. It would be difficult to have that on our consciences, knowing that we could have done something to stop it but we held back."

"So?"

She was silent for a long time. Cane was conscious he was breathing very shallowly.

"You've put us in an impossible position, Mr. Cane," she said with dignity. "You seem a very personable young man. No doubt you're very competent. And, yes, instinctively I suppose I do trust you. In time I'll discover if my faith was misplaced. You'll either be a hero, or I'll curse you to my grave. But I suppose that's what your job's about, isn't it?"

"So?"

"So the answer is yes, Mr. Cane."

He sat back in his chair and exhaled slowly. "Thank you, Mrs. Ross," he said. "Thank you very much."

THE RAIN EASED OFF JUST BEFORE
dawn, but the chill turned their breath to vapor. They left the quarters assigned to them at the DIA's Fairfax training ground and jogged down the grassy slope toward the woods, 500 yards away and almost lost in the mist. The grass was wet and spongy, and their feet splashed into half-hidden puddles, sending streaks of muddy water up over the legs of their track suits.

Ross was aware that Cane, slightly ahead of him, was deliberately moving slowly, barely warming up, while Ross already felt the sharp pain of unaccustomed exercise in his lungs, and before they reached the trees, his thigh muscles were weak and sore. His back ached.

Cane halted in the last stretch of open ground. A path led through the trees, visible for a few yards before being lost in the mist and the darkness. "Keep going," he urged. "A bit of running in place . . . shuffling in place if you want. Just keep the blood circulating."

He isn't even short of breath, Ross thought, already wishing he was back in their room and disgusted by his own puny performance.

"You're doing fine," Cane encouraged. "Don't push yourself too far the first day, that's all. You've got a lot of catching up to do, and you have to take your time . . . Okay, let's go. Follow me."

He set off along the path, and Ross pulled in behind him, determined to keep up. His breath was coming in gasps. Leaves slapped wetly across his face, and he felt cold water soaking through his running shoes. Cane moved easily and without effort a few yards ahead. Occasionally he looked over his shoulder to see how the professor was doing. Ross thought, *It's fine for you, you're thirty and fit; I'm fifty-eight and almost an old man.*

But soon he found himself incapable of thinking at all. His efforts were concentrated on keeping his body going and ignoring the tightening muscles in his legs, until his breath hissed out in pain as calf muscles cramped up, and he came to a sudden halt.

Cane was beside him immediately, kneeling in the wet and putting a hand beneath his shoe as Ross grimaced and gasped. "Straighten your leg now," Cane ordered, "and push against my hand . . . push . . . push . . . that's it."

The cramp eased miraculously, but the muscle was left feeling tender.

"You okay?" Cane asked.

"Yes, I think so. Thanks for that."

"We're going to walk now. Just take it easy. Let me know if you feel it cramping up again."

Ross was conscious of the pounding of his heart and his labored breathing as they moved off, but gradually his body quieted and the muscle pain was only a dull ache.

Cane picked up speed slightly, into a slow, steady jog, and automatically Ross followed.

The forest was superb. Dense and deserted. At least, Ross thought, he was noticing that now. The trees rose high around them, with ferns and foliage thick around the trunks. It was obvious the area wasn't much used because vegetation flourished close to the path. Somewhere in the distance there was a birdsong, but the dominant noises were the thudding of his own footsteps, the splashing of water, and the scraping of branches as he brushed past. Ross noticed how much quieter Cane was, for all his size: a natural animal. Ross's track suit was wet through now, but warm from body heat.

They took a path to the side and reemerged into the fields leading up to the Fairfax buildings. The mist was lifting, and it looked as if the sun would soon break through the low, scudding clouds.

They jogged slowly toward the deserted gymnasium, where they stripped for a hot shower, which was followed by a sauna and a plunge in the icy pool. Immediately afterward, Cane made Ross lie on a marble slab and massaged him hard and professionally, kneading old muscles that would be stiff and painful by evening.

"Okay, Martin," he said cheerfully, straightening up. "That's not too bad for the first day. Let's get some breakfast."

Ross was surprised at how much better he felt after he had dressed and they were walking over to the cafeteria. *I must have dropped a few pounds already,* he thought, although, as Cane said, there wasn't much point in weighing himself because most of it was only water, which would go back on when he had his orange juice and coffee.

Ross was ravenous, but Cane allowed them both only the juice, two boiled eggs with one slice of dry toast, and a single cup of coffee.

"Hell, David," Ross complained, "we've got a day of very hard work to do. How can I think about our problem if all I see before me is a succulent piece of rare steak and a pint of milk?"

"You'll get used to it," Cane said unsympathetically. "Anyway, you've got enough fat to live on for a month."

"I'm going to hate this. I know it already."

"Sure. Everyone hates it until it's finished. Then you'll feel great. We'll have another workout tonight . . ."

Ross groaned. "I definitely won't be able to make that."

"You'll make it. We'll have steak for dinner."

The DIA had set aside an office for their use, with files of abstracts of all references to Soviet computers and missile programs going back ten years. Ross sorted through the openly published references first, discarding most of them as being too circumstantial or straightforward nonsense, and then began poring over reports from agents, jotting notes and references in a notebook.

Cane sat with him, concentrating closely on the documents, asking questions, and occasionally pointing out things he felt the professor might have overlooked or attached insufficient weight to. Ross rebutted or explained his decision in every case, and Cane found his respect growing. He was a remarkable old guy. Nothing seemed to escape his scrutiny, and his powers of concentration over a long period were extraordinary. They spoke only in Russian, familiarizing themselves with technical terms and jargon, which they would need when the plan went operational. Cane became aware of a rapport growing quickly between them.

In the late afternoon, he took Ross back into the gym and put him through a series of simple exercises. It would take time to get the professor back into condition—three or four months of solid work before he could complete what Cane considered to be the most basic physical regimen for a man of his age, and *that* fell far short of the standard demanded for the job. Add another four months, and he might just pass.

Ross was certainly game. As he worked out, his face became red and sweat poured off him. His movements slowed, yet he would not give up. Cane shouted encouragement and commands, barraging him with a wall of sound to focus on, to distract his mind from the contortions his body was now putting itself through automatically.

At the end Ross leaned gasping against the wall, and then walked to the lavatory without a word. Cane could hear him vomiting. He fetched a glass of water, pushed open the door, and crouched in the stall beside him, holding the older man's head, and encouraging him with his voice. Body contact. Male bonding. No secrets. The stuff of Plebe Year at West Point brought up to date for a fifty-eight-year-old who in a few months would be going clandestinely into Russia, and whose trust and loyalty for the agent accompanying him had to be absolute. In that first appalling year a West Point plebe would forge personal links with his comrades in Beast Barracks that would last an entire career, even into retirement. The links weren't easy: forged in fire. But they were strong.

Ross slumped on the floor, breathing heavily, his eyes closed in exhaustion. "Sorry," he gasped. "Sorry, David."

"You're doing fine, Martin," Cane said, genuine warmth in his voice. "Most eighteen-year-olds end their first day puking their hearts out as well. Think you can stand up?"

The professor nodded slightly and made an effort to rise. Cane guided him limping out of the stall and into the shower. Then he got him back on the marble slab for another massage, and before he had finished, Ross was asleep. Cane covered him with a towel and went back into the gym for his own workout.

He was through in an hour and found Ross did not seem to have moved. Cane shook him gently awake.

"How do you feel?"

"Bit sore. Otherwise fine," Ross said.

"Hungry?"

"Steak?"

"Yup."

"Very hungry."

Cane clapped him on the back. "Let's get changed and hit the cafeteria," he said. "You've earned your dinner."

Both men ate well, and Cane allowed a glass of wine each. By the time they reached the room they shared, it felt past midnight, although Ross's watch showed only nine o'clock. He slept deep and undisturbed.

The days settled into a familiar pattern. Ross's body accepted increasing amounts of exercise, with muscle soreness a constant. He was losing weight, although not as quickly as he had hoped, and there was no sudden dramatic improvement in his physique. He supposed it was a little late in the day for that. Cane varied the exercises to avoid boredom and to bring different sets of muscles into play. He also introduced the first elements of self-defense, taking special care in this because the last thing they could afford now was a clumsy fall onto the mats and something getting broken.

Cane was sensitive to the atmosphere between them. It was difficult moving into someone else's life, particularly as closely and as personally as he had done. He watched for signs that Ross was beginning to resent the intrusion. It would be natural for them to get on each other's nerves at some point during training. Because of the age difference, the trick in this case would be for Cane to back off in time and keep ordinary annoyance from building into a real grudge.

Yet Ross appeared not only to accept the enforced intimacy but to enjoy it. There were strong elements of a father-son relationship there, even though for some of the working day it was Cane who was the leader, yelling commands and occasionally, when he thought he could get away with it, cursing, threatening, abusing with parade-ground arrogance and volume. Ross knew, in some deep, instinctive way, the purpose of the bullying, and if anything it made him trust Cane more.

They worked carefully through the files, and Ross built up his own picture of the Soviet computer system, which differed in small but vital respects from the model outlined in a top secret joint CIA-NSA report. Cane, while supervising the professor's research and learning what he could from them, was mainly preoccupied with the logistics of the operation.

Vologda base was 500 feet underground in the Urals, an enormous and impressive command center dug out of solid rock and apparently impregnable. There was an airbase at Sverdlovsk, eighty miles away, and helicopters supplemented the road route through the mountains, carrying mostly VIPs.

Access to the underground citadel itself was through a series of well-camouflaged bunkers, which had deep tunnels leading from them. At intervals along these were huge, heavy doors, electrically controlled by independent generators, which would provide seals in the event of war and protect against a direct nuclear hit.

Electric cars transported important Soviet officials along these passageways to the high-speed elevators that serviced the citadel far below.

There was access to an artesian well, and the underground complex included bedrooms, dormitories, dining rooms, a movie theater, a war room, sophisticated communications, and of course the vital computer. The agents' reports indicated that the personnel at Vologda stayed underground for a week at a time, working eight-hour shifts. This was apparently done in an effort to cut down the problems of security, because anyone going into Vologda was strictly checked.

For Cane's purposes there was no way in which to avoid the system. They would have to obtain forged passes and an adequate cover story with appropriate immediate verifications. They could not be armed because the KGB checks were thorough. It would be a walk into the lions' den, in the hope the lions might be dozing.

He could not estimate how long they would have to spend inside the center because this depended on Ross's knowledge of the computer system. If the professor had unlocked all the Soviet secrets, they might be lucky and be in and out within a few hours.

There was also the difficulty of how to deal with the personnel inside the computer room. Clearly Ross would have to be left alone to reprogram the missile systems. The others must be lured from their posts somehow. When Cane saw the scope of the problems, he found himself unconsciously grinding his teeth. The pivot had to be the cover story. If they could assume unchallengeable identities and reasons for working on the master computer, everything would flow naturally from that.

Cane involved Ross in the logistics at every stage, taking him over rough-sketch diagrams of the Vologda layout, which they both realized were not to scale or entirely accurate—they were layout maps drawn from memory by a Defense mole who had worked at the command center. Cane tried various possible cover stories on Ross, inviting objections and reservations, rejecting and rethinking when the professor uncovered some flaw which could trigger a deeper than usual security scrutiny, or alert the KGB that something was amiss. Again they worked entirely in Russian.

It was six weeks before Ross had prepared a preliminary list of questions, which required detailed answers not supplied in any agent's report. Cane announced a week's leave and suggested that the professor get back to Princeton and his wife, and he would spend time with his own family. Neither man had moved out of Fairfax since the first day, and Ross's cautious letters to Elaine were taken by special courier to San Francisco for mailing.

The three KGB *rezidenturas* in the United States kept a watch on their rivals, and the DIA were anxious to avoid the possibility that they might spot Martin Ross and discover after further investigation that he was at Fairfax. It would make him a marked man.

Cane took the list of questions to DIA headquarters in Washington and handed it to General Yardley with a preliminary report on Ross's progress. Not that there was much Yardley didn't know from his own monitoring. Cane was aware of this, of course, but still there were formalities to be observed.

Later, he telephoned Maryann from the office to tell her he would be home in an hour, and he knew, as he drove along Massachusetts Avenue and headed for the suburbs, that she would farm Timmy out to one of their friends for the afternoon, and that when he pulled into their drive, she would be waiting for him.

"SOVIET GEOLOGISTS! EXPLORE OUR
country's wealth more rapidly! Discover new deposits of iron, coal,
oil, gas, and nonferrous and rare metals!"

The parade marched briskly down the east side of Red Square,
past the line of Russians waiting between painted white lines for
their chance to enter the mausoleum and stare briefly at the waxy
corpse of Vladimir Ilyich Lenin in its solemn, dimly lit chamber.

Filipp Ivanovich Levin was in a hurry and glanced quickly at the
well-behaved, restrained parade, taking in a few of the slogans and
the brightness of the clothing. Young women wore blue pants and
yellow sweaters. Others had on purple gym suits and bright orange
stocking caps. Around them the ordinary Muscovites looked drab.

"Workers in literature and art! Strive for a high ideological level
in literature and art! Tirelessly perfect your artistic skill!"

Levin crossed to the south of Red Square, past the desanctified
church of St. Basil the Blessed which, beneath nine bulbous, convo-
luted domes, now housed a museum, and headed for a Metro. He
had one hour before the designated pickup time, but he was hurrying to see if he could flush out a tail by turning a corner and immedi-

ately entering a shop. The indecision shown by anyone following him would probably be apparent, and he would abandon the pickup and give the prearranged signal for an abort. It would then be up to the Americans to retrieve their message.

There was a fruit store just beyond the next block, and he headed for it with brisk determination. Once inside, he pretended to examine a box of apples from one of the southern republics while keeping an eye on people coming on both sides of the street. He could see nothing suspicious.

The shopkeeper ignored him, attending instead to other customers, and after a minute, Levin strolled out, maintaining a relaxed pace to the Metro. He glanced at his watch and found he had fifty minutes.

He changed trains three times, giving himself further opportunities to ensure he was not under surveillance, until with fifteen minutes to spare, he emerged from a Metro station and walked toward the Vagankovskoye Cemetery. Birch trees with piebald trunks lined the perimeter, and Levin wandered slowly among the graves until, almost exactly on time, he was in sight of the plot where the poet Sergei Yesenin had been laid to rest in 1925 after killing himself in Leningrad's Angleterre Hotel.

Levin glanced around him, taking in the silent, bleak scene: tombstones, ornate or simple; dead, colorless wreaths, some fresh flowers. A few people, quiet beside the graves of those they had once loved, preoccupied with private thoughts. Nothing to worry him.

He approached Yesenin's grave and saw that a wreath had recently been laid. Levin took his time, first studying the formal inscription on the stone, and then bent down to read the card on the wreath. No one was near.

The card read: "The written word remains." It was not signed. He dug gently at the soft earth beneath the wreath, and his fingers found a small, cylindrical package covered in plastic. It was about the size of a half-smoked cigarette and fitted neatly into the palm of his hand. He stood up and turned slowly away, pensive in the manner of a visitor to cemeteries.

Levin inspected several other tombs on his way to the gate, but once outside he headed quickly for the Metro.

His apartment was on the third floor of a block a half-hour's walk from the Chief Artillery Directorate headquarters where he had worked for the last eight years.

Levin had graduated from the Second Kiev Artillery School as a lieutenant and later attended the Frunze Academy, but although he had always shown above-average aptitude, his career had virtually stalled. Promotion to captain came grudgingly five years later with the job of special assistant to his benefactor, Colonel General Georgi Borisovich Stupar, the head of CAD.

Levin was particularly well-qualified for this position, as Stupar well knew. CAD had responsibility for the production and safekeeping of all the Soviet Union's nuclear equipment. The Central Committee and the Supreme Military Council had also assigned to it the task of supplying nuclear weapons to military districts both within the motherland and abroad.

Levin combined a sound theoretical knowledge of nuclear physics with a remarkable organizational ability. Quite simply, he showed Stupar off to best advantage.

Yet he was aware of insurmountable personal drawbacks which would stop him rising much further. It was only *General Polkovnik* Stupar's patronage that had got him to his present level, and kept him there.

Levin's problem was his grandfather, a stern and bearded figure in the old photographs, who had been a soldier in the White Army fighting against the Soviets. Filipp Ivanovich had sensibly not advertised this fact, but the KGB uncovered it during an additional security check while he was at the Frunze Academy. In a series of unpleasant interviews, it had been made clear to Levin that under the circumstances, he could not expect his military career to benefit from his background, and that he would have to work very hard indeed merely to maintain the position he had already achieved. Any subsequent minor promotions would depend on an extraordinary and consistent display of merit.

In the years following, Levin learned bitterly what that meant. The apartment he had been allocated was smaller and of a much poorer quality than he would normally have been entitled to, and in routine interviews with the KGB, no opportunity was lost to remind him of his grandfather and to stress the careful watch that was being kept on him.

But the scrutiny was not particularly careful, Levin knew. No more so than for any other Russian with a similar security clearance. Otherwise his contacts with the Americans would have been found out.

The threat was simply an example of petty persecution, one of millions performed daily by the KGB. A frightened man is a docile man: That was the rationale.

Filipp Ivanovich Levin was not frightened. Beneath a calm and apparently open exterior, he was often angry.

It offended his sense of justice that he should be made to pay for the sins of a grandfather who had died a decade before his birth. His father had no doubt suffered too, but he had done so without complaint, or without apparently considering alternatives.

Levin daydreamed about America, about the movies he was permitted to watch when he accompanied the *General Polkovnik* on a tour of the Ukraine or to some of the bigger military bases. He remembered the first one particularly. Senior KGB officers had screened it after a long dinner and several toasts in vodka and Armenian cognac. It was a comedy—he couldn't remember its name—and the others laughed uproariously, but Filipp Ivanovich Levin sat in silent awe. The shops. The clothes and cars, the music . . . well, the freedom. For a boy from Kiev, it was unimaginable.

When it ended Stupar clapped him roughly on the back, guffawing: "What did you think of that then, Filipp Ivanovich?"

And he had replied stiffly, saying the first thing that came into his head: "Laughter from a decaying society, comrade General."

Everyone laughed then, and Levin knew he had answered correctly. Still, he saw that particular movie in his dreams sometimes, and when he was awake and alone, he reconstructed scenes in his mind. America. That was where he wanted to be. And that is what they had promised him. When he had done enough and the opportunity arose, he would go to America, and they would give him a car and a house like the one in the movie, and he would meet an American girl and raise a healthy, free family.

Meanwhile, there was the cylindrical package in his pocket, the next step in a dangerous journey.

Levin climbed the stairs to his one-room apartment, with its small kitchen and bathroom, and let himself in. Through the wall he could hear the children next door, shouting and crying, and their mother's voice raised in reprimand.

He took a knife from the kitchen, slit open the plastic covering, and went to lock himself in the bathroom. If anyone burst into the apartment, he would at least have the chance to flush away the incriminating paper.

Levin dropped his trousers, sat on the toilet, and began to read, frowning over the single sheet and the questions it contained. He already knew some of the answers. Others he could discover fairly easily. But some were impossible. They wanted Minox film of a specimen program from the Vologda computer, and this he could not obtain.

He doubted whether the *General Polkovnik* himself had access to such things. Beyond the strict security of the Chief Artillery Directorate, overseen by the KGB, was the totally separate Vologda security, also a KGB responsibility, specially designed to guard their precious communications, their war room and their computer.

Levin had visited Vologda several times with the *General Polkovnik*, and he knew that in the event of war there would be a safe place underground for Stupar, his family and his special assistant. Although not, of course, for any member of the special assistant's family. His parents and sisters would take their chances with the others.

Levin could certainly provide the Americans with a full account of security procedures at Vologda—at least those in force during his previous visits. He also believed he had kept a special identity card from several months ago and that it was in his office desk. It was useless now—invalid. The colors of the cards changed periodically, and anyway they were clearly stamped with expiration dates. He would describe that to them too.

He wondered what the Americans intended to do. Was it just information they wanted? Did they plan an operation? He would advise strongly against one. It would be nothing more than a suicide mission. Vologda was impregnable.

When he had memorized the contents of the paper, Levin chewed it carefully until it had virtually disintegrated, dropped the sodden pulp into the toilet, and pulled the chain. He stayed to ensure that no pieces remained.

Two hours later, when it was time for him to verify receipt of the message, he let himself out of his apartment and took the Metro to a stop near the Balchug Hotel. He sauntered casually along the Sadovnicheskaya Embankment in the gathering dusk, staring at the canal barges and paying little attention to others on the street. It was only necessary for him to be seen walking along the embankment and past the hotel, and his chances of identifying the person sent to spot him, even if he wanted to, were slim.

The following morning Levin, in his captain's uniform, went

through the routine chore of screening the *General Polkovnik's* in-tray before Stupar arrived, removing the great weight of interdepartmental trash that could be delegated to other staff members or done by Levin himself, and placing inside a leather folder items of top-level interest. There was a third folder, for matters about which Levin was unsure and which were placed before Stupar as supplementary material, but this was usually empty.

One of Levin's assets was an ability and a willingness to use his own initiative and, more important, usually to be right. Initiative was not a quality often found or encouraged in the Soviet bureaucracy, because of the personal risk involved. An incorrect decision could mean the end of a career. Almost as bad, a series of correct decisions might make the immediate superior nervous about his own position. Far better that everything be done exactly by the book and that individuals—except for the insatiably ambitious—stay out of the firing line. Let those with the power and the position take the risks and look out for themselves when they did so.

But Filipp Ivanovich was a special case. He posed no personal threat to the *General Polkovnik* because, however ambitious he might be, everyone knew his was no rising star. The ghost of a grandfather saw to that. Even Levin's son, if he ever had one, would find fingers from the past snagging at him as he tried to climb his career ladder.

It suited Stupar to have an efficient, intelligent, brave—*and blighted*—special assistant. Levin made his life easier, and a crucial department ran more smoothly. It was rare now that the Chief Artillery Directorate came under criticism from the Central Committee or the Supreme Military Council.

Stupar, in his turn, protected Levin. On the few occasions the young Captain had made mistakes by taking a wrong initiative, the *General Polkovnik* himself assumed the burden of responsibility and merely pointed out to Levin, without rancor, where he had gone wrong, knowing the man was sufficiently perceptive to avoid a similar error in the future. It was a comfortable, friendly office.

A telephone call from downstairs alerted Levin that the *General Polkovnik* was on the way, and he crossed to the large door of the outer office to salute him and take his coat.

Georgi Borisovich Stupar was a large, seemingly amiable man whose balding gray hair was cropped close to his scalp. Like so many Russians, he was overweight, although in his case the food and drink which caused the problem were of a superior quality.

"You are well, Filipp Ivanovich?" he inquired pleasantly, returning Levin's salute. "You had an enjoyable day off?"

"A quiet day, General," Levin replied formally.

"I am sorry to hear that." He allowed himself to be helped out of his thick, well-cut woolen coat. "When I was your age . . . oh, well, it was different."

Levin followed him through to his office, picking up the leather folder on the way and placing it before him as he settled into his chair.

"What's in there for me today, Filipp Ivanovich?"

"New security requirements on the convoy to Alma Ata, comrade General. We are instructed to observe changed procedures from tomorrow."

"The *Komitet Gosudarstvennoy Bezopasnosti.*" Stupar's voice was noncommittal but tired. The sudden KGB rearrangement would cause considerable logistical problems. Levin's problems. He brightened up, opened the folder, and began reading.

"What else?" he asked.

"Production difficulties at Dnepropetrovsk," Levin said, referring to one of the Soviet Union's largest missile plants near Krivoy Rog.

"Are they serious?"

"Yes. On the face of the report, there seems evidence that incorrect tolerances have been built into a batch of SS-19 missiles."

Stupar stopped reading and looked up incredulously. "How can that be?" he asked. "Why were they not picked up at an early stage?"

Levin shrugged. "The report does not say, sir. The deficiency was detected during a spot check on SS-19s being shipped out to Kasputin Yar. The whole batch has been recalled."

The *General Polkovnik* leafed through the folder until he found the report. Levin watched him read, brow furrowed in anger, and knew orders would shortly be sent summoning the head of the Dnepropetrovsk plant to Moscow, where a verbal assault from Stupar would be one of the more pleasant episodes. The report would also have gone to the KGB, who would begin their own inquiry into possible sabotage. Unless there was a satisfactory explanation, the career of a senior officer would shortly reach an abrupt end, and some of the technicians involved, or suspected of involvement, would leave the factory for the final time in the company of the KGB, and would effectively disappear.

"In your opinion, Filipp Ivanovich, what would happen if one of the defective SS-19s was actually fired?" Stupar asked.

"I would really need more information to be sure, General," Levin replied, "but it seems that the detonation sequence is affected. Probably the missile would fail to explode on impact. There would be some contamination, but not much else."

Stupar nodded, his own suspicions confirmed. "What's all the rest of this stuff in here?" he asked, indicating the leather folder. "What other surprises have you in store for me, Filipp Ivanovich?"

"Nothing unpleasant, comrade General. The dates for your visit to Kazakhstan have been cleared. An underground nuclear test is scheduled for oh nine hundred on the twentieth, which works out well. The dates for the visit to Finland have also been set: June fourth to the sixth. It means you will miss Yelena Yakovlevna's birthday, I'm afraid."

Stupar growled disapprovingly, although Levin could not be certain whether it was over the prospect of being away for his wife's birthday or the fact that she was having one at all. Yelena Yakovlevna may have been a handsome woman once, although Levin himself could not see how, but now at fifty-four she had a face that was at once hard and bitter, and a plump, ugly body. She was not, Levin knew well, the sort of woman the *General Polkovnik* liked or sought the company of when he was away from Moscow.

Levin said: "I'm sure you'll be able to buy your wife a very agreeable gift in Helsinki, comrade General."

"She hates the things I bring her, Filipp Ivanovich," Stupar said matter-of-factly. "Even things from the West, she does not like. Other women like them: Yelena Yakovlevna—no. I think I will send you to shop for me in Helsinki. Perhaps your taste will be better."

Levin felt his heart lurch. "Am I to accompany you, General?" he asked as neutrally as possible, but he knew from the way Stupar grinned at him that he hadn't fooled the old man for a moment.

"Your first trip outside the Soviet Union, I think," Stupar said. "Don't tell me it doesn't excite you, Filipp Ivanovich, because I won't believe you."

Levin felt a smile spreading over his face. Helsinki! It seemed too good to be true. "It sounds wonderful, comrade General," he said simply. "There are things I can bring back for my parents and my sisters . . . and it will be good to go abroad."

"You'll need a foreign passport. I will sign your application. It would be best to do it right away. Our comrades at the KGB do not like to move quickly on such matters."

"I will, comrade General. I will get the forms today."

"What else awaits my attention, Captain?" Stupar gestured at the folder.

"Invitations, General. I have taken the liberty of expressing your regrets for some of the more tedious, but there is one you might find interesting."

Stupar leafed deeper through the file and came up with a batch of stiff embossed invitation cards.

"Surely not the Bulgarians," he said.

"No, sir. I have accepted for that. It is for your information."

Stupar groaned. "You are a hard man, Filipp Ivanovich," he said, flipping up the next card. "Oh, my God—the Afghans. I suppose I will have to go to that too."

"I am afraid so, comrade General."

The *General Polkovnik* paused at the third card and raised his eyebrows. "So," he remarked quietly, "the American Ambassador requests the pleasure. . . . Do I want to go?"

"I think so, comrade General. One never knows what one can pick up from such occasions, and I know there is more than the usual KGB and GRU interest in this case. The new military attaché, you remember. I imagine that acceptance will have their support."

"Very well, Captain. Check with the KGB, and if you have their agreement, accept for both of us."

"Yelena Yakovlevna? But she . . ."

"No, you fool. I would not want to show my wife off to the Americans. She would confirm all their prejudices. I want *you* to come with me. If you are going to be in Helsinki, you had better get used to mixing socially with the West. It will be part of your training. And you can keep your ears open too. You are more likely to hear something of interest than I am."

Levin felt a flush creeping up the back of his neck. He nodded. "Very well, comrade General. I will reply as soon as I secure the necessary permission."

"Nothing else?"

"Nothing, sir."

"Very well. I will go through these documents properly. Please see that my coffee is brought to me as soon as possible. When I ring for you, I will be ready to dictate instructions."

"Very good, comrade General."

Levin bowed stiffly from the waist and went into the anteroom, closing the doors quietly behind him. His mind raced with the possibilities brought by the morning.

Helsinki! A chance to reach the West! The first golden, wonderful opportunity. In a few months he would be free. He would tell the Americans in the next message.

And it would be strange going into the American Ambassador's house. A taste, no doubt, of what he could expect later. Levin wondered if he would see his contact at the reception, and whether someone would introduce them. It would be amusing to shake the hand of Michael Pitt under the eyes of the KGB, the GRU, and his own boss. But he doubted it would happen. The rules probably required that Pitt, if he was there at all, stay well away from his agent.

Levin telephoned the comrade colonel who dealt with liaison between CAD and the KGB and asked him to put in a formal request for a foreign passport and for authorization to accept the American invitation. A decision on the reception could be expected later that day, but Levin doubted that he would even be given the passport application forms in less than a month, and the document itself, if granted, wouldn't be handed over until just before the plane took off. That was the way the KGB worked. They liked to take their time, to keep people waiting, wondering if something in their past had been unearthed. Levin suspected that most of the time the KGB were doing nothing at all except fighting a war of nerves.

The morning passed swiftly. Stupar dictated a blistering message to the head of the Dnepropetrovsk missile plant, demanding his immediate presence in Moscow. It was couched in exactly the terms Levin expected. In fact, he could have drafted it himself without consultation. The comrade *General Mayor* when he read it later in the day would know to expect little understanding.

Levin made arrangements for the appropriate notifications to CAD personnel involved in the missile convoy to Alma Ata, and for the distribution of new security documentation. He could not really see the point of the changes, as the KGB itself was responsible for escorting nuclear equipment and the CAD drivers and technicians had their own identification cards. Suddenly to impose an additional layer of security made little sense to him, but no doubt it looked impressive on paper, and that was an end in itself.

Levin toyed for a while with the idea of going down to the central registry and drawing the complete CAD file on the Vologda base to see if it contained information which would answer the Americans' questions more fully than he already could. His security clearance was certainly high enough to have it released to him, although he would naturally have to sign for it, and this in turn could well lead to a cross-check with the *General Polkovnik*. At the moment there was no legitimate reason for Levin to be scrutinizing the complete file.

He decided he would be better off refreshing his memory with the less complete files held in his own office strong room, to which he had unlimited access.

He waited until Stupar left for the midday meeting with his counterparts at the Ministry of Defense—no doubt to rake over the Dnepropetrovsk matter and begin apportioning blame—and he was reasonably sure he could work in peace for a while.

Other members of Stupar's immediate staff were in a larger office leading off Levin's own. Usually there was constant coming and going, but he knew that now they would be frantic in their efforts to cope with the changed security for the Alma Ata convoy, scheduled to leave the following day, and he was unlikely to be disturbed.

Levin unlocked the strong room and collected three files—two of which he did not require—and settled back at his desk to go through the Vologda documents. He had learned it was always better to be as open as possible in order to deflect suspicion. If someone came into the room, he would close the file with unmistakable deliberateness, to signal that it was forbidden for *their* unauthorized eyes. Only a senior KGB man would ever dream of challenging this.

Levin went swiftly through the Vologda file, memorizing facts. There were three printouts from the center's computer network which contained technical information outside his understanding, and he decided to photograph these.

He walked through to Stupar's office, carrying the files. With a key that the Americans had made for him from an impression he provided. Levin opened the *General Polkovnik's* bottom left-hand desk drawer as far as it would go, and reached behind the back of it for the Minox camera he kept hidden there.

He locked the drawer again in case he should be disturbed. *Everything should have its own rhythm and routine,* he could almost hear Michael Pitt saying. *Cover your tracks. You might have to improvise suddenly. You might not have time to go back.*

With the Minox in his pocket, he glanced through the door to check his own office. He placed the open file on the desk facing the window and began photographing. Click . . . wind on . . . click . . . wind on . . . click . . .

It was a matter of perhaps two minutes, then he was finished. The Minox, wiped for fingerprints, went back behind Stupar's drawer, and the files were replaced in the strong room. He wrapped the film cassette in a plastic bag and dropped it behind the cardboard pockets into which the files slotted, confident that only a major search would reveal it, while he himself could make a retrieval in less than twenty seconds.

Getting it out of the building was another, less pleasant matter. There were periodic searches of pockets and briefcases, and Levin could not take the chance of being caught in a spot check. But if he pushed it deep enough inside himself in the bathroom just before going home, he could walk normally past the guards. However, it was messy and not without pain.

That night Levin wrote his report for Michael Pitt, detailing what he knew about Vologda and explaining why he could not answer certain questions. He told him of the proposed visit to Finland in June and announced his decision to defect when he was there. He asked Pitt to make the necessary arrangements.

He added a paragraph about the problems with the SS-19s at Dnepropetrovsk and another on additional KGB security for the nuclear convoys.

The final line of the cramped handwriting on both sides of the single sheet of paper said that in five days' time he would himself be attending a United States Embassy reception with the *General Polkovnik*. KGB permission had been received for this, and reports would have to be submitted later of anything significant learned at the occasion and personality profiles of Americans spoken to.

Levin folded the paper into a small square, wrapped it around the Minox cassette, which he then wrapped in plain paper. Remembering his previous drop at Pushkin Street, he attached a tiny magnet just inside the last fold and bound the package with thin fuse wire. In case the magnet didn't work, he fashioned a small hook.

Levin checked his watch and found it was 9:30. If he hurried, he would be able to make the cache before it became too late.

He used a phone at the Metro station for his warning call. He dialed first one number and let it ring three times, and then a second number, allowing it to ring four times. Then he caught a train.

There were still people on Gogol Boulevard as Levin strolled along in his captain's uniform. He turned into a house entrance where there was a public telephone. The hall was deserted, but he picked up the phone anyway and pretended to call a girl.

The magnet on the package stuck securely against the underside of the metal base of the telephone, out of sight to anyone standing in the confined space.

Levin finished his call, strolled out, and headed for the Baku Restaurant on Neglinnaya Street, where he knew the headwaiter and was sure of getting a table. He felt light-headed and happier than he could remember. He needed a decent meal. Stupar was right. He should have more fun. He should find himself a permanent girl friend instead of using the KGB whores the *General Polkovnik* occasionally passed on to him and whom he was both too polite, and too hungry, to refuse.

Everything would change when he reached America, he told himself. Once he was there, everything would be all right.

Levin felt poised and secretly amused as the Chakya limousine carrying Stupar and himself turned into the drive of the American ambassador's residence and rolled to a stop at the entrance. None of the others knew it, but he felt he was coming home.

The doors were pulled open, salutes exchanged, and he fell into step two paces behind Stupar, up the stairs and into a well-appointed entrance hall where the reception line waited. Beyond, Levin could see waiters passing among the guests, carrying silver trays of drinks and canapes. The atmosphere immediately seemed to him more relaxed and informal than on a comparable Soviet occasion, even with the KGB among the guests.

The ambassador shook his hand firmly and murmured a welcome. Levin wondered: *Does he know?* He passed on down the line, a few words in English to this person, some words of Russian to that.

Nearly at the end, Levin, with a shock, found himself looking into the calm brown eyes of Michael Pitt and his hand being grasped firmly and held. Stupar was a few feet away, engaged in conversation by the wife of the naval attaché. The next guest behind him had been detained, exchanging greetings with the new military attaché. No doubt a watch was being kept on the reception room by at least one member of the KGB, but for the moment Levin was in a vacuum, confronting his American contact.

Pitt smiled pleasantly, but the words were not the expected formal ones of welcome.

"There's a bathroom off the main reception room, to the left of the President's portrait." Pitt said in an easy, low voice. "You'll find a can of bleach behind the curtain. Unscrew the base and there's something for you."

Then he released Levin's hand and propelled him along the line to be greeted by his wife, who, if she had noticed anything, gave no sign. Levin was conscious of his heartbeat, and his hand had begun sweating.

The maneuver had obviously been prepared. The reception line was waiting for him, and Pitt had passed on the message in a deliberate, unobtrusive, professional manner almost impossible to detect. And it had been done immediately, at a time the KGB would least suspect it. It had taken perhaps ten or fifteen seconds. No longer.

Ahead, the *General Polkovnik* was entering the main room, and Levin joined him quickly. A waiter paused while they selected drinks from the tray, and another hovered with canapes. Stupar spotted some military colleagues and walked over, exchanging loud greetings. Levin stood on the fringe of the group, not being introduced and not expecting to be.

He glanced around the room, quickly locating the portrait of Ronald Reagan, looking photogenic and trustworthy, with the Presidential seal behind him. Doors at the side were open. He would wait a few minutes. Perhaps Stupar would head in that direction and make it easier for Levin to slip out.

He turned his attention politely to the conversation from which he was excluded and sipped his whiskey and soda.

What could the message contain? Almost certainly news about his defection: how it would be accomplished, perhaps. Where in the United States he would be sent.

Stupar was laughing with his colleagues, widening the group to admit two American diplomats and switching the language to English.

Levin could wait no longer. He walked toward the door and accosted an American he knew was talking to two KGB officers.

"Excuse me," he said, "but I wonder if you could direct me to the bathroom?"

"Sure," the American replied, pointing. "Right through that door there. It's facing you."

"Thank you." Levin smiled pleasantly at him and the KGB men, and moved away. *Act openly whenever possible.*

The bathroom was neat and brightly lit. Levin glanced around briefly, crossed to the window, and cautiously pulled back the curtain. The windowpanes beyond were of frosted glass.

Levin picked up the bleach can and examined it. From the weight it obviously still contained some cleanser. He turned it upside down, making sure the lid stayed on, and studied the base. There was nothing to show it had been tampered with. He gripped it firmly, gave an exploratory twist, and it began to unscrew.

Inside a false bottom was a small square of folded paper. Levin toyed with the idea of reading and destroying it right there, when suddenly, from the corner of his eye, he saw the door handle begin to turn. He froze, his eyes wide, and sweat broke out again on his palms. He wished he was certain he had locked it.

Levin heard himself calling out: "One moment, please," and he was surprised at the normality of his voice. He slipped the paper into his pocket and began screwing the base back onto the can, but he misjudged the threads and his hands began to slip. A small trickle of white powder escaped from the lid and dusted over his trousers. He started again, slower this time, forcing himself not to rush, not to panic. The base screwed into place, and Levin replaced the can on the windowsill, feeling weak and sick.

He flushed the toilet and dusted the powder from his clothes as best he could. Then he went to open the door.

"Excuse me, comrade General," he murmured to the bulky Russian waiting outside, but avoided meeting his eye and returned immediately to the reception room, where the buzz of conversation and occasional laughter restored his sense of normality. Levin helped himself to another whiskey from a passing waiter and went to stand near Stupar's group. The *General Polkovnik* did not seem to have noticed his absence or his return.

The note felt electric in Levin's pocket, as if it were emitting rays detectable by anyone in the room who cared to pick them up. Were the KGB watching? He looked around at the men he knew and at those he didn't but who he suspected were either KGB or their military equivalent, the GRU. Most of the Russians, except very senior men like Stupar, seemed to be keeping an eye on other Russians, and that was normal.

"Good evening." A young woman's voice interrupted his train of thought. He looked around to find her smiling at him, hand outstretched. He took it. "I'm Jean Buchanan, with the Embassy," she said. Her voice was warm, with the soft American accent Levin liked.

"Filipp Ivanovich Levin." He inclined his head, feeling immediately awkward. "I am a captain in the army."

"I wasn't sure whether you were looking lonely standing there by yourself, or surveying the battle scene," she said, teasing gently.

"It is my first visit here," he smiled back. "I was looking at the scene of festivity."

"A captain and a diplomat." She raised her glass in a silent toast, and Levin did the same. He noticed a KGB man detach himself from a group a distance away and move closer. Time to work, Levin thought.

"What do you do in the Embassy, Miss Buchanan?" he asked.

"Oh, I'm nothing very important," she said. "Just a secretary in the military attaché's office."

"That sounds very important to me," Levin replied, conscious of the figure nearby, just behind the girl's line of vision but close enough to pick up the conversation. "What is he like, this new boss of yours? We hear many excellent reports."

"Ken's a darling!" she exclaimed. "Just the nicest man. Your reports are all correct. What about you? What do you do in the army?"

"As little as possible," Levin said, remembering the old joke, and when she smiled, still waiting for an answer, he added, "I'm special assistant to *General Polkovnik* Stupar."

He was aware of the KGB man moving closer still, but he refused to let his eyes focus on him.

"That sounds very interesting," Jean Buchanan said. "Have you been there long?"

"A few years."

"By the way, what does *General Polkovnik*—have I said it right? —what does it mean exactly?"

"Your accent is beautiful. In the Soviet Union, it means colonel general. In America the ranks are different, I think. He would be a lieutenant general—what do you say, a three-star general?"

"That's what we say. I must compliment you. Your English is excellent."

"You are kind, Miss Buchanan. I have little chance to practice, I'm afraid. Have you been in Moscow long? Are you learning to speak Russian?"

"Six months. I'm trying to learn, but I find it so very difficult. I can't come to grips with the Cyrillic alphabet, I'm afraid. And my accent is appalling."

"I can't believe that," Levin said. "Your tutor must be very poor. Russian is a language of warmth and beauty. It would suit you very well." He found himself looking at her with a boldness that surprised him. Surely not all for the benefit of the KGB? Nor to cover up the note in his pocket which, if it was discovered, would mean his death?

Jean Buchanan held his glance a second too long before looking down at the carpet with a small laugh. "You Russian boys certainly know how to use the sweet phrase," she said. "Filipp Ivanovich, your wife would not like to hear you talking like that."

"If I had a wife. But I do not."

She smiled fleetingly at him and held out her hand. "Excuse me," she said. "I'm afraid I must circulate."

Her skin was warm and soft, and he was aware of a delicate perfume. He'd gone too fast and had lost. "Enjoy your stay in Russia, Miss Buchanan."

"I'm sure I will. Perhaps we'll see each other again." She withdrew her hand.

"I hope so." Levin gave a small bow and watched her move across the room, not looking back and being quickly absorbed into a crowd of Americans. The KGB man walked away too, but caught his eye briefly with what Levin thought was probably the nearest thing he'd ever get to a look of approval from the secret police.

For the remaining hour Levin spoke to no one, but hovered on the edge of Stupar's group until it was time to go. He glimpsed Michael Pitt once on the other side of the room, deep in conversation.

When Stupar began taking his leave, Levin stepped in behind him, and they were soon in the Chakya.

"Did you enjoy your evening, Filipp Ivanovich?" asked the *General Polkovnik* as they pulled away.

"Very much, sir," Levin replied formally.

"I noticed you spending time with a beautiful young woman. Who was she?"

"A secretary to the military attaché, General."

Stupar laughed uproariously. "Very good. Filipp Ivanovich! Very good!"

"She said nothing of interest, I'm afraid."

"Not this time, my boy. Some other time, perhaps?"

"Perhaps," said Levin noncommittally, knowing he would probably never see her again. This was Moscow, not New York.

The driver delivered Stupar to his apartment on Kutuzovsky Prospekt, then dropped Levin back at his own much more humble rooms. Normally the comparison would have caused the bitterness to resurface, but tonight Levin was concerned only about the note. He locked his front door and, following his routine, went into the bathroom to read it, first with excitement, then dismay.

> GOODS RECEIVED IN EXCELLENT CONDITION. CANNOT REPEAT CANNOT APPROVE HELSINKI PLANS. IMPERATIVE YOU STAY A FEW MONTHS LONGER. REPEAT IMPERATIVE YOU STAY. QUESTIONS FOLLOW AT NEXT DROP WHICH RELYING ON YOU TO ANSWER. HARD WORK NOW: RED CARPET TREATMENT LATER. TRUST ME. MIKE.

Levin chewed the paper to pulp and flushed it away. He lay on his hard, narrow bed in the dark, sick at heart.

At the American Ambassador's residence, the last of the Russians had gone, and the security men moved systematically through all the accessible rooms, sweeping them electronically in case one of the guests had left a bug behind.

7

MARTIN ROSS PORED OVER THE
photographs, making notes and calculations in a notebook beside
him. He had been working for three hours without pause, trying to
understand the computer language used by the Soviets in the four
examples produced by Cane shortly after their return to Fairfax.
Nothing made sense. He constructed his own flow charts, but the
printouts did not seem to relate to each other, and it was impossible
for him to imagine what they did relate to. Yet it was their only lead,
their first communication from the Vologda computer, and somehow
the code had to be cracked. At least the printouts weren't in the
Cyrillic alphabet, so the chances were that the master computer was
based on a Western model with a similar keyboard and special-key
characters.

"Do you mind if we take these over to the NSA?" Ross asked at
last, half-turning in his chair.

Cane looked up from his own work. "Got you beat?"

Ross nodded. "I'm afraid so. Part of it looks very simple, as if it
might be based on the old BASIC system."

"What's the BASIC system?"

"An acronym. You know what we computer whizzes are like.

BASIC stands for Beginners All-Purpose Symbolic Instruction Code. It was invented twenty years ago by a couple of professors at Dartmouth. BASIC was the real beginning of computerspeak. Of course, it's been developed since then, and there are a lot of dialects."

"Wouldn't BASIC be too simple for a sophisticated missile system?" Cane asked, tapping his pockets automatically for a pack of cigarettes before remembering he had given up smoking.

"Not necessarily. There might be a place for it, or a variant, somewhere along the line. The master computer is sure to be a pretty sophisticated machine but, don't forget, the onboard missile computers are fairly simple gadgets. They only have to perform a limited number of tasks. Keep the missiles on course, avoid obstacles if they're going in under the radar, bring them onto target. And trigger a destruct if they get the order. You don't need complex language for simple functions. The only calculations the onboard computers have to do are navigational. But it looks as if they're using other languages as well."

"I didn't know you could mix languages in a computer."

"Sure you can. If the translation software permits, you can actually write programs using several high-level ones. And by high level, naturally I'm excluding BASIC, although that could be there too. From these printouts it looks as if the Soviets have gone for a mix of low and high level. They've probably used a bit of BASIC, or a derivative, for the ordinary Ivan stuck out at a missile base somewhere in case he ever has to intervene. So if something goes wrong with the master computer at Vologda, for example, and the Kremlin wants to alter the missile's target, they'll still be able to pass the order to the programmers at the base and it wouldn't be beyond their capabilities to make the change. Moscow would want everything kept as simple as possible at that stage, I think. At least, if I was advising them, that's what I'd recommend. When you're dealing with programmers under stress, the last thing you want is an error."

"Yes, I can see that," Cane said with a grin. "Take out the Kremlin instead of Washington."

"Crash them into the sea more likely. Or, depending on how they've constructed their missiles, they might just push the red button and find their nukes still sitting in the silos, blowing smoke, while the VDU, the visual display unit, asks the programmer ?WHAT?"

Cane laughed. "Does it really do that?"

"It can."

"So why use other languages if BASIC will do the job?"

"Security probably. They'd want to make it as hard as possible for unauthorized personnel to break into the system. Everyone does this: every bank, corporation, departmental store, or whatever. If you can afford a computer, you need security," Ross said. "There are rules we try to get everyone to observe. For one thing, programmers ought never to be allowed to use the computer without supervision, in case they alter the program deliberately or by mistake. Secondly, there should always be two operators on duty whenever a computer is on-line. Third, every individual has his own code which identifies him to the computer, and there's a password as well. That sort of thing. And that's for the Wells Fargo Bank. We haven't started thinking about the Kremlin yet."

Cane gave a low whistle and gazed out the window at the fields leading down to the forest and, far beyond that, the security fences which protected the DIA ground. They'd really got themselves a bitch this time.

"So what do you want to do next?" he asked thoughtfully.

"I want to take these things down to the NSA and get them run through the computers. We don't have to say what it's for, of course. I want to identify the different languages in use for a start, and see if we can get some clue if these printouts are part of a sequence, or mavericks."

"I don't think there'll be any trouble over that," Cane said, turning back from the window. "I'll get clearance from Yardley, and we can go along to Fort Meade tomorrow morning."

"Fine. I don't think there's much more I can do with these right now."

"Feel like a jog?"

"Not much, thanks."

"Great," Cane said. "I'll give Washington a call and we'll go for a run after that. Say ten minutes?"

"Sadist," growled Ross.

"Nonsense. You feel better already, don't you? Better than you've felt for years."

"No."

"See what I mean?"

Ross watched him go. He did feel better, of course. His trousers were loose on him for a change, and perhaps he was imagining it, but when he inspected himself in the bathroom during his week at Princeton, he seemed to detect a slight improvement in muscle tone. Not much, but slight, and at his age anything was a blessing.

He had felt too diffident to ask Elaine if she noticed anything, and she hadn't mentioned it, beyond saying when he arrived home that he looked well.

It had been a good break, he thought. Nice to be home. Elaine was cheerful and supportive about his assignment. No sign of second thoughts there, although she was careful not to inquire too closely into any of the details. That wasn't unusual. Throughout their married life, one or the other of them had been involved in some sensitive government project, and although the broad outlines were shared, the details and findings seldom were.

And yet something at home had changed, and he still wasn't sure what.

She had accepted him into her bed on the first night, and on the last she came over to his own room while he was lying in the darkness wondering whether to make a move or go to sleep. She hadn't done that for more years than Ross cared to remember.

But that wasn't what preoccupied his mind as he sat in the impersonal, cream-painted office, which had become as familiar to him as his own comfortable book-lined study.

It really hadn't been a very good week, he thought to himself suddenly. A bit of a disappointment, in fact. The constituent parts, examined separately, were everything they should be. The totality was much less.

He had not been able to settle down. His work was in Fairfax with David Cane, and the books he read to take its place were unsatisfying and inconsequential.

He spent too long pacing moodily around the house while Elaine worked on her own projects, and he avoided seeing their friends more than he had to because he had almost nothing to say to them and no patience for cocktail gossip.

He found he drank little and woke naturally before dawn, feeling refreshed. Cane had suggested that he take home a track suit and have a thirty-minute jog every day, and he was surprised to discover he really wanted to do this. The suburban roads of Princeton, darkness patched with streetlights, the predawn chill, silent except for the sound of his running shoes on the sidewalks, filled him with a strange contentment. He had a sense of the physical, of tightening muscles, the warmth of sweat. He missed Cane most on these mornings: a strong, encouraging, young presence, setting the pace in the gathering light.

He realized he had actually spent the week waiting to get back to Fairfax. Had he communicated this to Elaine? He didn't think so. On the surface, nothing had changed. There were no sharp words or strains between them. No misunderstandings.

Ross stood up abruptly and went to prepare for his workout with Cane. There was no point in brooding, the change was within himself. He felt as if he was in a period of growth, and people he loved and familiar things were being left behind.

The next morning Ross and Cane drove into Maryland and headed for the National Security Agency, the biggest government installation in the Washington area, larger even than the sprawling CIA complex at Langley and staffed by many more men and women.

The NSA specialized in cryptography, the science of communications intelligence. In one part of the Operations Building, teams eavesdropped on conversations between Soviet pilots on training sorties thousands of miles away. But it was in the Office of Production —PROD to those who worked in or used it—that electronic espionage was practiced in its purest form. Several billion dollars' worth of assorted decoding machines and computers processed intercepts from the NSA's net of more than 2000 positions around the world. It was this technology that drew Ross and Cane to Fort Meade, armed with special clearance from the Pentagon requiring that they be given, on a top priority basis, whatever assistance they asked for.

Ross was well-known to the cryptoanalysis teams and the security men in PROD, and Cane was immediately aware of the cheerful acceptance of their requests and the respect the balding professor commanded.

Ross handed over the photographs of the Soviet printouts and explained what he wanted. There was some discussion about whether it would be better to run them through the IBM or the group of UNIVACS, but Ross thought the Atlas computer, built to NSA specifications, would probably best fit the bill, and this was immediately accepted.

In the air-conditioned quiet of one of the PROD computer rooms, Cane and Ross drank coffee and chatted with the chief of the cryptoanalysis team while the Atlas began spewing out paper.

Ross ignored it. The results would eventually be as fat as a telephone directory, with the final pages setting out balances of probabilities. He doubted the Atlas would come up with a clear-cut solution, as the sample fed into it was too small. What they really needed were further printouts from Vologda—one complete program if possible. That would give a better idea of the Soviet system.

Meanwhile, in a few minutes the Atlas would save him months of painstaking calculations and provide a series of results on which to do his own detective work. The beauty of computers was that however many security obstacles might be set up, every program was essentially chained, split into small linked segments. Solving problems was a matter of logic, as beautiful and mathematical in its way as a prelude by Bach, and Ross had been seized by the heuristic passion for his entire adult life.

When the Atlas had completed its work, Ross glanced at the final pages of the printout, with Cane looking over hs shoulder.

The cryptoanalysis chief and his team kept a discreet distance. The Pentagon message made it clear that, for them, this was a "hands-off" operation, and in any case they were well aware that Professor Ross required no assistance.

The printout was meaningless to Cane: a jumble of letters, figures and symbols filling the sheet in apparently random order; but Ross read, eyes bright, finger following the lines. Occasionally he gave a small grunt of satisfaction.

Finally, he straightened up and turned to the others. "Gentlemen," he said, "I think I've got enough to keep me busy for some time. Thank you for your help. We're very grateful."

"Anytime," the chief said. "Do you want to try it through the IBM?"

"Not at this stage, Jim," Ross replied. "I have to think this through properly first. Maybe later we'll rerun it with a few variables and see what comes out. Thanks for the coffee."

He handed the printouts to Cane to lock into a black case, and they all shook hands.

When they were through the security gates and on the road back to Fairfax, Cane said: "Well? Are you going to share it with me or aren't you?"

He glanced at the man beside him, buckled into his seat belt and utterly relaxed.

"It's looking good, David," Ross said simply. "Better than I hoped. Of course, there's nothing conclusive, but the probabilities . . . It looks as if we're dealing with two high-level languages and a variation on BASIC. I'll have to go carefully through it to see if we can find out what the originals refer to. And I can't be sure yet if the Russian printouts are part of a sequence or not."

"But you've got something to work on?"

"Oh yes. Weeks of work. The first real clues, David. Everything we've done so far has been secondhand: reports from agents on how they think the computer works, the occasional bit of bugging. Some of the facts fitted, some didn't. And we've got to be a hundred percent sure. This is the first time we've had a chance to look at primary material. It's invaluable. Of course, we must try to get more."

Cane accelerated to overtake a line of cars. "Well, we can try," he said thoughtfully. "I don't know how easy that's going to be. We have to move carefully. Can't have Moscow Center even know we're interested. Let's see what can be done."

The weeks that followed saw a step-up in activity at Fairfax. The professor was immersed in the Atlas printouts during days that were punctuated at each end by intense physical activity. Cane was putting on the pressure, taking advantage of Ross's improved condition and hyped-up mental state. The gentle morning jog through the forest at first became an unbroken run. Then Cane changed the course to take them over rough ground and up a steep hill, which had Ross's breath coming in gasps and his body aching as it had not done since the earliest days of training. Each session ended back in the gym with exercises, a shower, and a lesson in unarmed combat.

Ross learned slowly, partly because he had never been a physical person and had not since his school days been involved in a fight. He had the instincts of a gentleman, while Cane was gradually inculcating those of a street fighter.

They had not yet reached the stage where Cane would broach the subject of killing. The emphasis so far had been on the nonviolent nature of their mission, but Cane knew that if they were taken by surprise, they might have to fight their way out and that, although they would be unarmed, no witnesses could be left. He would need all the help he could get—whatever the professor was able to give.

Ross would have to reach the right psychological point before they moved into this phase, and it was Cane's experience that the fitter and more confident the man, the easier it was to take him over that final step.

Cane looked after the professor's body, judged when it could take no more without damage and when it could be pushed a fraction further. He massaged aching muscles, supervised a strict diet, and went with Ross on his weekly medical checkups to the DIA clinic in the training ground. His ECG was normal—excellent for a man of Ross's age—and his blood pressure was good.

Although neither articulated it, both were aware of the closeness and trust building up between them. Cane couldn't help liking and admiring the professor. Although his courage had never been tested —and no one ever knew how a man would react to extreme personal danger until the moment arrived and the answer was there for all to see—Cane had a hunch that he wouldn't fail. The operation seemed to fill a gap in his life, a gap he probably hadn't even been aware existed until the proposition was put to him, and he found he couldn't turn down that ultimate challenge.

It was partly machismo. Ross himself could feel that now. But he also felt deeply committed to the operation itself, its reason, and its consequences. So much, so many lives, hung on the outcome.

When Ross thought about it, it seemed melodramatic and absurd that he and David Cane might, if luck and planning were with them, literally save the West. No two men in history had ever gambled for such stakes. The nearest example Ross could come up with was the Kennedy show-down with Khrushchev over the introduction of missiles to Cuba.

Ross was also aware that he and Cane might forfeit their lives in the attempt. The end could come in a sudden burst of bullets, or slowly in the Lubyanka Prison just off Dzerzhinskiy Square when Ross told all he knew as fast as his mind and his voice could go, not hoping to save his life but to persuade the KGB to end it more quickly. He knew enough about himself and about interrogation methods to realize that in certain appalling circumstances there would be no secrets. Perhaps Cane was different. Every person had his own threshold, perhaps a personal hatred that could keep him enduring beyond reason.

Yet even these risks seemed puny in comparison with the importance and simplicity of the project. And when he wasn't being introspective, Ross felt good. Cane's strength and competence—and intelligence—bolstered his own confidence. As the days went on, this grew.

If any team could get into the Vologda base undetected, doctor the master program, and leave quietly, they were it.

And so Ross worked out in the gym, sometimes aware of Cane standing close, veins bulging in his neck and forehead as he screamed commands and cursed him, until Ross's elderly body moved only because Cane commanded it to. But if he ever hit real trouble, Cane was there, releasing cramps, massaging exhausted muscles, encouraging.

It wasn't as if the professor's regimen was particularly taxing; not in comparison with Cane's. Occasionally Ross, at the end of his workout, would sit against the gym wall, limp as a rag, and watch the young agent go through his own paces. He felt admiring but a little ashamed. The gap in performance was almost as wide as the one in age.

But what Ross lacked in his body, he made up for with his mind. He worked on the Atlas printouts as doggedly—Cane would have said brilliantly—as he had ever in his life. Slowly, one by one, the secrets of the Vologda computer were being revealed.

After a couple of weeks, Ross was certain that the Soviets had devised a master program split into three main sections, each of which used a different language. The reason for the complexity was clearly security. He had identified, on the basis of overwhelming probability, that the high-level languages in use were FORTRAN (FORmula TRANslation) and ALGOL (ALGOrithmic Language).

An operator entered the system using passwords which Ross did not yet know. Perhaps there were even two separate security systems, only half of each being known to any one team, so that two programmers, sitting at separate VDUs, would have to act together to enter the system and run the master program in an operational mode, thus enabling them to make alterations.

The same restrictions would probably be necessary to order the missile bases to fire their weapons. No one, neither Moscow nor Washington, would want there to be a mistake about starting World War III. Ross was reasonably certain that the orders to fire could be passed through the computer system, as well as by more conventional communications methods such as teletype or radio link, from places other than Vologda. Any Soviet president, like his American counterpart, was followed everywhere by a secret service man carrying a black box through which the order could be given to begin hostilities.

The Vologda computer was a sophisticated device for monitoring the condition of any individual missile, determining whether it was fully fueled and ready to go, whether the nuclear device was armed or not, and, most important from the American point of view, where it was targeted to hit. Naturally the target would have to be variable, and it was his job, and Cane's, to get in and vary it.

The Vologda printouts did not contain the firing sequence, Ross was sure of that. Instead they consisted of reports on operational readiness at three missile sites, identified by code numbers which were impossible to crack without more information.

Once through the initial security barrier, the language used was FORTRAN and it dealt with the targets. Ross established that of a battery of twelve missiles detailed on the first printout, six were zeroed in on New York, the rest on Washington. When he fixed the translated coordinates on a map and discovered this, it was as if a frozen hand had touched him. Everything became real, not merely theory. Other printouts showed twelve additional missiles were targeted for New York—eighteen in all, just in these random examples, enough to level the entire city—while the others were set to detonate in Chicago and Detroit.

After that there was a language switch to ALGOL. The information contained in this section was about operational readiness. From what Ross could make out—and Cane confirmed it after technical discussions with experts—the thirty-six missiles were ready to go.

The final section of the printouts was in a BASIC dialect, repeating the target coordinates. Presumably any of the bases had the capability to alter individual targets for the missiles under their command if appropriate orders came through. But only Vologda was able to change everything at every single base. And this master control, deep underground, was protected as determinedly as if the fate of the Soviet Union hung upon it, which in fact it might.

Ross had made a good start. Because of the logical way in which a program was put together, once he knew the language and the results being sought, he was able to construct flowcharts—diagrams of the steps in a program showing their connections—which provided him with an insight into the minds of the Soviet data-preparation operators. He found himself quite impressed. There were a couple of improvements which he would have suggested had he been employed as a consultant, but certainly the program did what it was designed to do.

When he was ready he laid everything out and explained it to Cane, line by line. Even as he talked and was aware of the enthusiasm he was generating, Ross felt a growing dissatisfaction within himself. It was good, but it wasn't enough. They had reached the point where they could look through a keyhole, whereas they really needed to swing open the whole door. And they had just run out of information.

"David, we've got to do better than this," Ross said dejectedly when he had finished. "I've learned just about all I can from these printouts, and I'll tell you frankly, I wouldn't go near Russia on that basis."

"What's the problem?" Cane hoisted himself to sit on the edge of the desk, instinct telling him that Ross, from an emotional high, was about to experience his first crisis, and that helping him through the subsequent depression would be the immediate priority. What he said was true. And there would be very little intellectual stimulation available to him until agents in the Soviet Union came up with new information, and God knew when that would be.

"The problem is," Ross said, "that we know the bread-and-butter parts of the Vologda operation, but none of the real secrets. What are the passwords? They're not on the printouts. Maybe they were torn off for security reasons, but they're absolutely crucial. We have to know precisely how to log-on—gain access to the computer. We've also got to know how to log-out. Again, that's not on the printouts. There's a special procedure for leaving any computer, and if you don't follow it exactly, the next people in will see at once that it's still on-line, and they'll know someone's been tampering."

Cane began scribbling notes on a sheet of paper. "Okay," he said, "let's make a list of what we have to know. One—logging-on: procedure, passwords . . ."

"User numbers, user names, don't forget those. Every operator must identify himself to the computer." Ross's voice was agitated.

"Right, got it. Logging-out." Cane remained deliberately cool and confident. "What else?"

"Use of special-key effects."

"What the hell are those?"

"They're keys on the terminal which don't print characters on the visual display unit. Carriage return, for example, or pressing down the control key at the same time you type an ordinary character. You don't see them on the screen or the printout, but they're there all right, and if you don't know where they're used and how *many* there are, the computer will reject your program."

Cane's pen scribbled the list. "Fine," he said. "Anything else?"

"And the master program. I need a complete breakdown of that."

"Isn't that what you worked out on your pieces of paper over there?"

"More or less. But I have to have it confirmed, and I'm sure we'll find some vital differences."

"Right," Cane said. "We'll get this list off to Moscow as soon as possible. It'll take a while, because it's got to be hand delivered. I don't think we'll trust it to the codes by themselves."

Ross stared at him somberly. "What are our chances, David? Are we going to get in?"

Cane looked him confidently in the eye. "We're going to get in, Martin," he said. "We've got people in place over there we haven't really called on yet, and we're going to call on them now. It might take a bit of time. I can't tell you how long, because we have to move carefully. Weeks perhaps. Maybe a couple of months. While we're waiting, we'll concentrate on our other work."

"How to get into Vologda? That'll be a bitch."

"You bet. But it's my bitch. That, and getting you into shape. You've done pretty well so far. We're all pleased with you. Me particularly. I think you're doing a great job on yourself, and I know it hasn't been easy. I'd better tell you now that it's not going to be easy in the future either. We've got to start working on your reactions, speeding them up. You're not doing too badly on self-defense. We'll go get changed now and have a run. Then I'll start teaching you some new principles—how to attack."

"Do I have to know how to attack?"

"Yes," Cane confirmed. "We're not going in as aggressors, I know, but the point may come when that's what we have to become. If it's our lives or theirs, we'll try to save ourselves. That's fair enough. So, Martin, I want to teach you how to fight dirty. I'm going to teach you how to kill."

The men looked at each other: Cane calm, determined; Ross initially uncertain, quickly glancing away to some undefined point on the floor while his mind raced over all the standard objections. Both knew this was a watershed.

Ross's mouth had gone dry and he had difficulty getting the words out, but when they came they were firm. "All right," the professor said. "Teach me."

Cane got up without a word, and Ross followed him to their room to change, an elderly man trailing after a young one, feeling both inadequate and excited, with a slight tremble in his legs.

THE KGB CAME A WEEK AFTER THE American reception, at a time when Filipp Ivanovich Levin least expected them. He had written his report the following morning when the knot of disappointment at Michael Pitt's message had not yet subsided and he was fighting off waves of depression. The report was brief and concise, and he showed it to *General Polkovnik* Stupar before delivering it to the KGB. Stupar read it without comment but handed it back with a grin.

Levin half-expected to be summoned for another interview with the KGB and questioned about the evening, but when the call did not come that day or the next, he presumed the officer who overheard the conversation with Jean Buchanan had given his own version, and that the matter had been closed. It was an inconclusive encounter which netted nothing of value. What else could be expected from a crowded cocktail party?

Over the next few days, Levin did his work automatically, without enjoyment. The prospect of Helsinki no longer seemed so exciting, and, of course, his application papers for a foreign passport had not even been given to him. If the KGB thought they were keeping him in a state of nervous anticipation, which would only increase the closer the scheduled departure date, he had news for them. He no longer cared very much whether he went or not. But Pitt's words nagged at him: Questions follow at next drop. Which questions? Why was it imperative that he stay in Moscow? He knew with a sinking feeling that as far as he was concerned, the reverse of "imperative" was "dangerous."

Trust me, said Michael Pitt, secure with his American passport and his diplomatic immunity.

Levin left the Chief Artillery Directorate offices and walked through the icy, crowded, dark streets to his apartment, determined to finish half a bottle of vodka to warm himself and improve his spirits before getting something to eat, and more to drink.

His room was on the fifth floor of a block inhabited mostly by minor state servants and their families. Although it was far below the standard he would ordinarily have been entitled to by virtue of his rank and job, the other occupants of the building were envious of him. Levin had a room to himself; a kitchen and bathroom he did not have to share with others. To people living three or four to a room, that was luxury.

Levin was regarded with diffidence and respect, mostly because none of the others knew what to make of him. The fact that he had his own room meant he was a man of some importance. And he was a captain, which made him more so, although neither of these squared with living in such a low-quality building. Also Levin was a loner. He appeared to have no men friends, no army comrades who visited his quarters. In one way this was generally considered to be a blessing, otherwise there would certainly have been long evenings of vodka and songs, which would have been vicariously shared by the families on the other sides of the insubstantial partitions who would have been kept awake but unable to complain.

There were few women visitors either. Only twice in as many years could those who lived in adjacent rooms remember those unmistakable noises filtering through the walls: the low voices, a bed that squeaked, a cry.

There was much speculation about the comrade Captain, and it was believed he had something to do with the KGB, a man therefore to be treated with caution, who was probably keeping watch on the rest of them.

There was, of course, no elevator to his apartment, and Levin climbed the flights of stairs past the flaking green-and-cream painted walls.

"Good evening, comrade Captain." An old woman in black with a shawl around her head made her obeisance on a landing as if he had the power of life and death and might one day be inclined to use it if he found her insufficiently respectful.

Levin paused. Two flights to go. "Good evening, Irina Dmitriyevna," he replied formally. "Is everything well with you?"

"Of course, comrade Captain. Except for the cold. But even the Central Committee can do nothing about that."

Levin smiled thinly. "Indeed not," he said, resuming his climb, feeling her eyes watching him out of sight.

Levin turned his key in the lock and went in. The room was dark, with only a glow of the lights from the city filtering through the window. He closed the door after him and felt for the light switch. It really was cold. He would need both the heater and a glass of vodka to feel comfortable enough to remove his coat.

Light flooded the room, and Levin found himself staring at a KGB colonel, sitting relaxed in his only armchair, and he froze, his mouth opening and closing like a goldfish.

Levin's stomach felt hollow and sick. *Trust me.* They know, he thought. Dear God on high, they know. And now they had come to get him. He thought instinctively of running to the window, hoping his weight and momentum would be enough to smash through the wooden frame so that he could die quickly on the icy pavement below. But he had frozen and his body was made of lead.

The colonel watched dispassionately. It was a scene he had witnessed many times before: proof of the power and effectiveness of the *Komitet Gosudarstvennoy Bezopasnosti.*

Levin's eyes flickered around the room. The colonel appeared to be alone. If the room had been searched, it had been done neatly because nothing was obviously displaced. But there wasn't anything for them to find: not there. At his offices, yes. And presumably at that moment, the KGB were going systematically through it, finding the Minox and the small supply of film in the recess behind the *General Polkovnik's* bottom desk drawer. Everything else was committed to memory.

Levin drew a breath. "Comrade Colonel," he said in a voice which, even to him, sounded unsteady.

"Sit down, comrade Captain." It was an order.

The colonel was a stocky man with black eyes in which it was impossible to distinguish iris from pupil; one only knew that the gaze was lazy and cold.

Levin sat on a hard upright chair, the only other available, back rigid, hands on his knees. The colonel let him wait.

He took a pack of cigarettes casually from his coat—imported cigarettes, Levin noticed—and lit up. "You don't smoke, of course, Filipp Ivanovich," he said, stating a fact.

"No, comrade Colonel."

"No vices? Girls, perhaps? Yes, a few. Boys? No, in your case, I think not. You see, we know everything about you, Filipp Ivanovich. *Everything*."

Levin felt his heart lurch painfully, and he thought for a moment he would be sick, right there on the floor in front of the colonel. He nodded. It was finally finished. His life, and whatever hopes he had for finding freedom, would end, probably in a KGB basement.

And yet, in an unexpected moment of self-revelation, he found he did not regret what he had done. He regretted being discovered, of course, deeply, and he feared what was to come. But not to have attempted to reach for something better, a more honest life, to have turned out eventually like old Irina Dmitriyevna out there on the steps with her wheedling voice and obsequious manners just because she thought someone else might have power and influence—that would truly have been a betrayal. Later of course he would be broken, but now, while he could, he would be tall. He lifted his chin and stared at the colonel. Let him play it in his own way and his own time, Levin thought. God knows, they do every day. Well, let's see how they unmask a traitor.

Levin waited patiently and found the colonel's cold, blank stare turning to something more thoughtful. At last, the KGB man said abruptly: "Tell me about your grandfather, comrade Captain."

For a moment Levin couldn't believe his ears. His *grandfather*? For God's sake—what about Michael Pitt? What about the dead drops? He felt a surge of hope, almost as nauseating as that of the shock and despair a few moments earlier.

He took a couple of deep breaths to settle himself, then said in a shaky voice: "My grandfather died ten years before I was born, comrade Colonel. He was a White Russian, as you know. He fought against the Bolsheviks."

"What do you think of him, Filipp Ivanovich?"

"I never knew him, comrade Colonel. I have only seen his face in old photographs. Our family hardly ever discussed him."

The colonel stood up. "Don't fence with me, Captain," he said shortly. "What do you think of his actions?"

Levin gained confidence. "I think he was mistaken, comrade Colonel."

"Only mistaken?"

"We are looking back now with the benefit of hindsight. To us everything seems clear. I doubt that it was clear in the early part of the century, not to the aristocracy, or to the middle class, of which my family were members."

The colonel gave a mirthless smile and gestured round the cold, sparsely furnished room. "And where are your middle-class pretensions now, Filipp Ivanovich?"

Levin replied calmly: "I did not say *I* had middle-class pretensions, comrade Colonel. As you know, there is no middle class today, or upper class, or lower class. We are all Soviets, and equal. The Constitution guarantees that. I was talking about the situation at the beginning of the century."

"But some are more equal than others, eh?" Again, the colonel stared disdainfully around the room.

"My quarters were allocated to me, as they are to everyone who is registered to live in Moscow," Levin said with dignity. "No doubt there was a reason. I have not complained."

The colonel resumed his chair. "No," he said at last, "you have not complained. Your patron would probably have seen you got a better apartment if you had."

"My patron, comrade?"

"Georgi Borisovich Stupar."

"I would not bother the *General Polkovnik* with such matters," Levin said with finality.

"You do not care for comfort, Captain? You do not mind living in this hovel?"

Levin looked at the colonel with a flicker of amusement. "If I had comfort, I would no doubt enjoy it, as you do, comrade," he said. "As I do not, I make the best of what I have."

The colonel dropped his cigarette onto the wooden floor and stubbed it out with a well-polished boot. "Come with me," he said abruptly. "It is time."

Again, Levin felt the surge of panic. He wanted desperately to ask where he was being taken, what was happening, but he thought he knew the answer in his heart, and he feared hearing confirmation.

Both men stood up. The colonel gestured to the door and followed him out into the passage. Levin turned to lock it.

"Don't bother," the colonel said. "There's nothing left inside."

Levin stared at him. It was true then. The KGB ruse: allay suspicions, then strike. He straightened up and led the way down the flights of stairs, conscious of Irina Dmitriyevna and others watching from the landings of the lower floors.

A KGB car was parked in front. It had not been there when Levin arrived home. Without being asked, he climbed into the back, the colonel beside him, and the uniformed driver accelerated away.

Levin took a final look at the shabby building. It was a hovel, overfull of life. It had been his home, and now it seemed infinitely dear to him. He settled passively back in the seat. No one spoke.

After ten minutes Levin noticed they had turned down Kutuzovsky Prospekt and were heading toward the building where the *General Polkovnik* had his apartment. Perhaps they were going to confront his patron with the traitor.

It would reflect badly on Stupar, having an American spy as his special assistant, and Levin was sorry for that. He had not meant to harm him, although when he thought about it, he realized it was of course inevitable. If he had succeeded in defecting, not only his boss but his parents and sisters too would have felt the repercussions.

Yet the car passed Stupar's apartment block, and Levin had no idea where they could be going. They were traveling in the wrong direction for the Lubyanka. But perhaps there was another interrogation center of which he was unaware.

Still in Kutuzovsky Prospekt, the car drew to a halt.

"We get out here," said the colonel. And this time it was the KGB man who led the way, apparently confident Levin would follow and not try to run for it. Not that there was anywhere for a fugitive to go in Moscow. Not for long. They entered a luxurious lobby with marble floors, freshly painted white walls, and a Socialist Art mural —youth marching steadfastly to victory or something similar—and potted plants. Whoever lived there would have to be of the importance of the *General Polkovnik*.

The colonel pressed a button for the elevator and immediately doors slid open. It took them to the sixth floor, and they emerged into a carpeted—Levin could hardly believe it—a carpeted public corridor. They stopped at the door to room 611, and the colonel produced a key.

"Go in," he ordered.

Levin found himself in a beautifully furnished living room. The sofas and easy chairs were of tan leather, surrounding a huge chocolate shag carpet. The walls were hung with originals, none of them showing youth marching anywhere. There was a large color television set and an impressive imported stereo with what looked like hundreds of records and tapes.

The colonel flung wide his arms. "How do you like it, Filipp Ivanovich? Not bad, eh?"

So it was the colonel's. He might have guessed. "Very nice, comrade."

"Better than that hovel we've just been in."

Levin inclined his head. "Yes, comrade Colonel."

"Have a look around." He led Levin into the dining room—a dining room!—and showed him a kitchen the size of his entire old apartment.

"This one washes the dishes," the colonel said, pointing out the sparkling equipment. "That one washes the clothes, except there's a maid who actually does it. That's an American stove with a wall oven. Well, Filipp Ivanovich?"

Levin had nothing to say. It was unthinkable luxury.

"And here's the refrigerator." He opened it: full of items obtainable only in the stores for the Party hierarchy and VIPs.

"Come, I'll show you the bedroom."

Levin stood awkwardly at the door of a large room, taking in the king-size bed, the built-in closets, another color television set. What the hell was going on?

"I congratulate you, comrade Colonel," he said stiffly. "It is a beautiful apartment."

The KGB man looked at him amused. "Oh, it's not mine, Filipp Ivanovich. My wife and I live in a rather more modest style, I'm afraid. No, this is yours."

Levin turned to him incredulously. "I don't understand," he said faintly.

"We'll talk tomorrow. I am Mikhail Ilich Malik. You'll still be doing your ordinary work for Georgi Borisovich, but he knows you'll be going out at eleven o'clock tomorrow morning. One of my men will call for you. Oh, there are clothes in the closets—your own, and new ones. You must take more care how you dress, comrade Captain. You'll find everything fits, I think. If there's a problem with the clothes or anything else, ask me about it. And I haven't shown you the bathroom—but it's through there, see for yourself later. Now I must go. Good night, Captain."

He held out his hand, and Levin found himself shaking it. Then he was gone, and Filipp Ivanovich stood dumbly in the living room.

It was a trick, a trap. Colonel Malik had left, but the KGB were still there somehow—listening, probably watching. But from where? Levin looked for a mirror fixed to an outside wall from the other side of which KGB teams would be able to spy on and film him. But the only one was on an interior wall, and it hung on ordinary hooks. In the bedroom then—yet the full-length mirror he found there was screwed to the inside of a closet door.

Well, certainly the apartment would be wired for sound, built into the actual construction—microphones Levin would never be able to find, and he didn't bother to look.

Instead he inspected the enormous bathtub, and the separate shower. He ran the water and found it so hot after a few moments that it almost scalded his hand. The apartment even had two toilets.

Levin went through to the kitchen and opened the refrigerator. There were cans of American beer:—Budweiser and Schlitz—French wine, and a bottle of top-quality vodka. Levin hunted through the kitchen for glasses. As he carried the vodka and a couple of beers through to the living room, he realized he was so hot he was starting to sweat. Of course, the apartment was heated. He removed his coat and scarf and dropped them on a chair.

Levin poured himself a half-glass of vodka and downed it in two gulps. He opened a can of Schlitz and drank that.

He sat on a brown leather sofa and leaned back, testing it. It was the most comfortable piece of furniture he had ever sat in. Levin stared around him in wonder. It was all really quite funny.

Suddenly he began to giggle, then to laugh uproariously, and finally, with relief and shock and bafflement, Levin started to weep.

Later he felt ashamed. If the apartment was bugged, and he was certain it would be, the KGB would have heard everything. Mikhail Ilich Malik would have a piece of paper on his desk the following morning saying; "Filipp Ivanovich Levin laughed for a few moments and then cried like a child." It was demeaning.

Levin knew he had to eat something, but he wanted urgently to get out of this new apartment in which he felt so strange, so he decided to follow his original plan when he left his office (it seemed like a week ago) and to visit a restaurant.

He was about to pull on his old, fairly shabby coat when curiosity drew him to the bedroom to look through the closets. He discovered them full of clothes: overcoats, raincoats, suits, a black dinner jacket, a blazer, shirts, socks, shoes, each an item of quality. He fingered cloth of different weights and textures. He found himself murmuring appreciatively, then he was on the verge of giggling again, but with an effort he pulled himself together. He did not want to repeat his earlier performance.

His hands, seeming to move independently of his brain, fumbled hurriedly at the buttons of his shirt, his trousers. He pulled off his shoes and socks, stripped off his underpants, and stood naked before the fantastic array of garments. What to wear? There was so much.

Levin chose a silk shirt, a dark, pure-wool suit, and a silk tie. The socks were made of thick wool and the shoes completely of leather. He inspected himself in the mirror. Everything fitted, just as Mikhail Ilich Malik had said they would, and they felt incredible. Because he remembered how cold it was outside, he selected a cashmere scarf and overcoat. A different man looked back from the glass, grinning like an idiot.

From his old coat Levin collected his wallet with identity cards and money and left the apartment, locking the door after him.

In the street only his face and hands stung with the cold. His body was in a cocoon of warmth. He wished he had looked for a pair of gloves. He had no doubt there would have been a choice.

He thrust his hands into his overcoat pockets and headed briskly down Kutuzovsky Prospekt, beginning to enjoy himself. He made his way to Neglinnaya Street and his favorite restaurant, the Baku, relishing the walk, being seen like this. A man engaged him in conversation, thinking he was a foreigner, and was obviously about to make an offer for his shoes or some other item of clothing when Levin addressed him in Russian, and he hurried away, apologizing profusely.

The headwaiter took in his new appearance at a glance and with considerable deference ushered him to a table.

The meal would be a celebration, Levin decided. He was still a free man, against all the odds, and he was being rewarded in some strange way. Rewarded, or enticed. It did not matter. He was in no position to argue. No one argued with the KGB, least of all when they were handing out luxuries. One merely accepted what was given on account, knowing that repayments would have to be made later.

For as long as it lasted, he would enjoy his luxurious circumstances. After all, was this not what life would be like in America?

Levin ordered caviar and duckling cooked with sour cabbage and pork. He had vodka and a bottle of wine. At the end, feeling replete and a little drunk, he signaled for the bill, knowing it would cost virtually all he had. But who cared? The refrigerator was full, and there was more where that came from. He could eat in the apartment every night for the rest of the month. Watch television. God, lie in *bed* and watch television! Listen to music. Have his family in and just see their faces! The headwaiter hurried over.

"Dmitriy Petrovich, where is my bill?" Levin demanded ebulliently.

The waiter leaned close and spoke in a low voice: "Oh no, comrade Captain, there is nothing to pay. It goes on the account."

Through the pleasant haze that enfolded him, Levin regarded the man with good-natured doubt. "I have no account at the Baku, my friend. I pay as I go, with rubles."

"But the other comrades gave specific instructions . . ."

"What other comrades?" Levin looked owlish.

"The two who came in just after you. They said you were not to be troubled with bills in the future."

"KGB comrades?"

The waiter nodded yes. Levin sat totally still. He hadn't noticed he was being followed, but then he hadn't particularly looked. And they obviously weren't making any secret of it.

"Are they still here?"

The waiter looked surreptitiously around the restaurant and back at Levin. "Over there in the corner near the door."

Levin felt himself sobering up. He glanced in that direction, at the two whose plates were being cleared away and who did not seem to be paying him any attention.

"Very well then," he said, rising to his feet. "Our comrades will have their way, as always. My coat, please, Dmitriy Petrovich."

The headwaiter hurried to get it and helped him put it on, his fingers almost caressing the soft fabric. "It's beautiful," he murmured. "Truly beautiful."

Levin pressed some notes into his hand, and the waiter's eyes widened with alarm as if he was being burned. "Oh no, comrade Captain, please . . ."

"Take it. You are hidden from their sight, my friend. Quickly now."

The money vanished as if in the hands of a magician.

Levin, as he left, did not look directly at the KGB men, but noticed from the corner of his eye that they did not appear to be preparing to leave. Still, it would take them no time. Their bill would also go on the account.

During the walk back, Levin checked over his shoulder several times to see if he could identify them, but the street was virtually empty and they were nowhere in sight. But they *were* out there somewhere. Levin became thoughtful. He had believed it would be fairly easy to spot KGB surveillance. That was the basis on which he had worked before in making the caches. Now, when he actually knew he was being followed and had seen the men doing it, he could not find them. The effects of the vodka and the wine had dissipated, and Levin realized how lucky he was not to have been picked up before.

What would he do when Michael Pitt sent the signal that a message had been deposited at the next drop? A message with the questions it was imperative he answer? He stopped and turned to stare back down the street. Nothing.

He was not going to commit suicide. Before he made a new contact with the Americans, he would have to know precisely how the KGB were tailing him. And how he would discover *that*, if their men were invisible, he couldn't begin to imagine.

He let himself back into his new apartment, walking from room to room, inspecting once again its luxury and elegance. He filled a bath to the brim with hot water and soaked, then fell asleep almost at once in the enormous bed.

He awoke in the unaccustomed space and comfort and lay still, remembering where he was. The sheets had a clean, new smell. It was still dark outside. The unfamiliar objects in the room were black shapes, edged in gray shadow. At this time of the year, Levin was used to waking in the cold, but now he lay undressed under a sheet and a light blanket, warm and relaxed. He tried and failed to see what the time was, and groped over to where he remembered there was a bedside lamp.

As he fumbled for the switch, he became aware of movement in the next room. Levin subsided onto the bed to listen. The KGB again, having discovered it was all a mistake? No, they would have burst right in. He swung his feet onto the carpet, found a towel to wrap around himself, and opened the door cautiously.

A uniformed maid was moving efficiently through the living room, dusting. She was middle-aged and her face, or as much of it as Levin could see from that angle, seemed pleasant.

He clicked the door shut and turned on the light. Seven-fifteen. Time to get moving.

Levin washed and shaved, and went to the closet for a clean uniform. His old clothes had been moved, just as Mikhail Ilich Malik had said, and were hanging there or neatly stacked on shelves. But beside them were the new ones, uniforms as well, carefully tailored in superior fabric. There really was no choice.

The maid greeted him cheerfully when he emerged. Levin saw the table had been laid for breakfast with silver, china, and good linen, and she disappeared into the kitchen to reemerge quickly with a cooked meal.

Levin, finding that his capacity for astonishment had been blunted, sat down as if he were used to this sort of treatment every day of his life.

A driver presented himself smartly when Levin walked out through the spacious foyer of the building, and took him to the Chief Artillery Directorate as if he were a member of the Politburo. There was a dreamlike quality about everything, and Levin wondered if it would end at eleven that morning when he was taken to see Colonel Malik. Somehow he thought not. The KGB did not act without reason, and in his case the reason was that they wanted something badly. The only question was, what?

Levin worked swiftly and with a purpose, ensuring that the *General Polkovnik* was briefed as usual, that his mail had been properly screened, and that routine tasks had been delegated to those most likely to perform them efficiently.

The driver returned at eleven, and took him in the direction of Tchaikovsky Street and the United States Embassy, before turning off into a side street and drawing to a halt outside what seemed like a large warehouse, five stories high. A watch was obviously being kept because a door swung open and the car passed through into the building.

They stopped in a concrete parking space, surrounded by gray walls, but when Levin was led through he found himself in a well-lit foyer served by modern elevators. The "warehouse" was just a facade behind which operated a major KGB section.

Levin followed his escort mutely, conscious of the maze of corridors, the personnel mostly in plainclothes, and the echoing sound of footsteps in the old, high-ceilinged building.

The escort opened a door and stood aside. "In there, please, comrade Captain."

Please. An excellent word, Levin thought, used all too infrequently.

Colonel Mikhail Ilich Malik looked up from his desk, gestured wordlessly to a chair, and resumed his writing. Levin sat, filling in time staring round the office.

There was, of course, a picture of Lenin above Malik's head, but on another wall there was also a Western calendar showing a woman wearing few clothes sitting on a car. The carpet, thin, stretched to the walls, and the comrade Colonel had on his desk a framed photograph of a family group—presumably his own. Levin could make out four children, none older than ten, and a woman who looked tired but must once have been very beautiful.

Malik screwed the cap onto his pen and sat back in his chair. He regarded his visitor with a level, impassive stare. Levin looked into the pure-black eyes, which he thought could easily be humorous, or gentle, or loving, but were now impenetrable, and he wondered if Malik had seen the report from those bugging his new apartment and knew that he had wept.

"Welcome to the First Department of the Second Chief Directorate, Filipp Ivanovich," Malik began formally. "This is where I work, and as you have seen, we do not advertise our presence. You are comfortable in your new quarters, I trust?"

"Yes, comrade Colonel. Thank you."

"Good. The clothes fit, I see." He gestured to Levin's new uniform.

"They are excellent. Thank you."

Malik nodded. "And now you are wondering what it is we want in return."

It was time for straightforwardness. "Yes, comrade Colonel," Levin replied without equivocation.

"First, tell me what happened when you went to the American reception last week. Whom did you speak to?"

"A woman. Jean Buchanan. She is a secretary in the office of the military attaché. I wrote of her in my report."

"I have seen it," Malik acknowledged.

"And you will have heard about it from a KGB comrade who came and stood close enough to listen to our conversation."

There was a brief flash of humor in Malik's eyes. "Was she aware of him?" he asked.

"I don't think so. He was out of her line of sight, and I didn't look at him in case she noticed."

Malik nodded thoughtfully. "Describe her to me," he invited.

Levin conjured up an image of the girl presenting herself to him at the reception, and found he remembered her clearly.

"She is about five foot five, with brown hair down to her shoulders," he said, "and light brown eyes. I would estimate her weight at about a hundred and twenty pounds."

"Yes. Go on."

"She was dressed well. She seemed intelligent. She spoke highly of the new attaché, but I did not form the impression that there was necessarily . . . anything . . . between them."

"And?"

"She is learning Russian, apparently with little success."

Malik's voice was cordial. "Does she have good breasts, Captain? Surely you noticed that."

Levin felt himself reddening. "She seemed . . . nicely built, comrade Colonel, as far as I could tell," he said evenly. "I would say she had a good figure. As I have told you, she is of medium height and slender."

"Did she wear perfume?"

"Yes, comrade, she did."

"Did you recognize it, Filipp Ivanovich?"

"I regret I am not familiar with Western fragrances." What the hell was Malik up to?

"Well, what did the perfume smell like to you? Describe it."

"It was—not sweet particularly, but it seemed to be around her faintly. I smelled it when I shook her hand. It was . . . deep, I suppose." Then abruptly: "It was good. I liked it. I'm sorry I'm not better at describing this sort of thing."

"No, you have done well. I congratulate you, Filipp Ivanovich. How would she be in bed, do you think?"

"I'm afraid, comrade Colonel, I have no idea."

"You wouldn't mind her in bed? You wouldn't reject her?"

"No, but . . ."

"You would be able to . . . perform?"

Levin felt himself flushing again. This really was a most disagreeable conversation, and he wished Malik was an equal so he could tell him to fuck himself. But instead he said carefully: "That would depend. On the circumstances. On how she felt. Whether she wanted to. It is not the sort of question a man can answer in a simple way."

"Not a man like you, Filipp Ivanovich, no."

Levin raised his head and looked squarely at the colonel.

"No, comrade. Not a man like me."

Malik's eyes allowed themselves to be amused. He murmured:

"That is good. That is very good." Then he paused. "Permit me to ask you a personal question, comrade Captain."

Levin waited—as if he had any choice.

"Months go by," Malik said, "during which you do not have liaisons with women. Months. I find that curious. You are young, and when you do make love, you do not leave the women, or yourself, unsatisfied. I know this, Filipp Ivanovich, because I tell you frankly, they've all been right here in this office, sitting where you are now, and they've told me about you. In detail. And yet, as I say, months go by between these . . . episodes. How do you explain that to me? Are you perhaps deeply in love with your hand?" Malik raised a quizzical eyebrow.

Levin hunted for words, civil words, to explain to this officer things he really had no right to know, while the colonel's black eyes bored into him, frank and unrelenting, waiting for an answer.

Levin said quietly: "You have no right to ask me this." And still the silence lasted. Malik's manner was of polite but insistent inquiry. At length Levin spoke again. "You saw where I lived, comrade Colonel," he said. "You yourself called it a hovel. It was not a palace. I accepted it because it was what was given to me, and I felt I had no choice. The women who have shared my bed have mostly been offered to me by the *General Polkovnik*. Yes, I enjoyed them. Yes, I satisfied them. Or, at least, they gave me to believe I did. They were KGB whores, comrade Colonel. I didn't pay them, but someone did. You, perhaps. I saw them only once. Do you think for a moment I could ask a girl I loved, I respected, to come with me to a place like that, so that the men and women and children on that floor could hear us through the partitions as we have to hear them?" Levin's voice was fierce now. "It was a place for those without hope and without pride. It was a place for whores who did not care, and for one's own hand, as you say." His mouth was dry when he finished.

Malik decreed another silence. Then he began clapping slowly in mock applause. "Bravo, comrade Captain, bravo." He picked up the telephone. "I think we need some coffee."

While he gave the order, Levin sat, still and drained.

"I ask you these things for a reason, Filipp Ivanovich," Malik resumed conversationally. "We have work for you. That is why you have been moved to more . . . amenable surroundings. They suit your temperament, I think. You will perform better in them. Our interest is in Jean Buchanan. Let me explain to you about the First

Department. We are large, and we have resources, as you have seen. We are divided into five sections. The first section is the one that concerns you. It concentrates on recruiting members of the United States Embassy to give us information and help us in any way possible to further the aims of the motherland. Your task will be to recruit Jean Buchanan."

Levin looked at him incredulously. "What makes you think she is willing to be recruited," he asked at last.

"Nothing in particular," Malik replied, "except she was attracted to you. It will be *your* task, Filipp Ivanovich, to make her ripe for recruiting. It may be a fairly long assignment, and it will require all your powers of persuasion, in bed and out of it, to bring this about. You must make her love you if you can. I stand ready at any time to give advice on how to proceed from there. Clearly it is not something that can be rushed, but she still has eighteen months of her posting in Moscow, and that is enough. You find her attractive?"

Levin nodded his head.

"So it will not . . . disgust you?"

"No, Colonel. It will not disgust me."

"You are not an unattractive young man yourself. This is not only my opinion. Others have studied you. Perhaps you have been neglected unfairly, Filipp Ivanovich, because of your background, your grandfather. Very unfortunate. You have talents which can be useful, and now is the time for you to use them. We reward talent." Malik let the message sink home, and the implied corollary. "You will meet Miss Buchanan again. You will become acquainted. In time, you will be intimate. That is all you need concern yourself with at this stage. Later we will advise you further. Is that understood?"

Levin nodded slowly. "How do I meet her?"

"We will advise you of that also," Malik said. "We are watching her movements. Many afternoons she goes alone to Gorkiy Park. She walks around. It is a good place for a chance encounter."

"Yes, comrade Colonel."

Malik stared across his desk, not unkindly. "How do you feel about this, Filipp Ivanovich?"

Levin considered the question. First—was there really a choice? If he refused he might simply be sent back to his old apartment. But equally he might be dismissed from his job and forced to leave Moscow. They would make sure no one employed him elsewhere, and if he wasn't employed, he'd be liable to arrest as a social parasite. Acceptance at least bought time. He would live well. He would go to

Helsinki. He might have a chance to receive and answer Michael Pitt's imperative questions, and perhaps there would be an opportunity to defect.

He would certainly enjoy the company of Jean Buchanan, whether she consented to share his bed or not, and whether she was prepared to help the KGB or not. If she did—well, that was her own business, a bridge both she and he would cross when they came to it. Meanwhile, time was the crucial commodity, and it was on sale now.

"I will do my best, comrade Colonel," Levin said.

"Excellent. Please stand ready to leave your office at short notice if I call. Naturally a car will be at your disposal. You drive, of course."

"Yes, comrade."

"You will be allocated a vehicle for your own use. It will be delivered to you this afternoon, so you can take it out and get used to it. You will entertain Miss Buchanan whenever possible at your apartment. Please make sure you familiarize yourself with your surroundings before you ask her up there. Particularly the little things. I want you to know exactly what records you have, what tape recordings. If she asks to hear a Beethoven concerto, or some country and western music, I want you to know immediately if you've got it. You must know what's in the refrigerator, what drinks are in the liquor cabinet. Where the light switches are. It's *your* apartment." He reached into the desk drawer and tossed over a brown envelope. "There's a thousand rubles. I expect you to spend it, but you must account for it. If you want to take time off from your office, you are authorized to do so, but it must not be unreasonable amounts of time so that she becomes suspicious. You must calm her prejudices about the Soviet Union. You must be more Western in your outlook, less conservative. Have you used marijuana? No? Well, you must try it. It's not bad. But try it first by yourself before you offer her any. We don't want you throwing up everywhere. I'll have some delivered to your apartment. I know you don't smoke, so you can have it baked in cookies, and it's just as good. Give it to the maid; she'll do it. She knows how these things work."

Levin felt dizzy. What Malik was suggesting carried the death penalty in the Soviet Union. But then, he recalled, so did spying.

"If that is an order, comrade Colonel," Levin murmured.

Malik smiled and his black eyes softened, transforming him for a moment into that totally separate identity which must be known to the people in the photograph on his desk. "Try not to think of it as an order, Filipp Ivanovich," Malik urged. "Think of it as a pleasure.

You must be relaxed. Try the marijuana. If you don't like it, don't use it again. But you'll probably find it makes listening to music a very special experience. And making love . . . incredible.''

Malik reached into his desk drawer once more and brought out a file which he passed over. "Read it here," he instructed. "It cannot be removed from this building. Facts about Miss Buchanan."

There was a peremptory knock on the door, and a woman brought in two cups of coffee. Levin sipped as he went carefully through.

The file began with photographs: The formal one accompanying her visa application showed her looking stiff and self-conscious, quite unlike the woman he had met at the Embassy. It would have been difficult recognizing her from it, except perhaps for the full, wide mouth. The second was of her walking through immigration at Sheremetyevo Airport on her arrival in Moscow. It had been taken looking down, presumably from a fixed camera position in the ceiling, and was more typical. Because it was a full-length photograph, it was possible to get an idea of her size and of the relaxed, confident way she had of moving. She had arrived in summer and so was lightly but fashionably dressed. Miss Buchanan really was most attractive, Levin thought. He would not be at all . . . disgusted . . . to make her further acquaintance.

The third picture showed her emerging from the American Embassy. Levin recognized the entrance. It was a rather grainy shot. The photographer had presumably been on the other side of the wide expanse of Tchaikovsky Street, either in a car or a building, and had used a telephoto lens. Levin was conscious that only Jean Buchanan had been blown up from the negative, but others must have been with her. Her face was half-turned, and she appeared to be saying something. The frozen fraction of a second indicated an animated, cheerful conversation,

The fourth showed her in the GUM store, again with a friend, cropped out of the picture, except for a feminine arm that joined hers in feeling the quality of a fabric; the wry expression on her face made it clear she did not plan a purchase.

She was naked in the fifth photograph. Levin stared transfixed and felt his breath stop. Malik was watching him, of course, impassive again, aware of the point he had reached.

Jean Buchanan looked straight at the camera lens as if inspecting her reflection. Levin knew at once it had been taken in an hotel room, not in her own apartment. The bed, the picture on the wall, the overelaborate and shabby furnishings were things of Russia, not the West.

If there was anyone with her, she—or he—was not in evidence. Levin thought she was probably alone. She seemed to have just had a bath because her hair was slightly tousled and the ends looked as though they might be wet. She was giving her body a critical inspection. There would be a mirror, of course, the ubiquitous two-way mirror, with the KGB surveillance team and their cameras on the other side.

She was beautiful, particularly at this private, vulnerable moment. Her breasts were full and the nipples large, which he hadn't expected. Her waist was slender, which he knew, and from the delicate dark triangle beneath, her legs were perfectly shaped, without a trace of fat. Her feet were small and dainty, the toenails painted.

Levin's mouth was dry. He lifted his coffee cup and found he had to grip it tightly because his hands were slicked with sweat.

Jean Buchanan. There, exposed before him in black and white, her eyes inquiring but with a hint of humor, as if in the next second she would laugh at herself for her own conceit. And beyond her vision, the men, watching. Aroused? Bored by the repetition of their job? Watching her as the comrade Colonel was now watching him, with eyes so impassive they blocked any sense of what might be going on in the brain behind?

Levin looked up and met Malik's stare. *Do you like your work, Colonel?* he wondered. *Do we live on in your mind, men like me, women like Jean Buchanan, when you're in your own bed and you turn to your once-beautiful wife? Is your mind a private screen on which you rerun movies, filmed through two-way mirrors, of muscles and flesh and hair and sweat? Do you need us to be able to . . . perform?*

Malik looked away.

Levin turned the photograph over and began reading the dossier. Jean Margaret Buchanan. Aged twenty-eight. Born May 8, 1957, in St. Louis, Missouri. An only child. Unmarried. There were details of her school and college careers. She had joined the State Department five years earlier. She did not appear to have any political ambition and no known political affiliations. For the past three years, she had worked as a secretary to middle-rank Pentagon officials, and this was her first foreign post. She was interested in reading, music, swimming, the ballet, and the theater. And that appeared to be all the KGB knew; or, at least, all they were telling Levin. Perhaps they also had details of former lovers. Even present ones. And that, he felt, he had to know.

Levin closed the file and handed it back to Malik. "Does she have a . . . lover at the moment?" he asked, feeling embarrassed at the question.

Malik shook his head slowly. "Not as far as we know. She lives in the foreigners' compound just near your apartment, and we maintain some surveillance there, of course. But nothing has been reported."

Levin rose to leave. "Is there anything else, comrade Colonel?"

"Just some advice. Take your time. Don't rush things at the beginning. Be discreet. We don't want the Americans to know we're interested in her, otherwise they might send her back to Washington immediately. Or use her to feed us false information. We'll give you two or three days to get used to your apartment. That is most important. Then when we call you, you are to go immediately to see if you can contrive a meeting. If it is difficult, or you feel the circumstances will make her suspicious, you are to return to your office immediately. Is that understood?"

"Yes, comrade."

"And after every meeting I want a full report in writing."

"Yes, comrade."

"That is all. Enjoy yourself."

Levin drove back to the Chief Artillery Directorate, lost in thought. It could have been worse. He might have been ordered to sleep with a woman he abhorred. Whichever way their relationship worked out, Jean Buchanan would be a pleasure. She was exactly the sort of girl he would have looked for in America. And who knew, perhaps it would work out for them too in some way. He had no idea what his chances were of recruiting her, and he could not imagine what would motivate someone like her to betray her own country for the Soviet Union. Malik felt she might do it for love. Levin did not have a sufficiently high opinion of himself to believe that: he, a Russian officer, weighed in the balance against the reality of life and death in his country? But then, of course, she wouldn't know the reality. Her world would be the foreigners' compound, the Embassy, and the sugar frosting he had been given to provide: his luxurious new apartment with its Western atmosphere, dinners at top restaurants, the Bolshoi. She would never see the inside of the building where he had lived until yesterday, would never meet Irina Dmitriyevna and the others, would never be invited to lie down on his hard, narrow bed while the neighbors talked and moved on the other side of the partitions, or snored if it was late enough, knowing that every squeak and murmur of their lovemaking could be heard equally loudly. Jean Buchanan could live out her two-year assignment in the

Soviet Union without coming closer to the real people than occasional encounters with those who wanted to buy her Western shoes or jeans. Everyone else she would meet would be "official." Trusted government men. Employees of military intelligence, the GRU. The KGB, of course. And *agents provocateurs* like himself.

When he got back to his office, he went to see the *General Polkovnik* to tell him that in the future he would have to spend some time out of the office, and that he would have to leave without warning. Stupar brushed aside his explanations. "I know, I know," he said. "They have told me everything. Congratulations, Filipp Ivanovich. This will be good for your career, I think. If you succeed, there will be promotion. That is the way our comrades work. At last, you'll be able to forget the ghost of your grandfather."

That night Levin drove himself back to Kutuzovsky Prospekt in a metallic-blue Volvo which had been delivered to him two hours before.

It was a long time since he had been behind the wheel of a car, and he had never had the privilege of anything as meticulously engineered and magnificent as this. The engine produced a surge of power that astonished and alarmed him, as the streets were icy and the digital readout showed eighty kilometers an hour, and climbing fast, in the space of half a block. Levin touched the brakes, and the Volvo responded without any indication that he might be losing control.

Levin parked near the entrance to the building. His step was jaunty as he passed through the doors and nodded to the doorman.

The apartment itself didn't feel quite as strange and foreign this second evening. Levin checked out the stereo system, and flipped through a pile of records, finally choosing an American rock group.

A slender box caught his eye, and he discovered it was a remote control unit for the stereo.

Levin stepped back, pointed it at the set, and pressed a button. The power light came on. He gave a hoot of delight. Another button, and he could see the arm lift and settle itself just above the record. The turntable revolved, and the apartment was filled with rich, incredible sound. Levin adjusted the volume and, still grinning, went to the kitchen for a beer. However things went with Jean Buchanan, he would certainly take his time. To hell with whether she gave him any information; just as long as the KGB thought she might, that was all that mattered.

Levin worked with a will, if work it was, going through the music collection to see what he had been given, sampling this classic, that musical, these love songs.

Early in the evening the doorbell rang briefly, and Katya, the maid, let herself in, producing from her shopping bag a plastic packet containing a blackish-looking substance, which she waved meaningfully at him. The marijuana, it seemed, had arrived.

Katya busied herself in the kitchen while Levin played with the stereo and tested the television set. He noticed that almost nothing in the apartment was Soviet. The set was Japanese, the superb stereo, Danish. A few of the recordings were Russian—classical, of course, but also Red Army Ensemble albums and folk songs—but mainly they came from America, West Germany, and Britain.

Levin knew that the kitchen equipment was all imported, and he felt, simply from the quality and design, so were the apartment's furnishings.

Curiously the paintings and prints were all Soviet—of a style one never saw in public, or if one did then the KGB could be expected to be close behind, smashing up unauthorized exhibitions and arresting avant-garde artists whose works were banned from public exhibition. It was odd, to say the least, that the secret police could simultaneously be patrons of that same art.

Levin found he liked the paintings. They were so much fresher and more vital than the officially approved works in which all the men were muscular, with thrusting jaws, and all the strong-bodied women stood right beside them, urging everyone on to final victory, or to be first in line at the store when decent-quality meat came in, or to demand proper housing or any of the things Levin sometimes found himself fantasizing about.

A delicious smell of baking came from the kitchen, reminding him that he had not eaten. He decided to wait until Katya had finished. He helped himself to another beer and began searching through the bookshelves. Almost the first volumes he came across were the works of Alexander Solzhenitsyn, neatly arrayed. He had heard about these but had never managed to get hold of any copies. Now, with the compliments of the KGB, he could begin with *One Day in the Life of Ivan Denisovich* and work his way through *Cancer Ward* and the others, right up to *The Gulag Archipelago*. Other books on the shelf included American authors whose names he had never heard—John Irving and Tom Robbins—and some who were familiar, like Gore Vidal and Truman Capote, but whose works had never actually been in his hands before.

The next few weeks—months, he hoped—were going to be wonderful.

Katya came through from the kitchen with a single cookie on a plate. "Chew it well, comrade," she advised. "It is better that way. The others are cooling. I will put them away in the morning. Do not eat more than this one. I think you will find it powerful enough."

Levin took it doubtfully and nibbled a corner. It had a strange but not unpleasant aftertaste. "Thank you, Katya," he said. "Are you going now?"

"Yes, comrade Captain. I have my own family to feed. But if you wish me to stay on at any time, I am at your disposal. I cook Western food and I can wait on table. If you want a special dinner, a proper chef will come."

"I'll remember that. Good night, Katya."

He ate the cookie slowly, and after he had finished he sat waiting for something miraculous to happen. Nothing did. He felt perfectly normal. Levin changed the record, choosing a British rock group, and sat back to enjoy the barrage of sound. His eyes flickered around the room. Leather sofa—soft, tan. Really beautiful. He felt the texture of the shag carpet, marveling at how thick and soft it was. A detail from one of the paintings caught his eye. He hadn't noticed it before, and he went over to study it closeup. At the edge of a golden wheat field, far in the distance, were three people, also painted in predominantly wheatish colors so that they tended to merge with the whole. But when he studied them, Levin could see that one was in uniform—a policeman? a soldier?—and that he had a gun. No jaws outthrust here. The future the other two were heading toward, a weapon at their backs, was obviously a prison cell, a firing squad, or a hangman's noose. It was really a very sad painting. Levin studied it intently. It was extraordinary he hadn't noticed this drama being enacted earlier. What had he missed in the other paintings? He went carefully from one to another while the drums, guitars, and trumpets kept their own insistent rhythm. There was the anger of the artist in an urban scene, in which the people were overweight and badly dressed and had little hope. He hadn't noticed the anger before. Next, a family group walked past one of the massive monuments to socialism, going steadfastly sideways even as the statues urged them forward. This made Levin laugh at lot.

When he turned to the next painting, the room dissolved into a blur of movement, as if he were spinning around on a carrousel, but in a moment it stopped, and there was the next work in front of him.

He inspected it critically. Not much there, he decided. An artist of poor caliber, obviously still afraid.

Levin's hands began to tingle as if lacking blood, and he felt very hungry. Hungry. Cookie. That damn marijuana cookie! He began to laugh with happiness and self-knowledge. No wonder they awarded death sentences for the sale of marijuana! What would happen to the Soviet Union if all the people were so relaxed they laughed at the ridiculous posturing of the KGB and the petty bureaucrats? "I sentence you," he said sonorously, "to be taken to a basement of the Lubyanka, and there shot in the back of the neck with a marijuana cookie." He laughed so much he had to sit down.

But he really was hungry, and he needed another beer. He helped himself to cheese and pâté from the refrigerator, and a jar of stuffed green olives, and a Schlitz.

He hadn't been aware before of the entirely different tastes and textures of food, but he savored the richness of every olive with its slightly spicy stuffing, and the sharp crumbliness of the cheese. Bubbles in the beer tickled his palate. Everything was wonderful.

Levin woke the following morning, not entirely remembering how he had gotten to bed except that for long periods of almost sexual pleasure, he seemed to have been plunging through space, causing extraordinary feelings in his groin and the pit of his stomach. He had no hangover. He was at peace.

He felt he did his work particularly well that day. Afterward he decided to take the Volvo out for a longer drive so that he could become completely familiar with it and what it could do. He took it down Gorkiy Street, headed for the terminus of the Moscow-Volga canal, and turned back toward the main street of the city, Gorkovo, and into the Leningrad Chaussée. Once clear of Moscow, he put his foot on the accelerator, and the spruces, pines, and piebald birch trees flashed past. Inside the car there was little sensation of speed, although the digital readout on the dashboard told him he was going 140 kilometers an hour and climbing. Levin smiled with pure exhilaration and pleasure. The rearview mirror showed there was nothing behind him, no KGB car following. He had been permitted a sort of freedom, a parole from the prison of ordinary Soviet life. He wondered how he would ever be able to give it up.

He pulled into a side road, and turned the Volvo around to head back, more slowly, toward Moscow.

Colonel Malik's call came on Friday after Levin had returned from his lunch break.

"I take it you are fully prepared, Filipp Ivanovich?" Malik asked without preliminaries.

"Yes, I think so, comrade Colonel."

"Good. Well, if you go right away to Gorkiy Park, you should arrive at about the same time as your friend. Walk around the area of the restaurant. If you have no success, go in and speak to the doorman. He will have further information for you. Good luck."

Levin hurried to Stupar's office to tell him he was leaving.

"Good hunting, Captain," the *General Polkovnik* said cheerily, waving him away.

Levin drove the Volvo to the Gorkiy Park for Culture and Rest, and cruised the perimeter. He could not see Jean Buchanan. There were a few people, muffled against the weather, taking exercise, but none looked as if they might be her. He parked, wrapped his scarf carefully around his neck, and pulled on a pair of fur-lined gloves. He began to walk.

In a few days it would snow, but now in the short afternoons there was just the faint gleam of ice in crevices, left over from the bitter nights.

Levin skirted the restaurant, trying to identify the girl, looking for the foreign clothes that would immediately mark her out from the others.

He took a path down toward a pond which had almost completely frozen over and would later be used by skaters. It was a lovely day, Levin thought, lovely if you were wearing warm, good clothes, and you knew that later you would go to a warm, luxurious apartment and eat and drink as much as you liked. The cold against his exposed skin reminded him of that other world from which he was, temporarily at least, freed.

He stopped at the pond, staring left and right, debating which path to take. Mikhail Ilich Malik had said they should both arrive at about the same moment. Perhaps he had made good time and was there ahead of her. So he sat on a bench, staring at the bleak, beautiful scene and at the birds which still scratched and pecked in the grass for what little they could find.

Levin rose and looked around. Time for another circuit of the restaurant. If he didn't spot her, he'd ask the doorman. She might have changed her route and gone somewhere else.

But there she was, in the distance; it was definitely and unmistakably her. As he recognized her, Levin was seized with awkwardness. He realized he didn't know how to make the approach. He felt his greetings would be so obviously forced and stilted that she would know immediately he had been waiting for her, and it wouldn't take long to figure out why.

Levin automatically began walking, closing the gap, pretending indifference. Jean Buchanan was small and slight, even more so than he remembered. Her brown hair showed under her fur cap. Into Levin's mind, unbidden, flashed the photograph of her, naked, in front of the mirror, but he pushed the image aside. What would happen now would be one of the most important moments between them. If he spoiled it, as he had their first encounter at the ambassador's, by being too forward, he might find himself out of his new apartment by nightfall, his Volvo a mere dream. Someone else would finish the marijuana cookies, and notice the people with the gun at their backs in the corner of the wheatfield, and read Solzhenitsyn, and listen to Mott the Hoople, and make love to some other girl, or some other man, in the king-size bed. The thought made him even more nervous.

Levin tried for eye contact while they were still a dozen paces apart, but she was looking the other way, toward a flock of pigeons, their feathers plumped out, waddling on the icy grass, searching for something to eat.

They were almost abreast. He tried to speak, but the words stuck in his throat. She hadn't noticed him.

Then it came in a rush: "Miss . . . Miss Buchanan? Excuse me, I'm very sorry, I thought . . ."

She turned to him inquiringly, as to a stranger. "Yes?"

He began to blush. "You don't remember me. You must think I'm very rude. We met at your ambassador's."

Recognition dawned and he felt a wave of relief. "Oh yes, of course. Captain . . . uh . . ."

"Filipp Ivanovich Levin. Special assistant to *General Polkovnik* Stupar." He grinned at her and she began to laugh.

"Right, right!" she said. "The Russian three-star general. I remember."

"It is . . . most pleasant to see you again. And unexpected."

"Nice to see you too, Filipp Ivanovich."

"Are you keeping well?"

"Yes, thank you. And you?"

"Yes," Levin said, searching for a way to end the banalities of ritual exchange, but unable to think of anything else to say. "Yes, very well. How's your Russian coming along?"

"Oh, I've almost given up."

"That is a pity."

"I'm not really very good at languages. I even have trouble with English."

"I can't believe it. You should change your tutor."

"I remember you saying something like that at the reception." She looked at him with a slightly arched eyebrow, and he laughed in embarrassment.

"I'm afraid you thought I was rude," he confessed. "I'm sorry."

"Don't be," she said cheerfully. "I thought it was wonderful. The nicest thing anybody's said to me for . . . oh, a long time."

Levin pressed his advantage. "Are you going anywhere in particular, or may I walk with you for a moment?"

"No, please. I'm just wandering around. So much to see in Moscow. I've done lots of the tourist sights, but there's always something more."

"It is a beautiful city," Levin said as they fell into step. "Or parts of it are, anyway. The country outside Moscow is really lovely. Have you seen much of it?"

"Well, no. It's not easy for foreigners to travel outside. There are quite a lot of restrictions beyond the twenty-five-mile limit, and we need special permissions. It takes time getting them."

"That is terrible," Levin said sincerely. "It must be possible. Perhaps I can do something through my office. You know what bureaucracies are like. Pull the right string and the locked door falls open."

"Could you? Oh, that would be great," Jean Buchanan said. "Do you really think you can do that?"

"I can try. I've never asked before, but I'm sure it must be possible."

"Without creating a diplomatic incident?"

"On my honor." Levin put a gloved hand on his heart.

"Okay, I'll take you up on that." She was as cheerful and open as if she had been walking in Central Park with the New York skyscrapers as a background.

"I have a car," Levin said. "Perhaps you would permit me to take you. I know some beautiful places only an hour or so from Moscow. Tourists never go there. I would suggest a picnic if it was another season, but there are excellent restaurants where you can taste real Russian cooking and meet the ordinary people."

"Oh no, you mustn't do that. It would be far too much trouble." She laughed lightly, making Levin realize it was just a token refusal.

"My dear Miss Buchanan," he said warmly. "It would give me the greatest pleasure. You would be doing *me* a favor. I only rarely get to practice my English."

"Well, that would be lovely," she said. "In six months I've hardly met any Russians at all. Americans, British, Swedes, Canadians . . . no Russians. Except for some officials, and they don't really count."

They both laughed. "We must change that," Levin insisted. "You will like the people. Except they might try to buy the clothes off your back."

"I've noticed that." She smiled. "The stores aren't very good, are they?"

"They're better for foreigners than for Russians," Levin admitted. "I suppose our priorities have been elsewhere. And, of course, we have an enormous population. We must seem very unsophisticated to you, I'm afraid."

"Not at all," Jean Buchanan said politely.

"But you should be exposed to us anyway, warts and all. That is how we will get to know each other. Have you ever been to a *pivnoyzal?*"

"What's that? *Piv* . . .?"

"*Pivnoyzal.* It's a beer parlor. Working people go there. Have you finished at the Embassy? Do you have to go back?"

She sounded interested. "No, I'm through for the day."

"Then perhaps I could take you to a *pivnoyzal.* I know one where they even serve vodka, and that would warm us up."

"Well, I don't know . . ."

"And you will see real Muscovites. No tourists, that's a promise."

She grinned. "Okay then. Take me to a *piv* . . . whatever it is."

Levin led the way back to where he had parked his car. When Jean saw him unlocking the metallic-blue Volvo, she stopped in her tracks and said: "Oh wow!"

"Do you like it?" Levin's enthusiasm was boyish.

"It's fantastic! What a beautiful car! Filipp Ivanovich, how on earth did you get such a thing in Moscow?"

"I saved up," he said.

"For about a hundred years, I think. I didn't even know you could get Volvos in Moscow."

"Oh, everything's available if you know where to go for it. You know how it is. The story of the world."

He held the door open for her and went around to the other side. The car started immediately, a low, powerful throb coming from the engine. Levin had a sudden desire to put his foot down on the accelerator and impress her with the car's speed and maneuverability, but he realized at once this adolescent urge could end up in an accident or with her thinking him a reckless driver, best avoided.

They cruised passed the trolleybuses, trucks, and taxis, of which Moscow traffic mostly consists, down toward the drab older section of the city where Levin was fairly sure she had never been. They parked fifty meters from a *pivnoyzal*, and Levin guided her in, avoiding the communal stand-up counter and selecting one of the tables for two in a corner.

"What will you have? Vodka?"

She smiled. "Why not?"

Levin brought back two glasses and slipped into a bench across from her. The *pivnoyzal* was filling up with factory workers, street cleaners, petty bureaucrats. The atmosphere was steamy, and the level of noise, which had been high when they came in, quieted to a murmur. Everyone was aware of Levin and Jean Buchanan because of their clothes. The immediate assumption was that one, or both, were KGB.

Levin lifted his glass. "Your good health, Miss Buchanan," he said.

"If I'm going to call you Filipp, you must call me Jean. Cheers."

She sipped the vodka. "Mmmm. It's good. Very smooth."

"You must drink it as we do in the motherland," Levin instructed. He tilted his glass back, drained it, and put it firmly down on the wooden table.

She stared at him thoughtfully for a moment, then shrugged good-naturedly. "If you say so." Her empty glass came down on the table, and she said: "Oh boy. That feels so good."

"Another?"

"Not right now, Filipp Ivanovich. You're used to this stuff, but I'm new here."

Levin began shooting her questions about America, partly to get the conversation going along personal lines, and partly because he genuinely wanted to hear a firsthand description. She told him about St. Louis, her college days at Vassar, and Washington. She described the apartment she had left behind, and a vacation she'd had in San Francisco. It was exactly as Levin had dreamed.

And Jean herself was as nice as she had seemed that first evening at the reception: warm and amusing. After a while she turned the discussion to Russia, and Levin found himself telling her about his childhood in Kiev, his sisters, what their husbands did, and his career, suitably edited, in the army. He did not mention his grand-father. He did not talk about the KGB.

"Where do you stay in Moscow, Filipp?" she asked.

"I have a place. Do you know Kutuzovsky Prospekt?"

"Sure. It's just a few blocks from the foreigners' compound, isn't it?"

"My apartment is there. Perhaps I will be able to invite you to dinner one evening? I can offer you a Schlitz or a Budweiser if you get tired of vodka."

"Or a bourbon?"

He shrugged. "Or bourbon. My own cooking is very simple, but Katya, my maid, can make Western food."

"I don't believe any of this," Jean said. "Here I am in the Soviet Socialist Republic, drinking vodka with a Russian who drives a Volvo, has a maid, and drinks Schlitz. I might as well be in New York."

Levin thought he ought to put in some time on Malik's behalf. "There are many misconceptions about the Soviet Union," he said. "The Central Committee blames Western propaganda, I know, but I think it is our own fault. Everything in your country is so open. Here, we pretend we have things to hide. We like to make you believe we have big secrets. So you can't go far outside Moscow without permission. That is ridiculous. What is there to see outside Moscow? Apart from beautiful countryside and warm-hearted people? I will show you that myself. Tell me any place on the map you would like to go, and I will take you there. Everything is possible."

A flash of amusement crossed her face. "Gorkiy?" she asked innocently.

"The park?"

"No, the city. Sormovo?"

There was silence for a second, then Levin began to laugh so genuinely and warmly that she joined in too. "*Touché,*" he said. "Closed cities both."

When their laughter subsided, she said, "I like talking to you, Filipp. You're very Western in your outlook. I thought for a moment there I might have offended you. I'm glad I didn't."

"But it's true," he insisted. "Why should truth offend me?"

"Truth can be very offensive. In my country too."

"We are friends. I hope we are friends?" He looked anxiously at her, and she nodded. "Friends should be able to talk frankly." He leaned closer, his voice confidential and serious. "You should be able to say to me: 'Filipp Ivanovich, how is it that, in your equal society, you have a metallic-blue Volvo, an apartment on Kutuzovsky Prospekt, and Schlitz beer"—she began to laugh—"while these other equal people here in this truly delightful but very basic *pivnoyzal* will be lucky to be *run over* in the street one day by anything as beautiful as a metallic-blue Volvo?"

They both roared. Some of the other customers in the *pivnoyzal* who had been watching them began to laugh too, without understanding what had been said. The sound itself was infectious. How could these people be KGB? Someone brought them another two vodkas. The drinks just appeared on the table without them noticing who was responsible.

"You see?" Levin said triumphantly. "The most valuable commodity in all Russia is laughter and comradeship!" He lifted his glass in salute to the unknown host, and Jean Buchanan did too. Around the *pivnoyzal* glasses were raised and everyone drank. Levin immediately ordered a general refill, paying out of a wad of notes in his pocket, and the second toast was more exuberant.

"That's enough," Jean said, putting her glass down and pretending to be having trouble focusing her eyes. "I'm a simple Missouri girl, Filipp Ivanovich, and if you give me any more, I'll think you're trying to get me drunk. And it's much too early for that."

Levin recognized it was time to go, and he ushered her cheerfully out into the cold street. "Did you like it?" he asked as they headed for the car.

"It was wonderful. I haven't done anything like that in all the time I've been here. One dull Intourist visit to Leningrad and a few of the Kremlin sights. Thank you for showing me something a little more real."

"There's more, Jean. I can show you more. I hope you will allow me to."

She looked sideways at him. "I'd like that," she said. When they were in the car, she asked suddenly: "What are you doing tomorrow night, Filipp? Saturday."

He shook his head. "Nothing."

"Would you like to have dinner at my place? In the compound? I'm having a few friends in. Nothing big."

Levin hesitated. What would Colonel Malik say? Perhaps he would argue that exposure in the foreigners' compound would alert the Americans and she might be warned off him. Good-bye Volvo. Good-bye apartment. Good-bye Jean.

"Now come on, Filipp Ivanovich," she said sternly. "If I'm brave enough to go into a *pivnoyzal* with you"—she'd got the word right at last and he grinned approvingly—"you can be brave enough to come into the compound with me. I'll look after you, I promise. No one will eat you. All my guests are personally screened by me. And I'm a terrific hostess."

"I would love to come," Levin replied honestly. "It would give me the greatest pleasure."

"Great. Eight o'clock." She reached into her purse and pulled out a small printed card with her address and telephone number. "Casual."

Levin slipped the card into his pocket and steered the Volvo out into the street. "Is there anywhere I can drop you?" he asked.

"Back home, I guess," she said, and they drove in silence, Levin feeling elated. It had gone far better than he had ever dreamed, and she was so nice. He caught the scent of her perfume again. *Describe it to me*. Well, comrade Colonel, I'll tell you frankly, it's indescribable. It's like her. Soft, and warm, and friendly. Not at all . . . disgusting. She saw him grin.

"Does vodka do that to you all the time?" she asked suspiciously.

"No, I'm used to vodka," Levin said, shooting her a quick look sideways. "My mother used to feed it to me when I was a baby to keep me quiet."

"Well then?"'

He said lightly: "I think it must be the company. Don't people always look happy when you're around?"

"Not that I've noticed. The silver-tongued Russian again."

"I must teach you some of the language. I think you will fall in love with it."

"Well," she observed, "you can try. But I warn you, I'm a very slow learner."

"I don't mind," he replied. "I'm a very patient teacher."

He caught her looking at him speculatively. They finished the journey in silence. He drove through the entrance in the high mesh fence enclosing the foreigners' compound, past the Soviet sentry box with its glass observation windows, stopped, and went around to open the door for her. They shook hands formally under the gaze of two blue-coated militiamen.

"Until tomorrow then," Jean Buchanan said.

"Tomorrow."

Levin returned to Kutuzovsky Prospekt in a glow of happiness, and when he let himself into the apartment, he discovered he had started feeling as if it really belonged to him. He put on a tape of country and western music, and remembered he was supposed to report to the comrade Colonel. What would Mikhail Ilich Malik say about the invitation to dinner? Levin shrugged. What could he say? It was the next logical step. A girl would usually invite a man to her own place first before consenting to visit his.

Levin turned the sound down, picked up the telephone, and dialed the special number at the Second Chief Directorate. Malik answered immediately, as if he had been waiting for the call. His voice was relaxed.

"It went very well, comrade Colonel," Levin said. "I have been invited for dinner at her apartment on the compound tomorrow at eight. I have accepted."

Malik showed no hesitation. "Excellent," he said. "I want a full report on what happened this afternoon. I will send a messenger to collect it in one hour."

Levin got to work as soon as he hung up. He kept the wording neutral, not communicating any of the delight he felt in her presence, and censoring some of the exchanges he felt it would be better for Colonel Malik not to know.

After the messenger had come and gone, Levin spent the evening reading Solzhenitsyn and listening to music. No wonder the Politburo and the KGB feared the written word, he thought bitterly. Short of war, it was the only real weapon being wielded against them. What Solzhenitsyn so vividly described was far worse than even his own imaginings, but he had no doubt it was true. That *was* the way they would operate. That *was* the fear they instilled.

And yet they had left the books there for him, a Soviet officer, to read. Did they think he would emerge unchanged? Or was it that they just didn't care. If one more man, in a strictly controlled society, knew the reality while tens of millions of nondissident, nonintellectual Soviet citizens could only guess at it, did that change the equation in any way?

It seemed an unwinnable fight, and Levin went to bed depressed.

That Saturday night he had a long, hot bath and dressed carefully. He chose a white cotton shirt with a scarf, a cashmere sweater, a pair of dark slacks, and a blazer. Their afternoon together had been fun, but for her it must have seemed a little bizarre. On this night, among her Western friends, he must impress her as an *international* man, not just a Russian, even though he had never been outside the Soviet borders and his only current prospect was a visit to Helsinki as part of a delegation.

But Levin thought he knew how to behave, that when in doubt it was better to be quiet than assertive, and that it was a good quality to be able to laugh at oneself.

He drove the Volvo to the compound a few minutes after eight. He had learned somewhere that in the West it was better to be slightly late than to be early or exactly on time.

The militia guard—KGB, of course—stared as he went through but did not challenge him. Nobody asks questions of a Russian who drives a Volvo in Moscow unless directly ordered to. If you have the car, you obviously have the authorization.

Jean Buchanan's apartment was on the tenth floor of one of the compound blocks, and he heard the doorbell chime inside.

"Filipp! Come on in! Welcome!" She looked to him as if she really *was* pleased. He handed her a large bunch of flowers he had bought during the afternoon from one of the shops reserved for VIPs and senior Party functionaries. A week ago he would not have been permitted inside it, nor would he have dreamed of trying. Now, whenever he wanted an official door to open, he clicked his fingers and people were anxious to be of service.

"Filipp, they're beautiful!" she exclaimed. "Where do you get flowers like these in winter? My God! You really amaze me, you know that?"

"You deserve flowers," he said simply.

She caught his eye, slightly embarrassed. Was he moving too fast again? "Well, thank you," she said softly. "Thank you so much." Then she brightened up. "Now come and meet the others."

He followed her into the living room and was conscious of a silence falling over the party as the four people waited to be introduced.

Two men were standing, and one of them was Michael Pitt.

Levin felt himself give a nervous start. Pitt smiled casually.

Levin didn't know the other man, a tall, crew-cut American wearing a bow tie. The women sat expectantly in their armchairs.

Jean Buchanan made the introductions. "Filipp Ivanovich Levin —a guaranteed genuine Russian who drives a guaranteed genuine Volvo. I'd like you to meet Joe Barron, from our Political department . . ."

"Hi," said the crew-cut man, taking his hand in a strong grip.

" . . . and his wife, Sue . . ."

A blond woman, with a silk scarf knotted round her neck, who looked older than her husband, extended a cool hand.

" . . . Michael Pitt, Second Secretary, Information, whom you might have met at the reception last week. Don't listen to a word Michael says. He's in the Propaganda department . . ."

"Mr. Levin," Pitt said gravely, shaking his hand. "I think we did meet briefly."

" . . . and his wife, Denise. Denise is not just a very pretty face. She paints, does some pottery and a bit of sculpture. Very classy stuff. You might want some for your apartment."

"Pay no attention to Jean, Mr. Levin," Denise Pitt said, her voice a slow, very appealing Southern drawl. "If she was a man, she'd qualify for being a chauvinist pig."

"She is right that I would like to see your work, Mrs. Pitt," Levin said. "I have a small collection in my apartment. I should be glad to add to it."

"That's very kind. Please call me Denise, by the way. We're all on first-name terms here."

"And I am Filipp."

Jean was at his elbow. "Do you drink anything other than vodka, Filipp? I have some, but I don't think it's as good as the stuff we were putting away yesterday."

"A beer? Schlitz, Budweiser, whatever you have."

"Schlitz coming up."

Levin sat beside Joe Barron on a sofa.

"What exactly is it that you do, Filipp?" Barron asked.

"I work at the Chief Artillery Directorate. I am special assistant to Georgi Borisovich Stupar, our three-star general."

"Oh, very good." Barron sounded impressed. "It must be very interesting."

"Much of it is bureaucratic routine. You know how the Washington bureaucracy works, so perhaps you can imagine what the Soviet one is like. Awful. But I enjoy it."

Pitt asked casually: "What's this about a Volvo, Filipp? Did Jean say you had one?"

From the kitchen door, her voice called: "Does he ever have one! A blue job." She came across with a glass of cold beer. "Digital readouts, stereo sound. A pleasure to be knocked down by. A great pleasure to drive in."

"I got it recently," Levin said. "It's a marvelous car."

"Not many of those around Moscow," Pitt observed.

"I don't think I've seen another one. Not of this type," Levin admitted.

"I asked how he got it," Jean said. "He told me he saved up."

Levin felt uncomfortable. He knew what Pitt must be thinking and wondered how he would be able to get him alone to explain what had happened.

"Well, you know how it is, Jean," Pitt said philosophically, coming to the rescue. "Look after the rubles, and the foreign exchange will look after itself."

Everyone laughed and the conversation turned to other subjects: art, ballet, books—Levin contributed some thoughts on Solzhenitsyn —the world economy, the strength of the dollar, the state of the Reagan presidency, and the elections which were due the following year. Levin found it exhilarating to be in the company of men and women who were knowledgeable on so many different subjects, and who expressed themselves freely. without fearing their government in any way.

The dinner was excellent and they ate by candlelight. Filipp found himself placed on Jean's right, which he recalled was a sign of particular favor.

When they had finished and coffee was being served in the living room, Jean invited: "Anyone like to dance?" There was a chorus of agreement.

The men shifted the furniture, clearing a space, and Pitt chose a record that had a good solid beat. Levin hoped they would change to something slower later.

He and Jean began to dance. She moved well, unselfconsciously. The ceiling light was switched off, leaving just the lamps at the side.

Michael Pitt and his wife were also on the floor, but Joe Barron had disappeared and Sue was drinking coffee in an armchair by herself.

When Levin noticed Joe Barron again, he was standing at the side, apparently listening to the music through padded headphones, his face intent. From time to time, he changed position.

Levin watched, baffled, but kept on dancing. When he caught Jean's eye, she put a finger over her mouth and shook her head.

The record stopped and Jean called out: "Michael, let's have some more like that. See if you can find something with a really good beat."

Sue asked: "Does anyone remember the Beatles?"

Michael Pitt said: "Baby, I remember the Andrews Sisters. I could sing a few verses of 'Buttons and Bows' if you asked nicely."

"No, don't," Sue cried in mock horror. "I've heard all about your singing, Michael. It sounds like the sort of thing that ought to be kept private between man and wife."

Joe Barron circled closer to them, brow knotted in concentration. Levin watched in astonishment. Barron was carrying a black case at the top of which dials and buttons were visible.

Jean, beside him, said: "Well, what about the Rolling Stones? Filipp, what's your favorite group?"

Levin, momentarily at a loss for words, finally collected himself and said: "Do you have any Mott the Hoople?"

"You mean Mott the Hoople made it big in Moscow?" Jean asked.

"In some circles," said Levin stiffly, wondering what the hell was going on.

"Isn't that amazing, Sue?" she called across the room. "Mott the Hoople in Moscow! Who else from the West is big around here. We hardly know anything about you people. Isn't that too bad? But the Beatles were big news, weren't they?"

"Yes, they were. Also Neil Diamond."

"Neil Diamond! For God's sake!"

Joe Barron stood directly in front of Levin now, black case in hand. Their eyes met and Barron winked gravely at him.

"Wasn't there a Neil Diamond concert in Moscow a few years back?" Jean persisted, right at his shoulder. "I seem to remember reading something about that, in *Time* magazine, I think. Or the *Rolling Stone*. I forget which. Did you see him, Filipp?"

Barron put his case on the floor and gestured to the others.

"No, I didn't have tickets," Levin said.

From across the room, the others took up the conversation:

"I think Neil Diamond's pretty passé . . . well, I like him, he always has a good melody . . . you've got to go a long way to beat country and western . . . you only say that because of what's her name and her big boobs . . . that's a terrible thing to say, Denise. She'd be a great singer even if she had small boobs . . ."

Joe Barron tugged at Levin's jacket buttons and gestured for him to take off the coat. He did so automatically. Barron carried it over to the group, listened through his headphones, shrugged, and placed the coat on a chair. He came back to Levin and pulled gently at the cashmere sweater. Transfixed, Levin stripped it off and handed it over.

The same procedure was repeated. The sweater was tested in front of the group, who spoke on animated and unconcerned, and was then dropped onto the chair. Barron returned for Levin's shirt.

Filipp Ivanovich began to feel embarrassed and humiliated. What were they doing to him? He glanced desperately at Jean, and this time she placed her finger over his own lips and gave him a look of total understanding and sympathy. *Trust me.* Pitt's words came back to him, and Levin began unbuttoning his shirt. He would probably end up naked in the middle of the room, a fate he would not have minded in other circumstances.

The shirt failed whatever test Barron was making. Levin's hands, unbidden, were already pulling at his belt, but Barron grinned and shook his head. *Not yet.* He pointed at Levin's shoes. Levin slipped them off and stood in his stocking feet.

"Do you know, I once stood in line for three hours, *three hours,* to get tickets for a Rolling Stones concert and then found my fifty-dollar seat was half a mile from the stage . . . I got caught on one of those and the sound was terrible . . . but my God, they know how to stage things . . . has anyone ever seen a laser light show they've actually enjoyed? . . . or a comedy where the newspaper critic laughed until he cried, and you found it hard to stay awake . . . ?"

Levin's new leather shoes were placed before the group. Barron, hunched over them, suddenly gave a grin and the thumbs-up signal. Then he came back and stood in front of Levin again, listening.

Immediately Jean joined in the conversation: "That's one thing I really miss about living in Moscow—live theater."

Levin started to speak, to mention the Bolshoi, but Jean looked alarmed and shook her head emphatically. She went on: "I used to go to the theater almost every week when I was in Washington, and some of it was very good. I think a good play is so much more rewarding than a movie."

Barron nodded, satisfied, and called across to the others: "Hey, Michael, where the hell's the music? At least put on something we can dance to, and *then* you can hunt for the Andrews Sisters."

The loudspeakers began to blare. Barron squeezed Levin's shoulder—*thanks*—and walked off, taking his case and the earphones out of range of the dancers. Michael Pitt motioned Levin to follow him, and Jean took up the rear.

They went into a bedroom. Pitt pushed the PLAY button of a tape-casette deck which lay prepared on a table, and more music filled the room.

The three sat close, speaking quietly. "Thanks for cooperating, Filipp," Pitt said. "You did that very well. You've probably guessed we were looking for a bug, and we found it in your shoe."

"Where?"

"Buried in the heel. It's a pretty old dodge, but still effective. It could have been anywhere, though. One of your buttons, for example. This room's been swept, by the way, but we've got the music on just in case. Now Jean here"—he nodded at the girl—"works for me. You probably guessed that. But apart from the others out there tonight, very few people, very few Americans at the Embassy, know about her. She's going to be your contact in the future. I take it the KGB asked you to see if you could have an affair with her?"

Levin blushed furiously, feeling humiliated. He refused to meet her eye.

"And try to recruit her or use her to get information?"

In a low voice: "Yes."

"Don't feel bad about it, Filipp," Jean said softly. "That's what we wanted to happen. The KGB set you on to me. But only because Michael set *me* to try and snare *you* at the reception. And it worked. So we're even. If they hadn't taken the bait, I don't know what we'd have done."

"Who's your control, Filipp?" Pitt asked.

"Mikhail Ilich Malik."

"Ah. Head of the First Department, Second Chief Directorate. What's he like?"

"He has eyes as black as sin."

Pitt grinned. "Bad as that, huh? Where've they put you?"

"An apartment in Kutuzovsky Prospekt."

"Comfortable?"

"Unbelievable."

"Fine. Enjoy it while you can. Now we haven't got too long, so this is just to lay some ground rules. No more dead drops, okay?"

"Excellent." Levin was relieved.

"Everything goes through Jean in the future. Your apartment, beautiful as it may be, probably has more electronic gadgets in it than you've ever dreamed of."

"No mirrors, though. I mean, two-way mirrors. I checked."

"Doesn't mean a thing. Work on the assumption that everything you do and say in *every room* of the apartment is heard and seen. And when you go out, you're going to be a walking radio transmitter, like tonight."

"But I have orders to submit a written report to Colonel Malik after every meeting."

"A matter of form," Pitt said dismissively. "They don't want you to know what sort of tabs they're keeping on you. It gives them a chance to compare what actually happens with what you tell them. Lets them assess your accuracy and trustworthiness. Useful for later."

Levin nodded bitterly. He saw what Pitt meant.

"So any messages that pass between the two of you have to be in writing, out of the apartment. Maybe in your Volvo, Filipp. And they must be destroyed, burned or eaten, before you leave the car." Pitt grinned. "So don't make your messages too lengthy, and we won't either."

"I'm on a diet," Jean said. "I have to cut down my paper intake."

Pitt glanced at his watch. "We've got three minutes before the record ends. I chose the longest cut I could find. Seems like it'll never stop, but it does after eight minutes twenty. And Filipp's got to be back in his shoes and talking by that time, or they'll wonder why he's been keeping so quiet. One last thing: You've both been set up to establish a personal relationship. The KGB are going to be watching for results, but I'm not. As far as I'm concerned, you're adults and what you do in private is your own business. But I'd strongly recommend . . . well, I leave it to you. There may come a point where Colonel Malik tries to blackmail Jean directly. Don't be upset. That's fine with us. We're prepared. Eventually when you ask her, she'll start feeding you bits and pieces from the Embassy. Now I'm going back to join the dancing. The two of you have got"—he checked his watch—"a minute and a half before you'd better do the same."

Michael Pitt left them alone.

Levin looked over diffidently, and Jean placed a gentle hand against his cheek. "Don't feel bad, Filipp," she said. "We've got to believe that it's just *us,* that we've met, and we like each other, and let it run naturally from there. There's nothing we have to do if we don't want to." She removed her hand and said in a voice which he could only just hear: "And I do like you, Filipp Ivanovich. If I'd met you in other circumstances, I'd like you just for yourself, and I'd hope you'd ask me out. Do you feel that way about me at all? Or is all this because Malik asked you?" Then, hastily; "I'm sorry, I had no right to say that. Please forget it."

Levin shook his head. "No," he said. "It's that way with me too. I liked you when I saw you at the reception. It was because of that . . . it was obvious to the KGB . . ."

Jean stood up. "We must go."

When Levin rose he was standing very close to her, and as she did not move away immediately, he kissed her very gently on the forehead and her hand touched his chest.

Levin followed her into the living room to find his shoes. His mouth was dry, and he needed another beer.

after midnight feeling so drained that he went immediately to bed and slept until late Sunday morning. Katya wasn't in, or perhaps she had been and gone. He fixed his own breakfast, and his mood was preoccupied. In fact his mind was almost completely blank. Levin was going through the routines of daily life—shaving, the food, brushing his teeth, getting dressed—almost in a dream, instinctively giving himself time to assimilate the new forces that had bombarded him and would now dominate his life.

Were the KGB watching? Michael Pitt certainly thought so, although Levin couldn't see how. But perhaps they were. Levin stayed naked for an hour, strolling through the rooms of the apartment, effectively saying, *Here I am, and I don't care.* Without consciously acknowledging it, he was reinforcing the psychological barrier that had existed throughout his adult life between himself and authority.

You want to watch me? Go ahead. Don't think I'm embarrassed. You want a performance? Fine. I'll perform, and I'll do it better because you might be watching. And you're certainly listening. You

*think you know everything? That I have no secrets? Well, comrades,
there's a surprise for you. Inside the glass prison you've constructed,
things are going on that you don't even dream about, and if you did,
you would feel sick.*

He sat in the warm living room, relaxed. Matters had passed
beyond his control. Levin did not have to worry about basic things
such as whether Jean would come into his bed. It was a foregone conclusion that she would, whenever he called. There need be no tension of uncertainty, no wondering about false moves and whether he
might be fended off when he tried to kiss her. It would be a relaxing
progression. He would dictate the timing to fit what he felt was best
for them, and for the KGB who permitted them to be together in the
first place.

He sat on the leather sofa, staring at the wheatfield and the tiny
figures in the far distance being threatened with a gun, while the
realization and the acceptance settled down in his mind.

The painted man with a gun reminded him of Malik and of the
report he would have to write. He might as well get that over with.

Levin roused himself and went to find paper and pen. He gave a
full account of the public conversations in Jean Buchanan's apartment and his personal assessments of the other guests. He left out
nothing that the bug in his shoe might have picked up.

Denise Pitt had made a critical comment about President Reagan,
and he quoted that. Joe Barron appeared hawkish about the Middle
East situation. Jean Buchanan mentioned the military attaché's fond-
ness for blondes, although that might just have been a joke, as Levin
remembered from the reception that his wife had black hair. And
Jean Buchanan had agreed to meet him the following Saturday afternoon for a drive outside Moscow. Levin proposed bringing her back
to his apartment for dinner afterward.

He added that everything appeared to be progressing well. He had
found the evening very congenial, but he thought it might be better
to avoid other Americans in the future in case their suspicions were
aroused. Unless, of course, the comrade Colonel advised otherwise.

Levin had no idea whether Malik would be in his office at midday
on a Sunday, but he dialed the number anyway, and a stranger's
voice answered. The colonel was not in. Levin left his name. An
hour later a messenger arrived to take away the report.

After that, it was a lost day. Levin ate lunch, read awhile, drank
beer, and on impulse had another of the marijuana cookies, which
Katya now kept in a flowered can labeled POT.

It suited his mood. He watched television until he found himself beginning to laugh at the news announcer. He wasn't *that* far gone not to know that open laughter at Politburo statements would be dangerous. One remote control unit beside him banished the news, while another summoned up from the stereo the first Tchaikovsky Piano Concerto.

How nice to be able to give oneself totally to pleasure, Levin thought vaguely. Must be careful not to spoil it. Must be sure not to rush.

Malik called him to the Second Chief Directorate the following morning to congratulate him on his progress, and to agree that in the future he should avoid other American contacts.

"I am pleased, comrade Captain," Malik said. "You and the girl are well-suited in many ways. Yet there are dangers. The Americans now know that she has at least an acquaintanceship with you. That much was probably inevitable. But if they see it continue, they will take evasive action—perhaps forbid her to meet you again. An order like this is more easily given in the early stages of a relationship, before any bonds have been cemented. Do you understand what I'm saying?"

"Yes, Colonel, I think so."

"The Western mind does not take kindly to such instructions when emotions are involved. But Miss Buchanan's emotions are not yet involved. Only her interest is."

Levin observed calmly: "You think I should sleep with her as soon as possible?"

"Yes, comrade Captain," Malik replied after a fractional pause. "That is exactly what I think. If she is ready, naturally. But your progress has been so good up to now that it would not be an unreasonable object to hope for."

"I will try, comrade Colonel."

"To other men I would stress how important it is not to move too swiftly. The fruit must by itself be ready for plucking. But you do not seem to be . . . violent in that way."

"I will not rape Miss Buchanan, comrade. You may rest assured of that."

Malik shot Levin a calculating look. He did not like his people to be too self-assured in his presence, particularly not those who were new and untried, like this grandson of a traitor. However, the captain did seem to be in a special category. It was difficult to make him out. He clearly enjoyed luxury and accepted as his due everything that went with it. Yet he had not once complained in all the years he was obliged to live in more spartan conditions, and Malik thought that if tomorrow Filipp Ivanovich found himself returned to his room in that same building, he would absorb the blow in silence. He was personally secretive and very proud, qualities the KGB mistrusted but Malik himself found he rather admired.

So he said dryly: "I'm glad to hear it. I believe you have a batch of marijuana cookies in your kitchen. Katya tells me you tried one out. How did you like it?"

"I found it very pleasant, comrade Colonel. Very relaxing."

"Good for sex?"

"I should think so, yes."

"Then do not forget the cookies if you feel that something . . . extra . . . is needed to get Miss Buchanan over the final hurdle."

"I won't, Colonel. Is that all?"

"I take it you need a chef to cook dinner on Saturday?"

"Yes, please, but I'd rather he wasn't around when we got back. Could he prepare the meal in the afternoon? I will heat whatever is necessary when we get in. Also, there's no champagne in the refrigerator. I think we ought to have some."

"Georgian champagne?" Malik asked politely.

"Oh no, comrade Colonel, And not Californian either. French, please. If possible."

Malik's mouth twisted into a kind of grin. "You shall have it, Filipp Ivanovich. And I, in return, shall expect results. I wish you a pleasant and successful Saturday."

"Thank you. I take it there will be no problems or restrictions about my driving Miss Buchanan outside the twenty-five-mile limit?"

"None. Orders have gone out that your car is not to be stopped or intercepted at any point."

"Then I will take my leave of you, comrade Colonel. I shall report as soon as possible after the event . . . after Saturday."

"Do that, comrade Captain." Malik's face crinkled with genuine amusement as he watched Levin go. From that bleak room in a run-down building one week, to turning down Georgian champagne the next. Rags to riches indeed. He presumed the captain was sufficiently realistic to realize that once he had served his purpose, he might easily revert. But, in a way, Malik hoped not. Depending on how useful the girl turned out to be, he ought to be allowed to keep at least some of the advantages he had been given.

With the approach of the weekend, Levin became aware of rising anticipation. He tried to imagine Jean in his apartment: how she would look, what things would interest her, whether she would feel she was being watched.

He worked on Saturday morning as usual, knowing the chef would be in to prepare dinner and that Katya would be busy cleaning and setting the table. At noon he returned to Kutuzovsky Prospekt to change for the afternoon.

He had arranged to meet Jean at Gorkiy Park, where their first contrived encounter took place. She planned to spend the morning at the Pushkin Museum and would walk there afterward. It set a useful precedent for future meetings, away from the foreigners' compound.

When he was still a half-block away, he spotted her waiting on a park bench, and there was genuine gladness in his heart. She noticed the Volvo pulling in—it was not the sort of car people tended to miss —and came over quickly.

Levin leaned over the passenger seat to open the door for her, and it slammed shut, enclosing them in the warmth and quiet of a . . . well, he thought, a moving recording studio.

Levin had brought a few cassettes from the apartment to play on the Volvo's stereo equipment, thinking it would make life more difficult for the KGB and might even allow some free conversation, but he was not entirely surprised to find the built-in tape deck was not functioning.

"Right on time, thank God. It's freezing out there."

"Not a good day for a picnic?" He was smiling at her with such obvious admiration that she grinned impishly back as she settled herself in the seat.

"Depends where you're thinking of having the picnic, my friend."

"I thought we might eat at my apartment this evening. Let's break the twenty-five-mile barrier, get a couple of vodkas inside to warm us up, and see what the chef has come up with."

"The chef? What happened to the maid?"

"The *dejournaya* set the table. The chef cooked the food."

"My God. How many people are you having around tonight, Filipp?"

"Just you. Is that not a reason for good food?"

Her fingers brushed his arm lightly. "That's a darn good reason."

He pulled into the traffic, heading past the airport and along the road to Kalinin. The sprawl of Moscow, with its eight- and ten-lane avenues, was behind them and the early winter landscape opened up.

The scene was barren, almost desolate, waiting for the snow. The occasional grove of evergreens provided the only color that seemed to belong to something living.

The digital readout on the dashboard showed them traveling at a steady hundred kilometers per hour, although it felt half that. Houses with gingerbread shutters—*dachas* for the well-off, the influential—were dotted among towering trees and were soon left behind.

"We're past the twenty-five-mile limit," Levin said, taking his eyes off the road to glance at her. "This is where the KGB arrive to arrest you for being a spy." He grinned.

"Oh, stop it, Filipp," she said anxiously. "You promised to protect me, and I expect you to do just that. Did you get permission? Seriously?"

"Seriously. They said to be sure to bring you back safely. *They* didn't want a diplomatic incident. Mad Russian Kidnaps Beautiful American Diplomat."

Jean laughed. Her hand touched his, resting on the floor gear shift, and stayed. Levin shot a pleased look at her. She settled closer.

"What *would* your Embassy say about us, Jean?" he asked for Malik's benefit. "Don't they mind you going out with a mad Russian?"

"Mad Russians are the only kind they'll allow me to go out with," she said lightly. "Sane Russians scare them."

"They don't mind? I'm glad about that."

"Well, I haven't actually told them I'm going out with you today. They certainly wouldn't approve of me moving beyond the magic twenty-five miles without official approval in triplicate on their desks, so I thought it best they didn't know. They'll only find out if I get locked into one of your nice warm-hearted Soviet jails."

"You won't. On my honor."

"Then they won't know," she said. "I don't have to check out with them or tell them where I'm going. I'm a big girl now. What I do outside working hours is my business. That's a basic American right, and just because I'm outside the States, it doesn't change."

"I liked your friends, by the way. It was a wonderful evening."

"Good. They liked you too. They were especially impressed with your dancing." She paused. "So was I actually. Particularly that part right at the end."

Levin grinned delightedly. He enjoyed conversations which took place on two simultaneous levels. "I enjoy dancing," he said. "The more I do it, the more I like it. Especially with you. In fact, I was sorry that particular one didn't go on for longer. I know a few other steps."

"Well, we'll have to do it again some other time. You can teach me."

"Soon?"

"Whenever you like."

He squeezed her hand and felt an answering pressure.

The road was flat and straight now, and Jean swiveled around to check the traffic behind them, but the black Tarmac ribbon behind them was empty. She presumed a KGB radio vehicle would be tailing a couple of miles farther back, monitoring transmissions from the Volvo—unless of course the recording apparatus was all on board, and they would merely send someone later to collect the tape. But this was not the sort of thing she could check—not without taking the risk of tipping Malik off that they were more aware of what was going on than he had assumed.

Jean said suddenly: "Oh, Filipp, look! It's so beautiful! Listen, can't we pull in to the side for a couple of minutes? It's a shame to speed past scenery like this."

"Yes, of course. I'll stop up ahead, near those trees."

He had been aware of her looking back. He knew himself the road was clear because he was constantly monitoring the rearview mirror for any vehicle keeping a steady distance. In other circumstances he would have thought the KGB had left them alone.

The Volvo's wheels crunched over loose gravel, and they halted near a plowed field. In the silence immediately after the engine died, Levin felt Jean touch his hand, and he glanced down to see a small folded piece of paper being pressed into his palm.

She began talking, filling the gap while he read the message with exclamations about the scenery and comparisons with the United States. Occasionally Levin murmured some noncommittal response. It was a one-sided conversation that required nothing more. Jean half-swung around in her seat so she could keep a watch on cars coming up behind them, although she suspected the radio vehicle would also have stopped. A truck appeared in the distance, but she paid it no attention. Trucks do not tail Volvos.

Beside her, Levin was reading with a sinking heart.

MUST HAVE DETAILED INFORMATION ABOUT VOLOGDA BASE COMPUTER.

1. WHAT MAKE, WHAT MODEL COMPUTER? ANY MODIFICA-
TIONS?

2. NEED EXACT REPEAT EXACT PROCEDURE FOR LOGGING-ON,
INCLUDING PASSWORDS, EXAMPLES OF ACTUAL USER NAMES,
USER NUMBERS.

3. EXACT REPEAT EXACT PROCEDURE FOR LOGGING-OUT.

4. ANY SPECIAL KEY EFFECTS INCLUDED IN ABOVE PROCE-
DURES?

5. PRECISE DETAILS OF MASTER PROGRAM FOR MISSILE
LAUNCH AND TARGETS.

6. WHAT PROCEDURE IS USED TO GET THE COMPUTER SIMUL-
TANEOUS ACCESS TO ALL REPEAT ALL ONBOARD MISSILE COM-
PUTERS, IF DIFFERENT FROM ABOVE.

IMPERATIVE WE HAVE THIS INFORMATION. WHEN WE DO, GET-
TING YOU OUT WILL BE OUR NEXT PRIORITY. TAKE CARE. MIKE.

Levin read it through three times, committing it to memory,
although he wondered why he bothered. He could certainly get the
answer to the first question. But the others would be known only to a
handful of select men with top security classifications, most of whom
would be based at Vologda.

It was possible he would be able to discover the names of these
people, provide Michael Pitt with a list to do with as he liked. But
Levin was certain he knew none of them himself, and even if he was
to pay another visit to Vologda with the *General Polkovnik*, it was
most unlikely he would come within conversational distance of any
of this select team, let alone begin pumping them for information
which had to be among the most secret in the Soviet Union.

And he didn't much like the ending. Pitt seemed to be linking his
defection directly to the procurement of the information. Was he in
effect saying: no information, no escape?

Levin grimaced, tore the paper in half and half again, and began
to chew the pieces. It was surprisingly edible. Trust the Americans.
He would probably be able to request a flavor next time.

When he had finished swallowing, he waited for a suitable pause
in Jean's monologue before asking, "Do you want to get out and
walk about a bit?"

"I don't think so, thanks, Filipp," she said. "It looks freezing outside, and it's a shame to leave this nice warm car. Anyway, I think I've seen enough. Let's go."

Levin drove for another hour, much of it in thoughtful silence. The day's unofficial business had been transacted. Soon would come the official part, and they could just relax and enjoy themselves.

He had in mind a village hotel patronized by owners of the sprawling clapboard *dachas* nearby, which he had visited in the company of the *General Polkovnik*. The hotel served Starka—a special type of aged vodka, very strong—yellow, herb-tinted *pertsovka*, Beluga caviar, and *blinis*.

It was about ten kilometers off the road, in hilly country. Levin slowed the Volvo because the road was narrow and winding and it was difficult to spot oncoming traffic until the last moment.

The village itself was small and poor. They could see inside some of the shops they passed, the cracked yellow tile walls, in worse condition even than the ones in Moscow. The selection of goods was just as paltry: the usual bags of salt, sugar, and flour were stacked on the floor, with clusters of dried sausages hanging from hooks. There were some cans on the shelves, and Levin was prepared to bet most contained smoked fish.

At the hotel they entered another, more comforting world. A log fire roared in a large grate, casting a yellow flickering glow onto the old carpets, the rich velvet furnishings, the heavy and ornately carved wooden tables. Levin and Jean checked their coats and hats and briefly warmed themselves near the flames. But it quickly became too hot, and they retreated to velvet-covered armchairs where Levin ordered two glasses of Starka and something to eat.

There were five other people in the room, at the other end, who glanced at them curiously but returned to their drinks and talk.

Jean settled back in her chair. "So this is where the ordinary people come, eh, Filipp?" she asked, amused.

"That is correct," he said stoically. "If I were to introduce you to them, you would soon discover how very ordinary they are. Ordinary conversation, ordinary intellects, ordinary dullness. For that reason I will not introduce you. We will view them from afar, and talk about each other."

The Starka arrived, and she accepted her glass, laughing at him. "Cheers, Filipp," she said, "you ordinary old fraud."

"Your health." He knocked back the drink and pushed the silver tray of red and black caviar, arranged in net squares, toward her. "Eat," he said. "It's very good."

"I know. I'm developing a taste for caviar. When I go back to Washington, I won't know what hit me."

"I will send you food parcels from Moscow. I shall ask the International Red Cross to deliver them."

"Why not deliver them yourself? You'd be very welcome. Do you ever get over to the States?"

Levin shook his head with genuine regret. "So far, I never have," he admitted. "But perhaps some day it will be possible."

"I'll drink to that," she said and tossed back her Starka. "Oh wow!" she exclaimed as it hit her stomach. "That's fantastic!"

"It is one way of keeping out the cold."

"But not your favorite, by the sound of it."

He shook his head slowly, the corners of his eyes crinkling.

They had a second Starka, and finished most of the caviar, before Levin called for the bill and escorted her back to the Volvo. As she settled in Jean noticed a man standing a block away, hunched on a corner, hands in his pockets. No one in their right minds hung around outside in that sort of weather, and she realized at once he must be part of their surveillance. She could not see his vehicle. Presumably it was parked down a side road.

With Filipp himself bugged, and the car almost certainly also wired for sound, there was no easy way of drawing it to his attention, and she preferred not to take the risk of the man seeing her pointing him out.

But the KGB were at least being discreet, which was not always their style.

For the most part the drive back to Moscow was completed in silence. The Starka had made them feel mellow and content, not needing words but aware of each other's physical presence.

Filipp parked near the entrance to his apartment building in Kutuzovsky Prospekt, and took her arm to escort her in.

When he unlocked his door, Katya and the butler had long gone. The wine and champagne were on ice, the table was set for two with heavy silver cutlery, crystal glasses, fine Irish linen, and candles waiting to be lit.

Jean stood just inside, surveying the scene, while he watched her with pleasure.

"Filipp, it's . . . it's . . ." she paused for thought. ". . . it's exceptionally ordinary," she said. "An ordinary Bang and Olafsen stereo. An ordinary twenty-eight-inch latest-model Sony television. Ordinary Italian leather chairs." She walked farther in, eyes mischievously sweeping the trappings provided by the KGB. "And am I deceived or is that ordinary Soviet Baccarat crystal on the table?"

"You have a good eye, my Jean," Levin said.

"Lucky for you I'm an ordinary Missouri girl, or I might not like any of it."

Anxiously: "But you do like it?"

"It's fabulous! You have good taste."

Levin hesitated. "Well, actually, someone did it for me. I know the things I like. I'm just not very good at assembling them myself."

"This must be the part where I say, 'Why, Filipp, you need a good woman to organize you.' "

"And I'd say, 'But I've got Katya, my trusty *dejournaya*.' "

"Can she cook?"

"Yes."

"Is she pretty?"

"Er, no. She's more the homely middle-aged type."

"Well, there you are. Not at all suitable."

"I do have a good barman, though."

"Oh, who?" Jean asked.

"Me. What would you like? Schlitz, Bourbon, vodka, wine, brandy, marijuana cookies . . ."

"Marijuana cookies? I'm hearing things again."

"Well, it's because I don't smoke, you see."

Jean laughed. "Don't tell me Katya made them for you?"

"Of course. I explained it was a special ingredient from America which gives them a particular flavor."

"And naturally she believed you."

"I am a very plausible man."

"A silver-tongued Russian."

"Will you have one?"

"Are they strong?"

"Quite strong. For me, anyway. But very pleasant."

"Then I'll have half with you. And a glass of white wine, please."

Levin grinned. Half a cookie would probably be perfect. Enough to set them flying, not too high.

They ate the cookie sitting together on a sofa, listening to Bach and sipping chilled Pouilly-Fuissé. The drug worked gently, heightening senses, leaving them in control.

Outside the light faded, and the apartment became gray and black with shadows, deep and rich with sound. Levin stroked her hair, the softness of her cheek. The tip of her tongue licked his fingers as they passed over her mouth. There was no urgency, only a sense of having time.

By candlelight they ate creamy sturgeon on dark pumpernickel, a hot, spicy veal dish, and a cold, sharp lemon soufflé.

They took the remains of the champagne into the living room. Levin chose a record and asked if she would like to dance. The music was slow. They scarcely moved on the floor, just touched, explored very gently, with tongues and lips and the tips of their fingers.

When the record ended Levin took her hand and led her to the bedroom. It was as if he had been waiting for this moment the whole of his life.

10

DAVID CANE CAME AT ROSS WITHOUT warning, suddenly whirling as they walked along the corridor from the Fairfax gymnasium, right hand rigid, fingers extended, edge of his palm slicing toward the professor's larnyx. Ross was aware only of the sudden inexplicable threat before his body turned instinctively and his forearm went up to ward off the crushing blow. There was a pain as their arms collided, and he was thrown against the wall. Ross fought to recover, knowing another blow would follow quickly.

Cane's body blocked the passage in front of him. Ross needed distance. He was too close and he could see from Cane's stance and balance that his foot would kick out and smash into his belly. Ross leaped back as the foot grazed past. He landed, off balance, shouting, "For Christ's sake, David, what are you doing?" Cane kept coming.

For the first time Ross could see in the implacable set of his features the face of a killer. After a day of personal coldness and outright hostility, it was suddenly clear. His stomach contracted in fear.

"David, you crazy fucker!" Ross screamed.

Cane swung his foot and Ross retreated. A fist hit out at his temple. Ross dodged. Cane was getting nearer the mark every time. His hand came around in a chop and Ross could feel the breeze past his ear. Without thinking, he turned and fled back toward the gym. He made it through the door, breath coming in gasps, aware of Cane on his heels, and then he was caught in a tackle and was plunging onto one of the exercise mats, a great weight crushing him, pulling him over onto his back, powerful hands around his throat. He stared unbelievingly at Cane's stranger's face and clawed ineffectually at the mat.

Abruptly Cane rolled off him and stood up. "Get up," he ordered. Ross pulled himself to his feet warily. "Come and stand here." Cane indicated a point two feet in front of him. Ross complied, not understanding, unsure of what was to follow, feeling embarrassed as well as frightened. The flush was leaving Cane's face, and his eyes had become neutral. "It seems. you're having a problem hitting me, mister," Cane said. "So I'm gonna make it easy for you. I'll stand here and LET you punch me. As hard as you can. Really PUNCH, 'cause if you don't, mister, I'm gonna get mad and I'm really gonna hurt you. Understand?"

Ross nodded.

"Make fists. Now HIT! HIT, YOU FUCKER!"

Ross jabbed experimentally at Cane's stomach. The man didn't move.

"I said *HIT*, YOU PATHETIC SONOFABITCH!"

He punched with more force: still no reaction. Then again, as hard as he could, becoming angry because now he knew he'd been tricked. He'd believed Cane would really kill him, and it turned out to be an exercise, and he was ashamed of having run. He put his weight behind the punches, and Cane began to shift ground, to guard his stomach with his arms. Ross aimed a wild punch at his chin, connected, and saw his head jerk back, and before Cane could get his hands up, he smashed a right into the bastard's mouth and there was a smear of blood as Cane's lip split. Ross felt a surge of joy and rammed his fist into the now-unprotected stomach muscles and then suddenly down below the belt, going in angrily, punching to crush his balls so that when Cane doubled over Ross could bring his knee up into his teeth. And then there was a shout of pain, "JESUS! JESUS!", and Cane wasn't standing like a punching bag anymore, but was fighting back, tears streaming, really working. They tumbled to the floor, Ross in a bodylock.

"Okay, okay, break now, break," Cane gasped, maintaining the hold until he felt the professor relax. Then he let go.

Cane rolled off and lay on his back, hands lightly between his legs, waiting for the pain to subside. Ross, the anger disappearing as if it were a bathful of water with the plug pulled, began to feel ashamed and alarmed.

After a moment he raised himself on an elbow, his hand touching Cane's arm. His breath was labored. "You okay, David? David, I'm sorry. You okay?"

Through his teeth: "YOU FUCKING . . . DESPICABLE . . ." Cane's body began to shake, and Ross at first thought it was tears, then recognized it as the beginning of laughter. "DIRTY LITTLE BASTARD."

Ross relaxed with relief. "It was okay, huh?"

"It was WONDERFUL! I never thought I'd see you hitting anyone in the balls. Least of all me. Congratulations."

"Are you all right? You want me to get a doctor?"

Cane shook his head and pulled himself to a sitting position. "No, it'll pass. I dodged most of the punch. You got my thigh as well. But it was good enough. The intention was there and that's what counts."

Finally, Ross understood. "The whole of today—you being so damn impossible—was all leading up to this?" he asked.

Cane nodded. "I wanted to see your reactions. And they weren't too bad. I wanted to test what state your adrenaline was in: Were you going to run, or were you going to fight?"

Ross said simply: "I ran."

"Yeah, I noticed. I nearly killed you for that. I *will* kill you if you ever do it to me again. But I don't think you will. Once you've got your blood up, that's something else. Once you've started *enjoying* hurting someone, life's never the same again. Take my word for it, Martin. And you did enjoy it, you bastard. Don't sit there pretending to be sorry." He grinned. "I saw your face, man, and it looked like you'd found religion. That's great. That's what I hoped for. Next time I go for you, you'd better be ready, 'cause I'm a better fighter than you are and a lot younger, so you'll have to go in fast and dirty if you want to stop me, or I'm really gonna bust you. Okay?"

Ross stared back at the young man and nodded, feeling more than gratitude, more than admiration. They were brothers.

Cane lifted himself gingerly to his feet. "Let's go get something to eat. You want another shower?"

"No, I don't think so, thanks."

Ross noticed Cane limping slightly as they moved down the corridor, and he put a supportive arm around him. He supposed he ought to feel sorry about fouling like that. Everything from his childhood

on—more than fifty years of training—labeled it wrong and cow-
ardly. But those voices no longer called to him, not even muted
echoes heard at a distance. It was as if they had never existed. Ross
wasn't sorry. In fact, he felt glad and relaxed, and a sense of well-
being flowed through his body. He was, for the first time in years,
really alive. Princeton seemed another planet. Elaine—well, she had
her own work and he loved her, of course. But a gap was growing
between them of which Ross had become increasingly aware, and
now he doubted it could ever properly be bridged.

Things were happening to him that he couldn't explain. He imagined pulling up a chair in Elaine's study, brushing the cat off and
saying, "Darling, the greatest thing happened to me. I was in the gym
with David Cane just after I thought he'd tried to kill me and I'd
run away, and he stood there and let me punch him. First, I hit him
in the mouth and his lip bled, then I socked him in the testicles and
he shouted, 'Jesus! Jesus!' And he was really pleased with me, and I
felt—so fantastic, it's hard to explain. I felt at last I was learning how
to kill. Then we went and had dinner."

It couldn't be explained, that's all there was to it. It was something private between David and himself, and it couldn't be shared
with anyone who didn't understand the special milieu of fighting men.

They ordered steaks, no wine. Cane had taken them off alcohol
during the intensive training period, although it was understood that
they would begin drinking again before the mission went active.
Alcohol was an inseparable part of Soviet life, and they had to build
up a tolerance, particularly for neat vodka. Otherwise, as Cane
.pointed out, they would be like virgins on a date, finding before they
knew what was happening that they were flat on their backs.

Preparations for the Vologda mission had stalled while they waited
for further information from agents in the Soviet Union. Cane himself had no precise idea who was being tapped to provide data on the
computer operations. For him it did not come under the need-to-
know heading, and he doubted that it ever would. Of course, he
would have to be given some contacts, the vital ones necessary to get
them access to the underground citadel in the Urals, but the plan he
was formulating didn't take into account the presence of an accom-
plice inside the computer section. If the DIA had a mole down there,
they hadn't told him about it.

Cane at last had a clear idea of how they would get into Vologda
and gain access to the vital computer room. They did have a middle-

rank contact involved in security at the base who would provide details of the identification cards and the special passes they needed. These would be prepared by the DIA and sent to Moscow in the diplomatic pouch to await Cane and Ross's arrival. They might also be able to call on the Soviet contact for help in actually passing through the security checks, but after that they would be on their own.

Cane had prepared a number of different cover stories to get them into the computer room. The one they finally selected would depend on how long Ross estimated he needed for reprogramming. And that couldn't be judged until all the information was in from the Soviet Union. *If* it ever came in.

There was still the real possibility, which Cane never spoke about to Ross, that they would hit a blank and the mission would abort. Officially he was cheerful and optimistic. Yet he knew that the information they needed had to be among the most closely guarded secrets in the Soviet Union, and they depended on having exactly the right man give it to them.

In some private moments, Cane wondered seriously if they weren't wasting their time. He wondered also how much longer he could keep Martin Ross on ice, distracting him with physical training and unarmed combat from the indisputable fact that intellectually they were stuck, and that no breakthrough was in sight. He guessed that after nearly five months, Ross was nearing his physical peak for someone his age. It was certainly satisfying to see how much he had accomplished. The professor was being transformed into the sort of man he'd never believed he could be. The spiritual and physical change had usefully filled his days and made him sleep, exhausted, through his nights. Cane could carry on for several months longer with combat instruction, and no doubt his pupil would improve constantly. But once Ross settled down with the knowledge that, if necessary, he could actually kill, he would become bored. The concept had novelty value, nothing more.

Cane chafed for more information from Moscow. He drove to Washington several times, and on other occasions General Yardley came to Fairfax to watch training. But in private discussions with Cane, there was really nothing more to say. Every string available to the DIA was being pulled. There were one or two hopeful signs, but it was too early to be sure if, in the end, they would result in anything positive. Meanwhile, the mere fact that nothing had been ruled out was encouraging.

Yardley assured Cane of the President's continuing interest in the

Vologda operation. Reagan was receiving regular briefings on progress, or lack of it. His demand for results was becoming insistent.

This top-level pressure did not cheer Cane. The effects produced
by demands for progress, particularly from the Oval Office, could be
both profound and adverse. Generals shouted at their subordinates,
who yelled at *their* subordinates, until finally the poor bastard in the
field found the screws really turning. Results, or else. There had
been times, and Cane was aware of some of the stories, when this
ended up in reports that turned out to be false—totally or partially.
If the pressure was really bad, a man might just make something
up. Or take what he hoped was an educated guess. Or, if he was
more conscientious, settle for information from second- or third-rate
sources rather than moving carefully and surely and getting things
right. This was usually a CIA failing, and the reason they sometimes
screwed things up so publicly.

Cane believed the DIA were a lower-key, more professional operation. For all Yardley's other failings, he usually absorbed such pressures himself and made sure they weren't transmitted to agents in the
field. Cane hoped that, on this occasion, he would stick firmly to his
guns.

The final nightmare would be actually bluffing their way into the
Vologda computer room to discover that the logging-on procedure
they had been given was wrong in some detail and that they had triggered an alarm signal.

Meanwhile, as far as Ross was concerned, the only thing Cane
could do was step up the physical pressure and run again and again
through the details of getting into Moscow, how they would shake off
KGB surveillance once there, travel to Vologda, and penetrate the
security screen; and then how they would get out again safely. Those
at least were matters on which Cane was well briefed.

At the beginning of March, Yardley called Cane to DIA headquarters, saying something had come in and that it might be of interest.
He did not sound particularly enthusiastic, however, and there was
no feeling that their problems had been solved. So Cane went to
Washington, glad of the break, glad to be able to see Maryann and
Timmy again, but not expecting anything particularly startling to
emerge. Ross elected to stay at Fairfax.

At the appointed time Cane walked into Yardley's outer office,
gave his secretary, Lucy, a hug which made her face pink with pleasure, and was told to go on through: The others were waiting.

This made Cane pause a moment.

At no point in the planning so far had he dealt with anyone other than Yardley and Professor Ross. As far as he was aware, the Vologda operation was so classified that only a handful of people knew of its existence.

In his office Yardley was sitting on the sofa with two others, and as soon as he looked at them, Cane knew the number must have been enlarged.

One man he didn't recognize at all, but the other one stood to greet him: medium height, sandy hair, watchful eyes a very light brown. A compact, controlled body.

Cane stared at him thoughtfully. "Goddam, goddam," he said softly. "Clive Lyle."

"Hello, David," Lyle replied, a slight Southern accent in his voice. "Good to see you again."

Cane, still softly, almost in wonder: "Goddam Lyle."

They shook hands, for form's sake rather than anything else, but they maintained their grip long enough to cause Yardley, who was aware of their history, to interrupt firmly: "And this is Dr. Peter Barry, David. He's one of the DIA medical experts."

"Is Clive planning to get sick?" Cane asked pleasantly.

"Mr. Cane." The doctor had the familiar, competent air of highly paid medics the world over, but Cane knew that if he was on the DIA payroll, he actually would be good. And willing to cut corners.

Peter Barry must have been in his mid-fifties, with a full head of silver hair and a gray suit which had set him back a lot of money.

Cane settled into a spare armchair and tapped his pockets for a pack of cigarettes before remembering he wasn't smoking anymore. Clive Lyle made him do things like that.

Yardley spoke: "Clive and Dr. Barry are fully aware of the Vologda operation. I filled them in myself, and they have both seen the relevant documentation. They've also seen the latest report from Moscow, which is why I called you in, David."

He handed over a single sheet of paper and waited while Cane read it. As usual, it was an abstract:

VOLOGDA COMPUTER IDENTIFIED AS AN IBM 7090, PURCHASED
THROUGH ITALIAN COMPANY AND MODIFIED. USE LIMITED TO
MISSILE PROGRAM AND PERFORMANCE OF STANDARD SE-
QUENCES AND THERE NONO CURRENT PLANS TO CHANGE. FU-
TURE UPDATING LIKELY THRU FURTHER MODIFICATIONS TO
PERIPHERALS AND NOT REPEAT NOT TO COMPUTER CORE.

THUS BASIC PROGRAMS EXPECTED REMAIN UNCHANGED. OPERATOR'S CONTROL CONSOLES AND KEYBOARD STANDARD. ALPHABET ROMAN.

ITEM: SOURCE ADVISES NONO POSSIBILITY HIM GAINING AC-CESS COMPUTER PROCEDURES, LOGGING-ON, LOGGING-OUT, ETC., EXCEPT AT GRAVEST RISK DETECTION AS WOULD INVOLVE APPROACHING PEOPLE CURRENTLY UNKNOWN TO HIM PER-SONALLY AND WHO ARE NORMALLY INACCESSIBLE TO HIM. THIS BEING SO, STRONGLY ADVISE TELLING HIM KEEP HEAD DOWN UNLESS SOMETHING CROSSES HIS DESK. GRATEFUL CON-FIRM AGREEMENT.

ITEM: SOURCE LISTS NAMES OF VOLOGDA COMPUTER OPER-ATORS, DATA PREPARATION OPERATORS, SUPERVISORS, AND SENIOR OFFICERS WHO LIKELY TO KNOW PRECISE COMPUTER PROCEDURES, AS FOLLOWS . . .

Cane skimmed the names, recognizing none of them. It wasn't a lot of help.

The report concluded:

THERE MAY BE POSSIBILITY ONE OF THESE KNOWN TO YOU AND MIGHT REPAY SPECIFIC APPROACH.

And that was all. Cane expelled his breath in a frustrated sigh and handed back the paper.

"Not much there," he said, disappointed. "Looks like a blank wall." He noticed Lyle staring pointedly at the ceiling and wished he hadn't committed himself quite so soon. They, of course, were ahead of him.

"Not necessarily, David," Yardley remarked. "Something's hap-pened since I phoned you at Fairfax, and it's the reason I asked Dr. Barry and Clive Lyle to be here. We fed the names through the NSA computers and came up with at least one very interesting fact."

Another single sheet was handed over. Cane grimaced. The paper read:

VLADIMIR PETROVICH METKIN. MAJOR IN GLAVNOYA RAZVEDY-VATELNOYE UPRAVLENIYE (GRU). AGED 43. BORN MOSCOW. SENIOR SUPERVISOR COMPUTERS. CURRENT ASSIGNMENT UN-KNOWN. NAMED MEMBER OF SOVIET DELEGATION TO "INTER-NATIONAL COMPUTERS IN INDUSTRY" SEMINAR, LONDON, APRIL 1 TO 4.

Cane looked up hopefully. "Is Metkin one of ours? Have we had contact with him?"

"No," Yardley said. "But he's sure to know the computer procedures. They must be in his head. If the word ever comes to press the button, Metkin's going to be the man standing over the operator who gives the orders to the computer, and behind *him,* breathing down his neck, are going to be the entire goddam Politburo. So he has to know what's going on."

"Do we think he might want to defect?"

Yardley shook his head. "Even if we did, we wouldn't encourage it. Not now. We want him where he is. We don't need anybody screwing things up and making Moscow take a new look at their IBM. No, we like him just as he is."

"So?"

"So we need to find out what he knows."

It was becoming clearer to Cane. At least why Dr. Barry was there, not Clive Lyle. "And that's where the doctor comes in?"

Barry cleared his throat. "My understanding of the requirements in this case," he said in his medically neutral voice, "is that the subject has to be placed in a situation where he is totally relaxed and at ease and free to speak what's in his mind. In response to questions. There are a number of drugs that can be recommended for this. The best is probably a derivative of Innovar. It produces a tranquil state and the loss of the sense of pain, but not a deep level of unconsciousness. This means the patient can communicate. The drug is a new one called Pentovar. In controlled experiments patients have communicated very freely on matters which ordinarily they would have kept private. I think for our purposes Pentovar would be ideal."

"Do the patients have any recollection of what's happened when it wears off?" Cane wanted to know.

"No. Not as far as we are aware."

Cane crossed his long legs. "Exactly how far *are* we aware, Dr. Barry? How many people has this stuff been tried on?"

"We've had controlled experiments on thirty-two so far. Men and women of different ages and in different mental states. We have, as you may know, an unofficial interest in a psychiatric clinic in New York City, and fourteen of the experiments have taken place there without the patients' prior knowledge. With extraordinary results."

"But they've all been stories about bed-wetting, intercourse with animals, and jerking off Daddy?"

Peter Barry was not fazed. "They have, as you say, been disclosures of profound disturbances to the psyche, usually in childhood and early adolescence."

"I see. Nothing about how the patients are currently fiddling the books? Or the numbers of their secret Swiss bank accounts?"

Dr. Barry thought for a moment. "Certainly not in the fourteen psychiatric cases. We have also used Pentovar on what one might, for the purposes of a discussion like this anyway, be termed 'ordinary people'—let's define them loosely as those not currently undergoing psychoanalysis. They include DIA staff members who volunteered to cooperate rather than take the routine polygraph test."

"But by definition," Cane pointed out, "these are people who'd have nothing to hide anyway. If they'd cheated their way past the lie detector before and got a security clearance, they're not likely to want to be pumped full of a new truth drug, are they?"

"I could debate motivation with you, Mr. Cane, for a long time," Dr. Barry said. "But can I ask instead what you're driving at?"

Cane leaned forward earnestly, aware of Yardley disapproving on the sofa and of Lyle preoccupied with a cigarette. "I'm just giving you a gut reaction now, Dr. Barry. But it seems to me two main questions arise. One is: Let's say we get Metkin and pump him full of Pentovar. Is there a chance he'll remember something when he wakes up, enough to set alarm bells ringing in his head? Because if there is we're going to have to kill him. So it's important to know. The second question is directly related to this. Do you think there's a qualitative difference between talking under the influence of Pentovar about how you were traumatized somewhere along the line and how today you're defrauding your company out of a million dollars?

"For example, let's say you've got a DIA agent on your couch." Cane steadfastly did not look at Lyle. "And under Pentovar he comes up with all sorts of terrible incidents and feelings, buried way down deep inside his psyche, which go back to when he was in diapers, and he explains to a man like yourself how he turned out to be such a crumb. Now this guy wakes up, and he doesn't remember a thing. Why? Because of the Pentovar? Or because the secrets that were revealed to you are actually still hidden from his conscious self? They're back under lock and key down there in his psyche. You just had a private showing. Is that possible?"

Barry nodded slowly. "It could be," he admitted.

Lyle's expression was cold and distant, but Yardley had unfrozen a little, obviously deciding Cane wasn't just being gratuitously offhand because Lyle had been pulled into the operation. It *was* a legitimate inquiry.

Cane continued. "Fine. So in those circumstances we don't know why this guy doesn't remember. But let's go a step further and say he hasn't been talking about profound disturbances of the psyche. He's been telling you about *now*, about the people he fucks, physically, personally, and mentally."

"David, I really think . . ." Yardley broke in sharply, but Dr. Barry held up a silencing hand.

"No, no, General. Let him say what's on his mind in the way that's most comfortable to him."

Cane grinned despite himself. What a five-star put-down.

"Thanks. Okay, this guy lays it on you: the things he does to other men and women, and you soon get the picture. He's a killer, and he likes it. Then he tells you about this plan he's working on. Let's say he's got a married woman into bed, and all her husband's secrets are coming out 'cause she really thinks she's found love at last and she trusts this guy. So far, so good. That's his job, and no one would argue with it, certainly not me. But he knows, even when he sets her up, that he's going to pull the rug out from under her later. He's going to betray her to her husband who—again, for example—is a leading government official in some South American republic. A wealthy man and a jealous one, who'll be mad enough to pay some thugs to kill her." Cane was conscious of a profound silence in the room and of Lyle turning to watch him calmly. It was one of the things Lyle did best.

"The main reason he wants to betray her is because he's bored. He's tired of her in his bed and of her conversation. Worse still, she wants marriage. She wants to divorce her husband and have kids with him. These things are definitely not our guy's scene. How does he get rid of her *and* still learn secrets from her husband? That's the problem. Now under Pentovar, he says he's made an appointment with the husband the next day and he's going to tell him what's been going on. He'll point out that if the bloodthirsty dictator who heads the government ever hears one of his senior men has been blabbing secrets to his wife—and that she's been the mistress of an American agent—well, that official won't live too long. So he'd better cooperate."

"I think I get the picture, Mr. Cane."

"Okay. Now you, the doctor listening to all of this, are in a position to blow the whistle on him. It happens you're related to the wife and you can tip her off. Not only that but by nightfall you'll be leading a family posse to shut this little bastard up forever. And when he's not doped up with Pentovar, our guy knows that very well. He wasn't one of your volunteers, of course. So he wakes up. What does he remember? What does he think happened? Are his suspicions aroused to a point where, without quite knowing why, he takes evasive action? Or is it all an absolute and complete mental blank?"

Lyle had lit another cigarette and was busy blowing slow smoke rings. Yardley looked as if he'd have things to say later.

"It's an interesting hypothetical case, Mr. Cane," Dr. Barry observed. "But I feel I can answer it. In none of the thirty-two cases has there been the slightest recall of what took place. The subjects simply went to sleep and then woke up. Between those times—a blank."

"Fair enough. Is thirty-two a big enough sample, do you think?"

"No. Not ideal. It's all I can offer you, though. There are other drugs which have been better tested, but in my opinion they won't give the *level* of response you'll need in this case. You want the precise details of a computer program, with nothing missed. Pentovar will let you have them."

"Do we kill Metkin afterward to be sure?"

Dr. Barry shrugged. "That's up to you. I don't think there'd be much point. Unless of course you hit problems about administering the Pentovar. Naturally if he's awake at the time, he'll remember everything that happened up to that point."

Yardley interjected: "We don't want a Soviet military intelligence officer found dead in his hotel room or wherever it is, if we can help it. They're sure to be suspicious."

"Not if it was measles," Clive Lyle suggested lazily. "Air bubble in the heart? No marks. Nothing in the autopsy. Tiny pinprick somewhere not very obvious, like the foot?"

Cane looked across at him with wry amusement. Nothing ever got through to Lyle.

"They'll go over his body with a magnifying glass, Clive," Yardley said. "We'll do it if we have to, but it's an added risk. Much better if Metkin goes to sleep, and wakes up, and no one's the wiser."

"Exactly how do you administer Pentovar, Doctor?" Cane asked.

"Intravenously. It comes in a small vial, about the length of a matchbox but half the width. There's a sterilized needle attached, with a protective plastic cap that unscrews. You insert the needle into any vein in the hand or arm. You'll probably find the hand is easier. Have you given an injection before, Mr. Cane?"

"No, I'm afraid not."

"Well, you'd better put in some practice before you go. It has to be a neat job, or you'll leave a bruise which the patient might notice later."

"I'll practice on Clive."

"Dr. Barry said a neat job," Lyle replied evenly.

"Come over to the hospital someday—Tuesday mornings are usually good for outpatients, I don't know why—and you can blood-test everyone who comes in. You're not squeamish about that sort of thing, right?"

Lyle looked up, interested to hear the answer.

"Hardly," said Cane.

"Everyone has their threshold, Mr. Cane, even men with jobs like yours. Sometimes a surprisingly small thing throws them." Dr. Barry glanced across at General Yardley. "Is there anything more I can help you with at this stage?"

Yardley stood up. "No thank you, Peter. That's fine. We'll call again if something comes up."

Barry nodded courteously at Cane and Lyle and left the room.

"Peter Barry is a fine man," Yardley remarked, resuming his seat. "A great doctor. If he recommends Pentovar, I'll go along with it." Cane said nothing. Yardley inspected his fingernails. "Now I have to talk to the two of you very seriously," he said. "I know there's bad blood, and I know why. You've got different ways of operating. You're very different personalities. Bound to be a clash somewhere. That South American thing was a disaster, certainly as far as you two were concerned. Professionally I have to say that Clive's arrangements are still going rather well." Lyle gave Cane a significant look. "And now we've got the Vologda thing, and I've asked Clive to give us a hand."

"I wasn't aware we needed a hand, General," Cane said.

"Well, we do, David. What do you think we're going to do with Ross while you're in London dealing with Metkin? You could be away for a fairly long stretch, with preparation and everything. Ross has to keep up his training, and Clive's one of the best. Whatever else you think of him, I'm sure you'll grant that at least. He was a Fairfax instructor for a couple of years, after all."

"I thought I'd take Ross with me," Cane said quietly. That stopped Yardley in his tracks.

"Take him with you?" the general asked incredulously. "What the hell for? He's not a trained agent. He'll just get in the way."

"I'm supposed to take him into Russia," Cane pointed out. "No one's got any objection to that. In fact that's what the whole thing's about. And he's going to go in cold. So let's initiate him in London."

Lyle weighed in unexpectedly on Cane's side. "David has something there, General," he said, tapping a fresh cigarette on the side of the box. "It might not be too difficult either. They probably have to get into a hotel room in the middle of the night, that's all." He turned to Cane. "I presume that's how you were thinking of doing it?" Cane nodded. "That's much easier than getting into Vologda base. It'll give David a chance to see how Ross reacts under pressure. Another 'does he fight or does he run?' test. And it's a lot easier on the balls too."

Cane found himself grinding his teeth. Trust Yardley to have shown Lyle the video. Jesus, nothing was private anymore.

Yardley seemed deep in thought. "You could be right," he said. Lyle inhaled a lungful of smoke and sat back.

"I'm glad to find Clive and I are on the same side for a change," Cane said finally.

Yardley fixed him with a cold look. "We're *all* on the same side, David. Just try to remember that."

"Yes, sir. But the fact is if I don't take Ross to London, what the hell are we going to do with him for another four or five months? He's progressing well enough on the physical side, but there's been no mental payoff for a long time, and a guy like that needs stimulation. Clive's right. We ought to try him on a piece of fairly gentle action first. Of course, it'll depend what hotel the Russians book into. I don't suppose we know that yet?"

"No," said Yardley. "It hasn't even been confirmed that Metkin's coming. His name's just on the preliminary list, that's all."

"Well, if it's not going to be too hairy and involve abseiling down to a bedroom window or something like that, I'd welcome Ross along. Apart from the personal test it'll provide, he'll know exactly the questions to ask. I guess I've got a pretty clear idea of what's needed, but Ross'll realize right away if something doesn't figure in Metkin's answers, or if he needs to ask for additional information, or wants extra technical details. There's a minefield in there, I tell you."

Yardley nodded reluctant agreement. "Makes sense," he admitted.

"Okay, David, take the professor and let's see how he works out. And you can stay out of it for the time being, Clive."

"There's something that's worrying me a little, General," Lyle said diffidently. "It's this. What the hell would Metkin be doing coming over to Britain? Now, I'm not a Soviet specialist like David here. But aren't I right in thinking that no Soviet citizen leaves the country without specific clearance from the KGB—not even if he's a guy like Metkin, a major in the GRU?"

Lyle was trespassing, but he obviously had something up his sleeve. Cane didn't know what it was.

"That's right, Clive," Cane said carefully. "The GRU is part of the Soviet General Staff, and it's supervised by the Central Committee of the party, but the KGB take precedence. They run clearances on GRU personnel. They've got their own informants among military intelligence officers. Major Metkin needs the KGB okay before he can get onto that plane."

"So I say again, why's he coming? Isn't it also true that any Soviet scientist, engineer, or technician who works directly on the missile program is banned from going abroad until there's been a time lag of at least two years?"

Lyle had a point. "As a rule that's true, Clive," Cane said, hating to admit it. "Generally they figure that after two years, their technology will have advanced sufficiently to make any information these people have virtually worthless. There've been exceptions but not too many, I grant you. Still, if Moscow wants something badly enough, they'll take an occasional risk."

"So," Lyle went on, "two questions: one—what is it they want badly enough to send Metkin to London, where MI-6 or we could snap him up if he showed the slightest sign of second thoughts about the glories of socialism . . ."

"We don't want him," Yardley broke in. "I've already told you that, Clive."

"Only because of the Vologda operation. And Moscow Center presumably doesn't know about that, we hope."

"True."

"And MI-6 don't know about it either. So my point stands. They'd be gambling sending him over. What do they want? And question two is really for David to think about. If they're taking a chance on Metkin, they're going to be watching him like hawks. There may be a KGB man staying with him in the bedroom. A babysitter."

Lyle was probably right. He had a quick, methodical mind. Just seemed to be missing a few basic morals, that's all. Cane nodded almost imperceptibly. Yardley, noticing, decided not to let him off lightly.

"Well, David," he demanded, "what about that? Has Clive got a point? Even though he's not a Soviet expert? Let's hear you."

Cane raised his eyes to meet Lyle's. "Both good points," he agreed quietly. "I'll get Ross to work out what Metkin might be after in London. Can we get as much information as possible on the computer seminar flown over here, General? Clive's other point is well taken too. Security will probably be a lot stricter. They won't take a chance on Metkin. In a way it'll be just as easy if an extra guy is in his bedroom. The gas we blow in will knock out two as quickly as one. We'll have to make sure he stays knocked out while we've got Metkin on the Pentovar, that's all. The problem will come if the KGB are outside in the corridor."

"Of course, they might not let Metkin stay in a hotel at all," Lyle pointed out. "They could keep him in the Embassy and just wheel him out to the seminar from time to time."

Cane rolled his eyes. "Let's hope it doesn't come to that."

"Well, if you need any extra help, David, I'm happy to be called in," Lyle said easily. Cane wasn't immediately sure whether he was being offered a peace pipe or Clive was rubbing it in to Yardley that it had been he who had pointed out the hidden obstacles and not the so-called expert. He opted for the former.

"Thank you, Clive," he said politely, then added formally, "It's no secret what I think about you, but that's . . . well, personal, between you and me. Otherwise you're a good operator. I'd be glad to have you with me. From that point of view, anyway."

Yardley said: "Look, boys, why don't the two of you go out, have a drink, clear the air?"

"I'm off alcohol, General," Cane said.

"Don't be pompous, David," Lyle said quietly. "It's a good idea."

Yardley was becoming exasperated and angry. "Listen, I don't care what the hell you do, but for God's sake go and do something. And do it together. Get this damned nonsense off your chests, both of you. Especially you, David. I run a tight ship here"—Cane and Lyle recognized the beginning of a well-worn speech, made to new recruits on their first day at headquarters after completing the Fairfax course, and exchanged a look—"and I'm not going to have it screwed up because my field men turn into a lot of prima donnas. An operation like ours is preparation and teamwork, knowledge and teamwork, calculated risks and teamwork. The two of you had a rough time in South America. Well, bad luck, Major Cane. It happened five years ago now, and I'm not going to have you nursing grudges like this. You're going to get rid of this bad blood, today! I don't want it around my operation anymore. Is that clear?"

Yardley glared furiously at Cane. It seemed as if he really meant it. "Yes, sir."

"That is an order, mister!"

"Yes, sir."

"Now get out of here, both of you and straighten yourselves out!"

Cane and Lyle left silently. Lucy in the outer office raised finely plucked eyebrows at them. Yardley shouting was not an everyday event. Cane's face was pale with anger. They walked together down the corridor toward the elevators.

Cane spoke, his voice cold: "Did you ever hear how she died, Lyle?"

"They took her into the forest and cut her throat. You know that."

"Yes, I know that. I wanted to make sure you did."

Lyle shrugged. "Of course I knew. You want that drink?"

"No."

"You heard the general, David. We've got to do something to clear the air."

"You want to come down to the gym?"

Lyle stopped abruptly and Cane turned to face him. "Fight?"

"Yeah. Clear the air."

"Rules?"

"I'd like to say none."

A shrug. "If you want."

"But we're supposed to clear the air, not kill each other. I want to beat the living shit out of you, Lyle. But you've got to be able to walk out. More or less."

"Okay. Grudge-fight rules." They continued in silence, taking the elevator down to the basement and crossing a cement courtyard behind the main building. The gym was on the second floor, above the squash courts, and they could hear as they approached that it was in use: the metallic ring of a weight being replaced heavily on the floor, a low grunt of exertion. Cane and Lyle paused in the doorway and looked around. Three others were working out.

Cane led the way through to the changing rooms, where there were uniforms they could borrow. They changed quickly, avoiding looking at each other.

The two men were evenly matched and there was no way of predicting the outcome. Lyle had actually been a Fairfax instructor, which ought to have given him some advantage except that both were second *Dan* black belts, which evened the score. And Cane had never been Lyle's pupil, so they had no firsthand experience of each other's technique. Cane had a weight advantage of perhaps twenty pounds, which would have meant something had they been about to box, but as a factor in deciding the sort of bout they intended, it was meaningless. It was to be an anything-goes fight, which in practice meant trying to disable the opponent with karate and whatever else might conveniently present itself, and only when he was down or about to fall would the time really come to use fists. Beating, but not killing.

They went back into the gym on bare feet. The others glanced at them, nodding acknowledgment, surprised to see them together. Cane and Lyle ignored them.

The gym smelled of sweat and disinfectant.

They faced each other in *Zenkutsu-dachi*, the basic stance for many karate techniques, leading foot forward, knee slightly bent, rear leg stretched out straight, toes outward about a quarter turn. There was something about their deliberateness and expressions that made their colleagues realize they were about to witness that rare event in the DIA: a grudge fight. Without a word they moved the weights to the side and squatted out of the way, to watch.

Everyone knew the rules from early days at Fairfax: no interference whatever happened. If a man didn't like what was going on, he'd better leave.

Cane and Lyle had not shaken hands—not even the ritual brushing of palms to pretend there wasn't really anything personal in what was to follow. A bad sign. The antagonism between the two agents was legendary, and garbled accounts of what had caused it were routinely circulated. Even recruits in their first six weeks at Fairfax heard stories about Lyle and Cane which at first they found difficult to believe but later, as they learned more of what they were expected to do and how they were expected to do it, bcame accepted as the truth.

Cane was the first to cross the line of confrontation, which was probably fitting since it had been his challenge. He took advantage of his extra height, leading with his foot, kicking forward at groin level. Lyle jumped back, deflecting the main force of the front kick and unable to use an ankle sweep to unbalance Cane because he immediately snapped his foot back to the ankle and slid it forward to resume his stance.

Cane looked for an opening. Lyle stayed motionless, upper body relaxed, waiting. Cane led with his foot again, closing the distance between them and striking with his forearm toward Lyle's elbow joint to put his arm out of commission, but Lyle rammed a backfist into his stomach wall, and Cane felt an explosion of pain and some of the air being driven from his body.

He doubled over, and Lyle's fist shot out, hitting the side of his chin. In a burst of fury Cane realized the last blow was just an ordinary fist, a boxer's punch. Lyle thought he could begin to play with him. Cane launched a *teisho* attack against Lyle's windpipe, chopping up with the side of his hand, landing off target but near enough for him to hear the grunt of pain and see the other man pull back, and he followed with a side-thrusting kick at the solar plexus. Lyle began to fall and Cane was above him, smashing with his foot onto any vulnerable point he could see. The most devastating karate attacks come from the feet, with a power much greater than that of punches. Lyle rolled, getting distance.

The moment he was up he counterattacked ferociously, kicking high at Cane's chin, the ball of his foot glancing off the bone, half-deflected. Lyle followed up with a knee in Cane's lower abdomen and a clenched fist smashing directly into his elbow joint. There was a tearing pain in Cane's right arm, and he realized it had been temporarily paralyzed. Lyle had set him up, and Cane could dodge and weave and inflict some minor damage if he was lucky, but Lyle could move in for the kill when he wanted. The heel of Lyle's hand crashed low down Cane's side, striking the floating ribs, and then he eased off, just boxing now, pounding his body, snapping back his head, and Cane tasted blood in his mouth.

He retaliated, using his greater reach where he could, but he was badly hampered without the use of his right. The rules of a grudge fight dictated that the winner could keep hitting as long as he liked and that no admission of defeat would be accepted. He could even keep hitting or kicking, if he felt strongly enough, when his opponent was down, although in practice this rarely happened.

Yet Lyle did not make the kill. Cane was aware of him easing off the pressure. The punches he landed did not have force behind them. The silent spectators could also see this: Lyle, almost playing, teasing, goading, while Cane strove to keep up, blood running from his mouth and down his chin, his right arm making an effort to hit but lacking power.

Lyle was giving Cane a chance to recover. He knew the fight should not be over so soon, and not like this. The air had to be cleared, and it was Cane's grudge, so it wouldn't be cleared unless he felt he had acquitted himself honorably. That meant Lyle taking some punishment.

Gradually the paralysis eased in Cane's arm, and when he was confident it was almost back to normal, he lunged at Lyle's face, connecting with the cheek and the side of the nose. The sight of a sudden stream of blood gave him hope. He closed on Lyle, concentrating on his face and stomach, using his extra weight and his reach, trying to get at Lyle's eyes with his knuckles, hardly feeling the return punches.

There was a lot of blood on Lyle now, and it looked as if his lip had also split, so Cane aimed for the face when he could.

If Lyle had meant the recovery period merely to restore equilibrium to the fight, he already knew that the fine dividing line had been passed and that he was in trouble.

His left eye was closing, and he began feeling momentary periods of dizziness. He thought of going back to karate. He could still throw Cane, hurt him once, but he might not be able to cope after that, and there was a grimness about his adversary that made Lyle prefer being beaten up with bare fists to the possibly more permanent damage of karate. Lyle's mind was clear as he assessed his situation and his options. He realized that the power of his punches was diminishing and he was definitely tiring. He was outclassed in this sort of fight. And he lacked the stamina to sustain anything more serious.

Cane on the other hand was fueled by the years of hatred and the reality of paying off old scores. Lyle hoped he also would soon flag.

The next moment Lyle felt the breath forced from his lungs by a blow, and he was down, rolling, trying instinctively to get distance, and he could hear Cane's voice, as if far away: "Get up. Get up, you bastard."

Lyle pulled himself to his feet, choking, fighting for wind, conscious that Cane was coming at him again and that now he was virtually defenseless, then, suddenly seeing his opponent's stomach unguarded, he lunged. Despite his earlier decision to stick to boxing, Lyle didn't even have to think. He put what strength remained into a final karate punch and sank back to the floor, finished.

Lyle lay hunched, gasping, waiting to discover if Cane would keep hitting, kicking, as he had the right to do.

But there was silence, and no blows came.

He opened his eyes—one eye, anyway. The spectators had not moved. He rolled over to see where Cane was and found him also on the floor, chest heaving.

Lyle summoned enough strength to get painfully to his feet. It wasn't certain whether the fight was over yet. It would only be finished when someone had definitely won, which meant his opponent was unconscious or unable to move and the victor was prepared to stop. Or if there was mutual agreement. Could Cane still move?

Lyle stood panting. His last punch hadn't been a killing blow, he was sure of that, and Cane, although he looked a mess, was probably only winded.

At last, Cane opened his eyes and focused on Lyle standing over him. He made an effort to get up and made it as far as his knees. He tried again.

Lyle went to help him, hoisting him unsteadily onto his feet. Cane leaned for support, attempting to gain his balance, finally achieving it. They faced each other, spent but wary.

"Enough?" Lyle asked.

Cane thought for a moment, his breath harsh. "Enough," he agreed.

Lyle offered his hand. Cane found himself staring at it, incapable of reaching out. He looked up at the bloody, sweating face. Lyle's eye was closing, the cheek cut, his lip split. Lyle looked a wreck. Cane couldn't imagine what he looked like himself. Not much better. Lyle at least was steadier on his feet. And his hand was still out.

Why did he care so much about Lyle? It was so futile, Cane thought. What Lyle did was Lyle's business. And he was good. Did his job. Sometimes you were ordered to kill, and so you killed. Sometimes you chose to kill, to ensure your safety or protect your assignment. So you killed. Cane had done that more than once. He realized that in the final analysis the only real difference between himself and Lyle was one of style, and that he had no right to feel superior on the matter of morals. Lyle was more . . . flamboyant.

Cane wondered if the reason he reacted so strongly was that they were two sides of the same coin, and Cane wanted emotional distance from the man who was also himself.

Lyle's hand had dropped, but he had not moved. He stood silently to see what came next, his breathing easier, his left eye throbbing, the taste of blood still in his mouth.

The other three agents sat motionless, knowing they were witnessing what would become part of the Fairfax legend.

Cane took a step forward and Lyle tensed to fight. Cane's arms went around Lyle's neck and pulled him into a hug. They stood motionless, clinched in the middle of the gym.

Then Cane said quietly: "You gonna buy me that drink?" He felt Lyle nod. They broke and walked painfully to the showers.

The other agents resumed their workout.

Cane had some explaining to do when he got home to Maryann late that night, lip swollen, face cut, knuckles skinned, and smelling of beer.

As he undressed he tried to tell her what had happened, but it was soon clear it would have to wait until morning when, depending on the size of his hangover, he might be more coherent.

It had been two weeks since Cane's last weekend off. Maryann was aware that his latest project at Fairfax would entail lengthy absences for several months yet, but that was all she knew about it. She had learned to curb her curiosity about what assignments David actually went on.

When she could no longer resist them, her questions and remarks were generalized ones. Was it dangerous? He always said, no, not very. Not if you were prepared. Had he ever killed another person? He replied, yes, sometimes, when necessary. Never how many, never when, not who or why. Were there other women? A flat no.

Maryann knew he traveled to Europe. She once checked his passport for visa and entry stamps. He spoke fluent Russian, so presumably he was a specialist on the communist bloc. And that was almost the extent of her knowledge of his career.

Cane lay in bed next to her, face puffed with sleep and the bruising from an extraordinary fight about which she couldn't make head or tail, except that it seemed to involve Clive Lyle, whom she had met once and remembered as a very nice man.

It was just after dawn. Soon she would have to wake Timmy, get him ready for school, and put him on the bus. The boy had been asleep when David arrived home, looking as if he had been in a car crash, and she knew he would have been thrilled to see his father's bashed-in face. A typical small boy, Timmy loved the concept of fighting and war. Later he would probably grow to love the actuality. She decided not to tell him David was back, or there'd be no way of keeping him out of the bedroom. Better to let his father sleep. He looked as if he needed it.

As she prepared Timmy for school, she considered again, as she often did these days, whether the reality of marriage to a man like David, with long separations and the uncertainties of his work, was worth it. Whether it was what she had expected when she agreed to be his wife in those normal, long-ago West Point days. Obviously they hadn't known David would be selected for the DIA. But they had known his career was the military, and that he didn't propose giving it up to become an accountant or go into real estate. She had accepted then that there would be separations—long, enforced ones —but she felt now she hadn't fully understood what they would mean: Lonely mornings when Timmy was in school; lonely evenings and nights when David had—just gone, without saying where, and coming back, who knew when?

She had also known that there would be danger, of course; that was implicit. But the dangers she expected were those from a real war, which seemed remote then and was still remote now.

The war David had chosen to fight for the DIA was something else: a hidden, undeclared, deadly everyday game, played for goals which might never be apparent to those outside a select circle. That, Maryann supposed, was what she resented most—the fact that she and David couldn't be ordinary. He had a life she couldn't share, not even vicariously, complete with a different set of friends, colleagues, lovers perhaps, people she would never meet and whose names she would never hear.

She walked through their home, inspecting the suburban, domestic *things* they had collected. All the conventional symbols of affluence and convenience were there. They had everything except time together; the one commodity she really wanted. The routine of David leaving the house in the morning, coming back at night, with weekends off and friends around. Theater tickets. Being able to plan two weeks or a month ahead. Ordinary things.

Sometimes when an assignment ended, David did have time off, and he'd sit around the house. They'd talk, but not about his work. They'd make love, usually not gently, not the first few times while he shed the mental debris of whatever it was he had just been doing. Maryann would fill in the gaps of what had happened to her and Timmy since he left, and he would listen, but she never felt he was paying full attention. And as the days wore on, and they went out to play bridge in the evenings, she would watch him grow restless, waiting to get back to whatever it was he had to do next.

So she asked herself: Is it worth it? And she found it a question she could not answer. Perhaps it was part of the human condition. Friends whose husbands were bankers or executives of one sort or another, and who confided their problems, seemed to face a similar predicament. They had the routine, and yet they asked: Is it worth it?

She took Timmy down to the school bus and went back to look in at David. He was sleeping deeply and didn't appear to have moved. She stood uncertainly.

There was marketing to do, and she'd promised to go down to the library and change Timmy's books. And the house needed cleaning.

But there was David, a rare event in her bed these days, his face bruised and puffed.

Maryann took the telephone off the hook. She undressed and slipped in quietly beside him. into the pool of warmth, and lay waiting for him to wake.

The puffiness had gone from Cane's face by the time he returned to Fairfax two days later, but Martin Ross guessed at once he had been in a fight. Cane explained what had happened, the whole story, and the professor empathized. At home Maryann had called Cane crazy when he told her about it. Not the details of what Lyle had done, of course, but about the fight. She said he'd acted like an adolescent. And in her world she was right. In Cane's and Lyle's even a newcomer like Ross understood.

It hadn't been a good idea to leave Ross by himself for three days. Without someone to set the pace and keep him occupied, he'd gone into a psychological decline. He had again been studying the Vologda printouts, in case he'd missed anything on the previous dozen dissections, and the lack of progress depressed him.

But at least Cane had good news. He outlined the contents of the latest Moscow report and the discovery that Major Vladimir Petrovich Metkin, a senior supervisor in computers and reported to be posted at Vologda base, might be coming to London.

At first Ross could hardly believe Cane wanted him along on the London mission to break into Metkin's hotel room and drug him, and his mood became near euphoric. Cane cautioned that it might not be as easy as it seemed, and that, in the end, a difficult entry to the room might mean counting Ross out of the action and going in alone. Or if Metkin was staying at the Embassy itself, they might lose their chance altogether.

But Ross refused to be deflected. "We've got to get Metkin," he urged. "We'll hear it from the horse's mouth, the whole thing, open and shut. We can't let him get away, David, and I've got to be in there with you."

Cane grinned at his enthusiasm. "Well, let's see how it works out, Martin. We can't kidnap the guy, and really the only way of getting him alone is when he's in bed, late at night. During the day Soviet delegations always stick together. You've been to these things; you've seen them operate. No chance of getting him then, not unless he's going to catch measles. But that would mean Scotland Yard inquiries, KGB suspicions, the whole thing. Yardley's very much against it, and so am I."

"I don't understand. What's 'catching measles'?"

"Sorry," Cane said. "Company jargon. If someone catches measles, it means he's been murdered so efficiently it looks like a genuine accident or death from natural causes."

"Oh, I see. No, that wouldn't do at all. Pentovar sounds much more our style, especially if it does what it's supposed to do. Do you think we ought to try it out first?"

"What, Pentovar?"

"Yes. On me, for example. See how much I tell you and what I remember afterward."

"Not a bad idea. I'll suggest it to Barry when I go along for some injection practice. Sure you wouldn't mind?"

"Not a bit. I don't have any secrets worth anything. Not from you, anyway."

"Not even a secret hatred of cross-country running?"

"That's no secret."

"Well, you've got five minutes to change."

A package of brochures, press cuttings, and handouts dealing with the "International Computers in Industry" seminar was delivered the following morning. With it was a cable from the United States Embassy in London, in which an obviously baffled staffer gave as full a rundown as he could manage of the underlying significance of the seminar. It was clear no one had spared it much thought before, and from their inquiries there didn't seem any reason to do so now.

The Soviets had promised to send a twelve-man delegation, the cable said, but there was nothing unusual in that or in the names they had proposed. The Russians always attended such events mostly to pick up information from the West. It was well known they often waited while the United States, Britain, or some other European country conducted costly scientific or technical research work, and then lifted their information and results. Except that in the case of the seminar, it was not at all clear what Moscow wanted. Dozens of papers were to be presented. The report listed their titles and authors, pointing out that one third of the participants would be from the United States and would probably, if asked, provide advance copies.

But if a significant breakthrough of some sort in computer technology was to be disclosed, it was a well-guarded secret. There were not even any rumors about it. In fact, the report concluded, the seminar looked superficially tedious.

Ross flicked quickly through the brochures and tended to agree with this assessment. None of the papers would be delivered by men or women he considered leaders in the field. A number of commercial companies were making pitches for their own products, but that was routine.

Ross decided the first thing to do was to contact the American participants to see if he could learn something on the grapevine. He spent the day on the telephone, working slowly through the names. Everyone was happy to discuss details over the phone—not a good sign—and the few who had completed their papers offered to mail them to him. They were flattered that a man like Professor Ross was interested in their projects, and were willing to help in any way they could.

It looked as if the staffer in London had been right—not only superficially tedious but actually so.

Ross decided to start phoning delegates in other Western countries the next day in case they had anything to add.

Because surely there must be something, not obvious from the brochures and press releases, to explain why Moscow Center would consider sending a senior computer expert from the Vologda base to a Western country when he had information in his head which could strike a serious blow at the entire missile program. Whatever the Russians wanted had to have a military application, almost certainly for missiles, since that was Metkin's current field. There were no clues from the American participants, although Ross thought he would still like to study their papers in detail before ruling them out entirely.

Perhaps some new hardware or software would be on display? He looked at the brochures once more, together with the technical specifications supplied by manufacturers, but nothing significant suggested itself.

His calls the following day to London, Paris, Bonn, and Milan were not much more useful. Everyone wanted to help, no one appeared to know much.

In the middle of Ross's research came a further report from Moscow, confirming that the KGB had given approval for Major Metkin to attend the computer seminar in Britain. He would be leaving, with other members of the delegation, from Sheremetyevo Airport on the first Aeroflot flight on the morning of March 31. The KGB *rezident* at the Soviet Embassy in London was handling the hotel bookings, and no details of these were yet known.

Cane arranged to have an urgent signal sent to the DIA station chief in London asking for help, and was delighted to have a reply within twenty-four hours. The earlier request for a rundown on the seminar had gotten them moving, and without knowing quite what they were looking for, they had started keeping a closer watch on the event and its participants. Sixteen Russians—twelve delegates and four "guides"—had been booked into a central London hotel. The Soviet Embassy had asked for eight double rooms, which meant Metkin would be sharing with a KGB man, as Lyle had predicted.

But at least he was coming, and he wasn't going to be closeted inside the Embassy. Cane asked Washington for all available photographs of the hotel, and to send a request to London for a floor plan. He also inquired about DIA status in the hotel. Was it possible to arrange for particular rooms to be allocated to the delegation?

The photographs showed it to be a fairly old building which, if Cane knew his London, would almost certainly be built on a quadrangular pattern. There were no balconies in the front. The photographs gave him no immediate clues about how they might get access to any of the rooms.

The floor plan, when it came, was a little more helpful. The main hotel had been constructed around a central two-storied structure, which housed the ballroom-dining room and the administrative offices. There were emergency fire-escape stairs leading to the pavement on two sides, and the bedrooms themselves—480 of them—went up seven stories.

An accompanying note from the station chief pointed out that the hotel was used regularly by the Soviet Embassy for delegations and guests, and it was therefore reasonable to assume they had their own informants on the staff. The DIA had no status there.

However, a routine request for assistance had been made to MI-6. British intelligence had its own sources in the hotel and confirmed it was possible to know in advance which rooms had been allocated to the Soviets or even to arrange for specific accommodation to be given to them, provided there was sufficient notice.

That was what Cane wanted to hear, and he went back to pore over the floor plans.

A narrow ledge ran along the back of the main building at the window level of every floor which they might be able to use to reach a particular room. So the first things to organize were to make sure that the delegates got only odd-numbered rooms overlooking the central courtyard, and that these were not too high up. The third or fourth floors would do.

Cane did not mind much about heights, but he didn't know what Ross's capabilities would be. If he was a borderline case, it was clearly psychologically better to offer him the prospect of a fall of between twenty and forty feet onto the roof of the central buildings rather than one from the seventh floor. Also if they were low, they were more likely to be in shadow, particularly because of the dining room's domed roof. They needed all the cover they could get. As soon as they climbed onto the outside of the building, they were liable to be spotted. There was not much they could do about that except wear black and pick the least hospitable hours for their mission—Cane thought between two and four A.M.—and keep their fingers crossed.

The floor plans showed that at each corner there were interconnected suites, every room with its own number and door into the corridor, so they could be booked separately. Cane knew that locks on each side of the interconnective doors would be the only concession to security.

That was another possibility, the easiest of all. Try to get Metkin and his KGB guard booked into one of these rooms, and take the adjoining one themselves. But Cane knew from experience things rarely worked out that simply.

He had to cover as many alternatives as he could to cope with a string of possible variables.

Would the KGB maintain some sort of guard in the corridor? If they were doubling up in the room with Metkin and a couple of the other delegates, it seemed unlikely, but he couldn't be sure. The comrade Major was a very important property.

And even if they tried to get Metkin booked into a specific room, there was no guarantee he would take it. The KGB might as a matter of course switch the delegates around.

Cane explained the alternatives to Ross. There were four weeks until the seminar, and it would be necessary to check the hotel themselves. They had to be familiar with the furnishings, the general layout, what types of locks were on the doors, whether the windows had been double-glazed and, if so, by what method. A hundred tiny points on which the success of the operation might depend.

The men caught a London-bound flight the following day and took two double rooms on the third floor of the hotel. It was a gray, drizzly day, colder than either Fairfax or New York, but the rooms were stuffy and overheated. Old radiators, painted dark green, were attached to the walls. There was a lot less space than Cane had expected from the floor plans, and the furnishings were solid and dull.

Cane started with a close investigation of his room, checking security. The lock was a Yale, but would be easy enough to open. The door, however, also had a security chain. The windows were double-glazed, with ordinary handles opening the exterior ones, while the interior glass panels slid across, presumably for ease of cleaning. This made entrance by this route easier too.

He measured the space between the bottom of the door and the carpet when the pile was pressed down, and found it was not large enough to introduce the flattened nozzle of an anesthetic gas cylinder without scraping the wood.

The bathroom was old with white walls, white tiles, and thin towels. Enamel had worn away in patches in the tub and basin. The only modern accessory was strip lighting fixed to the ceiling. Cane studied the bathroom for a long time. Something was different, but he couldn't put his finger on what it was. And then he realized the ceiling was slightly lower there than in the bedroom. He brought in a chair, a flashlight, and a screwdriver, and loosened the inconspicuous painted screws on each corner of an access hatch.

Cane pushed gently and the hatch lifted. He shone his light around the narrow ceiling cavity. Ceiling board, about half an inch thick, had been nailed to stout beams to make the covering. But the cavity stretched from Cane's room a distance of about forty feet before coming up against a wall and a main conduit for the electrical wiring.

Cane grinned. Providing one kept strictly to the beam, it would be possible to reach the sealed hatchways of at least four other bathrooms.

He put on a pair of sneakers and a sweater and pulled himself, gently and easily, into the opening.

It was dark inside and cramped. Cane lay along a beam, flashing his torch around to familiarize himself. He began moving cautiously, listening for the noises of squeaking wood. He crawled as far as he could. There were, as he had thought, four other hatches, none of which he could budge.

He inched back to tell Ross what he had found and to mark on the floor plan the rooms to which they now theoretically had access.

Ross's bathroom on the other side of the corridor was even better. It led to six more sealed hatches. Cane filled this in on the floor plan. The Soviets needed eight rooms, and he could arrange entry to nine, not including their own two. It would simply be necessary to replace all the hatch screws with shorter versions that would not actually lock the board to the wooden frame. This meant getting into every room to make the switch.

Ross, who was tired after the flight, elected to sleep off his jet lag. Cane took a taxi to the United States Embassy in Grosvenor Square.

Nature had apparently decided, in spite of evidence to the contrary, that spring had come, and daffodils and crocuses grew in profusion in the middle of the square, beneath trees already covered by the fresh green of new leaves. Overhead the sky was like slate.

Cane spent an hour in the office of the DIA station chief whose nameplate identified him as a member of the naval attaché's staff.

It was agreed that instead of sending a DIA fixer disguised as a maintenance man into the hotel alone to doctor the hatches and run the risk of being challenged, it would be safer to ask MI-6 for help and actually rent the rooms involved.

A shy-looking American in a dark suit, and bearing the scars of a bad case of acne, visited Cane first in the early afternoon so he could see and approve the job. The heads of the new screws were identical to the originals, but the bodies ended half an inch short. When they were fully in, Cane could raise his hatch with ease. A workman, unless he was exceptionally sharp-eyed, might not even notice the difference. The screws went in tight. The fixer carefully color-matched the white of the ceiling and dabbed paint on the screwheads. It would dry in a few hours and no one would be any the wiser.

He went on to the other rooms.

Ross meanwhile was making contact with his computer colleagues in London. Because of his international reputation, those he wanted to see were glad to make time available at short notice. But as for the question of what Major Vladimir Petrovich Metkin hoped to get out of the seminar, that remained a mystery without clues.

Ross felt exasperated. Metkin. What the hell was he coming to London for?

But at least he was coming, and even if Ross couldn't discover why, he felt he might get the chance to slip in a question when finally they got him under Pentovar and talking about the Vologda program.

Two days later the last of the hatch screws had been replaced, and Cane arranged, through MI-6, that the Soviet delegation be allocated eight of the rooms, while he and Ross would take two. That left one spare, to give them some slack.

Cane and Ross returned to the States and, for a four-day break, to their wives.

Ross was not able to tell Elaine he had been abroad, nor did he give any clue that the first part of their project would soon go operational. As she couldn't know anything, it seemed unfair to worry and tantalize her with snippets.

Alone at night, his stomach burning with indigestion, Ross brooded about what was to come. He visualized crawling through that stuffy, confined space to drug and interrogate a GRU major while the KGB bodyguard lay unconscious in the next bed. Of course, if anything went wrong, if they were discovered, they would not pay the price they could expect once they were in Russia. But it would mean the effective end of the mission. The chance to save the West from a nuclear holocaust would have slipped irretrievably from their grasp. Ross found that these days he had to keep reminding himself of the extraordinary stakes they were playing for. The logistics, and the immediate risks, were dominating his mind.

He was glad to get back to Fairfax and the training program with Cane, although he found the break and a loss of appetite had cost him that physical edge he had fought so long for. He became aware just how quickly gains could be dissipated. Perhaps it was different at Cane's age, but Ross was approaching his fifty-ninth birthday, and every day was important.

For him it seemed as it had at the beginning: a grueling agony of aching muscles, painfully snatched breath, fatigue which crushed on his shoulders until his body sagged. Pains and cramps tore at tissues and would not be ignored. He found he was still not hungry.

Cane pushed him hard. There was no time to lose now. Ross bore it as stoically as he could. Anything less seemed to him an admission that he was unready, even for the London run, an admission of age, that time was slipping away from him. The pains came, and he slowed his pace to allow for them but kept moving nonetheless.

Two weeks before their departure, Cane spent a morning with Dr. Peter Barry at the DIA's Washington hospital, learning how to give an injection. He found to his surprise that there was a mental barrier for him to overcome: He had to reach the point where, without thinking, he could slide a needle cleanly into someone's flesh. He had to rely on the sensitivity in his hands to tell him when he hit the resistance of a vein, to apply extra pressure to make the point penetrate the wall, realizing sometimes he'd exerted too much and that the needle had pushed out the other side of the vein; then to pull it gently back, withdrawing the plunger to see if blood bubbled freely into the syringe and showed he had hit the spot.

Cane felt it would be easier with Metkin because he would be unconscious. The men and women he practiced on, in his borrowed white doctor's uniform and under Barry's professional scrutiny, had arms and hands that flinched at a hesitant needle; they jerked when it probed and said, "Christ, that's sore!" and "For God's sake, I didn't come here to consult a plumber"; and, in one case, the patient looked as if she was going to be sick.

"You've got to be more decisive," Dr. Barry said finally. "You're getting the general idea, and in the end you do find the vein. But if you went and had a look at any of these patients tomorrow, you'd find they were all bruised. That's exactly what you don't want with Metkin. Next patient in, just take that needle and push it—smoothly. Pretend you're looking for a piece of spaghetti. Get in there and slip the needle inside it."

Cane tried, ignoring the look on the woman's face as he gripped her wrist tightly with his sweating left hand and pushed the needle into the resisting flesh. But he made it, first time. He grinned triumphantly at Barry and extracted the blood sample. Then he slipped the needle out and pressed his thumb over the puncture mark, rubbing. She hadn't said anything: no protest or cry of pain. Cane felt he was getting the idea.

He took another six samples, four totally successfully, two near misses.

When the last patient had left, Dr. Barry handed him a fresh syringe. "I'll hold your wrist," he said. "Try to get some blood out of your own hand. That'll give you an idea what it feels like. I'd better warn you that it's harder doing it to yourself, so let's see a bit of mind over matter. Slide it in, in one smooth, flowing movement."

Cane hesitated, confronting his mental block again, while he pushed the needle against his skin so that the flesh indented. Barry gripped the pressure points, making the veins stand up clear. Then Cane held his breath, pushed, and in it went. He could feel it touching the vein wall which slipped to one side, out of the way, and he followed it with the point, painfully, and thrust and there it was, in place. Cane felt slightly ill at the back of his throat but pleased with himself nonetheless. Barry took over, extracting a few ccs of blood. He let Cane pull the needle out himself.

"Not bad," the doctor said. "Next time you'll be fine. Are you going to be able to come back for another session?"

"Sure," Cane said. "Same time next week. Then we're off to London for the real thing."

"Just remember, go in firmly and without hesitation. It only starts hurting and leaving bruises when *you* start fooling around."

As usual, the final days leading up to the mission threatened to drag but in fact they went swiftly. Cane discovered on his second session with Barry that he had become reasonably proficient with a needle. He passed on Ross's suggestion that they try Pentovar on him to see what effect it had, and Barry offered no objection. The professor seemed in good health for a man of his age, and it would give Cane an idea of what to expect in London.

"Pentovar takes effect within a very short time, a few seconds usually. Just push the needle in and leave it there. For God's sake, make sure you've got a vein. That's all you have to do. The fluid will drip in by itself at a steady rate, so just leave the whole thing attached to the vein. You've got enough Pentovar for about an hour. If you need more time, insert a second ampule into another vein. But only one ampule at a time, please. We don't recommend double dosages. Recovery rate varies, but you can bank on five minutes between removing the needle and the patient regaining consciousness. Is that enough time for you to get clear?"

"Plenty," Cane said.

"Fine. The office in London will supply you with as much Pentovar as you need. It has to be kept refrigerated, so there's no point giving it to you now to put in your suitcase. Anything else?"

"Don't think so, thanks. You've been a lot of help, Doctor. I'll let you know how it goes."

"Do that. Good luck."

Cane dosed the professor that night after dinner. Ross lay obligingly on the bed in their apartment while his hand was rubbed with surgical antiseptic. Cane pushed in the needle, conscious of the patchy discolorations of age on the skin. He felt the point break into a vein.

Cane smiled. "Okay, old friend. It's truth time. Count backward from twenty."

"I don't care," Ross said. "You give a good injection, David. Twen ..."

And that was it. His eyes turned upward, the lids closed. The ampule hung leechlike from his hand. Pentovar dripped imperceptibly into his bloodstream.

Cane watched in fascination. He said cautiously: "Uh, can you hear me, Martin?"

"Yes."

"How do you feel?"

"Fine."

Cane took a chair nearby. "Why didn't you ever have kids?" he asked.

"I'm sterile."

"Did you want children?"

"Yes, very much."

"And Elaine?"

"She wanted them too."

"Have you ever been unfaithful to Elaine, Martin?"

"Yes."

"Often?"

"Five or six times."

Cane raised his eyebrows. That was one in the eye for security surveillance. They only listed two. "I'm not interested in five *or* six, Martin, I want to know exactly."

"Six."

"Any of them hookers?"

"Four hookers."

"I want the dates you met them, Martin. Their names, where you went, and what they charged."

"June fourteenth, 1953. A blonde called Louella in New York City. She never told me her last name. Cost me fifty. I took her up to my room at the Roosevelt on Madison Avenue. June sixteenth, 1953, a girl by the name of Stella. They'd have asked questions if I'd tried to get her into the Roosevelt, 'cause she was a little tacky-looking, and I'd had a lot to drink. We went to her apartment."

"What was the address, Martin?"

"I never saw. I was pretty drunk. Somewhere over near St. Mark's Place, first-floor apartment, looked bad outside but quite clean and nice inside. Cost me two hundred notes."

"Jesus, that was a lot. Did she roll you?"

"I had her blow me."

"And she didn't want to?"

"No, she made a big fuss. So I had to pay extra. I told her it was okay. She wouldn't get a baby or anything."

"Afterward, did you think it was worth two hundred?" Cane asked.

"No. She'd obviously done it lots of times. If I'd held out, I think I could have gotten it for fifty."

Cane laughed. "Who was the third hooker?"

"Jeannie. San Francisco. October first, 1953, in my room in the Fairmont on Mason Street. Sixty bucks, and I got her back the next night for another sixty."

"Was there another or does Jeannie count as number four?"

"Number four was on December twenty-fourth, 1953, back in New York at the Waldorf-Astoria."

"Christmas Eve?"

"Yeah, that's right. I was on my way home. There was this nice-looking hooker in the lobby, so I thought I'd give myself a present. Girl called Maureen, claimed she'd come over from Ireland. I paid her forty bucks. She was out of the room in twenty minutes."

"What was magic about 1953, Martin? Why all these hookers over —what—a space of six months? And not after that, not ever?"

"No hookers after that. Nineteen fifty-three was a bad year for me. They told me I couldn't have kids. I got the report on June fourteenth. Ten A.M.. My count was about zero. No chance of children, ever. Elaine and I had been trying for a long time and we were both pretty tense. Whose fault was it? You know. She got tested first and turned out to be fine. I didn't believe it could be me, but it was. I didn't know how to tell Elaine. I felt inadequate, half a man. On top of that, Elaine didn't like sex too much, but she did it whenever I was in the mood because she wanted a baby. I thought once she had my number, there wouldn't be much reason for her to sleep with me anymore, and I didn't feel I could push it. I looked elsewhere."

Cane asked, "Why did you stop looking, Martin?"

Ross, eyes closed, voice neutral, replied: "Because I realized I had something going with Elaine that I didn't want to lose, and she was trying—really trying very hard. She knew what I was going through. I don't think she knew about the girls. Those, or the others. I didn't tell her. But she understood it was a bad time for me. It was a bad time for her too: no kids. We thought about adopting, but it never came to anything. She spent a lot of time looking after me, initiating sex, even pretending she liked it. And there were other things we had together which were also important to me. Research in the same field, similar interests. We laughed a lot too, except for that time in 1953, but that was my fault."

Cane checked his watch. Ten minutes into the session. The level of Pentovar in the vial looked about the same. He presumed it was still dripping away quietly.

He asked Ross about his sexual preferences and habits, his childhood, his career, how he felt about himself, how he felt about Cane. He particularly homed in on anything which might be distasteful, trying to detect hesitations which could indicate Ross was telling something less than the truth, and giving him things embarrassing enough to remember when he woke up.

But whatever the subject, Ross replied calmly and freely, making no attempt at self-justification unless Cane asked for it. By the end of the hour, Cane felt he knew the man as well as he had known anyone, and that enough deeply personal and professional information had come out to warrant Ross having at least some memory of it if the Pentovar was not doing its job properly.

As the last drops disappeared into Ross's bloodstream, Cane decided to try an experiment.

"Martin," he said, "listen, because this is very important. Do you really want to go with me to London?"

"Yes, very much."

"And into Vologda?"

"Yes. More than anything in my life."

"Well, I'm not going to let you go." He waited for a response, but there was none. Ross lay quietly. "To tell you the truth, Martin, I'm pretty worried by some of the things you've told me. I'm worried by the fact that you don't seem to be sorry about them. Now if you want to go with me, there's something you've got to do. If you do it, everything's okay. If you don't, it's all off and I'm going to kick your ass out of here and send you back to Princeton. You understand what I'm saying?"

"I understand."

"Okay. Now five minutes after you wake up, I'm going to be sitting in this chair. If you want to come on this mission, you're going to have to apologize. You've got to walk over to me, put your right hand on my shoulder, and say these words: 'David, I want to say I'm sorry.' That's all. 'David, I want to say I'm sorry.' Got it?"

"Yes."

Cane went over to the bed and slid the needle out of his hand. A spot of blood formed, and he rubbed it with his thumb. There were perhaps three or four drops of Pentovar left in the ampule. Cane dropped it into the wastebasket and settled down to wait. It was 9:55.

For fifteen minutes Ross did not move. He might have slipped from Pentovar into normal sleep, if Cane, beginning to feel worried, had not shaken his shoulder.

Ross looked around, disoriented, as if it ought to be morning but somehow wasn't. Then he remembered and gave Cane a sheepish smile.

"How did it go?"

Cane shrugged. "It went fine. Now I know all your guilty secrets."

"I couldn't share them with a nicer guy. Anything particularly alarming?"

"Not a thing. I reckon I've got bigger and better secrets myself."

"Have some Pentovar and share them then."

Cane laughed. "Not a chance," he said. "You'd be here all night, and tomorrow. How'd it feel?"

"It felt like nothing. You gave me the injection, and I was saying something to you, and then you were shaking my shoulder. How long was I out?"

"Over an hour. It's just after ten past ten. Think hard. Isn't there *anything* you remember?"

Ross sat silently, concentrating on the sixty-minute-plus blank. At one point the mists seemed to clear slightly, but before he could identify what it was they showed, the thought dissolved and was gone. He shook his head decisively. "You're going to have to tell me. What did I say?"

"You really want to know?"

"I really want to know. And unless I do, I won't be able to tell you if it's accurate or not."

Ross had a point. So Cane went through the interrogation as thoroughly as he could remember. Ross sat still and the color drained slowly from his face. Cane recounted the information in a matter-of-fact, nonjudgmental way. From time to time Ross nodded. He disputed nothing.

The five-minute mark, at which Cane's experiment was supposed to pay off, came and went, even though he looked pointedly at his watch and said, "Five minutes." But Ross gave no sign that it meant anything to him.

When Cane had finished, omitting only the abortive experiment, Ross looked harrowed, wrung out. He said softly: "I wish we could have a drink. Jesus, that's awful. I'd forgotten half those things. I feel pretty ashamed."

"It's all true?"

"I'm afraid so. Every word."

Cane opened his suitcase and brought out a silver hip flask. "Vodka," he said. "Knock back a slug. It'll do you good."

Ross gave a wan smile. "Thanks, David." He took a gulp and felt the warmth flow through his stomach, producing a burning sensation, but he said, "Good stuff." He handed the flask to Cane and watched while he swallowed.

"Listen, David," he said at last, "those things I told you. I hope they don't make you . . . think less of me."

Cane laughed. "Are you kidding? Look, Martin, everyone's got stuff like that in their lives. God knows I have. I liked you a lot before, but I actually like you a hell of a lot more now. You're a first-rate guy. I'm glad we're working together. I'm glad I'll be taking you to London, and when we get to Vologda, I'll be especially glad to have you there with me. Here, have some more."

"Thanks." He tilted the flask back. The vodka was hitting him. It had been weeks since his last drink. "It's just that I feel a bit raw. You know what I mean? You know more about me than I'll ever know about you. Things I'd never have told you in the ordinary course of events. Or if I had, at least not in those words."

"Yeah, I understand that, Martin. You trust me, don't you?"

Ross nodded. "With my life," he said. "It sounds overblown and dramatic, but that's what I feel."

"Well, all that stuff you've told me, it stops with me, you hear? I'm not going to tell another living person. You got that?"

"Thanks, David." Ross took another sip of vodka and handed back the flask. "In a strange way, though, it's *you* knowing I care about. Your opinion of me. You say it hasn't changed. Well, I hope that's true."

"Jesus, Martin, it *is* true. Believe me."

"Well, thanks. Anyway, David, if I offended you in any way, I just want to say I'm sorry."

"You did not offend . . ." Cane broke off and stared hard at him. "What did you say?"

"Huh?"

"What did you say just then?"

Ross looked baffled. "I said I'm sorry if I offended you."

"Your exact words. This is important. Try to remember them."

"Uh . . . I said, if you were offended in any way, I wanted to say I'm sorry."

Cane sat thoughtfully. Did it mean anything? An echo of the experiment, or mere chance? Christ, he made a terrible scientist. Imagine running a test like that and then allowing the conversation to follow lines which made it almost impossible to tell if you'd achieved any result.

He debated whether to see Peter Barry again to tell him what had happened as a precaution, but really, the more he thought about it, the more unscientific it became.

Cane grinned. "It's nothing really. I gave you a little test while you were out for the count, just a sentence to say in case anything did filter through to your consciousness later. You came out with something similar, that's all. But it's not the same, and it doesn't count. You still don't remember?"

"Not a glimmer."

"Then, my friend, Pentovar works. One little injection and Major Metkin's gonna be telling us the secrets of the computer and anything else we ask him, and all he'll know the next morning is that he had a decent night's sleep for a change and didn't notice the KGB man snoring."

They finished the vodka and went to bed.

Two days later they were back in London, Cane in room 309, Ross across the corridor in Room 312. Their ceiling hatches had not been touched since their last visit, and everything looked good for the arrival of the Soviets.

The Aeroflot Ilyushin from Moscow was due in Heathrow Airport at noon on March 31. Cane and Ross waited in 309 for a telephone call from the station chief to say their friends had arrived and were on their way. Cane gave it half an hour after that before going down to the lounge adjoining the lobby, where he read a newspaper and was able to see what was happening at the reception desk.

The only photograph he and Ross had managed to get of Major Vladimir Petrovich Metkin was five years old and grainy. It could have been any one of ten thousand men. It was an abortion. Cane had asked that a positive identification be made at the Heathrow immigration desk, and a decent set of recognizable prints be delivered to his room as soon as possible after that.

The delegation arrived an hour later, just as Cane was becoming restless. There was a limit to how long a man could spend reading a paper, so he pretended to work on the crossword.

The Russians milled around the reception desk, while two men, obviously KGB "guides," handed out registration cards and arranged for room keys. There were two women in the party. No one was in uniform. Metkin was supposed to have dark, probably black hair, which narrowed him down to one of seven, not counting the two known KGB men. In ten minutes they had gone up to their rooms.

Cane stayed where he was. He wanted to avoid face-to-face meetings with any of them as a routine precaution.

He continued the crossword. At last, just as he was about to head up to his room, three Russians returned to the desk and made a request, which was refused. An altercation followed. He strained to hear what it was about, his heart sinking. Had the KGB noticed the ceiling hatch?

The voices reached him too faintly to make anything out.

He saw the receptionist scan a list again, shaking her head slowly. Two of the Russians were insistent.

Cane strolled over to the newsstand and stood with his back to them. He was closer now and could hear. The argument was about the room. They were dissatisfied. It was not clear why. They wanted to give up 302 and move somewhere else—perhaps to another floor?

Cane changed to the other side of the stand, flicking through the books and magazines, his face half-hidden.

The third man in the group waited quietly, taking no part in the negotiations. His whole attitude was one of indifference. It could be Metkin. Cane would have to wait for the photographs to be sure.,

He willed the receptionist to offer them the other "floating" room with the modified hatch on the third floor, but either she hadn't noticed it was there or the MI-6 contact in the hotel had blocked it off in some way she hadn't been told about.

At last, the girl made a counterproposal. The KGB men considered it for a few seconds and agreed. The girl walked to the information desk and lifted a key from a hook.

The fourth floor. Cane cursed silently.

He turned on his heel, walked straight into the street, and hailed a taxi. If Metkin was being shifted to a different floor, they had to start again from the beginning. And there was not much time. The delegation was booked back to Moscow on the evening of April 4, so it would be in London for only four nights.

In the Grosvenor Square embassy, Cane explained his predicament to the station chief, who put in a call to his MI-6 contact. They had their answer in half an hour—just as Cane was studying the Heathrow photographs of Metkin and discovering he was indeed the third man at the reception desk.

Metkin and someone called Chersky were now together in 441. There was no possibility of moving them back to the floating room on the third floor, not after the fuss there had been.

Cane made a quick calculation and reckoned that if the same building pattern was followed throughout the hotel, he had to change his own room to either 433, 435, 437, or 439. Any one of these should give him the same possibilities of access through the narrow ceiling cavity into 441.

It would of course also be necessary to doctor the screws in Metkin's bathroom, or find an alternate way of opening the hatch from above. Cane considered prying it up with a crowbar, but this was unlikely to be silent, particularly late at night when the slightest sound carried. Otherwise they'd have to send in a DIA fixer during the day while the delegation was at the seminar.

Cane passed on his request to change to one of the other four rooms and then drank coffee, silent and morose, while he waited for the reply.

The DIA chief took the call when it came. and as he listened he caught Cane's eye and shook his head ruefully. "Well, see what you can do, Steve," he said. "We'd be very grateful. We've got a couple of days to play with, but obviously the sooner the better."

Cane held up his hand urgently. "Hold on a minute, Steve," the chief said into the phone.

"Ask him to find out who's in those four rooms—433, 435, 437, and 439," Cane said. "I need names and very basic descriptions."

The chief shrugged and relayed the request. "The thing is," he said, replacing the phone, "their contact at the hotel can't do anything that causes too many problems. It's not the manager or anything, so he has to operate carefully or someone's going to start noticing. Those fourth-floor rooms are all taken, but at least one of them will be free on the third of the month. The day before Metkin goes. Maybe earlier, you never know."

Cane shook his head. "That's cutting it too close," he said. "It doesn't give us any chance to maneuver. I'm going to have to try to get in earlier."

"Good luck. You planning to break in?"

"Only if I have to. It's risky. It'd be better if I could smile nicely."

The station chief grinned. "You gonna need help?"

"Please. Couple of things. I guess you'll have them in stock."

Cane put in his request and, as he expected, it was easily filled. He pocketed a couple of small cardboard boxes, removed from a wall safe, but had to carry a bigger one about the size of a flashlight.

"The next priority is to get a fixer into 441, to see about the hatch," Cane said. "You think you can fix that?"

"You want it today? Might be difficult."

"No, today's pretty much a write-off. But it ought to be done as soon as possible tomorrow."

"Will do. Have you noticed any maintenance men around?"

"Not one. Not many cleaners either. Service is pretty slack."

"Better and better. Okay, leave it to me."

By the time Cane left the Embassy, he had a list of occupants of the fourth-floor rooms.

A Portuguese couple called Costas were in 439. They had registered as tourists. Couples were no good to him.

There was a possibility in 437. A young Frenchman, Jean-Claude Levesque had checked in, giving his occupation as "student," and his age as twenty-four. He was not married. Cane decided to check him out. If Levesque looked straight the station chief could send along one of the sisters to try for a low-key fix—see if she could get herself invited into his bedroom. If he didn't Cane would handle it himself.

Room 435 was taken by an elderly British couple who were on vacation. No luck there.

Which left Room 433 and an Australian woman called Jill Farmer. She had listed her occupation as "graphic designer" and her age as forty-three. She was also single, so she presented the same potential problem as the Frenchman: gay or straight? A job for the sisters, or for Cane? The decision on which possibility to explore would be Cane's own, usually made on little solid information—a question of instinct.

When he asked for his key at the hotel desk, he could see that both the 433 and 437 keys were on their hooks, which meant Jean-Claude Levesque and Jill Farmer were out.

Cane bought the new edition of *Time* and settled down in the lobby to wait. It was 4:45, and people were starting to filter back to prepare for the evening's activities.

From his position he could see the information desk pigeonholes and room keys, and the exact locations of the two he was interested in were emblazoned on his mind.

A twenty-four-year-old Frenchman, a forty-three-year-old Australian woman artist. He screened the possibilities as people came through the revolving doors.

It was growing dark outside. A party of Japanese tourists descended from a bus and chattered their way into the hotel, laden with thousands of dollars' worth of camera equipment. A businessman who appeared to have had a bad day was abrupt with a reception clerk. An American couple with four children, ranging from a bored and resentful teenager to a demanding, acquisitive toddler, carried packages to the elevator and didn't seem to be having fun.

Behind them came Jean-Claude Levesque. Cane was certain of this even before the young man had collected his room key. He was handsome, with thickly curled black hair and a sensual mouth. He dressed expensively. A student son of well-off parents. Arrogant.

Cane walked casually toward the elevators, in time to watch Levesque being handed the key to 437. Together they waited for a car to descend.

Cane glanced sideways. "Did you have a good day?" he asked in his most charming manner.

"*Pardon?*" The young man looked at him with indifference.

"Oh, I'm sorry. You don't speak English?"

"Yes, I speak. A little." He held his thumb and forefinger a centimeter apart.

"Are you here on vacation?"

"*Touriste,*" Levesque confirmed. The elevator arrived.

"So am I," said Cane. "I'm from the United States." They stepped into the car. He held out his hand. "My name's David."

Levesque shook it coolly and did not introduce himself. Cane made small talk until they reached the fourth floor, where he watched the young man leave. A job for the sisters, he thought.

The elevator ascended to the fifth floor, and then back down to the third. Cane went to his room to telephone the station chief and set up the fix.

He described Levesque in a way which ought to help the selection of an appropriate sister. She would have to be beautiful, very feminine, and apparently from a good family. A French-speaker, of course.

That left Jill Farmer. Cane hoped for better luck with her. He hated the idea of handing over both his possibilities to others, putting them out of his control. Even if a job was disagreeable, it was still better to do it oneself, make sure everything was paced correctly and there were no misunderstandings or bunglings, rather than sit helplessly in a bedroom waiting for a telephone call that might not come.

Down in the lobby, the key to 433 was still on the hook. Cane settled into a convenient chair nearby, to flick through *Time* and wait.

He almost missed her. Cane saw with shock that her key had gone before he noticed her walking toward the elevators. She was taller than he had expected, more intense but not unattractive. She had dark hair, cut short. A good, trim figure. She had not come in from the street but out of a shop in the corner of the lobby where she had obviously been buying postcards.

He followed immediately, stopping abreast as she pressed the UP button. He made eye contact and smiled "Hello." Cane looked at the elevator indicator lights and back at the pile of cards in her hand.

"Looks like you're going to have a busy evening," he said conversationally.

She glanced down, as if surprised to see the postcards. "Oh, these," she said. "Yeah, well, it's one of the punishments for coming to Europe." Her accent was unmistakable.

"Are you from Australia?"

"Yeah."

"Here on vacation?"

"No."

Cane glanced up to see how the elevators were doing. If he was fortunate, he'd have another minute. Not long. He grinned at her. "I'm luckier than that. I've got a few days off. What do you do?"

She shrugged. Still no flicker of interest. "I'm an artist," she said flatly. "Graphic design." She looked at her watch.

"Hey, that's very good. You working on a project in London?"

"Trying to get a job."

"Thinking of leaving Australia then?"

"If I can. It's a bit far from town."

Cane laughed and said: "Why don't you try the States?"

She was becoming restless. "See how I do here first."

The elevator had stopped on first. Cane held out his hand. "My name's David Cane, by the way. What's yours?"

It seemed for a moment she would tell him to get lost. He remembered someone warning him once about Australian women, but he couldn't recall what the warning was or even who had given it. Not a lot of help for an agent trying too hard and getting nowhere. Then she took his hand. "Jill Farmer," she said.

"Hi, Jill." She had a firm grip. "What makes you like London?"

She looked him squarely in the eye. "I think," she said, "it's because the English are so reserved. They never bother you. They leave you alone."

Cane felt himself redden. "Ouch," he said. "American men push too much. Sorry."

"That's all right." She turned away.

"But I didn't know any other way of building up to ask you if I could buy you a drink."

She frowned. "You're not easily put off, are you, cobber?" she asked bluntly.

He shook his head. "Or dinner even?"

"Dinner's your final offer?"

"Dinner and a show?"

She looked at him, calculating. The elevator doors opened. She put her finger on the button to keep them that way. "You're wearing a wedding ring," she said. "I don't go out with married men."

"It's on the wrong hand," Cane lied. "Americans wear wedding bands on the other hand. Which means I'm not married. And I really am quite good company, when I'm not working against the clock. How about it, Jill? Join me for a drink. At the end of the first one, if you want me to take a flying leap, I won't bother you again."

Others were filing into the elevator, stabbing at the floor buttons and wondering why the doors weren't closing.

"Just one drink?"

"That's right."

"Your room or mine?"

Cane wasn't falling for that. "Neither," he said. "Public bar on the ground floor."

That decided her. "Okay," she said. "See you there in an hour."

She stepped into the elevator, Cane after her, and the doors slid shut. They rode in silence, and she didn't look at him when she got out at the fourth floor. Cane had forgotten to press the button for the third. He rode down again.

That had been hard work. He wondered if he had done the right thing. Would Jill Farmer have been better off in the hands of a sister? It wasn't too late to fix something. However, he'd picked up hardly any personal vibes from her, and there was still a fifty-fifty chance that she was straight. He couldn't estimate his odds on getting her into bed even if she was. He was usually pretty lucky if he wanted someone badly enough, but she was a new category for him. He wasn't even convinced she'd turn up in the bar.

Cane decided to bathe and change, feeling for the first time in years as if he was going on a first date. On his way he knocked on Ross's door to fill him in on what had happened. He could see from the professor's face the beginning of doubt. If they failed on this mission, the whole Vologda operation would be threatened.

"How did the Russians find out what we'd done?" Ross asked, trying to keep the disappointment from his voice.

"I'm not sure they did," Cane said. "I think it might just have been a security precaution. Metkin's pretty hot property, don't forget."

"I hope you're right."

"Anyway, we'll know when we get in to 441. If they did see how we'd fixed the third-floor hatches and kept quiet about it, they'll be waiting for us."

"That's not a very happy thought, David."

"No, but I don't really think it'll happen. If they suspected anything, we'd see Metkin inside the Soviet Embassy so quickly they'd pick up a dozen speeding tickets on the way."

Cane explained about Jill Farmer in 433, and that he had arranged to have a drink with her downstairs. He did not recount the coolness of their initial exchanges, or his doubts that she would keep the date. There was no point in worrying Ross more than necessary.

"We'll get in through her bathroom," he said. "It should interconnect."

"Won't she mind?"

"She won't know. I'll make sure she's asleep." He caught Ross's doubting eye. "I mean really asleep. But not tonight. We've got to wait until the fixer has taken care of the hatch in 441, and that won't be until tomorrow. So get a decent night's rest if you can."

Cane prepared for his drink with the Australian woman with as much care as he'd ever given to himself. He bathed, washed his hair, shaved, brushed his teeth, and chose his clothes carefully. He stared appraisingly into the mirror. Not bad. But was he the sort of thing she liked? He would soon find out.

He went down to the bar, managing to find a small booth from which he could see the entrance, and ordered a Bloody Mary. When his eyes became accustomed to the dim lighting, he spotted Jean-Claude Levesque on a barstool in the far corner, trying very hard with one of the most beautiful girls Cane had ever seen.

From the speed at which he was talking, he was not practicing his centimeter of English. Cane wondered if the girl was one of the sisters. Quick work if she was. But he wouldn't know that until the next day.

Six forty-five. Time for Jill Farmer to arrive, if she was coming. Cane sipped his drink. He'd give her thirty minutes. And then what? Then—nothing. Dead end. All the chips would be down in Jean-Claude's part of the roulette table, everything depending on whether that lovely redhead with him was a sister or not. And if she was, whether she'd have the sense to save herself for a few more hours. It would be just their luck if Jean-Claude got her into bed tonight and tuned out to be a joker who felt as soon as he had come that he no longer "respected" the girl and couldn't wait to get away. Before sex she would be able to do no wrong. Afterward, he'd find it almost impossible to say hello.

"Oh, that's bloody great. I come down here, against my better judgment, and you've already got your eye on someone else."

Cane looked round startled, and his face broke into a smile of genuine pleasure and relief. He stood up. "Jill! Fantastic! I'd almost given you up."

"Yeah, I can see that." But she was smiling too. She slipped into the booth. "What's that you're drinking?"

"Bloody Mary. Want one?"

"No thanks. I'll have a glass of wine."

"White? Red?"

"White. Dry."

Cane signaled a waiter and placed the order. "I'm glad you came. I was afraid you wouldn't."

He noticed that her eyes had softened and she was obviously feeling quite pleased herself. "Well, I don't usually do this sort of thing," she said, "especially not with younger men. You're not a gigolo by any chance, I suppose."

"No. I'm afraid not. Does that disappoint you?"

"Not on my travel budget, no. But I'm a bit past the age where attractive young men chat me up at lifts, so I thought I'd ask."

"Oh, come on," Cane scoffed. "I'll bet that happens all the time. That's probably why you left Australia."

"Would that it were so, my friend." The wine came and she raised her glass. "Cheers. I'm sorry, your name again . . .? I really didn't pick it up the first time."

"David. David Cane. I'm from New York, here for a few days on vacation. And finding it . . . until now . . . a little bit dull."

"Well, David Cane. When a man is tired of London, he's tired of life. That's what someone or other once said."

"I think it's just looking at things by yourself. Going to theaters, or restaurants. They're all better if you've got someone with you. Don't you think? What's the point of a play, or a ballet, or an opera, unless when you get out you can have a drink with someone you like and say, 'Well, what did you think of *that?*' 'Course you do enjoy it by yourself, but it's twice as good if you share."

"You like the theater?"

"Yeah."

"And ballet and opera?"

"Very much."

"Strange," Jill Farmer said. "You don't look the type. I can see you at baseball matches, or watching a couple of bruisers knock each other about a ring. But not the corps de ballet floating past in tutus."

"I like sports too. The two worlds don't have to be exclusive."

"They usually are."

"Ah, but I'm not your usual guy."

She looked thoughtful. "No, perhaps you aren't. You're the sort who picks up older birds waiting for the lift. I'm not sure if that's a good thing or not. Tell me about yourself, David Cane."

Cane gave her a much edited synopsis of his life, then asked about her, her work, her life in Australia. They ordered more drinks and began to relax. Cane had been aware, from the moment he turned and saw her in the bar that she had changed her clothes, so unless she had another appointment later which she hadn't mentioned, she was leaving her options open. After all, he *had* mentioned dinner.

Cane found himself growing to like her. Her natural directness was refreshing. If she thought something, she said it. She was, in that way, completely open. And she had a good sense of humor. She didn't take herself or her work totally seriously, and was soon telling him stories about people she worked with and about her assignments, which made him laugh. When next Cane sneaked a glance at his watch, it was nearly eight.

"Well, so much for the preview," he said. "What do you think of it so far?"

She smiled. "I've had worse evenings."

"It's too late for a show, I'm afraid. You know what time London theaters start. But how about dinner?"

"Sounds good. What did you have in mind?"

"Fresh fish? Oysters? Wheeler's near Piccadilly Circus? Manzi's off Leicester Square?"

"Mmmmm. Oysters. You're on."

"Wait here. I'll go make a table reservation."

Cane walked over to the door, noticing that Jean-Claude's face was now only two inches from the girl's and he was listening to her with such rapt attention that she might have been divulging the eleventh Commandment or the secret ingredient in Coke. Cane grinned to himself. Baby, if you're a sister, just take it slow.

He hunted through the telephone directories and made his calls.

"Wheeler's is full," he told Jill when he had threaded his way back through the crowd in the bar. "But we've got a table downstairs at Manzi's in half an hour. Let's grab a cab."

"Is it raining?"

"No, I don't think so."

"Then why don't we walk? You're supposed to be a tourist. There isn't a better way of seeing a place than walking it."

The night was cold, which Cane was glad of, because people tend to stay closer together in such weather. Their arms brushed from time to time. He was perfectly relaxed now, back in command. He felt he was able to make her like him, and that he could pace their relationship so it would seem natural to sleep together the following evening. That was the really good thing about older women, Cane decided. They weren't saving themselves for anyone. If they ever had, that man had been and gone. They weren't hemmed in by tradition. They knew their way around.

Dinner was excellent: a cheerful, brightly lit restaurant with gingham tablecloths, fresh oysters and sole, chilled wine, and courteous Old World service.

It was starting to drizzle when they left, so Cane tried to hail a taxi, with the usual bad-weather difficulties. Finally they walked toward Piccadilly Circus, keeping under shelter as much as they could, while streams of black cabs passed with their FOR HIRE lights off.

Cane managed to flag one down on Shaftesbury Avenue just as the drizzle turned to rain, and after two blocks they were in a traffic jam. He didn't care. He was in no hurry, and as the driver patiently waited, they sat close together, talked, and laughed, and their breath misted up the windows.

When they went into the lobby, Cane suggested a nightcap, so they strolled to the bar for cognacs, and he brought up the subject of the next evening. Would she go with him to see a show and have dinner afterward? Sure, she said. She wasn't doing anything.

Cane saw her to her room and knew from the hesitant way she turned the key that she was wondering whether he might make a pass or whether she should. If *she* did he would accept, and if she didn't he would save his own move until the next evening.

"I enjoyed tonight," Cane said softly. "Thank you for taking the chance."

She gave him a fleeting, shy smile, went into her room, and closed the door.

Cane felt like singing. It was as good as done. They'd be in Metkin's room the following night.

She was more slender and her skin was softer than he had imagined. His lips brushed lightly across her breasts, down her stomach, and she began to move, her eyes half-closed, hand distractedly stroking his hair, gripping tufts when his mouth or his tongue touched particular spots.

Cane took his time, liking his work. She had a long, elegant neck. He liked that. She kissed well: a lot of tongue. He liked that too. Her body smelled faintly of scented soap, and around her very sensitive ears there was a faint musky, expensive perfume.

At last, he rested on his elbow and looked at her. "Your turn now," he murmured, and he rolled onto his back to let her go over him, gentle and expert. She was good. A natural, inquisitive explorer, finding out what felt nice, running hands, mouth, over muscles and hair, knowing when to go hard with teeth, and when to touch with tonguetip pressure so light it was almost unbearable.

Then: "Christ, David Cane. You are beautiful," and she sounded as if she meant it.

"Gigolos have to be," he said, "or we don't eat."

"You do take American Express?"

Cane, with lazy eyes, nodded slowly. He reached out and she came into his arms. He rolled onto her, very strong, sure of himself, and soon she began to cry out with pleasure, shutting her eyes tightly while he moved, faster, with more force, and suddenly she knew she was going to come and her teeth bit into his shoulder. His hands held the top of her head as if he was pushing her down onto him, then they released. Her body bucked and her breath came in gasps, and she wouldn't have heard the breaking of the glass phial near her ear even if it had been fifty times louder than the discreet crack it made because a force was building up inside her, insistent, dominating. She didn't even notice Cane wasn't coming too, that he was pulling his shoulder from her mouth and was leaning back away from her while his hips thrust automatically, because she was gasping, uncontrollable, and it was only for a moment that a sudden strong hospital smell overwhelmed her with bright flashes, and she was engulfed in the explosion and she subsided, relaxing, into blackness.

Cane lay on top of her, face turned away from the phial so none of the vapor would reach his eyes, his breath held to keep it from his lungs.

... eighteen, nineteen, twenty.

He pulled out of her, dropped the phial into an ashtray, and went to the other end of the room to get distance from the gas before he exhaled and fresh breath came in pants. There was really only enough in the container for one person and it would dissipate quickly, but he wanted to avoid having his reactions affected in any way by careless inhalation.

Time to move. He felt in the pocket of his jacket for the injection ampule. Not Pentovar, which wouldn't last long enough. Jill Farmer had to be unconscious at least two hours, and it certainly wouldn't be necessary to ask her any questions.

What do you think of it so far? Great.

Cane made a tourniquet with his tie, swabbed a section of her arm with antiseptic from a small plastic bottle—wouldn't want her to get blood poisoning—and pushed the needle into the piece of spaghetti in her arm. Lucky the first time. The drug disappeared into her vein.

One forty-five. The hotel was silent. He covered her with a blanket and dialed Ross's room. The phone was answered immediately. "Yes?"

"You want to come up now, Martin?"

"Right away."

A few minutes later there was a light knock on the door and Cane opened it, standing out of sight because he was naked and someone might be passing. Ross carried an overnight bag, which he placed at the end of the bed before peering intently at Jill Farmer. The smell of sex was strong in the room. The odor of the gas had gone.

"She's out for the count," Cane said. "Won't wake up for at least two hours. Probably nearer three."

"How did it go?"

He grinned. "No trouble. I don't think she knew what was happening." Cane flicked the combination of the lock and snapped open the case. Out of it he pulled slacks, a pair of sneakers, and a track-suit top. He dressed quickly while Ross watched in silence.

At last, this was it. Ross felt surprisingly calm, perhaps because everything that was happening now was so far outside his experience that it seemed totally unreal. But Cane—how many times had he been through this? Or something similar? Or something worse?

Cane caught his eye and grinned again. "You okay?"

"Great."

Cane carried a chair through to the bathroom and unscrewed the ceiling hatch. Apart from the gas masks that lay gray, businesslike, and ugly at the bottom of the case, everything else they would need had been prepacked into two black leather pouches.

Ross's contained a small cassette recorder, a notebook, a pen, a rubber-covered flashlight; Cane's held the gas, the drugs, a backup recorder, another flashlight, and other small pieces of equipment. They strapped the pouches to their waists, pulling them around to the side and out of the way for crawling. The gas masks were pushed up above their foreheads, straps around the backs of their necks.

"Ready?" Cane gave Ross a last visual check.

"Ready."

"Let's go." Cane gripped the sides of the hatchway and pulled himself up. His legs disappeared from view, and after a moment Ross could see his face dimly in the reflected light, looking down. There didn't seem much room in there.

Ross reached up, grasped the wood, and hoisted himself up. He found it suprisingly easy. The training was paying off. Cane helped him into the cramped darkness, guiding him onto the beam in which they would have to lie and crawl.

At first, Ross could see nothing, only smell the staleness of the air, feel the heat which had accumulated in the ceiling cavity, and be conscious of the confinement of the space. If he lifted his head, he grazed the cement roof. If he dropped his hand a few inches, he touched the ceiling boards. If he lost his balance or miscalculated and fell clumsily off the beam, he would make enough noise to awaken those below, and his weight could even take him crashing through.

Cane waited for the professor to adjust—long enough for his eyes to become used to the gloom and the basic layout, but not so long that he began thinking and became nervous.

He flashed his light around, focusing on the beams, the strong points, the cross-struts that had to be negotiated, the weak areas where there was either physical danger or the risk of making a noise. The silence was total. Ross fumbled in his pouch for his own flashlight and directed the beam at the brick wall at the end, the limit to which they could crawl, the far perimeter of Metkin's bathroom.

Cane began to inch forward, moving slower than he normally would, both for extra caution and to allow Ross to keep just behind him. It would be very easy for Cane to get so far ahead that Ross began to panic and rush his movements in an effort to catch up.

They were at the first hatch. Below them, asleep, would be a vacationing British couple. Cane shone his light at the cover, indicating to Ross that they were a quarter of the way. Ross glanced behind him at the now dim and receding square which marked the Australian woman's bathroom and—in an hour, two hours—home and safety.

Ross felt the hot, stale air beginning to catch at his throat, and he cleared it softly. Cane stopped, swung the torch onto him so Ross was aware of the briefly blinding light: Shut up.

I must pull myself together, Ross thought. *Concentrate on not coughing. Push it down.*

Cane was going forward again, cautious and calm, testing his weight on the beam with each movement, ready in an instant to pull back if there was a noise or something didn't feel right.

The light picked up the sealed hatch leading to 437, where Jean-Claude Levesque would be curled around the warm body of his beautiful fiancée. Cane had learned earlier in the day that the sister hadn't gotten to first base. Jean-Claude was already fully occupied. So everything had depended on him making it with Miss Australia.

In the corner, a noise. A sudden scratching. Cane and Ross froze, flashlights instantly off, ears straining. Ross thought his heart ought to be pumping fast, but he was totally calm. The training paying off once more, he supposed. *Life's never the same again,* Cane had said. The scratching stopped. Cane directed his flashlight at precisely the point he calculated it had come from, and he could see, although Ross behind him could not, a gray shape caught briefly in the beam before hurtling up the wall and vanishing through an almost invisible hole. Damn mouse.

Cane pressed in. Almost there. One crossbeam to negotiate. Perhaps ten feet to go. Absolute concentration needed for this final stage, which took them over the bathroom of 441 and to the hatch which that morning had been attended to by a young businessman in a smart black suit who carried a briefcase and let himself in, quite openly, using what appeared to be an ordinary hotel key. In and out in five minutes. A polite smile for a cleaning lady coming out of a room farther down the corridor. A slick, professional, Defense job. Easy, really, when you knew how.

Cane stopped and Ross knew they must be at the spot. His palms were beginning to feel clammy. He could see the flashlight being placed gently on the ceiling boards, its beam pointing out over the area of action and focusing uselessly farther away while Cane maneuvered his body into position to pry open the hatch.

Cane's hand went to his leather pouch and unerringly grasped the screwdriver. Carefully he slipped the point into the tight groove at the edge and levered. It gouged out some of the soft board at the periphery. He pushed it deeper and tried again. It raised slightly. Deeper.

And a sudden spill of light came through the hatch.

Jesus! A long, thin wedge of light where there should have been only darkness.

Ross could feel his heart now, and how slippery his hands had become, how dry his mouth.

Cane stayed still, maintaining the opening. No point dropping the hatch back because that way there would be no knowing what was below. Metkin in the bathroom? Or the KGB guard, Chersky?

Cane waited, face close to the crack. There was no smell, no sound. Had he been right when he half-joked that the KGB might be waiting for them?

What to do? Go back, wave good-bye to the Vologda program and probably the whole mission? But nothing could be worth that, not discovery now, nor capture and death later. There was no going back.

Cane lifted the hatch another inch and more light flooded in, but still there was no movement from below or any noise. Cane peered around as far as his sight lines allowed. Nothing.

He lifted it nearly halfway until he could see the entire bathroom. There was no one there. The door to the bedroom was closed.

Cane exhaled slowly. He pulled the hatch lid clear and placed it carefully to one side. The screwdriver went back into his pouch. He swung his legs through the hatch, gripped the sides, and lowered himself until he was hanging by his fingertips. With no chair beneath him, he faced a drop of two or three feet.

He let go, falling onto the balls of his feet as silently as a cat.

Ross saw him go across to the door, listen, and reach into his pouch for the gas cylinder. The room went black.

Cane waited in the darkness, hand on the light switch, collecting his courage. Then he pulled his gas mask into place. Alone in the ceiling cavity, Ross did the same.

There was a slight squeak as Cane turned the bathroom handle, and a momentary creak as the door opened.

Cane withdrew the canister safety pin and twisted the release valve. The gas began escaping with a low hiss. He held the canister in front of him, as if it were an aerosol can, and stepped silently into the bedroom.

The room layouts were identical. One double bed would be immediately to his left as he entered, the other farther away, separated by a bedside table. Above the faintly hissing gas, Cane could hear the sounds of breathing. Metkin and the guard were asleep.

Cane positioned himself between the two beds and crouched low, in case one of the Russians should awake before the gas did its work and see a dim silhouette. The gas seemed to take a long time escaping, although Cane knew this particular canister was timed at four minutes and, assuming a closed environment of the dimensions of this room, would keep a man unconscious for at least fifteen.

The hiss died away. Cane waited.

Slowly he closed the valve and dropped the canister back into the pouch. He stood up.

The breathing continued. Impossible to tell if it was at the same level or deeper, but by all that was holy, Metkin and Chersky ought to be dead to the world.

Cane walked cautiously over and sat deliberately on the edge of one bed. No response. He reached up and touched a man's face. Whoever it was needed a shave. No movement. Across to the second bed; same procedure.

Satisfied, Cane turned on the light.

Metkin was on the left, slack-jawed but peaceful. Chersky was lying naked, barely covered by a sheet, hairy and sweating in the overheated room. A big, powerful-looking man. Cane had the feeling Chersky would give him a run for his money if he ever had the chance.

Cane checked that the curtains were tightly closed. He went back to the bathroom and opened the door. He could see Ross was wearing his gas mask and that it seemed to fit properly. He motioned him to come.

When Ross was hanging by his hands, Cane grasped him around the waist to lift him the final distance. No sense risking a twisted ankle at this stage.

Back in the bedroom Cane busied himself with the injections. Chersky first, the pronounced veins on his hands an easy target. The KGB bodyguard got the same dosage as the woman. Cane would inject more if he thought it necessary later on.

Then it was Metkin's turn. Cane pulled back the sheet and stared through the goggles of his mask at the man who held the secrets of Vologda. Metkin—at last. He was aware that Ross, slightly behind him, was also watching with fascination.

Metkin was in his mid-forties. He must once have been muscular. but it had mostly gone now, leaving not so much fatness as slackness. His hair was dark but graying, and he was starting to lose it, particularly around the temples. His nose had been broken at one time and had healed, leaving a noticeable thickening at the bridge. He may have been a boxer when he was younger, perhaps at the Leningrad Artillery Academy when he was being trained, or during his spell at the Military Academy for Antiaircraft Defense in the city of Kalinin before he began specializing in computers. Cane recalled they were hot on boxing at both places.

Metkin had an aristocratic face, even-featured except for his nose, and Cane remembered the aloofness and indifference he had shown when the KGB were arguing to get the room changed. He wanted no part in that: They were the KGB, hated not only by those Soviets whose lives they touched but also by many in the Russian military intelligence organization, the GRU.

These Soviet intelligence rivals referred to each other as "the neighbors," but they cooperated as infrequently as they could get away with and rejoiced in each other's failures.

Yet the KGB were all-powerful. It was they who decreed whether or not Metkin could leave the Soviet Union, and there was no appeal from their decision. They sent Chersky to baby-sit him, and there the man lay, damp with sweat.

Metkin, in the other bed, wore cotton pajamas which Cane felt he would have discarded if the KGB had not been there. As it was, they illustrated the distinction between the services: the gentlemen, who never spied on their own Soviet comrades, and the KGB, who spied on everyone, including each other.

Cane fetched the ampule of Pentovar and swabbed clean a suitable area of Metkin's hand. He squeezed the wrist, making the veins protrude. The needle stabbed in and the drug began to drip.

Cane turned out the room light. He opened the curtains and then the windows, sliding back the double glazing to get at the handles. Fresh, cold air flooded the room. Ross shivered. They waited five minutes for the gas to disperse. Cane was the first to take off his mask, testing. His part was almost over now, and if he was affected by some residue in the room, Ross would be able to begin the interrogation while he was recovering.

There was a barrackroom smell of sweat from Chersky's body. "Okay," Cane said when he was satisfied, "let's get this show on the road."

Ross was startled to hear a voice after what seemed like hours of silence. He pulled back his mask while Cane closed the windows and made sure the curtains were properly drawn. Then he turned the bedside light on again.

Cane sat beside Metkin, checking that the ampule was safely attached to his hand and that the tape recorders were both running.

Very deliberately, and very hard, he slapped Metkin's face. It sounded like a shot in the room, and Ross jumped involuntarily. Metkin did not move.

"*Vladimir Petrovich!*" he said in Russian. "*Can you hear me?*"

There was no response.

"*Comrade Major!*" Cane's voice was sharp now, and his hand slapped down on the other cheek. Metkin's eyes opened slowly but hardly seemed to focus.

"Not so loud, David," Ross cautioned in English. "Someone'll hear."

Cane ignored him. "*Can you hear me?*"

"Christ, he's looking at us!" Ross exclaimed.

"*I can hear you, comrade.*"

"*There are some questions you must answer. Do you understand?*"

"*Yes.*"

"*What do you think of your KGB comrades?*"

"*Those who are not dogs are pigs.*" The tone was noncommittal, but the sentiments seemed deeply felt.

"*All of them, comrade Major?*"

"*All of them, comrade.*"

Cane grinned at Ross. "I think he's telling the truth, Martin. He's all yours."

Ross leaned closer. "*Vladimir Petrovich, I want you to tell me, precisely and in every detail, the procedure for logging-on to the master computer at the Vologda base.*"

Vladimir Petrovich Metkin began to talk, without any hint that the information he was calmly detailing might be other than routine —as if he were reciting the times of the trains to Leningrad, or what he had for breakfast.

He told Ross the operator numbers and names, how to log-on, passwords that gave access to particular banks of missiles in certain military sectors, and passwords that gave access to everything. The built-in fail-safe mechanism of special-key effects designed to prevent an unauthorized user—even one working from a printout of the program—from being in a position where he could begin a war. To fire the missiles from Vologda, Metkin told them, took two people. The operators knew only part of the program. He and the other supervisors knew the other hidden part, which was keyed in from a second console, twenty feet away and on whose VDU the master program automatically came up when the computer was running in the operational mode. The fail-safe sequence had to be punched in within ten seconds of it being due. Only the supervisors knew exactly where it was necessary for them to take over. They had to key in a series of three carriage returns, followed by eight space bars, followed by another three carriage returns. This was the signal which instructed the computer to go ahead with the next part of the program, and not activate an emergency alarm system which would bring armed guards stampeding in within seconds with instructions to shoot down anyone who did not immediately lie on the floor.

The Pentovar dripped into his veins. Chersky, in the next bed, did not stir. He had stopped sweating, and his chest rose and fell evenly.

Metkin had been talking for forty-five minutes.

He described the procedure for logging-out. There were no hidden signals for this, he said. It was assumed that anyone who had gotten that far was fully authorized. Ross's eyes, as he listened, were shining with absorbed fascination. Cane thought he probably wouldn't even need to refer to the tapes: Everything would be inscribed on his memory, every space bar, carriage return, letter, and digit.

It was 3:15. The ampule was running out, and Cane prepared another, ready to go into a vein on the other hand. They could spare a second hour, but no longer than that. Even if Chersky could be kept under control, Jill Farmer would be nearing the end of her own drugged sleep, and if she woke up she would find Cane gone but his clothes still by the bed, and a glance into the bathroom would reveal a chair and an open ceiling hatch. She might call the police or the manager. That would be bad for Ross and Cane. Or she might wait to confront Cane when he returned, and that would be bad for her. She would get measles, and Cane didn't want that.

But there was still time. The great thing about Pentovar, he thought, was that it did away with prevarications, justifications, and verbal fencing of any kind. You asked a question and immediately got the literal truth. An extraordinary amount of ground could be covered in a relatively short time. Cane stopped one of the recorders and changed the tape. Then he did the same for the other.

Ross was almost through. Cane took over the questioning, asking about security at Vologda, not only as it applied to anyone seeking entry to the underground citadel but the physical security within the computer room itself. Who was on duty, where did they stand, what did they do? What were the shifts?

The Pentovar ran out, and Cane jabbed a second needle into Metkin's unresisting hand. The answers came, detailed, straightforward. Metkin's eyes had remained open the whole time, occasionally blinking slowly but never seeming to focus.

Access to the computer room was severely restricted, and only holders of special identity badges were permitted to enter. The KGB routinely searched those coming in and going out, including the supervisors. In addition, the actual door to the computer room was controlled by a special security lock. It was necessary to punch a sequence of numbers onto buttons before the door would unlock. He gave the code.

The KGB guards normally stayed outside so the operators and programmers could get on with their business without having their concentration disturbed.

Cane glanced at Ross. "That's it, I think," he said. "Time to get going."

"One last thing, David. Won't take long."

Cane checked his watch. Four-oh-five. "Make it quick, Martin."

"Vladimir Petrovich, why have you come to London now? What is your purpose?"

It seemed for a moment that Metkin's eyes were slowly focusing first on Cane, then on Ross, but his vision wandered again over their heads.

"I have been sent by the Third Directorate to complete the recruitment of Professor Standish Smith to the GRU."

Cane looked surprised, but Ross was incredulous. He had known Standish Smith personally and professionally for over fifteen years, and considered him a man of complete integrity. Moreover, so did the British Secret Service. Standish Smith had a top security clearance and was based at Oakley in Cheltenham, where the Government Communication Headquarters, GCHQ, was situated. Standish Smith presided over a computer empire which, on a smaller scale, duplicated the functions of the National Security Agency in Maryland. He had at his command three UNIVAC 1180s, two IBM 360s, two ICL 1900s, and three CDC 6600s.

Almost the entire British codebreaking machinery was at his disposal. In time of war GCHQ at Oakley would play a vital role.

"Why do you say 'complete the recruitment'?" Ross asked, trying to keep the indignation from his voice.

"Professor Smith is known to me. We became friends when I was based in London between 1961 and 1963. I was not important then, nor was he. We corresponded openly at first, then as he rose in his profession, I suggested it was not advisable for us to continue in that way. Security checks would be run and our innocent letters would be misinterpreted. I suggested we correspond through a girl we both knew. She is a GRU illegal. She was how we were introduced and became friends. We shared her bed, together. It was a special, very close relationship, although we never spoke of it in letters, of course,

not even obliquely. And not face to face either. It was just something we did without words."

Cane asked: *"Photographs exist of you all in bed, I take it?"*

"Of course."

"The girl's name? And address?"

Metkin gave the information without hesitation, as he had everything else. He explained that once letters were being exchanged clandestinely, he was able to draw Standish Smith into more professional discussions. Of course, Standish Smith knew what was going on, subconsciously at least. He was being set up as a member of the Soviet orchestra.

Standish Smith was encouraged to bring a letter for Metkin when he visited the girl. If he had one, she would make a telephone call, and another charming and usually handsome man would arrive. After they had finished drinks and something to eat, they would go wordlessly into the girl's bed. If Standish Smith had no letter, she would be friendly but no call would be made, no friend would turn up, and she would say she had to go out.

It was obvious, of course, but Standish Smith continued to be drawn in. He had not yet disclosed any significant secrets.

Now the Third Directorate of the GRU, which dealt with Anglo-American strategic intelligence, had decided it was time to make a more formal arrangement. Metkin had met Standish Smith at the seminar that morning, and they had arranged to have "drinks" at the girl's flat the following evening. Renew old acquaintances. Everything would be concluded there, in a gentlemanly way.

Ross listened to the Russian, feeling sick. He would never have believed that a man of Standish Smith's eminence and intellect would ever allow himself to be maneuvered into such a foolish predicament—a man not only with a position in society but a wife and three teenage daughters.

"I've heard enough," he said to Cane. "Let's get out of here."

Cane nodded. They packed the recorders into the leather pouches, together with the expended Pentovar ampule and the injection given to Chersky.

Cane lifted Ross up to the ceiling hatch so he could get a firm enough grip to pull himself in, then he went back for a final check that the room was clean. He slipped the needle out of Metkin's vein and covered him up with the sheet.

"Good night, comrade," he said.

"Good night, comrade."

Cane remembered to leave on the bathroom light. He sprang for the hatch, caught the edges with his fingers, and hoisted himself up.

The ceiling was hotter and more stuffy than he remembered. Ross lay, a dark shape on a wooden beam a little distance off, shining his torch so Cane could replace the cover and press it firmly down. After that, because there was only one beam to crawl along, it was Ross who led the way back to Jill Farmer's room, the dull glow of light from the open hatch at the end of the claustrophobic, cramped ceiling cavity shining like a beacon to guide them home.

Ross and Cane shared something at that moment, a potent mixture of exhilaration and relief that they had actually done what they set out to do and that it had been easy. Adrenaline pumped in their bodies, but they no longer had use for it.

Without thinking or stopping to listen, Ross put his legs through the hatch into Jill Farmer's bathroom and lowered himself quickly onto the chair. Cane followed, pulling the lid down after them.,

It was done. He grinned at Ross in sheer delight and punched him lightly on the arm.

The woman's voice came from the bedroom: "David? You there?"

Cane's eyes went wide with dismay and disbelief. Then he moved, stripping off his clothes and equipment. He motioned to Ross to take care of them somehow and get out when he could.

"Yeah," he called back casually. He pulled the chain on the toilet and, as it flushed, walked out to face her.

She was lying quietly, head on the pillow. No way of knowing how long she had been conscious or what she had found out. Cane sat on the edge of the bed. He kissed her gently.

"Where've you been?" she asked, still sounding a little drugged.

"Where do you think?"

"Come back to bed." He felt a surge of relief. She pulled at his hand and he climbed in beside her. She rubbed his chest with heavy, sleepy strokes. "What did you do to me, David Cane?"

He nuzzled her neck. "What did it feel like, sweetheart?"

"It felt—just great. Fantastic. What did you use?"

His hand lightly touched her thigh. "Just a popper. Amyl nitrate."

"Amyl. Jeez, amyl hasn't done that to me before."

"You must have been in bed with the wrong guy," Cane murmured. "It's a question of timing. The stuff's all right, but you've got to know when to use it. Also you have to get the right purity. I bought it from a druggist friend in New York."

"Got any more?"

"Sorry, that was my last."

"Pity."

"Don't let it worry you. I know other ways of getting the same effect. Or pretty much the same. Nonchemical." He paused. "Like to try?"

"Oh God, I don't think I can. I feel so—full."

Softly: "Sure you can. It's another little secret I know. Handed on from father to son. Tonight's the night I'm prepared to reveal all."

His touch was becoming more specific, more insistent. There was poor Ross, sitting in the bathroom, waiting for an appropriate moment to make a dash for it. And here was Cane, lying beside this nice, sexy girl, his body still pumping adrenaline, his mind numb with what they'd done, what they'd found out and gotten away with, and he had this . . . this energy. *She* might be full, but so was he. And that was not the way he hoped to end the evening.

She began stirring under his hand, and he moved his position so he could work on her with complete and almost single-minded dedication. It would be single-minded once Ross had gotten clear.

For a woman who thought she'd had enough, Jill Farmer changed her mind quickly. At one point, when he heard a slight noise at the bathroom door, Cane stopped up one of her ears with his finger and took the other ear into his mouth, pushing his wet tongue deep toward the eardrum. The disbelieving, pleasured cries she made would have drowned the departure of men in boots, let alone one discreet fifty-eight-year-old professor with a black suitcase containing DIA equipment and two cassette tapes whose contents provided the key to an operation which, if it succeeded, would let Jill Farmer sleep more soundly in her bed. But on another night, and with another man.

Cane had a lot of catching up to do.

THE TAPE QUALITY WAS PERFECT. IT would have sounded amateurish and uneven on the Voice of America or the BBC, but for anyone listening hard to an ordinary Japanese cassette recorder, every word Metkin uttered was audible. And that was perfection.

Ross played it over the headphones when he awoke at nine A.M. and found to his surprise he was not at all tired, despite having had only four hours' sleep. His mind was crowded with images: Chersky, the KGB bodyguard, lying drugged, his body giving off an acrid sweat; Metkin with the magic ampule clinging to the back of his hand while his eyes moved slowly around trying to find focus; the rough, cramped, unpainted, stale-aired world of the ceiling cavity. And the noises at the end: David with the Australian woman. In all his years, and the thousands of times he must have made love (although admittedly mostly to Elaine), no woman had ever moaned like that beneath him. And none ever would. Ross, regretting that deeply, felt his mouth go dry. Cane could certainly teach him a few things—probably would if he asked. But what was the point? If he had been younger, perhaps . . .

No point in calling Cane now to listen to the tapes either. He'd almost certainly had even less sleep than Ross. Leave him alone. He deserved it.

The tape began with the noise of that first slap, and David's voice: "*Vladimir Petrovich!*" bringing the scene back so sharply that Ross, in a state of mild postmission shock, started to tremble. He listened to both sides twice through, the first time to relive the night, the second, trying the other tape, with a more detached, professional ear.

Before he had finished, Cane was at the door. He had obviously just come from the shower. His hair was damp and he had a scrubbed look about him.

"How does it sound?" Cane asked, the triumph still apparent in his face.

Ross just smiled, finding it difficult to choose words. Cane gave him a tight hug of congratulations, and Ross wondered if he had ever been happier or more fulfilled. To think that in the closing years of his life, he should have been chosen for such a mission and, more important, find himself able to do it! A new dimension to his personality had been revealed to him, he who once believed he possessed self-knowledge.

Cane released him and relaxed into an armchair. "Everything there you want?" he asked easily. "You don't have to go back tonight to ask a couple more questions?"

Ross laughed. "No, for God's sake. It's all there."

"Great. Have you tested both tapes?"

"Yes."

"Okay, let's have them. I want to send one back to Washington in the diplomatic pouch. I'll carry the other myself. That way, if one gets lost . . ."

Ross handed over both copies. Cane put the first in the inside top pocket of his jacket, which had a zip opening for extra security, and the second into the black suitcase with the rest of the equipment.

"I'll return this stuff to the Embassy now," Cane said. "Let them know about Standish Smith too. That'll be a repayment to MI-6 for their help. And maybe we'll be able to get the afternoon plane home. Nothing more for us here. Unless you want to stay on—do some shows, or see friends or something? I guess we could swing a couple of days."

"Whatever you like," Ross said diffidently. "Don't you want to . . . uh . . . see the woman again?"

"Don't think so. It's not necessary. Yardley discourages personal entanglements unless the job calls for them. That sort of thing can get messy if it goes on too long. Then you find yourself forced to decide what to do, how to break it off."

"Like Clive Lyle?"

"Clive Lyle is a special case. He tends to . . . overreact sometimes. In my view. But basically we prefer that agents avoid leaving lovers around in the sort of emotional state where they start asking too many questions, or making trouble, or trying to trace you back home. You know what I mean? God knows where that could lead. So it's better if I just check out. No explanations, no good-byes. She'll be sore at me for a while, but she'll get over it. I won't be the first shit she's ever come across. Or the last."

"I'll go with you then," Ross said. "There's no point sticking around London by myself."

"Fine, if you're sure. We're almost into the last lap anyway. We just have to work out the final details, get the documentation, and we're off—the shining silver bird to Moscow."

A chill settled over Ross. That would be the big test, of course. Last night was only a warm-up, with personal safety not a major factor. Cane seemed to read his thoughts because he said, "Don't worry about it, Martin. You're going to do just fine. I know that from yesterday. You were great. Made me proud."

Ross found a lump had formed in his throat, and he coughed to clear it. Cane waved cheerfully at him and left.

Time to pack. Ross knew that if David wanted them on a plane that afternoon, he'd like to be out of the hotel before the Australian woman returned, which meant leaving soon.

Ross thought he should try to eat some lunch. He had been off food for several days. He supposed the anticipation of the mission hadn't done his digestion much good, and if he came out of Vologda alive, it would probably be with a textbook case of ulcers. He hadn't eaten breakfast that morning either, but hadn't particularly missed it. A cup of coffee was really all he wanted.

He'd make an effort at lunch, and on the plane, of course, where they produced enormous meals in first class, and Cane would be watching. Anyway, he ought to build himself up for the final stage. When they got back to Fairfax, he had a feeling Cane would really pull out all the training stops, and the memory of how painful and unpleasant the workouts had been those first couple of days after the initial London visit remained fresh in his mind. That was the trouble with getting old: Your body kept reminding you it was starting to shut down.

When his suitcases were packed, Ross made telephone calls to his computer colleagues to say he had been called back to the States unexpectedly and thanking them for their help.

Then he went down to the coffee shop to order a light lunch. He decided on an omelet, followed by fresh fruit salad, and when it came he made a determined effort to eat, even though he did not feel at all hungry. In the end it wasn't worth it, because he was hit by sudden indigestion, and he pushed the fruit salad aside, untouched.

Ross bought antacid tablets in the drugstore down the road from the hotel and sucked on two. *All this excitement—not good for an old man,* he thought.

Cane was waiting in the lobby when he returned. They had seats on a flight leaving in two hours, and he had already checked out for both of them. Ross's suitcases had been collected from his room.

Ross shrugged. "Then let's go," he said.

As the cab headed over the Hammersmith Flyover and onto the Motorway for Heathrow, he noticed Cane staring at him with mild concern. "You're looking beat, Martin. I think we cut badly into your sleep last night."

"Actually, I don't feel tired," Ross said, "but I guess I must be."

"Try to rest on the plane. You want to go home to Princeton for a couple of days? It might be a good idea. No point trying to flog you until you get over jet lag and everything else."

Ross thought it over. It probably would be better, from a physical point of view anyway. He'd had enough stimulation recently to last him through a short vacation from Fairfax. He could go to bed early, do some predawn jogging to keep himself in basic shape, spend time with Elaine. Perhaps she'd come to his bed again as she had so unexpectedly that last evening. See if he could get her to make the sort of noises Cane probably took for granted. But that was a pipe dream. After so many years of marriage, they knew each other too well. Nothing so fundamental was likely to change. Even Cane would have trouble getting that sort of response from Elaine. She went along with sex because she knew it was necessary to keep him happy, but Ross felt she would not miss it if she never had it again.

And there *were* those other things they had shared more happily —the interests and the diversions. Even with Fairfax changing his life, there ought to be enough left of those to restore some of the old bonds and make "going home to Princeton" seem less like a sentence for bad behavior.

Yes, he would take two days off. Maybe three. And he would devote them entirely to Elaine. He might even try to tell her about some of the things that had been happening to him—edited, of course—to see if she could begin to understand. She was an extraordinarily intelligent woman, but that was part of the problem. Ross had a sneaking suspicion that the side of his personality Cane had cultivated with such success had nothing at all to do with intelligence. It involved deep-rooted concepts of manhood, of intense physical testing and ancient trials of courage. The point of the Vologda mission was to save lives, millions of them. But he now realized that the thrill and the impetus came mostly from the fact of the risk, the possibility of killing or being killed.

The norms of society were overturned. He had to remind himself constantly of the real reason for the mission. It was more seductive now that the Ten Commandments had officially gone into suspension, not that a lot of notice was taken of most of them anyway. But there were few circumstances in which a government considered it not only right but admirable for its citizens to kill, to maim, to steal and cheat, to commit adultery, to bear false witness, and hate their neighbors. And that, perhaps, was true freedom, for men anyway, instinctively, from the beginning of time. It was a miracle, Ross thought, that society had managed to advance as far as it had and to cover the inherent brutalities with such a smooth—thin—veneer. He himself was an object lesson: a respected, responsible, nonaggressive professor who had never seen combat except on television or in the movies, and had never felt the desire to do so—not even during World War II—who was nearing his sixtieth birthday when young David Cane took charge of him. The elderly body was put through a punishing training schedule and, to its owner's surprise, responded positively. The elderly mind was taught some new tricks involving wounding and killing. The elderly ego was then assaulted and taunted. And that was it—the civilized veneer, intact for nearly six decades, ripped apart. Ross could see himself that night in the gym, loving the blood on Cane's face—the face of a young man he hero-worshipped—and punching him between the legs with his bare fists, really trying to *hurt*. And enjoying it .

I saw your face, man, Cane had said, *and it looked like you'd found religion.*

Women weren't like that. Or at least they didn't appear to be.

They were much more civilized. Their weapons, when they fought, were usually words, not fists, or bullets, or bombs.

Except for women prime ministers who found themselves in command of armies of men, prepared to fight and die in exchange for the official suspension of the Commandments. *We're fighting for freedom,* they said, but which freedom? Whose? The freedom impelling them wasn't always the victory at the end, which would in fact mean the return of traditional restraints. It was the temporary permission to be savages.

And even women prime ministers—Golda Meir, Indira Gandhi—allowed them this. Perhaps because the rest of the world had been structured and dominated by men, and the rules of the majority, however distasteful, prevailed. One day it might come to pass that women ruled in two antagonistic neighboring nations. Whether they fought or just raged at each other would be an entirely feminine decision. Ah, that would be the test.

But he would speak to Elaine. He would try.

At the airport they checked in quickly, and after the immigration check, were taken through to the first-class lounge where they were offered drinks.

"Go on," invited Cane."You deserve it. We ought to get into practice again anyway. You know what it's going to be like later."

They both ordered Bloody Marys and halfway through his, Ross felt the hot acidity in his stomach. Automatically he pulled out a couple of antacid tablets.

Cane missed nothing. "Indigestion?"

"A little. Not serious," Ross replied. "This excitement's been a little too much for an old man, that's all. It takes getting used to. How about you? Don't you ever suffer aftereffects?"

"Not in that way," Cane said thoughtfully. "If it's been a particularly hard run, I come home pretty strung up. A lot of aggression in me. It takes a few days to settle down."

"How about food?" Ross wanted to know. "What's your appetite like?"

"Fine," said Cane. "I eat like a horse." That wasn't true actually, but it would have been psychologically bad to tell Ross that before some missions he went out immediately after a meal to be sick. Flaws like that made people nervous. Only another trained, experienced agent would shrug it off and make allowances. Later, when Vologda was all over, he would tell Ross about himself, demolish the heroic, invincible image he knew he presented. But for the moment it was a useful aid. *Follow me, Professor,* Cane could say, and for all his masterly intellect, Ross *would* follow, loyally, dumbly, to his death if necessary. That's what being an officer was all about, after all. Cane had been programmed for it, not only by the specialized Fairfax training but by what they had drilled into him at West Point, why they made life so damn hard there. *Get past us,* they said, *and you'll be ready to get past anybody. And when you can, other men will follow you.*

Their flight boarded. Immediately they settled into the front cabin of the Pan-Am jumbo, a stewardess offered champagne, and Ross accepted. His digestion didn't seem to be troubling him anymore, Cane was glad to see.

Later Ross ate well, although slowly. But while the movie was on and Cane dozed, the lack of sleep catching up with him, Ross slipped from his seat and went back to the bathroom, fighting waves of nausea. He was suffering the strangest reaction to tension, and he knew he had to find some way of combating it. Unless he did, he would have an impossible time in the Soviet Union, where the pressure would really be on. He ate more tablets, and slowly the nausea passed.

He went back to his seat and fell asleep. The announcement that they would soon be landing at Dulles Airport woke him, and he felt better after his rest. That was what he needed, of course—time to unwind.

A DIA car was put at Ross's disposal in Washington, and he drove directly to Princeton. How strange to be home, Ross thought, as he carried his suitcase up the darkened drive to the house, where lights shone through windows and chinks of curtain and where Elaine was waiting. Cane had promised to phone her that he was on his way.

She must have been watching for him, as they both had watched for Cane on his solitary visit all those months before, knowing that after he left, nothing would be the same. And now Ross was returning, a soldier on leave from fighting a war no one knew about, being given time off before the final offensive.

Light spilled out the front door as it opened, and Elaine stood silhouetted.

Suddenly he was truly glad to see her, and wordlessly he put his arms around her, holding her in a tight embrace.

"Welcome back, my dear," she said, her voice soft. She drew away and noticed the airline label on his suitcase. Her hand flew to her mouth. "Oh my God, you've done it!" she said. "It's finished!"

The relief was so clear on her face that Ross became aware for the first time what she must have been suffering, alone in the house, not knowing what was going on, whether he was in Russia or still training somewhere. He found it difficult to speak for a moment, but at last he shook his head.

"No," he said, "it's not over yet. Let's go inside."

As they walked in, she tried to cover her disappointment.

There, among the familiar but to him somehow strange things, Ross reached a decision. He had been authorized to tell Elaine about the mission. He had General Yardley's specific permission for that. And now he would. He would tell her everything, bring her up to date. To hell with whether she understood or not. He ought at least to try.

"Has the house been swept?" he asked.

"They come every three days," she said. "I hardly notice them anymore. They were in yesterday."

"Then we must talk."

Later, when Yardley read the monitoring transcript of their conversation, he was so intrigued he called for the actual tape, and listened himself to Ross's explanation of what had happened at Fairfax, how he had changed, and how he was actually glad of this in ways he could never justify intellectually. He described what had happened in London in such simple, graphic terms that Elaine—and Yardley —could almost smell the barrackroom tang of Chersky, feel the tension, the stifling atmosphere in the ceiling, and that moment at the end when they found the Australian woman was awake. Ross spoke about what happened then, the way Cane had pleasured Jill so that the noise she made covered his escape, and Yardley knew by the way his voice became halting and finally broke that Ross had begun to weep, although whether for the strain of the mission or for himself, it was impossible to say. There was silence on the tape for several minutes. And when Ross spoke again, his voice was stronger, more confident. That just left getting into the Vologda base, he said, which was Cane's department, and he trusted Cane to do it. Then it would be over. He would come back. He would be safe. But, of course, he would still be changed, and the tear in the fabric of his civilization would take time to mend. He would try to adjust as quickly as possible, and meanwhile he hoped she would understand.

After listening in complete silence, Elaine Ross's voice was even and composed. "My dear," she said simply, "I'm so glad for you. And for myself too. It seems that David Cane has taught you survival. That was the one thing I felt deep inside that you might lack."

"He taught me how to kill," Ross pointed out.

"No! To survive! He taught you that you *could* kill if necessary. You'll be going in without weapons. It's a mission of peace. You're there to save lives, not take them. You learned how to retaliate, that's all. And for that you do need aggression. But it's aggression in a cause—to defend yourself and to defend others. It's not the aggression of the bully or the psychopath but of King Arthur's knights. What you, my dear, are having trouble coming to terms with is something I'm afraid is common to many academics: their total concentration on one discipline. They take for granted the conditions they must have to work in freedom. You, fairly late in life, have been given the chance to play a part in the survival game, and you believe the experience has changed you. Well, I'm sure it has. For the first time in your life, you're a whole man. Do you understand what that means? Congratulations, my dear. I love you for it."

Ross, moved, sat beside her and took her hands. "Thank you," he said, "I'd hoped you'd understand just a little. I find you understand more than I did."

"And now, after that, I would like a drink, Martin. And then we can eat, if you're hungry."

"Not very. I'm afraid," Ross admitted. "They keep feeding you on planes."

"In that case you can talk to me while *I* eat, and perhaps we can share a bottle of champagne. I've never felt more like celebrating in my life. This is a special day."

Dawn at Fairfax, and Ross, back in his track suit at a familiar, calm hour, followed Cane out of the apartment and headed at a steady jog down toward the forest. Cane had told him they would start off fairly gently and build up over the next few days, but after five minutes Ross thought they might be able to step up the pace quicker than that. He felt well. His digestion problem had gone, although his appetite was small. And he felt none of the cramps and pains he had suffered almost immediately they resumed training following the last break. Some muscles were tight, but he knew they would loosen as he pressed on. His breath came easily, evenly. He had no trouble keeping up with Cane. They jogged through the trees, past the dew-wet bushes and the long grass, toward the hill which Ross had once thought of as impossibly steep and difficult. Now as they began their ascent, they passed, with ease, points which Ross remembered as places of virtual collapse in the early days of training.

Then they were at the top, and the path took them around to the south side of the hill before sloping sharply down, and Cane, seeing how well Ross was doing, let gravity speed his pace until he was racing when he reached the bottom, and he pushed himself to maintain the pace, lungs working like bellows, across the fields and back toward the gymnasium. Before he reached the building, he looked over his shoulder, slowing down.

Ross was nowhere in sight.

Cane halted, then immediately began running back, cursing. Stupid of him to have taken that downhill section so quickly. All they needed now was for Ross to break an ankle. If he was lucky, it would be something simple like a stitch or a cramp.

Suddenly Ross emerged from behind a rock, halfway up the hill, and began jogging down, picking up speed. Cane slowed to a walk, halted, and watched him come. No sign of a limp, and he was going too fast to have had a cramp a moment before.

Ross drew near, calling: "Sorry, David. My goddam shoelace was untied."

Cane felt a wave of relief and broke into a run beside the professor. Yet all the way back to the gymnasium, a doubt nagged at him. Why had it taken so long to tie a lace? And why go behind a rock to do it?

"How's your stomach?" he asked as they walked along the corridor.

"Fine. No trouble."

Cane grunted. "Okay, let's get our stuff together. Karate uniforms."

A few minutes later, they faced each other. "Revision," Cane ordered. "This morning we're going to have another look at striking. Where do you hit a man to cause temporary paralysis? The easiest place."

"In the testicles."

"Right. You discovered that a few weeks ago. Let's go up to the top, look at the head and neck area. The points which are dangerous."

He touched a place on his skull about six inches above his eyes. "The sphenoid. Strike downward here hard, and the jolt will carry all the way to the back of the neck. Man'll be unconscious. Two: nasal bone. Everyone knows that. Three: the maxilla, this point here . . ." Cane put his finger dead center between Ross's upper lip and his nose. "It's full of nerves. Get your index finger there, touch it. Okay, now press very hard. PUSH!"

"Ow! Jesus Christ!"

"See what I mean? So when you go in there, you go in hard with a single knuckle punch. Get the idea?"

"Yeah."

"Four . . ." Cane touched the area at the top of his Adam's apple. "The hyoid bone and the epiglottis. Strike here and you mean serious business." His finger moved lower down his neck. "Five . . . around the thyroid gland. A good strike here and you'll make your opponent choke." Cane turned sideways to continue the demonstration. "Six . . . back of the skull, around the transverse sinus. Hit it hard enough and he'll lose his sense of balance and maybe consciousness as well. But go a little farther down, to the base of the skull and you're right at the spot on the brain that controls breathing. Obviously that's a good target. So is farther down here . . ." Cane touched down the back of his neck. "This is the seventh cervical vertebra region. Strike it hard and you're hitting at the spinal cord itself. You'll also affect the nerves of the upper chest, neck, and face. Okay?"

"Okay."

"Now the side of the head: this soft part by your temples, here. The trigeminal nerve. They call it 'the seat of consciousness.' Go for it with the heel of your palm and you're in business. Now another experiment. Put your fingers here, between your jawbone and your ear. Found it? Right, push hard. Go on, don't be a sissy! PUSH!"

Ross exclaimed in pain.

"Feeling numb? That's the somesthetic nerve. It controls muscular activity and the sense of touch. Enough theory. Now some practice."

The two men worked hard for the rest of the morning. After showering and changing, they went to the cafeteria for lunch, and Cane noticed Ross was again picking at his food, although from the amount of energy he had expended, he should have been very hungry.

That afternoon, while Ross was transcribing the tapes into a computer flow chart, Cane went to the Fairfax clinic and ordered up a major medical. Something wasn't right with Ross, and he wanted to know what it was.

In the late afternoon he brought the professor to the clinic protesting he was fine.

"Bullshit," said Cane abruptly. "We don't give medals to heroes. If you're getting a stomach ulcer, I want to find out about it now. Then they can prescribe medication to get you through the rest of the mission, change your diet or something."

The doctor was waiting for them, and for thirty minutes he closely questioned Ross about his medical history, bowel movements, and digestion, how much food he ate and what sort, what he drank, about nausea, which he admitted, and about vomiting, which he denied.

Cane, sitting on a chair behind him, broke in suddenly: "You're a liar, Martin. You threw up this morning when we were running. That's why you went and hid behind that rock. Don't tell me you didn't because I sent someone back to check." Cane was guessing.

Ross hesitated and looked shamefaced. "It wasn't anything," he insisted to the doctor. "I was having my first workout after a break of several days. I overdid it, that's all."

Ross was told to strip. He was weighed. His temperature and blood pressure were taken, and his body pressed and probed. An ECG measured his heart, and an EEG charted his brain activity. The doctor took a blood test and a urine sample, and gave him a container and instructions to bring back a stool sample as soon as possible.

Ross hated it all, partly because he suspected there *was* something wrong with him and he didn't want some superefficient medic delaying the Vologda operation. He felt it was better to ignore the whole thing, do the job first and worry about an ulcer later. He told Cane so on the way out.

"Let *me* tell you something, Martin," Cane observed slowly. "This mission is so important that I'm not going to let *anything* stand in its way. When the doctor makes his report, he'll make it to me, not to you. If he says, 'Look, this guy's got an ulcer and we really ought to take it out,' I'll say to him, 'Can he last for another four months?' If the answer is yes, then you'll get only the treatment necessary to keep you in training and get you into Vologda. If the answer is no, then I'll fight that sonofabitch doctor, to see if I can't make him change it to yes and let you have stronger drug treatment."

Ross thought it over. "That sounds fair. But you'll tell me what the verdict is?"

"Of course."

"The truth?"

"Would I lie to you?"

"I don't know the answer to that, David," Ross said. "If it suited you, yes, I think you probably would."

Cane laughed. "You know me too well, my friend. But in this case I'll give you a cast-iron guarantee. I'll level with you. It's *your* body, and if there's something wrong, you'll have to know exactly what it is, if only to understand the reason for a particular treatment, or why you have to avoid certain foods or stay away from vodka or whatever. Now do you believe me?"

"Yes. Now I believe you."

"Dinner time. Feel like an early bite?"

"Sure. Let's get a steak." Ross was quite hungry this time, and when he ate he found to his surprise that he felt fine, no burning pains. Cane was watching closely, but he told him anyway.

The talk turned to the mission. Ross had completed the flow chart for the Vologda program and now wanted access to an IBM 7090 with two separate operators' consoles so he could reproduce it exactly. Metkin's disclosures had made it clear that Cane, too, would have to be taught how to use the supervisor's console so he could punch out the appropriate special-key code to prevent the computer triggering the alarm. There was an IBM 7090 available at the National Security Agency, and Cane had no doubt they could arrange to use it whenever they wanted.

"I want to get started tomorrow," Ross said. "It's not only a question of constructing a model of the Vologda program, but I've got to work out what we do after that. I have to program in a new set of instructions at the end of the launch sequence which must go into every onboard computer on every Soviet missile connected to Vologda, and it's going to have to be something that no one underground is going to be able to find. At least not until they've pressed the button and those nukes are in the air. Then it can flash up on the screen before their wondering eyes, and they'll have a few minutes to try to make head or tail of it." He began a flight of fancy. "I think I might give them a puzzle to work out, with a time limit of, say, twenty minutes. I'll have a lot of fun constructing it."

Cane laughed. "God, that would be funny. The Politburo standing round, waiting for the destruction of the West by missiles our radar can't even see, and suddenly their computer goes mad. I like it."

"I thought we might construct a program that asks them a number of general knowledge questions," Ross continued thoughtfully. "The words of 'The Star-Spangled Banner,' for example. The names of the first, third, fifth, eighteenth and twenty-second presidents. The name of Ronald Reagan's dog."

They both roared.

Cane said, still chuckling: "But wouldn't they just abort the attack if they knew they'd been set up? Pretend it was all a horrible mistake by a traitor who's subsequently been shot?"

"No, because I'll fix it so they have similar problems on an abort. That program might want to know the address of the Hilton Hotel in Chicago or the number of suites at the Pierre in New York. The first program of mine they'll see is the one they're going to have to work out if they want to stop their missiles self-destructing and put 'em back on target. The second is if they try to abort the firing themselves. You see, we don't know what the state of our own art is going to be. We have to give our side time to notice war's been declared."

"Don't make it too easy, will you? You might find a programmer who knows the answers."

"Leave it to me, David. It wouldn't just be general knowledge. There'd be one or two secret passwords as well. And no one will know those, except me."

In fact, Ross was far from sure he'd have time to program in a grim game for a panicking Soviet leadership to play as they awaited the destruction of their own society. It would depend on how much time he and Cane had available at the consoles of the master computer. If they could be alone for twenty or thirty minutes, Ross could have fun. If they had to snatch their opportunity to set up the computer ambush, it would be a brief code insert.

The following morning, as they had no word from the clinic doctor, Cane arranged their permissions to use the IBM 7090 at Fort Meade, and caught a light DIA plane to Washington to save the road trip. The NSA complex was only fifteen miles northeast of the capital, and they were there soon after lunch.

It took the rest of the day to set up the extra computer console into a position that roughly corresponded to the layout at the Vologda citadel and for Ross to punch in the basic program. It had been intelligently devised. After the system had been entered, utilizing the appropriate codes and passwords, the computer language used was FORTRAN, and to change from that to the next language, ALGOL, entailed an elaborate series of coded exchanges with the computer. There was a similar obstacle course before the final language change to the BASIC derivative.

Much of the program was duplicated, so it would be difficult to make unauthorized changes on targeting, for example. Yet it would be comparatively easy to slip in an extra sequence, a sudden hidden hurdle which had to be surmounted before the computer would pick up the remainder of the original program.

Ross gave Cane a preliminary lesson on the keyboard and let him play around until he started becoming familiar with it. They would get to work in earnest the next day.

The NSA had provided them with bedrooms in the complex—rather more luxurious than the DIA offered at Fairfax—and after finishing at PROD, the Office of Production, they went for their usual workout.

For Ross it turned into a nightmare. It wasn't that his body ached or his muscles were cramped, but that he was suddenly gripped with a deadening lethargy that glazed his eyes and made him jog slower and slower behind Cane. His legs moved first by force of will, then as that was sapped, purely because of his own momentum, he was walking, and then, not caring anymore, he halted on the grass and stared helplessly at the figure of Cane running back toward him to find out what the hell was going on. It was hard even to keep his shoulders from slumping. *What is it?* he thought, part of him not caring about the answer. *What is it?*

Cane, beside him, stared into his chalk-white face, touched his forehead for a fever, fingers pressing in the soft part of his neck below his jawbone to see if any glands were swollen, and then put a strong arm around behind his shoulders, supporting him, and walked him slowly back to the complex.

The journey seemed to take forever, but when Cane lowered him onto the bed in his room and he lay back, he felt so grateful and detached he just wanted to be left to sleep.

By the time the NSA doctor arrived to examine him, with Cane waiting strained and anxious at the door, Ross was feeling better. It had been extraordinary, as if he were powered by a battery which had inexplicably failed but was now flickering back to life.

The doctor was a young, cheerful man who asked many of the same questions his Fairfax colleague had and, like him, was noncommittal. He advised a light supper and rest.

When Ross was asleep, the doctor called Cane to his office and told him he had spoken to Fairfax. The results were in from the first batch of tests, and it was necessary for Ross to undergo others. In particular, they wanted a body scan. He could have it done at the DIA hospital in Washington, and they would be ready for him the following morning at ten. They also wanted to know what the hell had happened to his stool sample.

Cane tried to get from the doctor a preliminary indication of what the trouble might be, and how serious, but he came up against an impenetrable wall of professional caution.

"At this stage, we just don't know," the doctor said. "It could be one of several things, some bad, some not so bad. It would be foolish to guess, because I don't have enough information. We'll know better when we see the scan."

"When will that be?" Cane asked.

"We see it immediately. It comes up on a diagnostic display console and we record it onto floppy disc. It might take a couple of hours to interpret and get everyone's opinions. We'll have a better idea tomorrow."

Cane went back to Ross's room to look in at his comrade sleeping deeply. He seemed better. When he had slowed down during the run, Cane thought he was going to die. Now his color was back and he looked better.

Cane sat quietly in a chair, staring at Ross, and wished he had a cigarette.

They had been asking a lot of a fifty-eight-year-old body. Perhaps it was Cane's own fault. He had never trained anyone that age before and maybe he pushed too hard.

Don't quit on us now, he urged Ross silently. We're almost there. Stick it out a little longer.

Ross was breathing evenly, in a deep and dreamless sleep.

The following morning the two men presented themselves to Dr. Peter Barry at the DIA hospital in Washington. Barry was cordial and unhurried, putting Ross at ease and not going through the same questions as the others. Cane, who was skilled at reading upside down, noticed that on his desk was a report from the Fairfax clinic, and beneath it another—presumably from the NSA.

Barry took Ross's temperature and asked how he was. Ross, who felt himself still running at half speed, replied he was fine.

"We want to take a look at that stomach of yours," Dr. Barry said, "so we're going to put you on a body scanner. Ever had one of those before?"

"No," said Ross.

"Well, it's not a big deal. Takes about forty minutes, no injections, no pain. You're going to have to drink a couple of glasses of a liquid with a radio isotope in it. Tastes like anise. Not the sort of thing you'd offer people at home, but take it slowly and you won't throw up. If you do throw up, you're going to have to drink more until you've got enough into you for the scanner to do its job." Dr. Barry pressed a buzzer under his desk. "Might as well start right away," he said. "After you've finished, we have to wait twenty minutes for it to work down into your system."

A nurse appeared with a tray on which were three large glasses.

"All that?" asked Ross, surprised.

"I'm afraid so. Cheers."

Ross began to sip the liquid. It tasted sickly and he wondered why it didn't come in more pleasant flavors. While he drank Barry bantered about the day Cane came to give injections and how none of those patients had ever been back.

"Ah, but you should have seen me in London," Cane said. "I was fantastic. Not a single complaint."

"I hope you remembered to clean the skin first, or they'll all have lockjaw by now," Barry countered.

Cane clicked his fingers in mock disgust. "Goddam, goddam it, I *knew* there was something."

It took Ross longer to drink the isotope than he expected. It became harder to take with every mouthful, and he felt himself begin to hiccup back small amounts, which he knew was a prelude to being sick. The others chatted on easily, sometimes including him in their conversation and making sure he never felt he was being rushed. Two glasses were finished, and a half remained. Ross put his head back on his armchair and breathed deeply and slowly. Almost at the end, he told himself.

When finally he was through, Barry ushered them down a corridor to a room in which a CAT scanner had been installed. It was a large, high metal box with a circular opening in the center. The head of a black couch was placed lengthwise so that the X-ray detectors could travel right down it. At one end of the room, lead-glass double windows separated the scanner from the operator-radiographer, the viewing unit, and the computer.

While the isotope worked into Ross's digestive system, Peter Barry explained some of the intricacies of the scan and took them through to the operator's room to see what happened there. Although Ross with his training was a special case, Barry's policy was generally to make it clear to patients exactly what was about to happen to them and what it would feel like.

The only exceptions he made were on procedures such as angiograms, where the patient's hands had to be tied to the rails of the stretcher so he couldn't rip out the thick Pott's needle from his neck, and his head was secured with adhesive-tape strips to a platform so it couldn't move, and a dye was injected into the carotid artery, and it felt like a jolt of high-voltage electricity smashing into the brain. There were times when it was better not to know precisely what was going to happen.

But a CAT scan was not like that. The worst part was drinking the isotope, and Ross had already done that.

He was given a white hospital gown and told to change.

Then Barry arranged him on the couch, instructing him to lie very still while the machine did its work. He and Cane retired to the next room. When Barry gave the word, the radiographer pressed the button to START SCAN.

Cane found the next forty minutes fascinating, in the way that a space probe is fascinating. The scanner was taking thousands of X-ray readings of Ross's body, translating them into images on the screen, which showed him almost in cross section. Cane could not interpret the pictures, but he knew that something extraordinary and technically marvelous was going on.

Barry watched, saying nothing.

Through the window Cane could see Ross lying quietly, his breathing shallow, and wondered if they were looking at a stomach ulcer and finding the explanation for his running out of steam so suddenly the evening before.

On the console a green light displayed the words DISC BUSY, showing that the scan was being recorded automatically onto a floppy disc for reviewing and storage. Finally, the light switched off and another flashed on: ARCHIVE COMPLETE.

The scanner had returned to the head of the couch, and Ross was free to go.

"Excellent," Barry said, helping Ross to his feet. "I suggest you go and get dressed, and come back at four this afternoon. That'll give me time to study the scan, and I should have a better idea of what the trouble is."

Cane glanced at his watch. It was 11:30. Not really enough time to get back to Fort Meade and put in some useful work on the IBM, but too long just to hang around waiting. He suggested he and Ross take in a movie.

They chose a spy thriller and enjoyed it, but as Cane pointed out later, the trouble with most thrillers was that they couldn't keep up with life. Reality was far more bizarre than fiction. What author in the late 1970s would have dared write a book about a communist agent killing a Bulgarian exile in London by stabbing him in a bus line with a poisoned umbrella? But that's what had happened to a broadcaster for one of the BBC's East European services: fact not fiction. Even Scotland Yard and the hospital doctors didn't believe the man, as his life slipped mysteriously away, when he said he was being murdered. A tiny metal pellet was discovered in his thigh during the autopsy.

There were a dozen other bizarre examples Cane could cite, many of them from the CIA archives. His particular favorite was the plan to manufacture a special shoe polish for Fidel Castro that would give off fumes to make his beard fall out and so discredit him as a leader.

They headed back to the DIA complex, feeling in good spirits, to hear the results from Dr. Barry.

Afterward Cane drove Ross to his home in Princeton and went inside with him. They hadn't spoken since leaving Barry's office three hours earlier, and the purpose of going back was just to collect a few personal things and give Ross a chance to talk to his wife overnight.

Barry had given it to them straight from the shoulder. The professor's weight was down by eighteen pounds in six weeks, he said. He was running a minor but fairly constant temperature. A particular glycoprotein had been isolated in his blood sample and was found to be altered both physically and chemically. He recalled Ross saying that when he threw up during his training run a few days earlier, it had looked a bit like black coffee grounds. Ross had persistent indigestion, loss of appetite, and the previous night had been hit by a sudden lethargy. Although he claimed to feel fine today, Barry wouldn't bet a nickel on it. Ross did not contradict.

All these factors, combined with the evidence of the CAT scan, had been considered by Barry and three DIA consultants. Ross was of course at liberty to get other opinions.

"For God's sake, Doctor," Ross burst out at last. "Put me out of my misery. Have I got ulcers or haven't I?"

Barry shook his head. "Not ulcers," he said carefully. "We'll have to go in and take a look, but it's our opinion that you have cancer of the stomach."

Ross stared at the doctor in disbelief. David Cane sat as if turned to stone. Cancer. Ross whispered: "That can't be true."

"I'm afraid it is," Barry said. "I know how you must feel. But it needn't be as bad as you think. Patients still look on cancer as always being terminal, but it isn't necessarily so. Of course, we don't know how extensive it is in your case. That's why we have to operate as soon as possible—tomorrow morning, if that's agreeable to you. But I must tell you that in the United States, about fifty percent of cancer patients are cured either by surgery or chemotherapy or both. And it depends where the cancer is. Now in your case, we think it's in your colon. Well, if it is and it's localized, you've got nearly a seventy percent survival chance after five years."

"But . . . what about the mission? What about Vologda?" Ross demanded.

"Out of the question at the moment," Barry said firmly.

"David, talk to this man! We can't call it off, not now!"

Cane looked steadily at the doctor. "How about it, Peter?" he asked. "What if we don't consider the professor's chances later? What if we only want him in some sort of shape to get through this mission? Can you fix him up just for that? Two, three months?"

Ross backed him up. "I don't care about the cancer," he urged. "Let it grow. Let it spread. Let's worry about it later. There must be something you can give me to keep me going. Please. Please, Doctor."

Peter Barry fell silent a long time, considering the alternatives. Cane found himself holding his breath, and a quick glance at the stricken face of Martin Ross showed he was too.

At last, Barry said: "Look, I'm a doctor with the DIA. I cut corners as part of my job all the time. If some of the things I've done ever came out in public, I'd be struck off the medical register. Wearing my DIA hat, I don't honestly care whether you live or die, Martin. If I could I'd pump you full of something, give you a box of pills, and put you on a plane for Moscow"—he paused—"but I can't. I'm sorry. Your collapse yesterday is a late symptom. You could hardly move, am I right? Okay, you were in the middle of a workout at the time. But you needn't have been. It could strike when you're sitting at the computer. When you're sitting across from me now. *And no one can help you.* Not on the sort of time schedule you need. If you were going to be in Vologda inside of a couple of weeks, I might take the risk. But you aren't, are you?"

Cane shook his head. "No," he admitted. "It'll be another couple of months if we rushed it."

"So you see. And with the cancer progressing, it gets more and more difficult. We have to get inside you, Professor, to see what the trouble is. Maybe it's something we can fix easily. In that case you'll need a recuperation period of, say, six to nine months, plus chemotherapy. Then I'll tell Yardley he can send you to the moon if he likes, and you'll have a fighting chance of making the journey. But I wouldn't bet a nickel on you at the moment. Not if you ignore my advice and just keep going." He stopped to let his words sink in. Then he added the clincher: "Anyway, I've already spoken to General Yardley. He knows the prognosis. He agrees that we operate on you tomorrow morning."

"So the mission is off." Ross sounded as though his world had collapsed. Beating Vologda had become so central to him that even the diagnosis of cancer was important mainly insofar as it affected that.

"The mission is *postponed*," Barry said carefully. "That's all we can say at the moment."

Ross stood up, suddenly an old man. "Thank you, Doctor," he said. "I must go back to my wife now."

"We really have to keep you in the hospital overnight," Barry warned.

"No. Not tonight. I'm going home now. I'll come back tomorrow. You can operate whenever you like after that."

Barry shrugged. "Okay," he agreed. "Be back here by four tomorrow afternoon. Take it easy."

"I will," said Ross. "Thank you."

Out in the corridor, Cane put an arm around his shoulders as they walked slowly to the lift.

Ross stopped. "David," he said sadly, "I'm really so very, very sorry."

But Cane could not look him in the eye.

12

GENERAL YARDLEY'S MANICURED fingernails scratched his crew-cut head as they tended to do whenever he was disturbed. It was the only nervous mannerism Cane had ever noticed his DIA boss had. Yardley was a cold fish generally. What he thought or felt took place in some deep recesses of his brain, where light never reached, and only very occasionally a signal that it might be comforting to scratch his scalp came to the surface. So he scratched amid the gray, spiky hair, slowly and tenderly for fifteen seconds at a time, always on the same spot, right on the top of his head.

Cane had taken up smoking again. He thought Yardley would object, but either he had too much on his mind or he realized it didn't really matter what the hell Cane did now. Anyway, he gave no sign of having noticed.

Cane held in a lungful of smoke and blew it out slowly, watching it swirl around toward the air-conditioning vent and disappear.

Yardley was lost in thought at his large mahogany desk. Cane sat in an armchair at the side of the office. A cup of coffee had gone cold beside him, and the onyx ashtray was littered with the stubs of cigarettes. He hadn't felt so bleakly impotent since Maryann was having Timmy, and Cane had found to his very great surprise that being in the delivery room when she was hurting so badly for so long, and he was powerless to help, was making him feel faint. So he sat that early morning in the hospital lobby, waiting, and thinking, and wondering, and smoking too much, until a nurse told him he had a son, and they were both all right.

Who now was going to come into Yardley's office and tell them Martin Ross was all right so they could pass the news on to the restricted few who were authorized to receive it and waiting anxiously? For it wasn't only here, in the sanctum sanctorum of the Defense Intelligence Agency, that a special watch was being kept and normal operations suspended. Yardley had been on the phone to the Oval Office three times so far, and each time it was Ronald Reagan who had called *him*. Yardley replied in a deferential but firm leave-it-to-me-Mr.-President way, which Cane approved of. Reagan might be boss there, but Yardley was still boss here.

On Yardley's desk was a top secret file, which he read constantly. Cane figured he had been through it eight or nine times in the last hour and a half, but if the contents were especially interesting or worrying, no flicker of emotion transmitted itself to Yardley's unlined face. Naturally Cane didn't ask what it was.

The telephone on his desk rang—not the red scrambler phone, which would probably have been Reagan worrying again, but the white one, which meant it was an internal call.

"Yardley." A pause, then a grunt. "Okay, as soon as you can." He replaced the receiver. "Ross's out of the operation room," he told Cane. "Peter Barry's on his way over here."

Cane glanced at his watch. Ross had gone in before ten. It was now 12:45. Was a three-hour operation a good sign or a bad one?

Cane lit another cigarette. It would take Barry five minutes to walk from the DIA hospital along the corridor, to get an elevator and reach Yardley's office. Providing he didn't stop for a leak, or to wash the blood off his hands, or whatever surgeons did after digging around inside a man.

Barry arrived quicker than Cane had anticipated, and he rose to his feet, along with Yardley, to hear the verdict. Barry as always was immaculate, in a gray flannel suit, and looked calm and unflustered.

He spoke without preliminaries as he took a seat near Cane, and Yardley came over to join them. "It's cancer," he confirmed. "There's a primary in the colon and a few secondary growths in other organs."

"Did you take them out?" Cane asked anxiously.

Barry shook his head. "No point," he said. "It's inoperable. It's all

over his liver. Ross's going to die, and there's nothing we can do.
There are probably other growths, but I didn't bother looking."

Cane closed his eyes and whispered: "Oh Jesus."

Yardley said gruffly: "I'd better tell the President." They both
waited while he dialed the Oval Office on the scrambler phone. It
answered immediately, presumably by Reagan himself, because Yardley started right in: "Mr. President, the operation's over . . . Not
good, I'm afraid. There's cancer in his liver too . . . no, it's inoperable. Ross's finished . . . Yes, Mr. President, I'm well aware of that . . .
Yes, I've been through the report, many times . . . we must not be
stampeded in this matter, sir . . . I will . . . yes, yes, of course, Mr.
President. I know the time schedule . . . As I told you before sir,
there must be a fighting chance before I could agree to such a thing
. . . Yes, I know . . . I'll call you later, Mr. President."

Yardley replaced the phone and grimaced. Reagan was putting on
the pressure. He came back to the sofa. "Let's have it in detail,
Peter," he said.

"Technical, or layman?"

"Oh shit, layman."

"Well, I don't frankly know how the cancer went undetected for so
long, particularly as Ross has been having weekly medicals over the
last several months. But it didn't show up, at least not on any of the
tests we were running then. If we'd known what we were looking for,
it might have been different. And I really don't know how the hell
Ross got through his workouts without hitting bad trouble. Still,
that's the way it goes sometimes. Cancer can be pretty sneaky. It
looks like something else. The symptoms come and go, never long
enough to worry a person, or alert a doctor that anything particular's
wrong. Then . . ." He hit his fist into the palm of his hand with a
sharp report. "And he's dying."

"How long has he got?" Cane asked. "Any chance of patching him
up to have a go at Vologda? I'd make it as easy for him as I could."

Barry shook his head. "Not a chance," he said. "I'd consider myself
lucky if I got him well enough to leave the hospital and come in for
chemotherapy once in a while. Frankly I doubt that he'll ever go
home. But, as I say, for all the practice we've had with cancer, we
actually don't know too much about it. Sometimes there are remis-
sions we can't explain." He caught Cane's hopeful eye. "Enough so
he can go for short walks without pain, or prune the roses. Not
enough to crack Vologda."

A deep sadness fell over Cane. It really *was* finished. They'd never complete the mission. They had a cassette full of extraordinary, detailed information on the Soviet missile computer system, and no way of using it. Unless . . .

"Couldn't I go to Vologda by myself, General?" he asked hopefully. "Martin could teach me enough to get by."

Yardley shook his head. "Don't think we haven't considered that, David. As soon as I knew Ross was ill, I asked one of our computer guys to give me an assessment of your prospects. He estimated a success factor of less than fifty percent, and that's not good enough. It isn't just a question of pushing the right buttons for the existing program. We'd be able to teach you that here. The deal is going to be reprogramming. Working under heavy pressure. Having to cope with something unexpected that's out of your field. What if Metkin failed to mention some small point or symbol that would be self-evident to an expert, but would fool someone like you? The hotel tape doesn't even go into the modifications the Soviets have made to their IBM. Maybe it's got nothing to do with the main console, but maybe it does. You didn't remember to ask about that, did you?"

Cane shook his head, feeling ashamed. Jesus, they'd known before they went to London that there had been modifications. They could at least have found out what they were. Then an image of Jill Farmer came into his mind, and he remembered that if they had taken even a few minutes longer, either she would have reported them or she would have had to be killed. But no point explaining all that to Yardley, even if he thought it counted for anything.

"No, General," he admitted. "I didn't remember."

"So you see the problem."

"Yes, sir."

"I'm not complaining about the tape, David. I think it's a terrific job. First rate. But we didn't know then that Ross was dying, or that you might want to go in alone. Now that we do, we find we don't know enough. And *you* don't know enough."

Cane was despondent. He turned to Barry. "How long has Martin got, Doctor?"

"Hard to say," Barry replied. "Six weeks. Six months. Something like that. I wouldn't think longer. We might get some remission with chemotherapy, but frankly it's been my experience that once you go into the body with a scalpel, the cancer spreads very quickly."

"Does his wife know?"

Barry shook his head. "I came straight here," he said. "I'll go and tell her now."

Yardley broke in. "Perhaps *you* could, David," he said. "If you don't mind. She'll be anxious, and I want to keep Peter here a while longer. We have other business. Naturally he'll see her as soon as he's free. She'll probably have a few questions."

It was a dismissal, and Cane rose to leave. "What about Martin?" he asked. "Do we tell him?"

"Well, he's asleep now," Barry said, "and he'll be kept sedated for the rest of the day, so I don't think there'll be any chance to have a coherent word. It's up to you, of course. And Mrs. Ross. If you think he should know, then tell him. But I'd wait till tomorrow if I were you."

Cane nodded briefly. "Thanks, Doctor."

Yardley waited until the door had closed behind him before he said: "Okay, Peter, let's talk about the fallback position."

And while they did, in earnest, serious tones, Cane walked over to the hospital and found Elaine Ross staring out of the window of one of the waiting rooms in a calm, rather abstracted manner. She turned when he entered, and her face gave away nothing. Cane knew she was a strong person and that her courage would not fail her now.

"He's out of the operating room," Cane said. "The nurse says you can go and see him whenever you like. But he's still asleep."

"And it is cancer?"

"Yes. Inoperable, I'm afraid."

When he had finished telling her all Dr. Barry had said, she sat quietly for a moment, deep in thought. "I think we'll find," she said, "that what'll be worse for Martin than dying will be the failure of the mission. I wonder if you realize, David, how much the last few months have meant to him. Perhaps it's something you take for granted when you're young and so much is changing, but at our ages it's different. We were set in our ways. Our personalities had been molded and weren't developing any longer, unless you call growing old a development. And then you, David. That man loves you. He hasn't said so, not in so many words, but I can tell. It's obvious from his face when he talks about you. He loves you, and envies you, and I think he wishes that he could make himself in your image, even at this late point in his life. That was something very special you gave him. And now the chance has gone." She looked at him squarely. "I know you're very busy, and you'll probably be off on other missions before long. And I know it's difficult for a lot of people to be around while others are dying . . ." A half-amused look crossed her face and she looked at him slyly. ". . . I mean, dying slowly and by natural causes." Cane grinned, embarrassed. "But anytime you can spare to help him through the next weeks or months, we'd appreciate it very much. Both of us."

"I will, Mrs. Ross," Cane promised. "Anything I can do, you just have to ask. He's an extraordinary guy, very gutsy. He did much better than I thought he would. I was proud of him."

"One other thing. I'll say this to Dr. Barry as well when I see him, but I want you to carry the message to General Yardley if you would. Now I'm not talking about euthanasia, but I would consider it a great favor if no efforts were made to prolong Martin's life beyond its normal span. He's dying now, David, and we ought to accept that. Why not? It's as natural as being born. So let him die in peace, and with dignity, and with the minimum of pain." She paused. "If there had been the slightest chance of him recovering enough to complete the mission, I don't think there are any lengths to which both he and I would not go to see it done. But we don't have that option, so let's just . . . let him go and think to ourselves: Well, it was a nice try."

Cane took her hand. "I think that's right," he said. "I'll tell Yardley. There won't be any trouble about it. What about Martin?"

"I'll tell him as soon as he's able to listen and understand. Tomorrow, if what Dr. Barry says is correct."

"Do you want me around?"

She thought for a moment. "That would be kind," she said. "I think it would do him good to see you afterward."

"Well, I'll be in around ten. We'll talk then. You want to go in now?"

Cane escorted Elaine Ross to the intensive care ward. Two nurses sat in the center of a reception area, behind a long desk which enclosed them on three sides. Computers monitored the condition of their patients, with the readouts constantly displayed on television screens. If any patient deteriorated beyond a certain point, a warning buzzer would sound and a red light would flash above both the monitor screen and the door of the room.

The nurses smiled hello and pointed out where they could find Martin Ross.

Ross's face was ashen, and there was what looked like dried froth on his lips. A plastic tube went through his nose into his stomach, the other end terminating in a plastic bag hanging on a hook at the side beneath his mattress. An oxygen mask hung nearby for emergency use. Ross's hands lay, palms up, outside of the covers, with whole blood being transfused into one arm and a colorless drip through an intravenous line into the other.

Cane watched for several minutes, then hugged Elaine Ross and walked out.

It *had* been a nice try, he thought, but now, except for the dying, it was over.

Elaine Ross stayed by the bedside until after five that evening, waiting for Dr. Barry to arrive. She had no doubt he would come, and until she could talk to him and confirm what she already knew, she was content to sit and watch her husband, check that the drips were working properly, and learn to listen with acceptance to the low noises of pain which he made even through the sedation.

She remembered the first evening when he had told her of the mission the DIA had offered him and how, staring from her study window into the garden, she thought she had seen the possibility of his death, and her loneliness. And now it was upon her: ironically not from the Russians as she feared but from natural causes to which she had given no thought.

Meanwhile, Dr. Peter Barry remained in General Yardley's office, arguing, counterarguing, answering questions, and asking others in return. Two new files lay on Yardley's table: one related to David Michael Cane and the second to Clive Charles Lyle. Yardley kept flicking through them, examining photographs, reading aloud extracts from reports, and scratching the top of his head.

In one way there was nothing to choose between the two men. Both were fine agents, in peak physical condition. Cane smoked more than Lyle, which was a small minus. And Cane was married with a child, which was a major minus. But he was a bigger man than Lyle, which was a plus.

Finally, Peter Barry came as close to losing his temper as he ever had in his years with the DIA. "General Yardley," he said coldly. "You don't appear to have been listening to me. You don't appear to have been listening to me at all. I don't, frankly, give two cents whether Clive Lyle's more suitable because he doesn't have a family, or whether David Cane's better because he's got a bigger goddam head. In other circumstances it might indeed matter. And in personal terms, no doubt it does. In any case the whole thing makes me sick to my stomach. But that, with great respect, is not the issue. The issue is a simple one. David Cane has an Rh-positive blood group. You can see that for yourself on his file. Clive Lyle is an Rh negative. You can also see that on his file. That's where the argument stops: right at that point. I don't see how I can put it simpler than that."

At last, Yardley reluctantly accepted the argument. He'd known it all along, of course, but he couldn't avoid the struggle.

"Do I tell the President?"

"That's up to you. I myself am not a Republican, so I don't know how he'll react. He is, as far as I'm concerned, a different species of man. I imagine he'll have an orgasm for sheer joy. His beloved operation will be back on the rails."

"That's not what I'm talking about, Peter," Yardley said, giving him a reproving look. "Is it *proper* for me to tell him?"

Barry sighed. "Of *course* you mustn't tell him," he said. "*You* know that. For God's sake, Lyndon, weren't you ever in the field?"

"You know I was."

"Well, try to remember what it was like. You had to do something unpleasant, and you just went and did it. The President didn't want to know. He'd have wet himself if he *had* known. It implicates him and his high office. Nevertheless . . . . he's aware there's a fallback position, right?"

"Of course. He was pressuring me about it when I told him the verdict on Ross."

"So? What more do you want? An engraved invitation from the White House? He's as good as given you his orders. He doesn't have to spell it out. Remember what the king said about Thomas à Becket? 'Will no one rid me of this meddlesome priest?' All you have to do is phone the Oval Office, speak to his private secretary, and say, 'I think I've just hit on a way to complete the Vologda operation. Would you please tell that to the President, and ask him to leave it to me.' That's it. The end. No one will ask questions."

"I wonder. I *am* a Republican, and I'm damned if I can be sure what Reagan will do." He picked up the scrambler phone and dialed the Oval Office.

Peter Barry could tell from the glazed look that suddenly came over Yardley's face that Reagan hadn't switched the scrambler back to the outer office and had answered it himself. But he said stoically: "This is General Yardley, Mr. President. I wonder if I could speak with your private secretary. No, I'd rather not, sir. Yes . . . yes, I'll hold." Yardley and Barry exchanged wry glances. The general began talking again. "Oh yeah . . . would you please tell the President to leave Vologda to me? Tell him everything's under control. I think I know a way. No, I don't want to talk with him, thank you. Just pass on my message."

Yardley replaced the receiver and sighed. "You're right, of course," he admitted. "I shouldn't let this thing get to me. It's too bad about the cancer, it really is. Everything was going so . . . so well."

Barry stared at him compassionately. "Is there any way I can help?" he asked.

"Pep pills? Tranquilizers? No thanks, Peter. I never use them."

"Even another ramble through the options, if it helps you. We'll take it back to square one and go through again. You don't have any other candidates, I take it?"

Yardley grimaced. "I thought seriously about trying to get someone from the CIA. They've got a million."

"Well, why not? That would be a lot less painful."

"Because the CIA are as leaky as a goddam sieve, that's why. And this is just about the most secret secret we have. It *can't* get out. Not now, not for fifty years, until we're all dead and gone. I just can't trust it outside the family. It's like the Watergate thing: one small bungled special project and the President of the United States finds himself out of a job. If we crap out at any stage on our fallback position, there's going to be no way of stopping everything from coming out. Richard Nixon's going to look like Goody Two Shoes compared to us. We've got to do it ourselves. So that means David Cane, or . . . "

"Or David Cane." Barry rose to leave. "I'd stay and hold your hand a little longer, Lyndon, but I don't think you need me anymore. I'd better have a word with Mrs. Ross and look in on my patient."

"Okay, Peter. Thanks for your help."

"I won't say it's a pleasure, but it's what you pay me for."

"Yeah. Well, thanks anyway."

When Barry had gone, General Yardley studied the covers of the three files on his desk. One had the words VOLOGDA 2 stenciled on it. The other, the name CLIVE CHARLES LYLE, the third, DAVID MICHAEL CANE.

Yardley stared at them for many minutes, as if trying to conjure some magic out of the air. But as Peter Barry had pointed out so forthrightly, there was nothing to help him and nothing to hinder him either, beyond a conscience which had not been much used for years and which was now working overtime.

"God," he said, staring at the ceiling, "help us all."

Then, slowly and carefully, he took the file marked CLIVE CHARLES LYLE and dropped it into a drawer, which he locked.

The files marked VOLOGDA 2 and DAVID MICHAEL CANE he stacked on top of each other as if from now on they would be inseparable.

And then he began to read them, carefully, every word, as though for the first time.

Cane drove home, as depressed as he had ever been. The mission was in ruins, their work meaningless. And tomorrow Martin Ross, that brave old guy, would have to face the fact of his death. Cane knew that if the DIA could spare him, he would keep the vigil with Ross and his wife. It was a miserable thought. Cane was used to death but not to dying, and he realized there was a difference.

Was there something that could be salvaged now they had come this far along the road? Surely there had to be another computer expert who spoke some Russian? Give him six months, a year even, of intensive language training, a bit of unarmed combat instruction at Fairfax, and Cane would take him in. He might not be as nice a man as Ross, but he ought to be able to do the job.

But Cane was sure scenarios like that were already being discussed at the DIA. Yardley himself would be working on something, especially because of all the pressure from the White House. If there was a way to get into Vologda with a fighting chance of success, he would find it.

Timmy, his son, was playing baseball with a friend on the front lawn—at least making a good six-year-old attempt at it, lashing out wildly at a ball that went too wide or fell too short, but having fun anyway, and the sight of that made him feel a little better.

When he saw the car, Timmy dropped the bat and ran over excitedly. His dad being home was not a common event these days, and Cane hoisted him up so the strong, small arms could hug him.

"Ask your friend to come in for a Coke," Cane invited. "Is Mommy inside?"

"Yeah, she's in the kitchen, I guess."

She was. Drinking a beer and fixing dinner. A bit early for the beer, *but what the hell?* Cane thought. It was exactly what he wanted himself. She recognized how flat he was feeling. "Anything you can talk about?" she asked after she'd kissed him hello. Cane shook his head.

"Not really. A guy at the DIA is dying of cancer. I was working with him on a project."

"Oh Lord, I'm sorry. Does it mess everything up?"

"Everything," Cane confirmed.

Maryann snapped open a beer and handed the frosty can to him. "Here. Get your second wind."

He smiled weakly. "Thanks."

Cane was, as usual, either unwilling or unable to go into details, so Maryann did what she could to keep a cheerful one-sided conversation going, giving him a chance to shake his depression, but after a while when that showed no sign of working, she suggested he take Timmy to the park to play.

Cane brought the boy back when it was getting dark, and hung around the kitchen, content to be in his melancholy mood and to watch his wife going about her ordered, reassuring tasks while he adjusted to the new situation in his own disordered and cruel professional existence. He realized for the first time just how important his home had become to him. It represented stability and sanity, a base he could touch between missions to remind himself of the way ordinary Americans lived, but a base at which, ironically, he could not stay long. His job, and whatever personal demons drove him, saw to that.

In the morning Cane got a call from General Yardley asking him to drop around his office before going to the hospital to see Ross. Cane's spirits rose slightly. Perhaps Yardley had come up with an alternate plan, or at least the beginnings of one.

If he had it would certainly improve what would otherwise be a terrible day, and perhaps even Ross could take some comfort from the fact that the Vologda base might not be impregnable after all.

Cane sat in his usual chair while Yardley finished some paper work at his desk. Yardley's attitude was abstracted. He hardly glanced at Cane before motioning him to take a seat. Even when he walked over to him, he seemed to find difficulty meeting Cane's eye for more than a moment.

"You haven't seen Ross yet?"

"Yesterday, sir. After I spoke to his wife."

"Ah, yes. But not to talk to?"

"No. He was still asleep."

"Who's going to give him the news? You?"

"Mrs. Ross will. I'll see him afterward. See if I can help soften the blow."

"Good idea." Yardley stared fixedly at his nails. Cane waited for him to get to the point, say why he had called him in. The silence extended. It seemed as if Yardley was building up for something momentous.

Finally, he began, uncharacteristically diffident. "I had a long talk yesterday afternoon with Peter Barry. He seems to think there's nothing to be lost by trying to persuade Ross there's still some hope."

Cane was baffled. "What do you mean, General? Tell him he's not going to die?"

"More or less. Tell him we've got a plan up our sleeves to get him into Vologda."

Cane looked at him strangely. "Have we?"

"In a way, yes. Look, I don't want to go into it at the moment if you don't mind. It's something which is still very much in the planning stage. But we—Peter Barry and I—think if the professor could be persuaded that we were working on something rather . . . unusual . . . which might mean he gets a chance for a crack at the citadel, it could just give him the mental impetus to trigger off a remission." Yardley glanced at Cane briefly, then back at his fingers.

Cane said softly: "That sounds like bullshit to me, General, if you don't mind my saying so."

"Does it?" Yardley was neutral.

"And I think it'll sound like bullshit to Martin Ross, too."

"Why? Drowning men clutch at straws."

"Not *intelligent* drowning men. With respect. Ross's wife tells him, 'Martin, you're riddled with cancer. You'll be dead anytime between six weeks and six months.' Then I come along immediately afterward, and I say, 'Martin, General Yardley's got a secret plan to get you into Vologda. I can't tell you what it is, but it's very unusual.' And he'll say, 'What's the general planning to do? Mail them my ashes?' "

Yardley managed a faint grin. "Well, you'll have to make it a bit more convincing than that. Point one—and this is an order, mister, so listen good. You're going to give that guy some hope, and you're going to do it this morning. You're going to win an Oscar for acting if you have to. You've got to convince him that *you* believe it, and that you are personally involved in a way you can't tell him now, but that everything will become clear in time."

"I'm not hearing right," Cane said softly, staring at his boss.

"There's nothing wrong with your hearing, David. This . . . is . . . an . . . order. Do you understand?"

"Yessir."

"Now I've never told you to do anything before unless there's been a damn good reason for it. Correct?" Yardley's voice was even. His gaze flicked up at Cane and away to focus on a framed oil painting of giant redwoods on the wall.

"Correct," Cane conceded reluctantly.

"And there's a bloody good reason for what I'm telling you today. It might even get us into Vologda. And I'm *not* kidding you along. It's true. In the end we could accomplish what we set out to do."

"Get Ross down into that citadel? Dying of cancer?"

"We hope he won't . . . ah . . . be dying of cancer when we get him there."

"You have a secret miracle cure?"

"As you say. Now it's your job to persuade Ross that something is being planned and that you have a hand in it. In fact, you are going to tell him that *you've* actually suggested something which you're not going to disclose at the moment, but which ought to make it possible for him to get into Vologda."

"By himself, of course."

"No." Yardley gave a bleak smile. "You'll be going with him."

"He won't buy it, General," Cane said flatly.

Yardley's voice raised. "He *will* buy it, David. He'll buy it because *you're* going to tell him it's true, and he trusts you. For Christ's sake, is it so difficult?"

"Yessir. You're asking me to lie to a dying man who, like you said, trusts me to tell him the truth. I wouldn't mind if there was some purpose to it, but to give Martin Ross a flicker of hope and then stand by while the cancer does its work seems . . . inhuman."

"I'll say it again, David. There *is* some purpose in it, even if you don't know what that purpose is at the moment. And it *is* the truth. We *are* working on something. We believe it will get him into Russia. We can't say what it is yet. Not even to you. But we want Ross to believe it, to give himself a mental boost, and give *us* time to make the final preparations."

"Well, sir, why don't I just tell him that—that you're working on something or other and you're quite hopeful, but I don't know what the hell it is?"

Yardley shook his head emphatically. "That is exactly what you must *not* say," he stressed. "For the purposes of this . . . exercise . . . it is vital that you identify yourself closely with the plan. I repeat, David, this is an order."

It was the third time Yardley had said that, so Cane, working on the rule of thumb that what he said three times was true, didn't push it further. This was still the army.

"Yessir."

Yardley seemed to relax. At last, he managed to look at Cane levelly. "How much does the Vologda thing mean to you, David?" he asked bluntly. "I mean, is it just a job? Are you just doing it because you're assigned to it? Or is there something deeper, some commitment?" His stare was unwavering now.

Cane thought for a moment. It was an odd question coming from Yardley, who usually maintained it wasn't the job of any DIA operative to concern himself with the philosophy behind a particular mission, which was part of that wider picture only the boys at the Pentagon could see and which everyone trusted looked clearer and cleaner when taken as a whole than it appeared while inspecting one of the murky individual pieces. The commitment of men like Cane was supposed to be only to the successful completion of the mission, while those higher up and better qualified concerned themselves with the moral issues.

But Cane had grown to care about Vologda. He liked the nonviolent philosophy behind the mission, and if they pulled it off, it would be an overwhelming coup. They'd have literally saved the West.

So Cane said carefully: "It would have been the most important thing I'd ever done."

"Worth any risk? Any price?" Yardley pressed.

"Yes, I think so."

"Even if you died for the mission, would you have felt it worthwhile?"

Cane frowned. What the hell was Yardley driving at? "Well, sure," he said. "I risk my life on a lot of the missions I go on. We all do. You know that."

"Yes, but a lot of it, comparatively speaking, is garbage, isn't it?"

That was quite an admission from the general. Cane wished he had a tape recorder. The others wouldn't believe their ears.

Cane grinned suddenly. "Comparatively speaking," he said.

"Whereas Vologda isn't?"

"No. Vologda is in a category of its own," Cane agreed.

"Worth dying for, would you say?"

Cane began feeling embarrassed. "Well, I guess so, yes. But I don't plan on dying so easily, General. If you come up with your magic cure for Martin Ross, I'll give them a damn good run for their money."

"But if . . ." Yardley went on inexorably. " . . . you knew you were going to take Ross into the Soviet Union, and you had no hope of getting out again alive, would you still do it?"

The conversation was getting heavy, and Cane shifted to being both embarrassed and uncomfortable. "I'm not a no-hoper, sir," he said flatly. "I believe there's always hope, and I'll fight for it."

"So you rule out the concept of making the supreme sacrifice?" Yardley watched him intently.

"Do you mean in general, sir, or me in particular?"

"You, David. You in particular. Would you lay down your life for your country?"

Cane thought. "Yes, sir, I guess I would," he said finally. "If it was necessary."

Yardley nodded. "Thanks for looking in, David. You'd better go see the professor. And don't forget what you've got to tell him."

Cane walked down the long corridor to the elevator, shaking his head bemusedly. "Goddam, goddam," he said aloud. "What in the name of God is going on?"

He'd never seen Yardley in a mood like that before, and he'd been with the DIA quite a few years. Perhaps he was cracking under pressure from Reagan. Well, Cane thought, an order is an order, and no doubt it would all become clear in time. He hoped it would not be at Martin Ross's expense. When a dying man rests everything on a false hope and then sees it snatched away, it is a needless cruelty.

Cane stood uncertainly at the door of the hospital room watching Elaine Ross beside the bed, talking earnestly to her husband. If this was the moment of truth, Cane didn't want to intrude. And he felt uneasy about what he had been ordered to say.

Ross spotted him and said something to Elaine, who turned and beckoned him with a smile. Cane wished he'd brought flowers or something. Ross's lips twisted into a kind of welcome. He was obviously in considerable pain. He was no longer being given blood, but the IV drip was still in his arm and the plastic tube was up his nose.

Cane smiled hello to Elaine, then placed his hand softly on Ross's

cheek in a gesture of understanding and comfort. Ross pressed his
face into it.

"Hi, David." His voice was soft and his mouth was obviously very
dry. He was having difficulty talking, partly because his tongue was
sticking to the roof of his mouth.

"How are you feeling?"

"Sore. Sad. Sit down, David. Good of you to come."

Elaine said: "I've told him the news."

There was a wet shine to Ross's eyes. "Yes," he said. "That's a
tough break, isn't it? All that work for nothing. I've already said I'm
sorry, haven't I?"

Cane nodded. "Many times. But there's nothing to be sorry about.
It's one of those things. I couldn't have asked anyone to give it a
more gutsy try than you did." The message he had been ordered to
pass on flashed into his mind, and he tried to find the heart to deliver
it. He opened his mouth to speak, but no words came.

Elaine said: "Dr. Barry's been to see him this morning. He didn't
say much. Martin's got a bit of a temperature, and they say they want
to start chemotherapy in a few days."

Ross shook his head. "I told him I don't want any of that crap. I'm
dying. Chemotherapy's not going to stop me dying, so why do it?
Why do I want all my hair to fall out, for God's sake? Let them use
their drugs on someone who's going to benefit."

Another possible opening. Cane took a breath and plunged in.
"My friend," he said, "I've never given you a bum steer, have I?"

"No," Ross agreed. "You've been straight with me, David."

"Well, I just want to tell you something, and I don't want any
questions afterward because I won't be able to answer them. Okay?"

"Okay."

"I've had an idea. I've thought of a possible way of getting you
well enough so that we can get into Vologda and do the mission." It
sounded even lamer than Cane had feared. Ross looked bewildered.

"Now he turns into a joker," Ross said, trying to smile again.
"David, it's okay. I know the prognosis. I'm going to be dead in six
months. I'll be very lucky to leave this hospital alive, even for a
couple of days in Princeton."

Cane was aware of Elaine Ross gazing at him reproachfully.

"Just listen to me," Cane insisted. "You can believe it or not as
you like, but it's the truth. There is a plan. I suggested it, so it's my
plan. And it gives us a chance of getting you over to that computer."

"And you can't say what it is."

"No. You're going to have to wait and see."

"Or wait and not see," Elaine Ross observed dryly.

"Let's drop it now," Cane said. "I don't have anything more to say about it. Except to repeat I've never given you a bum steer before and I'm not giving you one now. Okay? Wait and see."

Thirty minutes later, when Cane excused himself from a visit that seemed to have lasted for hours, Elaine Ross walked with him to the door. It had been one of the most emotionally draining times of Cane's life. After he had delivered his idiot bedside message, he was at a loss for anything else to say, and both Ross and his wife were looking at him as if he had suddenly grown horns. What could they be thinking? A man they trusted, coming out with garbage like that.

Elaine Ross seemed to be considering what she should say. She turned to him in the corridor, her eyes frank and penetrating. "Now, what was that all about, David?"

"Mrs. Ross, I wish there was more I could tell you, but there isn't."

"It's not something you just made up because you were feeling embarrassed or sorry for Martin?"

"No, ma'am. I didn't make it up. It's real."

"Some sort of organ transplant?" she persisted.

"I really can't say. Not now. I'm . . . under orders not to go into it."

"It can't be a transplant. Surgeons decide about those, not DIA operatives. Anyway, Martin's too far gone for that sort of thing."

"I wish I could help you further, I really do. All I can ask is that you trust me. Just trust me. I've got something up my sleeve, and I think it'll surprise you."

Elaine Ross gave a short laugh. "It'll certainly do that," she said. She thought for a moment. "If you discover, later on, that this . . . plan of yours isn't going to work, you will tell us, won't you?" she asked. "I know Martin's trying hard to disregard what you said, but the human mind is a funny thing. It sometimes latches on to the most futile hope and builds it up into something which can never be justified. And then, it's dashed . . ." She put a hand on Cane's arm. "I don't want that to happen to Martin. Not another disappointment. If your plan comes to nothing, promise you'll tell us immediately? Promise."

"I promise," Cane said, feeling more despicable than he had for a long time.

He went back to his office, sick at heart. Yardley had better come up with something good, he thought, or I'm going to transfer out of here. Back to the real army, and a world where people are sane and don't play psychological games with those who are dying. It wasn't the first time Cane had considered returning to a regiment, but it was the first time it had seemed a relatively attractive option. Goddam Yardley.

Cane found an envelope on his desk with a note inside from Peter Barry asking him to drop around to the clinic for a medical checkup before lunch, if possible.

Cane cursed. He had just come from the hospital, and now he'd have to go back. But it would give him a chance to have a word with Barry and see if he could get more sense out of him than he'd managed from Yardley.

Barry was sitting in his office, neat in a pinstripe suit, and he appeared to be waiting for Cane.

"Thanks for coming over, David," he said. "I have to give you a thorough checkup."

"Afraid I've caught cancer?" Cane asked, more churlishly than he intended.

"VD's more like it." He pointed to a screen at the side. "Change over there," he said. "You'll find a hospital gown."

Cane emerged after a few moments, wearing the white cotton gown tied at the sides with tape. "What's this all about?" he asked. "It's only three months since my last medical."

Barry glanced over Cane's previous medical records. "Mmmm, I know that. This is a special."

"Whose orders?"

"Yardley."

"Oh. Listen, Peter. About Yardley. He had me in his office this morning for a very strange talk. Claimed he'd got some plan worked out with you to get Martin Ross into Vologda. Now what the hell's going on? Will you tell me, please? Has the good general finally flipped his lid?"

"Did you tell Ross?"

"Yeah. Sure I told Ross. I had no option. He ordered me *three* times."

"Did Ross believe you?"

"Of course he didn't believe me. He's not a fool. Although . . ." Cane paused, remembering what Elaine Ross had said, ". . . maybe he's ready to grasp at straws. I don't know. It made *me* feel pretty sick though. Now level with me, Peter. What's going on?"

Barry looked at him calmly. "Just what Yardley said. There is a plan, but we can't tell you what it is."

"It's not a joke?"

"No, it's certainly not a joke."

"And it's going to get Ross into some sort of condition so he can go into Vologda?"

"That's right. Now there's nothing more I can tell you, so can we get on with the examination, please?"

Cane shrugged and began answering a long list of questions. Then Barry came around to the other side of his desk, inspected his throat, and looked into his ears.

Cane lay on a couch while his heart was checked with an ECG. Barry prodded and probed him with great thoroughness. He tested his blood pressure and extracted 100 ccs of blood from his arm, and asked for, and got, a urine sample. He took his time and seemed almost to be waiting for something.

Finally, Barry sighed. "Okay, David," he said, "You seem to be in great shape. As good as I've ever seen in any man. No, don't get up, please. Lie there. I've got to give you a jab."

Cane grunted. "I thought I was up to date on everything. What is it?"

"A booster," Barry said dismissively. He tapped a glass ampule twice against the metal side of a cabinet and snapped the top off. He drew the liquid up the needle and into the syringe.

Barry inflated the blood-pressure bandage around Cane's bicep and had him make a fist so that the veins protruded in the crook of his arm. He swabbed clean a section of skin.

"This won't hurt," he said.

"How often have I said that to people?" Cane asked.

"Mmmm. I remember." The needle slid smoothly into the vein, and Barry pressed the plunger. When it was done he pulled it out and dropped it into a basin. "Just lie there for a minute," he said. "Don't move."

Cane did as he was told, staring at the acoustic tiles on the ceiling and thinking: *He doesn't give a bad injection;* he didn't have time to notice or be surprised when, without warning, he was engulfed by darkness.

Peter Barry lifted Cane's eyelids, checked his pulse, tested for reflexes. Then he went to the telephone and called General Yardley.

"He's under," he said tersely without preliminaries. "What now?"

There was a pause before Yardley said: "Go ahead."

Barry hung up without a word. The couch on which David Cane lay was on wheels, and Barry pushed it through the double doors at the other end of his office, down the empty corridor to a small operating room, one of three in the hospital. This, too, was empty.

He stopped next to the anesthesia machine, put a black rubber mask over Cane's mouth and nose, and turned the valves to pipe in a mixture of nitrous oxide and oxygen.

There was a movement outside. Barry glanced up to see that Yardley had arrived.

"How's it going?" the general asked.

Barry shrugged. "Help me get him on the operating table," he said. They pushed the couch into position and hefted Cane's body over.

"What do I do now?" Yardley asked.

"Nothing."

Barry connected David Cane to a cardiac monitor and watched the electronic blip trace across the screen of the oscilloscope.

The things he would need were already assembled, waiting. He injected Cane with d-tubocurarine, which paralyzed and relaxed his muscles so that he stopped breathing. Barry pulled the mask off Cane's face and, working swiftly, went into his mouth with a laryngoscope to push the tongue out of the way and clear a passage to the trachea. He squirted in some anesthetic and inserted an endotracheal tube, the other end of which he attached to the rubber hose leading from three gas tanks. He squeezed the ventilating bag. David Cane's chest rose. He released it, and the chest fell. He carried on like that for several minutes, until the paralyzing drug wore off and Cane was able to breathe for himself.

"Shouldn't I have scrubbed up or something?" Yardley asked.

"We're not operating, Lyndon," Barry said flatly. "I hardly think it's necessary."

He checked Cane's condition. His blood pressure had fallen to 90/60 because of the anesthetic, and his pulse rate was 70 per minute. The blip on the oscilloscope was regular and strong.

Peter Barry turned his face to Yardley. "Well?" he asked quietly. "You want to go ahead?"

Yardley closed his eyes. "We must!" he whispered. "We have no choice!"

When he opened his eyes again, Barry was turning a valve on

another gas tank and shutting off the oxygen. Yardley found he couldn't look at Cane, unconscious on the table, so he stared at what Barry was doing and at the green blip on the oscilloscope.

Cane's heart rate began speeding up. His brain and body were hungry for oxygen and were being fed instead a mixture of nitrous oxide and carbon monoxide. The room seemed filled with the urgent beep-beep-beep-beep of the monitor. The oscilloscope began to blip prematurely, as if Cane was on the point of a heart attack. His blood pressure fell sharply, and then Cane ceased to breathe by himself.

Barry automatically stepped forward to compress the ventilation bag.

After a moment he stepped back, turned off the carbon-monoxide cylinder, and increased the oxygen.

Cane's heartbeat on the cardiac monitor returned to normal. Barry eased off on the nitrous oxide.

"Make yourself useful," he said to Yardley. "Squeeze this for him."

Yardley stood beside Cane, depressing and releasing the ventilation bag, watching the rise and fall of the young man's chest, and looking, although he tried to stop himself, at his face.

Barry went around to the other side of the operating table and lifted the lid of Cane's eye. He shone a penlight into the pupil. It was so dilated, it almost filled the cornea. It showed no response.

David Michael Cane was clinically dead. They had destroyed his brain.

13

MARYANN CANE SAT AT HER HUS-
band's bedside holding his hand, her eyes flicking from his motionless
face over to the equipment that monitored his functions and
breathed for him. Peter Barry had spent a long time after David
came out of the operating room explaining what the screens showed
and what they meant.

His heart was strong: a regular, comforting blip on the green
screen of the oscilloscope. But the EEG waves were almost flat. Long
sheets of paper unwound slowly from the monitor and collected in a
bin behind it: the written record of the fact that there was no longer
any activity in his brain. It had been going on for five days now, from
that surreal afternoon when General Yardley arrived at their home
to break the news that David had had a stroke and was being operated on at the DIA hospital.

After that, and a breakneck drive into Washington, she had to wait
four more hours of nervous, restless pacing before they brought him
down from the operating room. She saw the procession pass in the
corridor.

David's head was wrapped in bandages. IV lines ran from plastic
packs of blood and clear fluid into his arms and neck. A tube came

from his mouth, and a doctor, walking alongside, rhythmically compressed and released a ventilation bag.

Although she had promised herself that whatever happened she would be brave, Maryann could do nothing to stop the tears that suddenly blurred her vision and rolled down her face, nor could she control the trembling of her body.

She wept for several minutes until she became aware of someone else in the waiting room, and as she pulled herself together with an effort, she saw Dr. Peter Barry watching her quietly.

"I'm sorry," Maryann said, wiping roughly at her eyes with a handkerchief and smearing a black streak of mascara across her cheek. "I promised myself I wouldn't do that."

"It doesn't matter."

She focused on Barry and found comfort in what she saw. He was the perfect image of a doctor. Middle-aged, calm, in control. He was good-looking in a rather suave way, with thick silver hair and quiet brown eyes. And he dressed impeccably. David had always told her that DIA doctors were the best in the country, and she could see what he meant.

"Mrs. Cane, I'm Dr. Barry," he said, extending his hand. It was warm and strong.

"How's David, Doctor?"

"Would you like to sit down?" They settled onto a sofa. "Your husband has had a spontaneous intracranial hemorrhage," Barry said. "A stroke, in other words. We operated to locate the clot and remove it"—he paused—"but I'm afraid the prognosis isn't good."

Maryann waited for the blow to fall.

"We know where the clot is, but we can't get at it. Not without an unacceptable risk. In any case, it's too late."

"David's not dead, Doctor. I saw him."

"No, he's in an intensive care ward. But I'm afraid the hemorrhage was so massive it caused very considerable brain damage. Your husband is in a coma, and it's unlikely he'll ever emerge from it. I'm sorry."

Maryann could feel the tears starting again, and she fought them back. "Is there no chance?" she asked, hearing the shakiness of her voice.

Barry said very gently: "I wouldn't like to give you false hope, Mrs. Cane. The fact is that David's brain appears to be gone. The hemorrhage just . . . destroyed the cells. It's a bit like a child's sand castle when the tide comes in. He can't even breathe for himself. The EEG—which measures electrical impulses from his brain—is almost completely flat. In my opinion, David is already clinically dead. His body functions only because it's on a life-support system, so when you see him you'll find his heartbeat is strong. But if that support was withdrawn, the heart would just stop."

Maryann looked at him with anguish so utter that Barry, who thought he was inured, felt his own heart jolt. "But can't it heal? He's a strong man! Young! His life ahead . . ." She could carry on no longer and wept again.

Barry took her hand in both of his and held it tightly. "The brain does not repair itself," he explained quietly. "Once the cells are gone, they are never replaced. However, we don't make any final decisions in cases like this until several days have passed. We watch and monitor constantly. If there is anything that can be done to save your husband, Mrs. Cane, rest assured we will do it."

Maryann whispered: "Thank you." After a pause she asked: "How did it happen?"

"In my office," Peter Barry said. "Your husband felt a headache coming on suddenly. In fact, he said he felt as if someone had hit him. He came to see me right away. His neck was stiff and the pain was becoming worse. Classic symptoms. As I was examining him, he collapsed and went into a coma. Obviously he received immediate emergency attention. It couldn't have been faster, happening just like that in the hospital itself. But, as I say, the sea had rushed in and we could do nothing. It's extraordinary how these things happen. Superficially your husband was in perfect shape. Splendid physique. Robust constitution. But deep inside his brain, a tiny flaw. Perhaps it was something that had been with him from birth. Or it could have been a lesion which developed as a result of . . . his work. Only a postmortem will tell us."

Maryann turned her head away.

"I'm sorry," Barry said again. "Would you like to see him now? Of course, you can stay as long as you want. We'll put an extra bed in his room if you like."

"Thank you."

"You have a son, don't you? Timothy?"

"Timmy, yes."

"Are there friends or relatives who can look after him? Should I ask General Yardley to have someone stay with him?"

"He's with friends. They'll look after him."

"Well, if there's anything we can do to help on that score, don't hesitate to ask."

"Thank you, Doctor. You're very kind."

Peter Barry put a comforting hand on Maryann's shoulder and guided her down the corridor to the intensive care unit. Cane was two rooms from Martin Ross.

He lay alone with his machines, his tubes, and his drips. Maryann gently touched his face and found the skin warm and familiar. She saw the nick on his neck where he had cut himself shaving that morning and next to it, going into a vein and held in place with a bandage, a needle connected to an IV tube.

She kissed Cane's cheek and said very distinctly into his ear: "Hello, my darling." The large square machine beside the bed hissed in . . . sssssssss . . . and out . . . sssssssss. Cane's chest rose and fell. "David, my darling. Can you hear me? It's Maryann." In . . . sssssssss . . . out . . . sssssssss. The cardiac monitor bleeped like a far-off Sputnik. She stroked his cheek with loving fingers. "Timmy sends his love," she said loudly, in case something was penetrating the destroyed cells, and suddenly she was weeping uncontrollably, her face pressed against his until the tears soaked the pillow. She kneaded his unresponsive hand with great strength.

Peter Barry turned on his heel and strode down along the corridor, almost colliding with a medicine cart in his anxiety to put distance between himself and the results of the day's work. He touched his forehead with a silk handkerchief. In his own office he broke the rule of a lifetime by taking a tranquilizer, and it was twenty minutes before he felt ready to return to the ward.

Maryann Cane had stopped weeping, but her head was still pressed to the pillow, her fingers stroking her husband's cheek, and she was staring at him with complete absorption.

"Is there anything I can get you, Mrs. Cane?" Barry asked. "A couple of Valium might be helpful."

She shook her head. "No thank you," she said. "I'm all right now."

"Are you sure? It'll help you get over the shock."

"No. I have to do it by myself if I can."

"As you wish." Barry looked across automatically to check the monitors, then back at Maryann. He had to get her away from Cane, stop her touching him like that. "I wonder if I could explain something to you," he said loudly, and when she looked up, he added, "Over here, if you don't mind."

He took her in detail through the various components of the life-support system, explaining the obvious things like the breathing machine and the less obvious ones like the electroencephalogram, which, as he had indicated earlier, showed that virtually no electrical activity was taking place in her husband's brain. Barry pulled from the bin behind the EEG the written evidence that this had been the case ever since Cane was brought down from the operating room—a long roll of paper showing virtually flat pen tracings.

"The EEG," Barry said, "measures the overall state of awareness of the brain. We've attached electrodes to your husband's scalp—they're under the bandages, of course, but there you can see the leads to them. The brain cells—the neurons—put out electrical voltages when they're working, which show up on the EEG. Now, an alert brain would make a tracing of peaks and troughs." His fingers sketched a squiggle on the paper, then he gestured to the reality of Cane's reading.

He pointed to the drips suspended above the bed. "That, of course, is whole blood, which he needs to make up losses during the operation. And that clear bag on the other side is a dextrose solution. Naturally your husband can't take anything by mouth. Now that we've got IV lines established, we can feed him, replace fluids, and administer injections into that rubber connector there."

Barry indicated a plastic tube curling down from under the sheet into a plastic bag hanging below the mattress. "And that's for urine. We keep a close watch on how much we collect there for signs of kidney failure."

Maryann nodded numbly. All this equipment. And David, unresponsive, unmoving.

"Outside in the reception area, everything that happens to your husband is being monitored on a television screen. If he suffered a heart attack, for example, or any of his vital functions were affected, a warning light and a buzzer would alert the staff on duty."

"It's very impressive."

"Yes, it is. This is one of the best-equipped hospitals in the United States, Mrs. Cane. We have access to the top neurosurgeons. No effort or expense is spared here. You know what the DIA are like."

"Yes, I know."

"When we were trying to remove the clot in your husband's brain, there were three neurosurgeons up there, advising and assisting. He couldn't have been in more competent hands. But . . ." Barry spread his hands philosophically.

"How long will you keep him on these machines, Dr. Barry?" Maryann asked.

"As long as necessary. We don't like to rush these things."

"But you think David's dead already."

"Yes. Yes, I do think that. But, nonetheless, we won't take any chances. It isn't only me who has to be satisfied. Three other independent doctors have to concur. That's the DIA rule, which is even stricter than the law. And *you* have to agree."

"Before what?"

"Before we . . . withdraw the life-support system."

"Pull the plug?"

A pause. "Precisely."

"And if I don't agree?"

"Then it stays on, for years if necessary. There are coma patients in the United States who have been on life-support systems for twelve years . . . sometimes longer."

"With no change in their condition?"

"No. No change."

"Is there never a change in someone like David? Not even a slight change?"

Barry pursed his lips. "Occasionally there are minor improvements. Some parts of the brain may not have been destroyed and function may return. But there'll be no miracle, I can assure you."

"Well, what does it mean, then, if function returns . . . ?"

"I mean perhaps he'll start breathing by himself. Maybe his eyes will open. But that's all. We'll never know if he sees anything. He won't speak or eat. He'll be . . . that unfortunate expression, a vegetable."

Maryann covered her face with her hands. The breathing machine hissed out . . . sssssssss . . . and in . . . sssssssss . . . while images piled into her mind. David laughing with Timmy. David sitting, melancholy, in the kitchen only last night, following her with his eyes. The fact that they had not made love: their last chance. She dropped her hands, and her eyes focused on the plastic bag hanging from the side of the bed, a small collection of yellow liquid in the bottom.

That was five days ago. The bag filled, and was changed, and filled again, and was changed. She seldom noticed the hiss of the respirator, and even the steady low-frequency beeping of the cardiac monitor faded in her consciousness as she became used to the hospital noises and routine.

Every few hours, nurses came to change David's position to prevent bedsores. They rolled him onto his left side, propping pillows against his back. His body remained limp. Later, another shift rolled him onto his right side. They undid the tapes on the white hospital gown to expose his broad, muscled back, which they rubbed with alcohol. Later still they settled him flat on the bed again. David did not stir, and neither the cardiac monitor nor the EEG registered change.

When she was alone with him, Maryann experimented, talking loudly into his ear about important, personal things, then hurried over to the EEG traces on the slowly unfolding paper to see if anything was awakening in his brain. There was nothing.

She spent the nights in David's room, in a bed beside his, falling into exhausted, haunted sleep while the monitor beeped, low and regular, and the respirator blew and relaxed, sssssssss . . . sssssssss, a sound that sometimes comforted her because it meant David was breathing and his body was still warm, but sometimes, particularly in the moments before sleep or upon waking, it seemed malevolent, as if death were with them in the ward.

Dr. Barry visited every evening, but spent little time. Cane's condition was unchanged, and that being established, there was nothing to do, and still less to say.

Maryann had left the hospital only once, to see Timmy at a friend's house where he was staying, unaware that anything had happened to his father. He was used to David being away for long, unexplained absences and asked no questions. Maryann realized with a shock how much alike David and his son were. She had been aware of the resemblance before, but now that David was . . . sick . . . it hit her with new force. Their coloring was identical, and although Timmy was still too small for his nose to have formed properly, his face was almost a carbon copy. It was clear from the size of the child's hands and feet that he would grow to be a big man. Some of the mannerisms—his way of holding his shoulders, his walk, certain gestures —were David's, part of the miraculous, detailed genetic programming he, too, would someday pass on to his own children.

As soon as she had established that Timmy was all right, Maryann drove back to the DIA hospital to continue her vigil. Nothing had changed when she returned except that the urine bag was fuller and the dextrose drip had almost finished.

From time to time the nurses brought her coffee and she drank, staring blankly at the oscilloscope, hardly hearing the noises that confirmed her husband was still theoretically alive.

When she finished the coffee she took the cup to the reception area and thanked the nurses. They were friendly and willing to talk, if she wanted to, although they never volunteered information about David or inquired how she found him. They had all that information on the monitor screens, of course. They seemed more concerned about how she was, and whether there was anything they could do to make things easier for her.

She discovered that one of the nurses was leaving soon to get married, while the other was divorced and swore she would never make the same mistake twice. It did Maryann good to have her mind taken off her own troubles, and she began to spend forty minutes at a time talking to them. They brought her books from the hospital library so she would have something to distract her during the long hours at the bedside of her unmoving husband. Sometimes she sat at the central reception desk, watching them working in one of the other wards, turning patients, administering injections, and she noticed that even in the cases of people who were unconscious, the nurses always spoke loudly and cheerily to them as if they might be able to hear. But to David, when they turned him or gave him a bed bath, they said nothing. The distinction had been drawn between the maybe living and the clinically dead.

On the fifth afternoon, as she exchanged small talk with the nurses, a woman in her late fifties emerged from another intensive care unit to return her coffee cup and stayed for a few moments to join the discussion about a new television series.

Maryann had seen her from a distance several times, and they had nodded greetings to each other in the mornings. The woman had a kind, handsome face, and was obviously highly intelligent. There was an alertness and an understanding about her which were immediately apparent. She dressed in understated expensive classic clothes. If she had worn a white coat, Maryann would have guessed she was a specialist of some sort. The fact that she did not, and the strain that was sometimes evident on her face, indicated she, too, was keeping a vigil.

The nurses on duty assumed the women had already met, so finally it was Elaine Ross who introduced herself and Maryann who replied.

"Cane," said Elaine Ross. "I know a David Cane. I don't suppose you're related?"

"He's my husband," Maryann said.

"Oh my dear! How nice to meet you at last. Where is David? We haven't seen him for several days, and Martin is always asking about him. He hasn't been sent off on an assignment somewhere, has he?"

Maryann shook her head mutely, and she found her eyes filling with tears. She thought she had gotten herself under control, yet she was constantly being taken unawares. She gestured to the ward. "He's in there," she said in a barely audible voice.

Elaine looked bewildered. "David is sick?" she asked.

This time Maryann couldn't reply at all. She sat motionless, summoning all her reserves to prevent herself from breaking down totally. The nurses watched sympathetically. One of them caught Elaine's eye and nodded.

"May I . . . go in?"

Without waiting for a reply, Elaine walked the few steps into the ward and stood at the door, staring in at the still figure in the bed. No one had to explain the life-support system to her. She went to the EEG, glanced at the unwinding paper, then pulled yards of it out of the box into which it had neatly folded itself and saw the virtually flat tracings. Blood drained from her face. It was beyond belief. Not David.

"Oh my dear," she murmured in genuine anguish. There was a movement in the doorway, and she glanced up to see Maryann standing there, almost defiant.

"When did this happen?" Elaine asked softly.

"Five days ago. Last Wednesday. He had a stroke at about lunchtime. It . . . they say it . . . destroyed . . ." She wasn't able to complete the sentence. Her voice trailed away.

"Oh my dear, I'm so very, very sorry. Martin, too . . . I don't know how to break it to him. David was a marvelous, magnificent man." Was. David was. "He and Martin were very close, as perhaps you know."

Maryann shook her head. No, she didn't know. "Martin . . .?"

"My husband. Professor Martin Ross. He and David have been working on an assignment together for months now."

A memory came back. "Your husband has cancer," Maryann said.

"Yes. Poor Martin is dying now."

"David told me. The last day he was at home. He came back very depressed. But I never knew any of the details of what they were doing."

"Neither do I," Elaine lied. "You know what these men are like. But I do know it made such a difference to my Martin. He . . . well, he almost worshipped David." She paused. "What do the doctors say?"

Maryann took a breath and forced herself to reply straightforwardly.

"That there's no hope. He's in a coma, and he won't ever recover."

Elaine gestured to the equipment. "The EEG's been like this the whole time?"

"Yes. Five days."

Elaine Ross walked over to Cane's bedside and ran a hand gently down his cheek. Maryann was surprised to see there were tears in her eyes, and she looked away because of her own tenuous hold on self-control.

After a moment Maryann said: "Do you think they're right?"

"Who?"

"The doctors. Dr. Barry."

"I'm afraid it does look like that," Elaine said. "Brain cells don't recover. Not like the rest of the body. There's no real regeneration. I take it he can't breathe for himself at all?"

"No."

"What's going to happen?"

"I don't know. Dr. Barry says he thinks David is clinically dead, although the machines could keep him alive for years if necessary."

"Providing he doesn't get pneumonia."

"Is he likely to?"

"Respiratory infections are very common in coma patients," Elaine said. "They can be treated with antibiotics, and quite often they respond, but pneumonia usually gets them in the end."

"Are you a doctor?"

"Yes, but not of medicine. I know a little about the subject because my mother died a few years ago at the ripe old age of seventy-eight. She was in a coma for almost a year."

Maryann's interest was aroused. "How did you cope with that?"

Elaine looked at her cautiously. "You really want to know?"

"Please."

"Well, every case differs, so what was right for me isn't necessarily right for anyone else. But I wished they had pulled the plug on her. It was terrible. A total waste of expensive, scarce resources on an old lady whose time was up and whose prospects of recovery were nil. They were anguishing months for the whole family. It dragged on and on, seemingly without end. When finally she got pneumonia and wasn't responding to antibiotics, I almost cheered. There comes a point when there's no dignity left. A dead old lady was being kept theoretically alive by machines. I wanted the doctors to switch off the life-support system. They wanted to do it too. But my younger brother had some doubts. He didn't want a decision like that on his conscience. So they fought like tigers to save her while I prayed that God would be merciful and let her die."

"It must have been awful."

"It was. One of the most grueling experiences of my life. And now Martin's dying. Both he and I are determined that he'll go with dignity. He's refused chemotherapy because there's no point, and he's given instructions that nothing must be done to keep him alive. All he wants are injections to kill the pain when it gets too bad. Otherwise it becomes bizarre and hateful for everyone. If there's a chance —fine, one fights for it. If there isn't, we don't see the point in postponing the inevitable at an enormous cost in money, facilities, and, most important of all, the tremendous toll it takes on the dying and the living."

"How long has your husband got?" Maryann asked, a little timidly.

"They say six months. But it could be six weeks. We'll just wait and see."

Maryann said: "I'm very sorry."

"Don't be. It's natural. It happens to us all. The thing we're mostly sad about—and poor Martin still agonizes over it—is the . . . the mission he was working on with your husband. It meant so much to him. And now David's . . ."—she gestured to the man in the bed, motionless except for the rise and fall of his chest—"like that, it seems the whole thing was jinxed. Perhaps it never was meant to be."

"No. Perhaps not. You don't know what they were trying to do?"

"No, I'm afraid not. The DIA code of secrecy, you know."

"David didn't tell me anything either. I wish I knew. There's so much of his life I was excluded from."

"It's probably better that way, my dear. Now I must get back to Martin and give him the sad news about David."

Maryann nodded and watched her leave. There was truth in what she said. David was unresponsive, and he never would respond. Everyone seemed to agree on that. There would have to be a miracle for him to recover—and recover properly, not just to the point where he was a breathing vegetable. Could she wait for a miracle? Could she keep the vigil by his bed for another few weeks until Timmy's demands reduced her visits to an hour a day, then an hour a week, an hour a month, for years; unable to pick up the threads of her own dislocated life? Peter Barry thought David was clinically dead. Three others yet had to agree. And she had to agree. And then the machines could be turned off. They would all formally accept the fact that stared them in the face. David was already dead, and modern science was keeping his body going unnaturally. Dignity, replaced by futility.

The cardiac monitor continued its low beep . . . beep . . . beep. The EEG tracings unwound without significant peaks and troughs. The dextrose dripped into the IV tube. Urine dribbled from a catheter inserted in David's penis into a plastic bag. The automatic respirator hissed sssssssss . . . and his chest rose, sssssssss . . . and his chest fell.

And it would be like this, with occasional alarms when pneumonia or some other problem struck, for years and years and years.

Maryann found herself staring at the wall plugs to which the life-support system was connected. The ordinary switches which would bring everything to a swift close.

How simple it would be to walk four, five paces from where she was standing and just flick them. One, and the cardiac monitor would fall silent. Two, and the breathing machine would end its obscene hissing. Three . . .

The warmth would go from David's body, and he would be taken away and buried, to live on in her heart as a man, not as a sapping, scarring terminal experience, remembered for its horror and its absence of dignity.

Maryann took the five paces over to the wall, touched a switch with the toe of her shoe.

And found she couldn't do it. She shrank from the act. Not now. Not yet. Not by herself.

She would wait and talk to Dr. Barry when he made his evening rounds. She would engage him in conversation, discuss the options once again, and unless something had changed, she would ask him to end the charade and let David die in peace.

With that decision made, she felt a weight lift from her shoulders.

Two rooms away, Martin Ross wept.

14

MARYANN CANE'S ANNOUNCEMENT came as a surprise to Peter Barry. He had not expected it so soon, and both he and Yardley had been prepared to wait at least another two weeks. Then if she showed no signs of moving in that direction, they would arrange for Cane's "death" from other causes: an infection, a heart attack. But now it had come, and he was both glad and at the same time not quite ready.

He told her it would take an additional day or two before the independent examinations could be completed and the final decisions made. There was no rush, he stressed. Everyone needed to be fully satisfied they were doing the right thing. But he made it clear that he personally applauded her bravery and common sense.

Barry knew, however, that the quicker they could proceed to the next part of the plan, the better it would be all around. As far as Ross was concerned, there was always the danger of metastasis—the cancer spreading to other parts of the body, perhaps even to the brain.

But Ross himself still had to be mentally prepared for the next step, and work on this—apart from the hint Cane had dropped at his last meeting—still had to be done.

Ross was being treated for depression with doses of Diazepam and with an antitumor drug, Diagoxin, which made him nauseous and scarcely able to eat. But he was getting out of bed for brief spells and walking short distances with help. Barry decided the time had come to take him and his wife outside the hospital for a demonstration.

He went to Yardley's office to advise him of the latest developments. For the first time since Vologda 2 began, Barry detected a spark of hope and enthusiasm in the DIA chief. The decision to sanction Cane had been a hard one, and Yardley, having taken it upon himself to break the news to Maryann, had then been unable to visit David in the hospital. The thought of it made him feel cold.

But now things were starting to move again, and action was a great healer.

Yardley immediately ordered his secretary to locate Clive Lyle in San Francisco, where he was on leave. Yardley had a pretty good idea what Lyle was up to. Still, he was a good operator and that was his own business. When he was found, he was to get back to Washington on the first available flight. There was urgent work for him.

Lyle presented himself for duty at 9:30 the following morning, relaxed and laconic as always.

"Had a good break, Clive?" Yardley asked.

"Yes, thank you, sir. Very pleasant. It might have been longer."

"Mmmm. Sorry to call you back, but something's come up." Yardley tossed across his desk the file marked VOLOGDA 2.

While Lyle read it, Lucy brought in coffee. Usually mission discussions took place in the comfortable leather chairs at the side of the office, but on this occasion Yardley wanted his desk between them to emphasize his authority. He anticipated it might turn out to be a difficult meeting, although one never knew with Lyle.

When Lyle had finished, he glanced briefly at Yardley, eyes expressionless, then started again at the beginning. He lit a cigarette absentmindedly as he read, never taking his eyes off the paper. Yardley scratched the top of his head and waited with as much patience as he could muster.

Finally, Lyle closed the file and dropped it onto the mahogany desk. "That's pretty heavy," he said. "Is it going to work?"

Yardley shrugged. "That's what the experts tell me. As you read, the preliminary experiments have all been completed, and apart from teething troubles with the first half dozen, there's been no trouble with the others. You're going to take Ross and his wife out there tomorrow to have a look for themselves."

"Does Ross know?"

"Not yet. It has to be broken to him slowly and carefully. Step by step, please. It's a little too much to digest all at once."

"Yeah, I can see that." He inhaled a lungful of smoke. "Who's the lucky donor?"

This was it. "David Cane."

There was a silence during which Lyle's mouth dropped open and he stared at Yardley in disbelief. "David?"

The other man nodded. "It's already done."

Lyle's eyes flared. "Jesus Christ! You sanctioned David! You actually sanctioned David!"

Yardley said coldly: "Pull yourself together, Clive. I did not sanction David. David volunteered. He chose to make the sacrifice."

Lyle was on his feet. "Have you got that in writing, sir? 'Cause if you don't, I might just break your fucking neck."

Yardley glared back at Lyle, willing himself to meet the outraged, disbelieving stare with his own confident, righteous one. "Of course I haven't got it in writing, Clive. What the hell do you think? Haven't we taught you anything in the years you've been with the DIA?"

Lyle slowly resumed his seat. "I don't think you realize, because you were only on the periphery of this operation, just how much Vologda meant to Cane. How much it means to the President of the United States, for Christ's sake. How much it means to the whole world. When we found Ross had inoperable cancer, Cane and I sat in this office, right over there, Clive, and we went through the fallback position. And Cane *volunteered*. I thought of using a CIA man. He said we couldn't risk someone from the outside because of the possibility of a leak. It had to be kept in the family. Of course, he was right." He could see Lyle didn't believe him, so he played his ace. "Cane even went so far as to go and see *Martin Ross* in the hospital and *tell him* what he planned to do."

That threw Lyle. "David told the professor he was going to let himself be killed?"

"Grow up, Clive. Martin Ross is a sick old guy. Of course, he didn't tell him in those words. It would have put Ross in an impossible position. What David told him was that he had hit on a plan to get the professor into Vologda base. He said Ross would recover to complete the mission, but that he couldn't give any details at that stage. And that was the last Ross saw of him."

Clive Lyle sat silently, staring at a point above Yardley's head. "I'm gonna check that out, General," he promised quietly. "I hope for your sake you're right."

Yardley said icily: "May I remind you, Major Lyle, that you are still in the army?"

"I'm aware of that, General."

"I could have you court-martialed for gross insubordination and for threatening a senior officer."

Lyle shrugged indifferently. It would never happen, and they both knew it. What would be more likely, he suddenly realized, was that Yardley would give the order to another operative that Lyle himself should be—that wonderful CIA jargon—terminally demoted. And whatever had happened to David Cane, there was little point in that. Lyle drew on his cigarette.

"How did you do it, General?" he asked softly.

"David had a stroke. His brain was destroyed."

"But how?"

"He went down to the hospital, of his own accord and by himself, and when he confirmed his readiness to go through with it, Dr. Barry gave him an injection of Pentothal. He was unconscious in seconds. Then Barry fed him a combination of nitrous oxide and carbon monoxide. It was totally painless, and over in a matter of minutes. David just went to sleep, and that was it."

"Jesus Christ. Poor David. Does his wife know?"

Yardley looked despairing. "Clive, are you going to take this seriously or aren't you?" he asked with asperity. "You think I handed her the fallback position file as if she was just another DIA operative and said, 'That, my dear, is what your husband's just volunteered for. He's in the next room, so why don't you go through now and say good-bye, and, remember, not a word to anyone'? As far as she's concerned, he had a stroke, and now he's clinically dead. She's prepared to give permission for us to switch off the life-support system. And that's why I've called you in now. We're ready to go to the next stage of the operation and, dammit, I need your help. And your full-throated, full-hearted help, or, by God, you can get out of here right now." Yardley's performance increased in emphasis. "Do I have to remind you of the importance of the Vologda mission? Have you forgotten the Special Collection doctrine? Have you given *five minutes'* thought to what would happen if the Soviets launched a nuclear strike against the United States and our cities and military bases were in ruins before we even knew what was happening?" Yardley fueled himself into a fury. "Is the concept of sacrificing your life for your country so foreign to you that you can't take on board the fact that David Cane had the *guts* to do it?"

"Okay, okay," Lyle held up a placating hand. "I'm sorry, I'm sorry. Let's take it back to the beginning. David Cane put his neck on the block without saying good-bye to his wife or kissing his kid. If we had a body to bury, we'd bury it at Arlington with full military honors. I take my hat off to him. He was a damn fine young American, and if anyone ever knew what he'd done, they'd compose songs to him and erect monuments on every Main Street in the country." Lyle lit another cigarette and sighed. "And where do we go from here?"

Yardley relaxed visibly. Lyle was hard work sometimes, but in the end he did adjust to new situations. "You take over where David left off," Yardley said.

"You want me to go into Vologda?"

"No. You don't speak the language. Ross's got to do it by himself. But you've got to train him for that point. Oh, hell"—Yardley sipped the coffee, which was going cold in the cup, and grimaced—"we're talking about a long time ahead. The first priority is to get the professor to accept the basic concept of Vologda Two and the point of David's sacrifice. That'll be difficult, but not impossible. He needs to have the next stage explained to him by an expert. Peter Barry will handle some of that. He's got a pretty good rapport going with Ross. But you've got a major role to play. The thing is that Ross's only just learned what's happened to Cane. He thinks it's a stroke. The truth has to be broken to him gently. Stress the opportunity it presents, not only for the mission but for Ross himself. We've got a psychiatrist standing by to deal with some of the basic guilts and identity crises we can expect, so you ought to have a preliminary talk with Howlett and get some pointers on how to proceed. We're taking Ross and his wife out for the demonstration tomorrow morning at nine. You'll have to go along on that. In fact, you ought to spend time with the professor this afternoon. Just a social call, nothing heavy. Take it from there."

Lyle nodded slowly. "Anything else?"

"Nothing," Yardley said. "Just take it easy, Clive. I know how you feel. I wish to hell you knew how *I* felt. I loved David."

Lyle stood up. "Yeah," he said. "I guess I did too."

Lyle picked up what he could from Dr. Geoffrey Howlett. In the bland, professionally decorated psychiatric unit, they went through videos of Cane and Ross together at Fairfax, mostly of them working out in the gym, walking, and talking. Howlett froze frames from time to time to underline various comments about the way their relationship had developed, and how Ross had subconsciously modeled himself on Cane. He had even developed gestures which were exact copies. They played monitor tapes, with a few months between them, and Howlett showed how the professor's phraseology, and in some situations even his accent, had altered to fit more closely with Cane's. It was an engrossing study, and Howlett had obviously spent a long time on it. Although Martin Ross had not yet met the psychiatrist, he soon would, and Howlett might turn out to be a vital lifeline over the next extraordinary months.

In the afternoon Lyle visited the intensive care unit. Having seen Ross on videos taken secretly at Fairfax, he was not prepared for the dramatic physical decline since then. The flesh seemed to have fallen away from Ross's face, and there were defeat and resignation in his eyes. His wife sat by his bed, reading aloud from an early Jane Austen novel. She stopped as Lyle approached and looked up inquiringly. Ross looked too, without interest.

"I'm Clive Lyle. I'm a friend of David's."

A tired spark lit up Ross's face. "Clive Lyle. Good Lord. I'm not sure you were a friend of David's, were you?"

Lyle grinned. "Not for a long time," he admitted. "It changed after he beat me up in the gym. Got rid of the bad blood. We went out afterward and got drunk."

Ross remembered and nodded, amused. "I'm glad to meet you at last, Mr. Lyle. David spoke to me about you."

"I hope not all of it was bad."

"No. Some was good. David said you were a natural bastard, but then he realized he was too." Ross chuckled. "I don't know what you looked like after the fight, but David was a mess. Poor David."

"Oh, I looked worse. One of my eyes had closed up. I was covered in blood. My face swelled up. It was pretty bad. After we showered and changed, there were three bars that wouldn't let us in at all. We got into the fourth only because we threatened to bust the place up if they didn't give us a drink. It was a great day."

Elaine Ross closed the book and put it away in the metal chest beside the bed. Clearly it was not to be an afternoon for intellectual refreshment.

"Pull up a chair, Mr. Lyle," she invited.

"Thanks, Mrs. Ross. How are you feeling, Professor?" he asked.

"About how I look, I guess."

If Ross expected sympathy, he was mistaken. "Well, it's time to straighten yourself out now," Lyle said. "We've got to start thinking about Vologda again."

"Not you too, Mr. Lyle," Ross groaned.

"Call me Clive."

"Clive. You haven't come to drop dark hints about miracle cures, have you? Dying men don't appreciate jokes like that. It was hard enough to take from David."

Lyle pulled out a pack of cigarettes. "Mind if I smoke?" Elaine fetched an ashtray, and Lyle lit up. "Would you mind telling me, Professor, exactly what David said to you that time?"

Ross said: "I really don't feel . . ."

"It's important, or I wouldn't ask."

Martin Ross sighed. "It was . . . inexplicable. He said there was a way of getting me into Vologda. He couldn't say much about it, but I should trust him. He'd thought of something, and I'd find out what it was in time. Elaine spoke to him alone afterward, and he just repeated the same thing to her."

"It was an idea of David's?"

"That's what he said. 'It's my plan. I suggested it.' I can hear him now."

"No hints of what it was?"

"Nothing at all. And then I didn't see him again. I spent the days lying here feeling sorry for myself, wondering where the hell he was, just wanting to *see* the guy again, and then yesterday Elaine meets his wife and finds David had a stroke an hour or so after he left here. He's been two rooms away the whole time, in a deep coma. His brain —finished." Ross's eyes glistened with tears, and he bit his lower lip. "Oh God," he said, "it's so terrible."

Lyle sat very still. He guessed he owed Yardley an apology. That Cane. What an awesome thing to do. The silence stretched as he waited for Ross to recover.

Then Lyle said: "David was right. You should trust him. Especially now, you must trust him. There *is* a plan. It's David's plan. And the time is coming when we're going to be able to tell you what it is." He was conscious of Ross and his wife staring at him, uncomprehending but no longer able to challenge what they heard. "You've been preparing to die, Professor. It's written all over you. You're giving up, flunking out. Well, you'd better stop that because you're not going to die. We're going to fix it so you can go into Russia and crack Vologda. You still want to do that?"

Ross nodded, numb. "How?" he asked.

"We'll tell you tomorrow. Or at least we'll show you. You and Mrs. Ross and I are going to take a little trip out of the hospital for a demonstration. We'll leave at nine." He paused and stared squarely at Ross. "Are you a fighter, Martin?"

"Well . . . I suppose so. If there's a chance."

"There is a chance. David's given it to you. Will you take it?"

"Yes, I will. If I can get to Vologda." There was a note of hope in his voice now.

"It'll be hard. The hardest thing you've ever done. You're going to have to make a big mental adjustment, and there's no guarantee of success, of course. Just a fighting chance. You ready for that?"

"Yes."

"Remember: this is David's plan. You're going to be in the hospital for months yet, and when you come out, you're going to work with me. I'm going to take over where David left off. But you'll be going into Vologda on your own. Does that scare you?"

"A little, yes."

"Good. David told you I was a bastard. Well, he was right. I'm the biggest bastard they've got at the DIA, and I'm going to turn you into one too."

Ross grinned. It sounded like old times. Elaine saw how his face had become alive again, and she felt her heart sink. What were they talking about? It wasn't possible to take a man, riddled with terminal cancer, and turn him into an agent capable of penetrating the most secret Soviet citadel. No one could do that. Not Clive Lyle and the DIA. Not even David Cane. But she sat silent. At least they were promising to show them something. Tomorrow they would have information on which to evaluate Martin's chances, so she would suspend judgment until then.

Meanwhile, it was extraordinary how a stranger like Clive Lyle could walk into the room, unannounced, and turn Martin's resignation into virtual euphoria in a few minutes.

Lyle wasn't a David Cane. He was shorter, smaller, and not nearly as good-looking. But it was comparative, of course. Next to Cane, Lyle came off second best. Next to most ordinary men, he would have an authority, an easiness, with his average-sized body that indicated he was totally in control of himself and possibly dangerous. She doubted that many men would be prepared to challenge Lyle.

When he left an hour later, after recounting a few of the Fairfax legends and some stories about David Elaine found difficult to believe, Martin Ross lay back against his pillows with a look of sheer contentment and was soon asleep—the first decent, undrugged sleep he had had since the operation.

Elaine left to get something to eat, to walk around Washington for a while. She took a cab down to Constitution Avenue so she could stroll on the lawns around the Washington Monument and beside the reflecting pool to the Lincoln Memorial. It was good to be out of the hospital, to feel the grass beneath her feet and look across the Potomac River. That was real. The other world of the DIA, Fairfax, baffling suggestions of miracle cures for a dying man, and the violence in the lives of people like Clive Lyle and poor David Cane, was a world light years distant. Cane had admitted he killed in the course of his duties. Did Lyle also? Did one get to be the biggest bastard in the DIA without killing? She walked thoughtfully for an hour.

When she checked her watch, she saw it was time to get back to the hospital. Martin might have woken, with his emotional roller coaster switched from euphoria to deep depression. She should be with him. She hurried to find a cab.

But Martin was still asleep, relaxed and apparently at peace. Whatever had happened, at least he had been given a few hours of rest.

The following morning, promptly at nine, Dr. Peter Barry and Clive Lyle walked into the ward. Lyle was pushing a wheelchair.

"How are you feeling this morning?" Barry asked.

"Still some pain. Otherwise fine. I slept well last night for a change," Ross said.

"Glad to hear it. Let's see you get out of bed by yourself. Try and make it to the wheelchair. We're here if you hit trouble."

Ross eased his legs gently over the side of the bed, careful not to strain the sutures which were still in his stomach, and pushed his feet into slippers which Elaine held ready for him. Then he stood up cautiously. He still felt very weak. Elaine helped him into a warm bathrobe, and he began to shuffle, alone, toward the wheelchair a few feet away. He made it and sat down with a smile of triumph. "It's not exactly a five-mile run," he said to Lyle, "but it's the best I can do at the moment."

"It's pretty good," Lyle replied. "Wait until I get you on the Fairfax assault course. I don't think David even showed it to you, did he?"

"No."

"Well, just wait and see. It's pretty grueling. You won't like it much, but I'll want you through it in four minutes. The average for a DIA agent is four minutes fifteen."

Ross chuckled. "You'll be lucky," he said.

Lyle wheeled him out of the ward and quickly through the reception area before he had a chance to identify Cane's room and glance inside. The elevator took them to the basement garage, where a limousine waited. Ross was helped into the back seat, and the wheelchair was folded up and locked in the luggage compartment.

As they pulled smoothly up the ramp and into the spring sunshine, Ross looked around with pleasure. "You know," he said, "I didn't think I'd ever see the outside of that place again. No more trees, or fields, or gardens of flowers. Where're we heading, by the way?"

Lyle said: "Northeast eventually. Toward Annapolis. We'll turn off before we get there. We've got a small facility just near Chesapeake Bay."

"What are we going to see?"

Lyle grinned. "A surprise. You'll have to wait."

Ross relaxed against the seat, content to watch the Washington traffic, seeing the familiar landmarks, the Capitol building, the Supreme Court, and the Library of Congress, then along Independence Avenue until they could take a route which led eventually onto the southeast highway, branching off toward Annapolis.

How good it was to be out of that hospital and to sample again the freedom others took for granted. He rolled the window down slightly to let the cool air rush in. He wished he'd been able to get rid of his pajamas and dress in ordinary clothes again. He felt he was in hospital uniform, more conspicuous than anything dreamed up by a prison. And what he wanted most of all was to be the same as everyone else again.

Elaine beside him, held his hand, and he could feel tension in her grip. He knew she was worried that after the buildup by David, reinforced by Clive Lyle, he would experience a crashing disappointment, and she didn't know how to protect him from it. But Ross was aware of the possibility, and he found he didn't care. Lyle had at least made him feel a man again. The emotional beating he had taken with the news of the cancer, the collapse of the mission, and then David's stroke had reduced him to a state of almost total demoralization. Now, even if the demonstration, whatever it was, offered good ideas but no real answers, at least some mental equilibrium had been restored and he could face death with calmness rather than defeat. It might be a fine distinction, but to Ross it was important.

They drove for an hour before exiting the highway and almost doubling back down the coast of Chesapeake Bay. Finally, they turned onto a dirt road leading to a farmhouse, and the DIA chauffeur gave a short blast on the horn to announce their arrival.

It was an old-style house, painted white some years earlier but now comfortably faded, with a wooden veranda running the length of the front. The door opened and a man—in his early fifties Ross guessed —casually dressed in Levis and a sweater, came out to greet them. Behind him was a younger man, also in casual dress, and at their heels charged an assortment of barking dogs, Labradors and German Shepherds. The young man called out an order, and the animals pulled back around his heels, obviously well-trained.

Lyle came around the side to open the door and help Ross onto his feet.

"Can you stand?" Lyle asked.

"Yes, I think so."

"Great. Then you can probably walk a bit too. I'm going to leave your wheelchair in the car. We'll get it later if you need it, but you ought to have some fresh air and exercise. That okay, Peter?"

"Sure," Dr. Barry shrugged. "No reason why not."

"So take my arm, Martin. Lean on me as much as you want."

The older of the two men, with thick black hair and a craggy face, held out his hand. "Professor Ross. Welcome. I'm Jeremy Howard. And this is Simon Olgin."

Dr. Barry explained. "Professor Howard is now with the DIA, working on a number of rather intriguing experiments. He used to be a senior consultant in the Neurosurgery Department at Cleveland Metropolitan General Hospital."

"Good to meet you, Professor," Ross said.

"And Simon Olgin's responsible for the dogs."

"Pretty well-behaved, I see. Very good. It must be more difficult training animals than it is training people."

"Simon's a fully qualified vet, of course, as well as a trainer," Barry said. "He's in charge of the DIA sniffer pack. They can find anything from a hand grenade in a suitcase to a buried corpse."

"How are you, Professor Ross?" Olgin's welcome was restrained: a man, Ross thought, who probably preferred animals to humans. And there were times when who could blame him.

"Would you like to follow me?" Olgin asked and led the way around behind the farmhouse to an area where chairs had been set out facing a field. Ross took his time, leaning on Lyle, conscious of the strength of the young man. It didn't surprise him. He'd seen some of the damage Lyle had inflicted on David Cane.

They settled in the chairs, and Olgin blew on a whistle which to human ears made no sound, but whose high-frequency tone was immediately picked up by the dogs. They raced in a pack to the end of the field and sat down obediently. A series of hurdles of increasing height had been set up along the field.

Ross did not see Simon Olgin blow the whistle again, as he was standing slightly behind the row of spectators, but an order had obviously gone out because, one after the other, the dogs began jumping the hurdles. When they reached the end, they sat in a line. After the final animal had completed the course, the dogs, again apparently on signal, lay down simultaneously, waiting for the next command.

Suddenly they took off in a pack, dropped to the ground, motionless, again leaped forward and dropped.

Olgin provided no commentary. The animals were perfectly drilled and totally obedient. It was rather like watching a superior circus performance. The dogs completed one trick after another for twenty minutes. At one point, a man—heavily padded for protection—emerged from the farmhouse and began running across the field. The dogs set off in pursuit until suddenly all except a large German Shepherd stopped in their tracks and lay down while the remaining hound went in for the attack, fangs snapping at the padded arm out to fend him off. Without warning, the dog ceased its assault and returned to the others.

Ross became aware that, from time to time, Professor Howard, who was seated next to him, glanced over to see his reaction.

Finally, Simon Olgin walked into the center of the field carrying a cloth-bound hoop on a stand and placed it in position. He poured fluid from a bottle in his pocket over the cloth, waited until it had soaked in well, then flicked a Zippo lighter. The hoop burst into flame.

The dogs went through it, one after the other. When they had finished and were sitting at the end of the field, Olgin took hard biscuits from his pocket and fed each animal, patting heads and praising them.

Professor Howard broke the silence. "Well, Professor Ross, what did you think of that?"

"Very impressive. Is this what I was brought here to see?"

"Yes, that's right."

"Well, it's splendid. Mr. Olgin obviously knows how to handle animals. But forgive me if I fail to see the relevance."

"I'll explain in a minute. Shall we go inside?"

Lyle offered his arm once more, and they climbed the stairs to the back door, down a wooden corridor, and into a comfortable living room. The dogs followed them in and sprawled out over the rugs.

Jeremy Howard again took his place beside Ross. Elaine sat in a chintz-covered easy chair and abstractedly stroked the ears of a golden Labrador bitch, which settled beside her.

Simon Olgin offered drinks, and as he poured them Professor Howard began his explanation.

"You're wondering what the hell this is all about," he said, "and now I'm going to try to explain. Please forgive me if I seem to be taking a long time about it, but a bit of background is necessary first. I'm a professor of neurosurgery, as you know. One of my primary interests over the last couple of decades has been research into brain-stem damage. We see a lot of patients—usually broken necks, dislocations—who have lost all spinal cord function and are paralyzed from the neck down. It's very tragic. An otherwise healthy young man, his mental faculties unimpaired, is condemned to a lifetime of effective imprisonment inside a useless body. He has no sensation at any point below the damaged cord. He can't control his bladder or his bowels. And until recently, there's been no hope we've been able to give someone like that. Unlike other parts of the body, including the peripheral nervous system, the spinal cord left to itself simply does not regenerate. A broken bone repairs with extraordinary precision. Even peripheral nerves, controlling fingers, for example, or in some isolated cases, even whole limbs, are capable of regeneration as long as the reconnection occurs between points which are fairly close together." Jeremy Howard accepted a glass of Scotch from Olgin and sipped it. "Thanks. Perfect. Now, Professor, may I ask how much you know about the structure of neurons?"

"Only what I remember from college," Ross replied. "You'd better refresh my memory."

"Okay. Well, I've got a couple of diagrams here you might like to see." Professor Howard picked up a file and opened it. He pointed to a drawing. "Now the nervous system is made up of nerve cells called neurons—that's this central part here. And this linear extension coming out here is called the axon. You get two neurons together, with their axons touching, and the junction between them is called the synapse. It's all pretty simple. One neuron wants to pass a signal to another neuron, so it goes down the axon, across the synapse, and that's it, on and on through the body. There's also a supporting structure, which is the neural sheath and some of the surrounding tissue. That acts as insulation. We've known for some time that there are differences in this supporting structure in the peripheral nervous system, which can heal itself, and the central nervous system, which can't. This suggested to us there was something in the environment of the neural pathway—and not the pathway itself—which inhibited healing. Okay, now these structural cells in the peripheral nervous system are known as Schwann's cells, but the ones we're concerned with now, in the central nervous system, are called the glia. You with me so far?"

"Sure. You bust your spine, and the reason it doesn't repair itself is because of the insulation and not the nerve cells themselves."

"More or less. The thing is, it wasn't always so in the human body. There is a point in the embryonic development of everyone when the nervous system goes through a phase in which radiating nerve pathways grow from the center of a pretty simple cylindrical tube, out to the periphery—a little like the spokes of a bicycle wheel. We call these things radial glia. But as human development progresses, for some unknown reason they disappear. This is not a good thing. Cold-blooded vertebrates, like fish and frogs, keep theirs—and *they're* capable of neural regeneration in their central nervous systems. So the bastards that turn people into hemiplegics are these radial glia— or the lack of them. We've been experimenting for . . . God knows how many years, finding out what goes wrong and what to do to correct it. The answer lies partly in creating the right cellular environment at the point of neural damage. Call it a nerve glue if you like. A man breaks his neck, and we inject nerve glue into the damaged area, and at that point, at least, the environment is changed so the central nervous system has the capacity for repairing itself. Of course, nothing's quite as simple as that. There are millions of individual nerve fibers in the spinal cord—too many to possibly connect up in the right order. So we did some more research, and we came up with a surprising result."

Jeremy Howard finished his whiskey and refused the offer of

another. Ross and Elaine, who were listening with complete attention, exchanged glances. *What's going on?*

Professor Howard continued. "Every neuron fires electrical impulses. As we know, these signals go down the axon, across the synapse, and trigger identical impulses in the interconnected neurons. There might be ten thousand other neurons along a single line, and the impulse goes down them like a spark along a fuse. The brain, by the way, uses about twenty-five watts of electrical energy: enough to power a dim light bulb. But in each neuron, the voltage is so small we measure it in micro-volts—one millionth of a volt. It was assumed for a long time that the same amount of electricity was used by every string of neurons. We now know that this is not true. For us, this was an extraordinary breakthrough. It meant that if every set of neurons used a slightly different voltage to perform their tasks—and, believe me, the difference is really tiny—then what we needed to work on was some sort of absorbent blanket which would recognize the voltage differences and match them up with the voltage needs of neurons on the other side of the damaged tissue. This, together with the nerve glue, could get the regeneration going. Do you see what I mean?"

Ross nodded. "Yes, I do, Professor. But with respect, I fail to see how it affects me. I also enjoyed the dogs, but I don't know what they've got to do with me. I was brought here this morning because Clive Lyle told me I was going to be shown something which would help me get well enough to go . . . to complete an assignment. I have cancer, Professor Howard. I do not have brainstem damage."

"I'm aware of that, Professor Ross. And I'm sorry to be so long-winded in my explanation, but you'll see why in a moment. If you don't understand the theory, you'll find it difficult to believe the actuality. Do you want another drink, by the way?"

"No thanks. Just the explanation."

"The reason we showed you the dogs is because they've all been patients of mine."

"I thought you were a professor of neurosurgery, not a vet."

"I sometimes wish I was. Animals are often easier to deal with."

"Sorry."

"Not at all. We might as well get straight to the nitty-gritty. The point about you, Professor Ross, is that you're dying because your body has given up on you. There's nothing at all wrong with your brain. Now, all these dogs you see here, and were watching earlier, are actually not those dogs at all. They're other dogs."

Ross looked incredulous. "I beg your pardon? I don't think I understand."

"I transplanted their brains," Jeremy Howard said casually. "We solved the problems of regeneration of a break in the central nervous system, and there's the living proof." He gestured around him.

Ross and Elaine stared at the animals, lying or sitting around the room. Simon Olgin called, "Cleo!", and one of the German Shepherds went across to him immediately. He fondled her head.

"All the tricks you saw, every one of them, were taught by Simon *before* the transplant. After the recovery period, the memory was unimpaired."

Ross said faintly: "And you want me . . .?"

"Exactly. I want to transplant your brain—that part of you that actually is *you*—into a suitable donor body. When that's done, you can complete your mission."

Ross, stunned, looked at Elaine for comfort and found her face as stricken as he imagined his to be.

"The idea is . . . obscene," Ross whispered.

"Is it? Are you opposed to kidney transplants?"

"No."

"Heart transplants?"

"No, I guess not. But that's different."

"Only in degree," Professor Howard said. "It's all basically spare-part surgery. Although in your case I do admit it's virtually a total refit."

Ross could think of nothing to say. Elaine broke the silence. "Let's put morals and ethics aside for a moment, Professor," she said calmly. "We've seen what you've done with dogs . . ."

"Monkeys too. Macaques. I've got a cageful of them which you can have a look at later. But obviously they're not as good for demonstration purposes."

"Monkeys . . . whatever. What about people. How many brain-stem-damaged men and women have you cured? And why haven't we heard about it before now?"

"The answer to that is simple," Jeremy Howard said. "None. We hope your husband will be the first human experiment."

"If it fails?"

"Then he dies."

"Or he becomes a quadriplegic."

"As you say. Or he becomes a quadriplegic."

"I'd sooner be dead," Ross observed.

"Well, you are going to be dead, Professor, and pretty quickly too, if we don't do something about it. I've been asked by the DIA, under whose auspices the experiments have taken place, if a brain transplant would give you a fighting chance of living to complete a mission they have in mind for you. I don't know what the mission is, and I don't want to know. My answer was a straightforward yes. I estimate the chances of success at about seventy to seventy-five percent."

"What about tissue-typing? What about the rejection factor?"

"Well, we're lucky there, Professor Ross. The brain does not possess an intrinsic lymph system, which means it is immunologically privileged. It cannot be rejected."

"Wouldn't it be better to try your cure out on one of your paralyzed patients first? And then if it works, come back to me?" Ross asked, unable to shake off the specter of an active mind imprisoned in a helpless body.

"I could do that, but it would be too late. You'd either be dead, or if by some miracle you were still hanging on by your fingertips, there would be a pretty good chance that the cancer would have metastasized to your brain. There's not much point in transplanting a cancerous brain into a healthy body, is there? Even now we're taking a chance."

Another silence fell. Ross snapped his fingers at a German Shepherd lying on the other side of the room, and the dog trotted over to him. He fondled its ears, ruffling the fur around its skull, where Ross could see the operation scar circling the head, bisected by another scar across the top of the cranium.

"The other problem," Ross said at last, "is finding the replacement body."

Professor Howard made no comment. Lyle, on the other side of the room, cleared his throat. "All we want you to do at this stage, Martin, is get used to the basic idea, and *think* about it seriously. Ask any questions about the mechanics of the operation you like. How long is it going to take? How's it going to feel?"

"Okay," said Ross, turning back to Professor Howard. "Let's have the answers to those two."

"The transplant itself will take twelve or thirteen hours," Jeremy Howard said. "We're obviously going to keep your own eyes and your own middle and inner ear. There are enough problems without worrying about vision and hearing, beyond the microsurgery techniques which will be necessary to attach them to the donor muscle and tissue. Oh, and I may have misled you slightly earlier when I said there'd be no rejection problem. There won't be with the brain, but there will be at tissue contact points. But we're not worried about that. Our knowledge of immunology has progressed to the point where a simple injection every three months will be all you need. And it will only slightly lower your resistance to infection. As for recuperation, well, we do use microsurgery for the thirty-one pairs of nerves that emerge from the spinal cord and then distribute themselves through the trunk and limbs, and the twelve pairs of cranial nerves that go out through the skull itself. This connects them through the nerve glue and the microvoltage blanket I was telling you about before, and gives a good start toward general regeneration. So you should have some function fairly shortly after regaining consciousness and the rest will return gradually after that. In three months you ought to have full function. Add another three for general rehabilitation, and after that you're off and—literally—running."

Martin Ross caught Clive Lyle's eye, and the agent grinned at him. He tried to smile back, but made a bad job of it.

"Well," Ross said at last. "That is . . . extraordinary. I don't know what to think, or what to say. I need time. I must . . . talk it over with my wife."

"Of course," Professor Howard said. "I understand that. But once you get used to the idea, I imagine you'll find it isn't a very big decision to make after all. You're dying anyway, there's no question of that. As far as the DIA are concerned, you're being offered this transplant simply so you can complete a mission on their behalf. I understand that the mission is not only top secret, but vital to the national interest. So if you want to do it, whatever it is, this is the only way we can help you. The only hope. Of course, no one will ever know you've had the transplant. There'll be no problems of publicity, which I'm sure you'd want to avoid anyway. I won't even be able to write about my stunning success in a medical journal. I've already had to agree to that. As far as everyone's concerned, your brain transplant won't have happened. You'll be given a new body and" — he glanced at Elaine Ross, sitting very still as the implications broke on her— "from that point of view anyway, you'll be a new man. But the essential *you* is your brain. That won't change. Naturally there'll be identity problems. You're far too intelligent for me to pretend there won't, and the DIA will make available the best psychiatrist they have to help you overcome them. To help you both overcome them. But General Yardley has asked me to stress, and I do stress it now, that as far as they're concerned, the mission is the vital thing. That's the reason for the transplant. How you pick up the pieces of your life after that is up to you. Of course, we'll help at all stages—for the rest of your days if necessary."

Martin Ross shook his head slowly, as if to clear it. He suddenly looked very tired.

Lyle said: "Have you got any more questions, Martin? Or would you like to get back to the hospital?"

"Let's get back."

Lyle came over to help him to his feet, the dying man in the thick woolen bathrobe and slippers, struggling to comprehend what was happening to him. And he hadn't heard the worst part yet.

"Thank you, Professor Howard," Ross said formally. "You have given me . . . much to consider." They shook hands. "And Mr. Olgin, thank you for the drink and the demonstration. Your dogs are extraordinary." He glanced around at them. With everyone standing up, the dogs were also on their feet, alert.

Lyle helped Ross back into the limousine, and the drive to Washington was completed in silence. Ross leaned his head against the seat, watching the scenery in a desultory fashion. His first instinctive reaction had been that the idea was obscene. But was it? Was it any more obscene than letting an active, useful brain destroy itself in a diseased body when it still had vital work to do?

Vologda. At every point there was the mission to consider, and Special Collection. He remembered the computer printouts he and David had worked on at Fairfax, and the target coordinates which showed nuclear warheads programmed to detonate on New York, Washington, Chicago, Detroit. That was what they were up against. *Oh God,* he thought, *I wish I knew what to do.* In some ways it was all so easy—Vologda took precedence. In others there were giant stumbling blocks. To take over the body of another man and become —what? Still himself? Was the brain all that counted? What about identity, and family, and friends? What about different muscles, different glands, triggering new responses?

And the transplant was still an experiment. At the end he might be a quadriplegic, longing for even the searing pains of cancer to deliver him to death, but physically unable to move a finger, let alone take his own life. Or his brain, damaged in the transplant, could turn him into . . . what? A pathological killer? A cretin? It could be noble and worthwhile, or it could be a Frankenstein experiment.

He closed his eyes while his mind thrashed over the options, discovering new subtleties, extra horrors, more complications. He felt a headache begin. Ross realized that Elaine, who had held his hand so supportively on the outward journey, was now keeping to herself. He glanced over and saw her face was a mask. He reached for her hand, and she gave him a brief smile, but he noticed her touch was limp, cold, almost lifeless. Ross sighed.

It was two by the time he was back in bed, and the nurses put his lunch in the microwave oven. Lyle left, saying he would return in a couple of hours to talk things over. Elaine sat preoccupied, staring out of the window. At last, she told him she needed to be by herself and would eat out.

Ross's food came in individual containers with cardboard lids on which the contents had been neatly printed. Chopped steak and potato. Egg salad. Jello and cream. He picked at each, but even the smells made him nauseous, and he pushed the tray aside.

Clive Lyle returned before Elaine did, to find Ross brooding alone in his room.

"How do you feel, Martin?"

"Fine."

"I mean about the transplant."

Ross shrugged. "I just don't know. I don't know what to think."

Lyle pulled back his sheets. "Come on," he said. "Out of there. You and I are going for a walk, and then we're going to talk, man to man."

Ross did as he was told. Lyle helped him on with his bathrobe and slippers and escorted him from the ward, a few yards along the reception area. The nurses on duty at the television monitors looked up but said nothing.

Before Ross realized it, they had turned into another room, and he was confronting a motionless figure connected to tubes and drips, a cardiac monitor, an EEG, and the slow, rhythmical hissing of the breathing machine. David.

No one else was there. Maryann Cane had been called up to see Dr. Barry, so she was safely out of the way for the moment.

At first, Ross didn't recognize Cane because of the bandages around his head and the equipment, and because his memories were of movement and strength and life.

But when he did he made an anguished noise, which sounded almost like a groan. Lyle put his arm around Ross and held him tight, for comfort as well as physical support.

Ross shuffled closer to the head of the bed and reached out in the exact gesture David had made to him after he learned he was under sentence of death, and held his hand against Cane's cheek.

After a few moments, Ross glanced at the oscilloscope. "His heart's strong," he said, his voice shaky.

"Sure," Lyle replied quietly. "His body's fine. It's his brain that's destroyed. The EEG's flat."

Sssssss . . . Cane's chest rose. Sssssss . . . it fell.

Ross sighed. "It's such a tragedy. It doesn't matter about me, I've had my life. But a man like David . . ."

Abruptly Lyle pulled back the sheets, exposing Cane. His white hospital gown had been removed and he lay naked. A tube drained his bladder. Leads from the inside of his thighs, his left elbow, and the front of his right shoulder connected him to the cardiac monitor.

"Do you think you ought to do that, Clive?" Ross asked anxiously. After a pause: "He'll get cold."

"I wanted you to look at him. Go on, look."

So Ross stared at the familiar body, remembering the months of workouts, the agonies, and the triumphs of Fairfax.

"David's dead," Lyle said. "Don't let anyone fool you. If we switch off that breathing machine, it's the end. David doesn't feel anything anymore. He doesn't know anything. It's funny, isn't it? He knew it was going to be like this. It's what he planned. A brave guy. Noble. I look at him, and I don't know what to say." They stared in silence. Lyle made no move to cover Cane. "What did he tell you the last time you spoke?"

"What about?"

"About his plan."

"His plan? He said he had one, that's all. He couldn't say what it was, but I should trust him. He'd never given me a bum steer. I'd find out soon what it was. It would get me well enough to go to Vologda . . ." Ross's voice trailed away, and he stared in disbelief at the figure on the bed. "Oh no!"

"No what?"

But Ross couldn't bring himself to say it. It was unthinkable.

"Did David know about the transplant possibility? Is that what you're wondering?" Lyle asked. "Sure he knew. *That* was his plan. It was the only way left of getting into Vologda. It was our fallback

position. The only way you—and he—could crack that computer."
He felt Ross begin to sag and held him tighter, pulling him against
the side of his own chest. "David didn't have a stroke, Martin. He
volunteered. He said we couldn't let it out of the family. The whole
Vologda thing's too secret, too vital. He sacrificed himself for the mission, and for you. David's offering you your chance, Martin. There
he is. He's your donor."

Tears poured down Ross's cheeks and his body convulsed. Lyle
eased him into a chair while he covered Cane gently.

"Come on," he said. "Let's get out of here." It was difficult to
move Ross now, as he seemed to have lost all control, but he had to
get back to his own bed because before long Maryann Cane would be
returning. Slowly Lyle coaxed Ross up and, supporting him strongly,
managed to get him out into the reception area, leaving David Cane
unmoving, except for his breathing, and feeling neither sorrow nor
pain.

When he got Ross to his own bed, Lyle did not let him lie down,
but sat next to him on the edge, holding the professor's head against
his shoulder, patting his back comfortingly as if he were a baby.
They were on the precipice now. A wrong move could send Ross
over the brink into mental instability, which would make Vologda
impracticable and Cane's sacrifice worthless. Ross needed to see Geoffrey Howlett. Lyle decided to phone the psychiatric unit as soon as
he could. But before that, if he was to build up any sort of relationship with the professor, he felt he personally had to persuade him
back from the edge and onto steadier ground. So Lyle talked, calmly
and soothingly, while he rubbed and patted Ross's back, and the
other man's tears soaked through his shirt. He talked about David,
the meaning of sacrifice, heroism, war, opportunity, duty, peace. Lyle
let his thoughts pour out, more honestly and freely than he had ever
done in his life. He spoke of the months Cane and Ross had put in at
Fairfax, the bonds that had grown between them. Cane's pride at
how Ross had handled the London assignment, and his guts at tack-
ling the difficult physical challenges.

"At the end, David trusted you," Lyle said softly. "He didn't spell
out what he planned doing. That would have put you in an impossible position. He just gave you a clue, and then he went and did it.
Don't mourn for him, Martin. It was quick and painless. David had
an injection and went to sleep, that's all. But he did it for you,
Martin. For the mission. He did it so *you* could carry on. You, with
your terrific mind and your guts. You thought David had everything.

You loved him. Well, he knew—we all knew—that none of us really had what it took to crack Vologda, except you. Your brain, your knowledge. Without you, there is no mission. If you flunk out now, David's sacrifice becomes meaningless. He'd have died for nothing. And if Special Collection hits, we'll probably all die—millions of us. The free world will be destroyed. But David trusted you. He knew you'd do the right thing. Accept his gift, Martin. Everything David had, his life, he gave to you so you could go to Vologda. You owe it to him to try. What do you say, huh? You gonna let David down?"

Ross's weeping had quietened, and Lyle could feel him shake his head.

He hugged Ross, held him tight. "That's the way," he said softly. "David knew you'd come through. He didn't misjudge you. But we've got to do it soon, right?"

A nod.

"Good boy. No time to waste. You know the score. We've got to get this mission back on the rails as soon as we can. I don't know how soon they can do the operation, maybe tomorrow, I don't know. But as soon as they can, we're going to get in there and *do it!* Right?"

Muffled: "Right."

"And then you and I are gonna get back to Fairfax. There's a lot of work to do. Remember that assault course I was telling you about? David holds the record for getting through that. Four minutes flat. My best time was two seconds slower. But Christ, with David's equipment you're going to equal his time, you hear? I'll see that you do. I'll be there to help you, every day, every step. Any problem you've got, whatever it is, talk it out with me. There're gonna be a lot of problems, and they'll all be personal and different. So you've got *me,* and you've got a guy called Geoffrey Howlett. He's a good man. Runs the psychiatric unit here, and there's nothing in the world he hasn't had to deal with sometime in his life. I'll ask him to come down and say hi this afternoon. He's gonna be a friend, like me. We'll see you through this, and we're gonna get you off to Vologda. And when you get back, we'll have the biggest fucking party you've ever seen. Okay, Martin?"

"Okay. Okay, Clive."

"Good boy. Now lie down—here, you have to wipe your eyes. Feeling better?"

"Yes."

"It's a lot to take on board all at once, but you're doing fine. You comfortable?"

"Yes, thanks."

"Shall I send Dr. Howlett down?"

"Sure. If you want."

"I do. Anything on your mind, talk it out with him. I'll tell Barry we're ready to go whenever they are."

"Clive?"

"Yeah, Martin?"

"When are they going to pull the plug on David?"

"When the operation's under way, I guess. But it doesn't mean anything, Martin. David's been dead a week now. What we've got is what he bequeathed to you—his body. The machines are just keeping it in top condition for the transplant. Don't worry about it, you hear?"

"Okay, Clive." Ross hesitated, his face anxious. "Before you go, there's one thing I want from you."

"Name it."

"A promise. If I go into this thing and the operation doesn't work out . . . I'm a hemiplegic or I can't talk at all . . . then I want out. I don't want to be a prisoner in some other man's crippled body for fifty years. Especially not David's. You understand what I'm saying?"

"Yeah, I understand."

"I know the legal position, and what I'm asking you to do. But I also know the sort of guy you are. I want you to kill me in some quick, obscure way. Measles."

Lyle grinned. "You're picking up the jargon," he said. "Okay, here's the deal. If the transplant flunks out and you're not able to go on the mission, then I'll come around to visit you. If you can talk and you tell me you want to quit, I'll respect that decision and do what I can. If you can't talk for any reason and the prognosis is bad, I'll just go ahead by myself."

"Will it hurt?"

"No, not much. I've had a lot of practice."

"David was right. You are a bastard." But Ross was at least attempting to smile."

"Is that a deal?"

"That's a deal," Ross said. He held out his hand, and Lyle gripped it. "Now you'd better send the shrink down, Clive. If my mind's all I've got left, I'd better keep it in some sort of shape."

"That's the spirit."

"What about David's wife, Clive? I haven't even met her."

"No. Oh well, that's a problem. She doesn't know what David did, or anything about the transplant. She can't ever be told either because it compromises security. We couldn't expect a grieving wife to understand the point of the sacrifice, particularly when there aren't going to be any visible signs of success and no public acclaim, even after Vologda works. And we couldn't expect her to shut up about it for the rest of her life. There'd come a point where she'd tell her best friend, or her new husband"—he saw the professor flinch, but it was true, of course; her life would go on without David— "and that person would confide to *their* best friend, and the next thing you know it's in *The New York Times*. It's too good a story to keep quiet. So Mrs. Cane believes David had a stroke. She's agreed to switch off the life-support system. In a few days there'll be a funeral at Arlington, and she can make a new start. She's young and pretty, and she's got a great little kid. It won't be difficult."

The professor cleared his throat. "About the funeral, Clive. How're you going to manage that?"

"We'll seal the coffin."

"Empty?"

"I don't know. We'll weight it with something, I guess. I haven't thought that far ahead, but I suppose Yardley has. The thing is that if you do see Maryann Cane before the operation, you mustn't even hint what's happening. As far as she's concerned, David died naturally, and she'll be shown the form he signed consenting to have any of his organs used for transplants, and that'll be it. If any shadow of doubt enters her mind now, it'll haunt her for years. That would be cruel. And it would be dangerous to the mission. Don't forget how many millions of lives hang on everything you do, every conversation you have. Anything else?"

"Yeah. One other thing. Have they already taken out David's brain? I saw he had an operation."

Lyle shook his head. "No operation," he said. "The only thing they did was shave his head, and they'll have to do that again before the transplant. The bandages are for his wife's benefit, otherwise she'd wonder why nothing was done to get the clot out of her husband's brain. It's part of the smoke screen."

"I see. Okay, send in the shrink. And don't forget our deal."

"I never forget deals. You can trust me. David trusted me, you know. Even when we were enemies. He trusted me as an operative. He thought I was an immoral bastard. He called me a killer. And I guess that's what you want me to be, isn't it?"

"I guess so."

Lyle waved briefly and walked out to phone Geoffrey Howlett. Ross was going to make it, he thought, providing there were no problems with the transplant. And just how big a risk was that? Jeremy Howard claimed a seventy-percent-plus chance of success, but he was theorizing after working on dogs and monkeys. A human brain was far more complex, and the room for failure correspondingly larger. In the end Vologda 2 might result in a case of measles, a depressing finale to an abortive, wasteful operation.

Lyle had made his call to the psychiatric unit, using the internal phone in the reception area, when he saw Maryann Cane emerge from the elevator and come slowly along the corridor toward him. The only time he had met her before was when, by coincidence, he spotted David emerging from a performance at the National Theater off Pennsylvania Avenue and, in an effort to mend fences, went across to say hello and offer a drink. David, if he'd been by himself, would probably have told him to fuck off, but with Maryann there, introductions were dutifully made, and they walked the few blocks to the bar at the Sheraton-Carlton on Sixteenth and K streets. David was being professionally formal, so Lyle concentrated on making his wife like him, and at the end of forty minutes, when Cane insisted they had to leave, he thought he'd succeeded. No progress with David, though. That finally had to be done on different territory, and in a different way.

Maryann looked drained and exhausted. Lyle walked over to greet her. She remembered and was glad to see him.

"You look like you have to get out of here," Lyle said. "Want a quick drink? Even a slow one?"

A wave of gratitude overcame her. "Oh God, that really is what I need, Clive. I feel I've spent my whole life in this hospital."

As they took the elevator to street level, Lyle pondered whether to take her back to the Sheraton-Carlton, where they had a reference point and memories, or to opt for somewhere different. He decided on a bar on Vermont Avenue where they could sit in a booth and talk undisturbed.

But Maryann said suddenly: "Look, would you mind if we didn't go anywhere public? I don't feel I could face that at the moment."

"Sure." Lyle pressed the elevator button for the basement garage. "We'll go to my apartment if you like. How's David?"

"Let's not kid around, Clive," Maryann said. "We all know how

David is. He's dead, and we're just coming around to formally recognizing the fact."

"I'm sorry."

"So am I. More than you'll know. But I guess that's the way it goes."

"What happens now?"

"I'll spend tonight at the hospital. Two specialists are coming to see David in a few minutes—one of the reasons I don't want to be around. The third comes in the morning. If they all agree, Dr. Barry will switch off the life-support system. It'll be over this time tomorrow."

The elevator reached the basement, and they emerged into the gray concrete parking garage. Lyle guided her to his twin-seater MGB sports car. You can always tell a bachelor, she thought. And Lyle was thinking, *It'll all be starting tomorrow. Jesus, what a risk. What stakes we're playing for.*

But as he drove up the ramp and into the beginning of the late afternoon rush hour, he said finally, "That's rough."

"Yes, it is."

"But just as well. There's no point pretending, hoping for a miracle that's never going to come, turning yourself and your family into wrecks."

"That's what I thought. Even if there was a chance of an improvement, I think I'd dread that even more. Imagine if David recovered enough so he knew what had happened to him but no more than that." She shuddered. "Anyway, I've spoken to Barry and given my consent, subject to the decision of the specialists. And they want to take some organs from him. Corneas, I guess, kidneys. I don't much like the idea myself, but David wanted it. Barry showed me a form he'd signed. David was a strange man in many ways, Clive. Very secretive. Of course, he had to be for his job—just like you probably. But he carried it into other things. He never told me about wanting to be a donor for a transplant, for example. But we didn't discuss that sort of thing. You know, death. The hazards of his work. We pretended they didn't exist. Do you realize you're the only one of his DIA colleagues I've ever met?"

Lyle glanced at her. "Is that so?"

"Apart from General Yardley. We went to dinner with him once, and he came and told me about David's stroke. Other than him—no one."

The MGB accelerated away from the lights, along Seventeenth Street and into N Street, where he had his apartment. "That's probably just as well," Lyle said. "What you don't know doesn't hurt you."

"Would I have been hurt if I'd known?"

Lyle considered this. "Not in the way you think," he said carefully. "But, for example, if the Russians thought David had been letting you into secrets, they might decide it was a good idea to lift you some morning and pull your fingernails out until you told them what you knew. Then they'd kill you."

"You're joking, Clive."

"No, I'm not. Sometimes I wish I was. If David didn't tell you things, it was for your own protection. People play dirty out there."

He pulled into a parking space and went around to open the door for Maryann.

Lyle's apartment was spacious, well-furnished, and very tidy, which surprised her, as she imagined bachelors lived in a certain degree of squalor.

"You got someone who looks after the place for you?" she asked as she took a seat on the sofa.

"A cleaning woman a couple of times a week."

"No girl friend?"

"No."

"Well, you know how to look after yourself. Can you cook?"

"Sure. What do you want to drink?"

"Whiskey, please."

Lyle poured two Scotches and flicked the PLAY button on his tape deck, not particularly because he wanted to hear anything but instinctively, because you never knew when someone had just been in to plant a bug, and music was an easy way of making listening in more difficult. He sat beside Maryann.

"Is there anything I can do to help?" he asked.

"Not really. Except, tell me about David. Not the secrets, just what he did, how he operated."

There was quite a bit she could know which would do neither her nor the DIA any harm, so Lyle, in his lazy, laconic way, told her stories about Fairfax and some of the non-Soviet bloc assignments Cane had been on in the early days. It was obvious she really knew nothing, and she was fascinated, and proud, and sad. They had more whiskey. Lyle changed the tape. The light in the room faded slowly, and he switched on lamps which gave out a soft glow. Then Maryann spoke about herself, life with David, and life without David.

There was a moment in the long conversation when the emphasis changed. Maryann made a point and as she gestured with her hand and dropped it, her fingers lightly brushed Lyle's thigh, almost by accident. A little while later, it happened again. The talk was routine, but the atmosphere became charged. Lyle, who rarely missed anything, knew exactly what was happening, and why, and where it would lead. The whiskey was an excuse, the music an unintentional counterpoint. The things that mattered were sadness, loneliness, need, and the ability to give comfort, which was his. He hoped, had the roles been reversed, that David would have done the same for him. He reached out and touched her lips with his fingers.

Maryann expected to feel ashamed when, around midnight, Lyle dropped her back at the DIA hospital and she hurried up to the intensive care unit to see David. But she found to her surprise that she did not. Perhaps it would have been different if something about David, or the ward, had changed, other than the relative contents of the suspended plastic bags. But it was as if she had never been gone, and it became clearer to her than ever that life, in any humanly intelligible way, had been extinct in David from the first day. She felt well, and happier. For her there was still a future, and it would be worthwhile, that much she'd discovered.

David had died quickly, and they were pretending he was dying slowly. Tomorrow they would ring down the curtain on the grim play they had been enacting, and the survivors would pick up the threads of their lives. She had loved David, more perhaps than she would love any man, but he was gone and there was no point prolonging the grief.

She sat by his bed, watching his face for almost an hour, imprinting his features on her memory, touching his skin and the matted blond hair on his arm, enjoying that at least for the last time.

Then she undressed and slept soundly in the bed next to his, caring no longer about the hissing of the breathing machine or the beeping of the cardiac monitor. She knew they were frauds.

Two rooms away Elaine Ross sat staring also for the last time at the motionless form of her husband. The operation was scheduled for ten A.M., although they had been warned there might be a last-minute delay. Martin was sleeping comfortably again, but she was too mentally alert and physically numb even to think of rest.

She and Martin had gone over the options with the psychiatrist and discussed superficially what the changes would mean. Martin had already made the decision, and Elaine couldn't help feeling that much of Geoffrey Howlett's talk and advice was for her benefit, not his. In some strange way Martin was moving on, and she was being left behind. If the operation worked, she would be a woman in her late fifties, and he would again be approaching the prime of life. What would happen to them? Could she look at the body of David Cane, even accept it into her bed, and see Martin there behind the strong young muscles and the different feel of another man?

She sighed. But that was in the future, a long way off. First, Martin had to survive the transplant. Second, he had to be turned into a functioning human being. Third, he had to become what David had been in his professional life—a trained agent and a killer. Fourth, he had to get into the Soviet Union and doctor the Vologda computer. Fifth, he had to come out again alive. And sixth . . . well, then would come the personal problems. Who would he be? Martin Ross? David Cane? Or a different third person? And what would it make her? A wife, or a widow?

Dr. Howlett hadn't pretended it would be easy or that he knew most of the questions, let alone all the answers. They were taking a step into the dark, and the adjustment would be hard. It needed to be taken slowly, and in many ways, Howlett thought it was helpful that they had the mission to concentrate on. That at least was a point of unity on which other things could be built. They should keep their eyes on the mission and work relentlessly for it. As they did, some of the problems would no doubt be resolved automatically, while others would benefit from being shelved until they could be looked at with fresh eyes after everyone had settled down and become used to the new situation, the changed circumstances.

The responsibility that David Cane had put on them both was awesome, and Elaine suddenly remembered her words to him at their first meeting when she was asked to agree to the Vologda mission: *You will either be a hero, or I will curse you to my grave.* Now she realized it might not be an either/or situation but a case of both.

Elaine Ross stayed up through the night, stirring from her chair only to return an empty cup of coffee. The door to David's ward was closed.

The hospital came awake before 6 A.M., with carts of medicines moving through the corridors and nurses talking. Martin had not been allowed to eat the previous night, and they let him sleep. Elaine could not understand how he could be so relaxed. The truth was that the increasing activity had actually woken him, but he continued to lie quietly, eyes closed, postponing the moment when he would formally have to face the morning. On this day the gamble would succeed or fail. He would die or be given new life. He lay, feeling the gnawing ache in his stomach from the operation and the cancer. That at least would be gone. This body and its corruption would be discarded. But would he inherit incorruption? And what else with it? After the first few hours of shock, Ross had blocked out thoughts of how a new form, a new identity, would change his life and his relationship with Elaine. He agreed with Geoffrey Howlett that they ought to concentrate on the mission. David's sacrifice and the transplant were for Vologda, nothing else. Later there would be time for agonizing.

But now Ross was afraid that by opening his eyes and sitting up, he would be expected to put on a brave, confident show for his wife, for the nurses, for Dr. Barry when he came down, and he feared they would see in his face only insecurity, timidity, and, worst of all, barely suppressed cowardice.

He wished David was with him. Or Clive Lyle. He decided he would try to keep his eyes closed until Lyle arrived to give him moral support.

Peter Barry came first. Ross could hear him talking to Elaine, then felt his hand being lifted and his pulse taken. It was becoming ridiculous. He couldn't maintain the charade for much longer. But, at last, Lyle's voice:

"Morning, Peter. Morning, Mrs. Ross. How's Martin?"

"Still sleeping," Elaine said.

He was conscious of Lyle's presence right beside him, and the lazy voice said, "You faking bastard. You're no more asleep than I am." Ross found himself starting to grin.

But he kept his eyes closed as he said, "I didn't feel like facing the day until all my forces were assembled."

"Well, they're assembled now. So rise and shine."

Ross sat up and looked around sheepishly. Lyle was smiling. Elaine seemed slightly reproachful as she greeted him.

"Already I know you inside out, Martin," Lyle said. "So you'd better not try anything when we get back to Fairfax because I'm on to you."

"Good morning, Professor," Dr. Barry said. "How do you feel?"

"Scared."

"That's natural. Oh, I've got a consent-to-operate form for you to sign." He pulled it off his clipboard and handed it to him. "You'll find it's worded pretty vaguely, for obvious reasons. It gives us permission to act as we think fit." He handed over a gold Parker pen, and Ross affixed his signature. It was done—the last official act of a dying body.

"Er, what about David, Doctor?" Ross asked.

"The formalities are being completed now. We ought to be able to start on schedule."

Ross nodded, feeling a stab of sadness and wishing he could take a final look at David—as David. His visit the day before had been too traumatic, too emotional, and he would have liked a quiet time by himself to say good-bye. But it seemed too much to ask, so instead he said, "Shouldn't I be seeing the anesthetist? Isn't that routine?"

"You're looking at him," Barry replied. "I'm going to do it myself. Don't worry—I'm fully qualified. I thought it would be appropriate. Now we have to shave your head. An orderly will come down in a few minutes to do it."

Ross hadn't thought about that, and it chilled him even more than signing the consent form. He glanced anxiously at Lyle.

"Why don't I do it for Martin?" Lyle offered, understanding instinctively what he was feeling and knowing that the presence of a stranger would make it worse. "I have to shave twice a week now," he joked, "and I almost never cut myself."

Barry shrugged. "Sure. If you want. I'll ask the nurses to bring the kit."

A few minutes later, Ross sat in a chair, a sheet draped around his neck, while Clive Lyle used electric shears on his thinning gray hair, cutting as close to the scalp as possible.

"You know, I thought I was going bald," Ross remarked. "But you seem to be getting a hell of a lot of hair off me."

Lyle grunted. "Hold still, can't you. I'm almost through with part one."

Ross, with uneven gray stubble on his scalp, looked so emaciated and vulnerable that Elaine felt a sickness in her stomach. Lyle, too, surveying his handiwork as he lathered the shaving brush, was aware of a wave of pity, but he said bluntly, "Shit, Martin, you look like something out of Belsen," and although Elaine recoiled at the cruelty of the remark, Lyle did appear to know how to handle Martin, because Ross laughed and said, "You wait till later, you bastard. I'll make you pay for that."

Lyle smiled. "You probably will too." He finished mixing the lather and smeared it over the scalp, then began shaving carefully starting at the crown. Although he had cut the hair as short as he could, the safety blade became clogged every few seconds and had to be run under hot water. The lather tinged red from small cuts, but Ross sat quiet and uncomplaining.

When Lyle had finished, including Ross's face, neck, and—very carefully on Barry's instructions—his eyebrows, the professor looked so much like a dying creature from outer space that Elaine had to turn away and left the small talk to Lyle who didn't seem to care.

"Yul Brynner, step aside," Lyle said, rinsing the brush.

"That's not a bad job, Clive," Barry approved. "When Yardley throws you out for incompetence, come and see me and I'll sign you up as an orderly."

"Gee, you really mean that? Oh wow!"

Ross felt strange. His head was naked and cold. There were no mirrors in the room, although he did have a small shaving glass in his bedside table. Half of him wanted to see what he looked like, but the other, more sensible half knew it would be a bad mistake. He could tell from Elaine's face, and from the way she avoided glancing at him, that he was not an agreeable sight. But he said: "Well, dear, how do you like it?" and she was forced to meet his eyes. He tried to look calm, brave, and reassuring, but he wasn't sure he made it.

"Ummm," Elaine replied gravely, playing along, although she could feel her hands had gone quite cold, "it's . . . different. I think it suits you. You should keep it like that."

"Yes," said Ross, "I think I will."

"And now," Peter Barry broke in, "it's time for some medication." He called a nurse who brought two tablets for Ross to swallow.

"What are these?"

"Sedatives. They'll relax you. You'll get an injection later, which will make you feel great. I'll give you the anesthetic upstairs."

"What's the time?"

Barry consulted his watch. "Eight o'clock."

Two hours to go. Jesus, could he make it till then? Ross swallowed the pills, and Lyle helped him back to bed.

Barry excused himself. "I'll come back about nine-thirty," he promised.

Lyle tried to make conversation, but it was difficult and soon they all lapsed into silence. Lyle chain-smoked. Ross stared at the ceiling and thought about Cane and Fairfax. And London. Oh Christ, London. That crawl through the ceiling. Metkin. Chersky. The Australian woman. Thousands of miles away, and a million years ago.

Elaine stared fixedly out the window. Ross felt great admiration. It was every bit as traumatic for her as it was for him, and she was bearing up with great courage.

So he said very distinctly: "My dear, I love you."

She looked round, startled, at the strange, nude face against the pillow, and after a moment she smiled: "I love you too."

Lyle watched the smoldering tip of his cigarette with an expression that gave away nothing.

In David Cane's room the third and final specialist had completed his examination and gone. Maryann was alone, feeling suddenly panicky. The moment was approaching, and an instinct told her she ought to resist longer, leave it another week, another month. What could be the harm in that? Perhaps there would be a miracle. She sat on the edge of her bed, her mind racing and confused.

David lay before her, as he had since his stroke, unmoving but for the rise and fall of his chest.

She walked over to him and bent close to his ear. "David," she said distinctly, "David, it's Maryann. This is very important, my darling. Very important. Can you hear me?" And even as she spoke, she felt ridiculous. Of course he couldn't hear, or understand. She crossed to the EEG and consulted the tracings. It was hopeless.

She went back and kissed his cheek. The skin was warm, and there was a stubble of heard which had grown since he was shaved the day before.

"Good-bye, my darling," she said softly. "I love you."

When she straightened up, Peter Barry was standing in the doorway, looking at her, she thought, with strange compassion.

"What's the verdict?" she asked in as businesslike a manner as she could.

"The specialists agree. Your husband has suffered irreversible brain damage. They have signed the appropriate papers."

"And so have I."

"Yes."

"Well? What now?"

"We switch off. The DIA have made appropriate arrangements for David's body after we've removed what we need for transplantation. If you agree, the funeral will be at Arlington the day after tomorrow, at ten A.M., with full military honors."

Full military . . . Maryann felt she would choke. She had learned to cope with the big things, like pulling the plug on David, but she was forever being taken unawares by the small personal details, poignant and sharp as needles.

Peter Barry reached in his pocket and took out a plastic container. He shook two pills into his hand, got some water, and held them out to Maryann. "Take these," he said.

She shook her head. "No, I . . ."

"Take them. It's an order."

She did as she was told. Barry glanced at his watch: nine o'clock. From his breast pocket he pulled a white envelope, which he handed to her. "This is from General Yardley. He asked me to give it to you myself rather than put it in the mail."

"Thank you."

Barry asked gently: "Would you like more time by yourself, to say good-bye?"

She shook her head. "No. I've done it."

"Do you want to leave?"

She took a deep breath, then another. "No," she said. "I'll stay. Do what you have to do."

Barry took two paces to the wall plugs, flicked the switches and the machines fell silent. The breathing machine ceased hissing, and Cane's chest no longer moved. The cardiac monitor stopped bleeping and the oscilloscope screen went dark. Peter Barry felt David's pulse.

After a minute he said: "The heart is stopping now." Maryann began to tremble. Barry's long, elegant fingers continued holding David's wrist, then he pressed a stethoscope to his chest and listened for what seemed like a long time.,

He straightened up. "That's it," he said. "It's gone," and to demonstrate he stepped back to a wall plug and switched on the cardiac monitor. The bleep had become a single, unbroken tone, and the line across the oscilloscope screen was straight.

Maryann turned away.

Barry pulled the sheet up to cover Cane's face and put a comforting arm around the young woman. "I think you'd better go and have a cup of coffee now," he said gently. "We have work to do."

He took her as far as the door and motioned for a nurse to take over. As Maryann was being led down the corridor, Barry turned abruptly.

Time was critical. He flicked on the wall switches with his foot. The artificial respirator began pumping, sssssssss . . .sssssssss, the EEG resumed its pointless measurements. Barry uncovered Cane and, putting the heel of the palm of his right hand on the breastbone, pushed down strongly, depressing almost two inches, then released, and pushed down again. The cardiac monitor blipped once and stopped. Barry pushed . . . released. Jesus, this wasn't the moment for Cane's body to give up on them. Push . . . release. Push . . . release. Five times more, then he would use the electrodes. Push . . . push . . . push . . . and the monitor blipped, then again, and the heart began beating finally.

Barry sighed with relief. Color was gradually restored to Cane's face. He waited several minutes to assure himself that body function was stable before checking on the whereabouts of Maryann Cane. She could not be allowed to see her husband's heart going again. But the nurse had taken her to another floor.

Barry telephoned an order to the operating room, and within five minutes orderlies lifted Cane onto a stretcher cart and, breathing for him with a ventilation bag, wheeled him to the elevator.

Nurses stripped the bed and made it up with fresh sheets. They took away the life-support equipment.

When Maryann Cane returned fifteen minutes later, there was no sign David had ever been there.

She was glad not to have to look at him again, or see the dead, sheet-covered shape.

Her mind was full of the phone calls she would have to make to friends who had to be told, and on whose moral support she would be relying over the next days. She even wondered where Clive Lyle was and whether she should tell him it was over, but she wasn't sure she wanted to see him again so soon. Then she remembered the letter from Yardley.

She took it from the pocket of her dress, turned it over, wondering if she should read it now or later when she felt stronger. Her fingers made the decision for her, tearing open the envelope automatically.

Yardley's handwriting sprawled across a single sheet of paper.

My dear Maryann,
David was one of the bravest men I ever met, and certainly one of the finest operatives in the history of this agency. You will never know some of the things he did for his country, but he lived and died a soldier. I share your grief, and your loss, deeply.

The attached acknowledges the debt which the United

States of America owes to David. In addition, you will receive his full pension for the remainder of your natural life, regardless of any future change in your personal circumstances, as well as the usual medical benefits. If I, or any member of the DIA, can be of assistance to you at any time, you only have to ask.

My prayers are with you.

Lyndon Yardley

Stapled to the letter was a check for half a million dollars.,

For the last time in that hospital, Maryann Cane broke down and wept.

Upstairs, in a preoperative room, the bandages were removed from Cane's head, and the stubble of hair which had grown over several days was shaved off together with his eyebrows.

In the interval before the operation began, the endotracheal tube was again connected to an automatic respirator to relieve an orderly of the chore of squeezing the ventilation bag. Screens were wheeled around Cane before Martin Ross, having been given additional premedication and now in a happy, drowsy state, was brought up and parked a few feet away while Barry and two neurosurgical teams prepared to scrub up and don their green sterile gowns and rubber gloves.

Two tables had been placed side by side in the operating room, with a scrub nurse responsible for each. The scrub nurses had been on duty since early that morning, wheeling what looked like supermarket carts into the sterile storage room and loading them with sterilized bundles of surgical instruments, double-wrapped in green linen sheets and secured with long strips of masking tape. They helped themselves to air drills, Bovie cords, sterile sheets, towels, gowns, pillowcases, silk sutures, dozens of boxes of bone wax, and all the other requisites of neurosurgery.

Many of these they packed on shelves along the rear wall of the operating room. Nonsterile instruments, such as Gigli saws and fishhooks, were put into the autoclave for sterilizing.

The operating room was divided into sterile and unsterile zones. Later only two operating room nurses—circulators—would be permitted to go freely between the zones, fetching necessary supplies for each team.

The scrub nurses made sure that enough Mayo stands were in position—adjustable steel tables about two feet square on which instruments, air drills, and fiberoptic lights could be kept.

In the scrub room Peter Barry, Professor Jeremy Howard, who was the overall leader of the teams, three other neurosurgeons, assistant surgeons, and a second anesthesiologist were scrubbing up to their elbows with hexachlorophene sponges for ten minutes, then washing in alcohol for thirty seconds to reduce their bacteria skin count even further.

The chief operating room nurse, who had already scrubbed, was in the operating room making a final check, and her assistants were helping the teams into sterile gowns, caps, and masks.

David Cane was wheeled in first and placed on a low table. The circulator slipped a metal Bovie plate under his naked buttocks, to ground his body to the Bovie machine and complete the circuit for the electric knife. Cane's legs were wrapped in elastic bandages from toe to groin, and a large webbing strap was fastened around his waist to hold his body to the table.

The surgeons began filtering in and, at their instructions, Cane's inert trunk was raised and propped until he was almost sitting up, his head cradled in a holder attached to the end of the table.

Peter Barry and the second anesthesiologist checked Cane's position to make sure it was balanced and that there would be a proper circulation of blood to and from the heart.

An assistant surgeon clamped a cotton ball in sponge forceps and soaked it in Merthiolate. He painted the scalp liberally while the circulator held a gauze pad over Cane's eyes to prevent the antiseptic from running in—not that they wanted the eyes for later, but there was a certain form to be observed. The assistant dropped used cotton balls into a stainless-steel bucket on the floor and turned his attention to swabbing the Merthiolate deep into Cane's ears, cleaning them thoroughly to get rid of bacteria colonies.

"Why aren't we taking his corneas?" the assistant asked. "I'm sure we could use them."

"Not enough time," Barry said shortly. "Too many other things to worry about."

Then a green linen square with a large hole in the center was draped over Cane so that only his skull, eyes, ears, and the top of his nose were visible. An assistant taped the sheet onto the flesh around his face and neck with waterproof adhesive bandage.

The breathing machine hissed regularly, and the cardiac monitor registered a strong heartbeat.

There was no point in anesthetizing Cane. It would only be necessary later when his body became alive again. When, or if.

Barry wrapped a blood-pressure cuff around a stethoscope on Cane's right arm. From that point on the second anesthesiologist would read the blood pressure every five minutes and record it on a chart.

Barry went out to the preop room to attend to Ross.

"How are you feeling?" he asked.

"Great. Whatever you gave me is good stuff."

"I know it. Okay, we're ready to go." Barry prepared a Pentothal injection. "A small prick in your arm, nothing to worry about." Ross felt the needle pierce his flesh. "Count backward from twenty for me."

"Twenty, nineteen, eighteen, seventeen, sixteen, fifteen, fourteen, thirteen . . ."

Blackness.

They wheeled Ross into the operating room and strapped him onto the low table while Barry pushed a needle into the vein above his wrist and established an IV line with a five percent dextrose solution dripping in. He covered Ross's mouth with a mask and opened the valves of the gas tanks to pump in a mixture of oxygen and nitrous oxide. When that was done, the blood-pressure cuff was attached to Ross's right arm and ECG leads taped to the inside of his thighs, elbow, and shoulder. Each beat of Ross's heart threw up a spiky light trace on the green oscilloscope screen and a second steady beep . . . beep . . . beep could be heard, matching Cane's cardiac monitor.

When Barry was satisfied, he moved on to the next part of the procedure. Seventy milligrams of tubocurarine chloride were injected into the IV tube's rubber connector, paralyzing Ross's breathing.

Barry opened Ross's mouth, checked automatically for dentures, although he already knew there were none, and slipped a nine-inch-long, slightly curved plastic tube smeared with local anesthetic into the throat, past the vocal cords, and deep into the trachea. Swiftly he attached a flexible rubber hose to the endotracheal tube and fastened the other end to a breathing machine. Two artificial respirators now hissed rhythmically in the operating room.

The others maneuvered Ross's body almost into a sitting position, with the metal Bovie plate under his bare flesh and his head cradled in a holder so that Professor Howard and his team could get at his brain. The webbing straps were tightened. The green linen drape covered his body and the lower part of his face, as it did Cane's, and was taped into position.

Barry disconnected the respirator and found that the curare-type paralyzing drug had worn off. Ross was again breathing for himself. It was important to maintain this state for as long as possible, as it was only in this way that they would know if they were causing damage to the breathing centers of his brain. And even this warning system would be of limited duration. From the moment the brain was removed, they would not know if they had been overtaken by disaster until after the transplant had been completed.

Barry lifted the lids of Ross's eyes and squirted in antibiotic ointment to seal them. An assistant taped the lids shut. This was a precaution to prevent the corneas from drying and becoming ulcerated during the next long hours.

It was exactly ten o'clock.

Across at Cane's table, Professor Howard, masked, capped, and gowned, took from the scrub nurse a bottle of an alcohol-based dye, methylene blue, and outlined on Cane's scalp the incision he wanted made. He kept it to the hairline as much as he could, not only for cosmetic reasons but for security as well. The fewer distinctive features, particularly scars, that an operative had, the safer he was. The blue line went around the skull, low to the point where the brain channeled down into the medulla oblongata and became the brainstem. Then it bisected the crown, from the line above the forehead to the back of the head.

Jeremy Howard turned to his neurosurgical colleagues. "Gentlemen," he said, "I think you can get moving with this one."

The neurosurgeon heading Cane's team checked to make sure the scrub nurse was ready and automatically looked over at the second anesthesiologist.

"Are you ready?"

The man shrugged. His patient was clinically dead and the question of pain did not arise until he became clinically alive, by which time Peter Barry would have moved across and taken over. But Cane's heartbeat was strong, his blood pressure normal.

"Ready," he said.

The neurosurgeon injected adrenaline deep into Cane's scalp around the cutting line marked out by Professor Howard, so that when he went in with a scalpel the blood vessels would be constricted and the bleeding reduced.

Jeremy Howard marked Ross's skull with his blue lines as he had for Cane.

He checked the scrub nurse. Okay. He looked over at Peter Barry. "Are you ready?"

Barry turned a valve, deepening Ross's anesthesia. "Ready."

"Right. Let's get this show on the road." Professor Howard began injecting adrenaline, working swiftly over these easy initial stages because soon they would be into painstaking, critical work and the hours would drag out. "Where's the circulator?"

"Here, Doctor."

"Well, where the hell's the music?"

"Sorry, Doctor. I wasn't sure whether you wanted it today."

"'Course I want it. I never operate without something to take my mind off my work."

There were grins around the table. Jeremy Howard was famous for this foible. Some surgeons tell jokes or talk about golf. Others are silent and snap commands. The ones who joke or listen to music are more popular with the operating room staff and their surgical colleagues because they help reduce the tension, and a delicate job can be done with greater ease and efficiency.

"You don't mind music while you cut, do you, Gordon?" Professor Howard asked his middle-aged colleague, who was making an incision deep down to Cane's skull.

"Not as long as it isn't the sort of crap my daughter makes me listen to at home."

"No, this is a different sort of crap."

The circulator found the cassette recorder and a tape of chamber music. The sound of violins, cellos, and a harpsicord filled the operating room.

"That's more like it," Professor Howard said. "Look, my hand's stopped shaking already."

There was laughter.

Above their heads, sitting alone behind glass in the viewing gallery, Clive Lyle grinned. He liked the man's style. Lyle had never watched a brain operation before, and he imagined it would be pretty bad. In fact, it already looked gruesome with Cane and Ross almost sitting up, with just the domes of their shaven, painted heads, their ears, and closed eyes visible through the green sheets. But Lyle prided himself on being virtually inured to anything the world could throw at him, and he was determined to sit through it. He heard a noise behind him and glanced around to see General Yardley coming in.

"Morning, Clive. How's it going?"

"Just starting, sir."

Yardley settled in beside him. "What the hell's that music?"

"Telemann, if I'm not mistaken."

"What's Telemann?"

"Eighteenth-century German composer. Chamber music."

"Jesus. Trust you to know that. How's Ross?"

"Seemed pretty good this morning. Considering."

Yardley grunted and peered down. Professor Howard's scalpel cut lightly across the incision made on Ross's head, opening a thin, red line. Then the knife went deep, cutting down through the scalp to the skull, and the skin separated and split wide, showing briefly the yellow layer of fat before it became masked with blood, which an assistant sucked out with an aspirator.

Yardley swallowed hard.

The identical scene was being enacted with Cane, although his neurosurgical team had advanced further. His scalp had been cut right along the marked lines, except for three-inch sections just above the ears. Unless a scalp flap remained attached in this way, it would be starved of its blood supply during surgery and would die.

Around the cut the edges of the wound were clamped with dozens of small hemostats to shut off the main blood vessels.

Small cotton pads, which had been carefully counted out by the scrub nurse and the circulator were pushed into the cut to sop up oozing blood and keep the operating area dry.

Professor Howard worked quickly and had almost caught up with his colleague on the other team. It was time to turn back the scalp and expose the skull, which meant severing a thin membrane.

"Tooth forceps," said the team leader working on David.

"Tooth forceps," called Jeremy Howard, holding out his right hand.

The scrub nurses, waiting, ready, passed the instruments. The forceps lifted both men's scalps, exposing the membrane. Both surgeons reached for their Bovie knives.

The Bovie electrosurgical unit is an invention that cuts tissues or coagulates blood vessels, depending on the strength of the electrical current selected. The SCALPEL setting on the Bovie's black box gives a higher voltage and lets the sterile electric knife cut brain tissue like a blade through fairly hard butter.

The COAGULATION setting produces a lower voltage and sears the ends of blood vessels to stop bleeding.

"Scalpel."

"Scalpel."

The assistants on both teams checked the settings.

"Cutting."

"Cutting."

The assistants stepped on the foot pedals, completing the circuit from the ACTIVE jackplug, through the metal Bovie plates under Cane's and Ross's naked flesh, to the GROUND jack, and blue sparks jumped from the knives to the wounds, followed by wisps of smoke.

In the viewing gallery Yardley closed his eyes, almost able to smell burning flesh. "I'll leave you alone, Clive," he said abruptly. "I've got a lot to do today. Drop in and let me know how it went."

Lyle, unable to take his eyes off the scene, nodded abstractedly. "Yeah, sure." Yardley went away, trying not to hurry and not looking back.

The procedure was repeated, then the halves of scalp on each man's head were peeled back like the skins of tangerines. Jeremy Howard was a little ahead now, ordering the Bovie setting to be changed to COAGULATION to seal the oozing blood on the raw, red inside of the scalp.

"Fishhooks."

The scrub nurse handed over two bent wires attached to heavy rubber bands, which Howard pushed into the raw side of the scalp. He pulled the rubber bands taut so they could be attached to the green drapes and would hold the right-hand scalp flap out of the way.

He did the same to the left side of Ross's head.

The white bone of the skull was exposed. Howard hummed with the music, preoccupied but relaxed, as if he were pruning the roses at home or putting together a model airplane from some fairly simple kit.

The circulating nurse rolled a nitrogen tank into position behind Jeremy Howard, and stood holding a large, fairly heavy drill fitted with a half-inch-diameter bit.

Professor Howard glanced over at the other team. "How's it going there?"

"We're winning, slowly."

Howard could see Cane's scalp flaps being secured.

The tape ended, and without being asked the circulator said, "Okay, okay, as soon as you've taken the drill, I'll turn it over. Don't bite my head off."

Howard smiled. "I cut heads, darling," he said. "I never bite them." He took the drill. "Now move, before my hand starts shaking again."

"You should take up smoking, Jeremy," one of the neurosurgeons said. "It'll calm you down, and I've got a friend who does damn good lung operations, cheap."

"I should give up drinking, that's what I should do."

With both hands he lifted the drill and placed the bit against the front of the skull, just by the edge of the wound. An assistant held Ross's head steady.

There was a scream from the nitrogen-powered motor, a hiss of escaping gas, and the bit chewed efficiently through the bone. The assistant dribbled saline solution from a syringe onto the bit to cool it and flush away chips. The liquid flowed down Ross's face, onto the green drape, and finally into the "brain buckets" at their feet.

The drill broke through the other side of the skull, just as the rival scream began coming from Cane's table, and the automatic chuck, with nothing to press against, instantly stopped the bit from turning.

Professor Howard wriggled the drill to pull it free and held out a hand. "Bone wax."

A small lump was passed to him, and he pressed it into the hole, which had filled with blood. The mixture of beeswax and formaldehyde plugged the gap and stopped the bleeding.

Silence from Cane's table as the procedure was repeated there.

Each team drilled a total of sixteen holes in the skulls of their patients while saline solution was squirted liberally over the bone and ran down the unexposed parts of their faces, carrying bone dust, chips, and small clots of blood. Jeremy Howard hummed happily. "How long have we been going?" he asked suddenly.

"Fifty minutes."

"Not bad. I've got to take my wife to lunch. Think we can get it wrapped up by then?"

"Sure," Peter Barry said. "As long as it's lunch tomorrow."

"How's Ross doing?"

"As well as can be expected."

"Shithead."

"Blood pressure one twenty over eighty. Pulse seventy, steady.

Blood pH, etcetera, fine at last look. I thought music made you good-tempered."

"It makes me less bad-tempered than I would be otherwise. Let's have the saw guide."

Clive Lyle, feeling queasy in the viewing gallery, watched the scrub nurse hand Professor Howard a long, thin metal strip. The surgeon cleared the bone wax out of two adjoining holes and carefully inserted the saw guide through one, pushing it along gently until it came into sight at the other. He retrieved this end. The procedure looked simple, but unless it was done with great care and skill, the saw guide could tear through the dura, the membrane directly beneath which was all that now separated them from Martin Ross's brain, and dig into the tissue itself.

"Gigli saw."

A flexible wire saw was put into Howard's hand, and he attached one end to a hook on the saw guide, which he then carefully pulled until the front end of the Gigli itself emerged from the second hole. Howard fitted wire loop handles and while an assistant held Ross's head firmly, he pulled strongly and steadily on alernate ends of the saw. The teeth of the Gigli bit into bone, raising a fine spray of dust.

"This is the part that reminds me of that old Bobby Darin number, 'If I Were a Carpenter,'" Howard mused aloud. "You know, Gordon, I put up some shelves at home last weekend."

A sound of sawing came from Cane's table. "How do they look?"

"Terrible. Fell out of the wall."

"Better stick to people."

Lyle was definitely queasy now, and he averted his face, just as the two assistants, holding the heads of Ross and Cane, were doing to keep the bone dust out of their eyes. Lyle considered going out for a while for some fresh air, but instead he lit a cigarette and inhaled deeply. It would be worse later coming in cold. At least he was watching the procedure stage by stage and he could follow what was happening and why. But to just walk in—Jesus. And surely this had to be the really bad part. It couldn't get worse.

They were only an hour into the operation. But what a distance that seemed from the morning when he'd shaved Ross's head. It might have been years earlier.

Jeremy Howard was starting on the next small piece of skull. Lyle realized it was going to be a long business, sawing through fifteen sections of bone. Assuming a constant five minutes on each section, they would be going at it for more than an hour.

He sighed. It was good practice for him, he supposed, and it would certainly get easier with repetition, as everything did. So Lyle watched and concentrated, and gradually his stomach calmed down. He noticed that Howard and Gordon what's his name working on Cane weren't just hacking away at the bone, but were carefully beveling the cut edge so that when they came to put it back, the flaps would sit flat and stable.

At last, one side of Cane's skull had been completed, and Howard lifted it off carefully, handing it to a scrub nurse, who immersed it in a saline-solution dish. Cane's team still had the final space to saw before they could do the same.

Lyle, Howard, and the first surgical team stared in at the half-exposed, shiny dura which covered Ross's brain—the last flimsy protection for the mind which held the key to the Vologda computers.

The assistant squirted water over it and the edges of the open skull, flushing away the last particles of bone, and Howard pressed bone wax along the cut to stop the ooze of blood.

When this was done, he started sawing the opposite section.

It was after midday before the brains of Martin Ross and Dave Cane had been totally exposed, and work began on cutting through identical areas of bone surrounding their middle and inner ears. When this was over the surgeons eased the brains back from the foreheads, holding them gently so they could saw through the frontal air sinuses, and then, working from the front, they detached the muscles of the eyes.

The neurosurgeons checked regularly on the conditions of their patients. Both continued stable. Lyle from his vantage point could see what they were doing in these latest stages and understood they were saving themselves the additional risk of having to transplant the eyes—and the extra time it would involve even if they had perfected the techniques. As it was, the operation would last the whole day and well into the night, and it was a question of how long the teams could maintain their concentration. People can drive themselves only to a certain point, after which efficiency drops sharply and, often, suddenly.

The Telemann had long finished, to be replaced by Hoffmeister and then by Haydn. From time to time Professor Howard hummed absent-mindedly.

He straightened up and stretched. "God," he said, "I'm getting too old for this sort of thing. How're you feeling, Gordon?"

"I'll have a stretch in a second. Then I'll be fine."

Jeremy Howard walked over to the other table and checked the progress on Cane. "Not too bad," he said carefully. "No one would think this was the first time you'd cracked someone's skull. You must have been watching 'General Hospital.'"

"All the time," Gordon replied. "I only go wrong when someone disturbs my concentration by humming."

"I could sing if you liked. Or whistle."

"Thank you, Jeremy. Humming will be fine."

"You ready to go?"

"Why not? Sooner we do it, sooner we get home."

The scrub nurses helped them strip their gloves, which were dusted with fine bone particles, and pull on fresh pairs.

The circulators mopped the floor beneath the tables to clear away water and bone fragments which are irritating to stand in for long periods as they crunch underfoot and make the surface slippery. A dolly was drawn up beside Ross.

Cane's brain was dead, but Ross's had to be kept in peak condition.

The functioning human brain needs glucose and oxygen in great quantities and in an uninterrupted supply. A three-minute break in blood flow will mean irreversible cerebral tissue damage unless the body temperature has been lowered. Blood, carrying exact quantities of nutrients, reaches the brain through two internal carotid arteries in the front and two vertebral arteries in the back. Professor Howard had to avoid interrupting the flow for more than a few seconds. His alternative, if he wanted more time, was to lower the temperature of the brain so that it required less nourishment, but this carried the risk of a slight degree of cerebral degeneration down to 20 degrees Celsius, and profound injury below that. No one was prepared to take the chance with Martin Ross. What if the slight degeneration affected his intellectual functions?

The neurosurgeons worked carefully, exposing the arteries of their patients, while around them the circulators arranged the reservoirs of blood, the oxygenators, arterial pumps, and venous pumps, and the heat exchangers necessary to ensure supplies to Ross's brain and Cane's body.

Jeremy Howard's degree of absorption increased. Lyle, watching from the gallery, noticed that after the mechanical, routine manner in which he had removed the scalp and most of the skull, he was now totally involved.

Lyle could only occasionally see the rapt expression in Howard's eyes when he raised his head to let the scrub nurse wipe his brow, but it was mostly in the hunching of the shoulders that the concentration showed. Lyle thought that if the music stopped and the circulator failed to change the tape, Howard would no longer notice. The only sounds he was listening for now were the bleepings of the monitors and the occasional announcements by Peter Barry of blood pressure, pulse rate, and the routine blood pH, Pco_2, and oxygen saturation measurements.

Howard checked the autoperfusion system drawn up around him, and when he was satisfied, he said to the scrub nurse, "Get ready with the cannula."

"I've got it, Doctor." She stood close with a small, specially designed, siliconized surgical tube shaped like a T. Howard clamped two sections of a carotid artery, then quickly sliced between them. He ignored the sudden, brief flow of blood, felt the cannula being slapped into his open hand, and inserted it, clipping the artery tight around it. He completed the connection to the reservoir.

"Run!" he ordered. Beside him, a pump began to hum, and warm, oxygenated, glucose-rich blood flowed into Ross's brain.

"Time?" Howard asked.

"Thirty-two seconds, Doctor."

Howard grunted. That was acceptable. He moved to the second carotid artery, clamped, cut, and inserted.

"Run!"

"Pulse sixty-five," announced Barry.

At the next table, he could hear the identical procedure being followed, at a more leisurely pace. They were providing alternate circulation to Cane's body, which could tolerate longer interruptions, and their pump was acting as a backup for his own heart.

Howard went around to the exposed vertebral arteries, moving swiftly but trying not to rush. Barry began intoning changes in Ross's pulse as his heart strained to push blood to a brain that had had two of its main channels suddenly blocked. The monitor bleeped slower, irregular.

"Cardiac distress," Barry said.

Clamp. Cut. "Cannula! . . . Run!"

One to go. Clamp. Cut. Spurt of blood. Cannula in place and secured. "Run!"

Ross's heart bucked, fibrillated. The oscilloscope line jerked impotently. The monitor tone became constant, monotonous. The trace went across the screen, straight and unbroken. The professor's heart had given up.

"Heart function terminated," Barry intoned formally.

Howard closed the circle at the base of the brain, providing even distribution of blood to all cerebral tissues from the reservoir.

The pump hummed.

Without the supply of nitrous oxide from his lungs to maintain Martin Ross in unconsciousness, his brain began to wake. Barry injected Nembutal into the blood reservoir to counteract this.

Professor Howard turned and stooped so that his forehead could be wiped free of perspiration. "How's your guy doing?" he asked the other team.

"Fine. We've just about got him hooked up. We'll be ready when you are."

"Okay." Howard gently prodded the dura covering Ross's brain. "Feels like a ripe Camembert," he said irrelevantly. "Where the hell are the EEG leads?"

"Right here, Doctor."

Howard took the sixteen electrodes and applied them to Ross's brain, over the motor strip running roughly across the crest between the ears, where specific sites controlled the tongue, the foot, the upper leg, the fingers, the hand; over the frontal lobe, where the intellectual functions and moral, ethical, and social behavior were located and personality determined. Then onto the second great cerebral hemisphere in the rear, which controlled sensation: the old brain, the seat of primitive emotions—pleasure, sex, fear, hunger. The preservation of the species. The impetus which would send Ross, if all went well, into Russia.

The jacks of the lead wires were inserted into numbered holes, and the EEG was turned on. Professor Howard walked over to peer at the tracings.

Allowing for Ross's degree of anesthesia, the squiggles on the unwinding paper were normal.

"Looking good," Howard said. "Anyone see any reason for not going on? No? Okay, let's give this guy a new body."

The team crowded around for the final, decisive cut: the division of the spinal cord near the point where it joined the medulla oblongata and became part of the brain.

Jeremy Howard's scalpel sliced cleanly through, and there was a flow of cerebrospinal fluid. This his assistant quickly stanched by pushing into the cut a thick pad coated with the fluid, which, more than anything, would make the transplant possible by altering the cellular environment and allowing the neurons to heal: the product Howard casually called "nerve glue."

"EEG?" he asked.

"Jerked a bit but settling down."

Lyle, staring at the scene, felt himself breathing shallowly while his cigarette burned down, forgotten, between his fingers, leaving a long ash.

"Time?"

"Nine minutes, twenty seconds since the beginning of isolation. Three hours, twelve minutes since anesthesia," Peter Barry said.

"How's it going, Gordon?"

"Fine, Jeremy. We're through now."

"What are Cane's signs?"

The second anesthesiologist answered: "Pulse seventy-two, blood pressure one fifteen over eighty."

Howard murmured: "Not bad." Then he said: "Okay, folks, let's take our prize cauliflower over and see if we can't plant it into new ground."

The team maneuvered supports around Martin Ross's brain, front and rear. Howard cut the flesh, including the cartilage of the ears, so it fell away, and then used the Gigli to saw through the final pieces of bone, which were all now holding the brain steady and in place.

Three weeks short of its fifty-ninth birthday, the brain was totally disconnected from a failing, diseased body.

The team lifted out the supports gingerly, as if the brain they held were an element as unstable and dangerous as nitroglycerine, and lowered it onto a dolly.

Everyone in Howard's team helped maneuver the various carts containing the linked parts of the perfusion system and the EEG into a group, ensuring that none of the leads or tubes got tangled. Slowly, cautiously, they moved together across the operating room floor to the table where David Cane's body was ready.

"Thank you, Gordon, ladies and gentlemen," Jeremy Howard said, glancing at the isolated, dead brain still in its skull. "Looks like good work."

The second team were thus formally relieved of their responsibilities for Cane. Their next task would be to sew Cane's brain into Ross's discarded body, and they weren't ready for that yet.

Howard wanted to make the final separation himself, to match it up as closely as possible to the cut he had made on Ross's spinal cord.

He studied the area for several minutes, then held out his hand for the scalpel. The stroke was clean and decisive. His assistant stanched the gush of cerebrospinal fluid.

Jeremy Howard did not bother with supports for Cane's brain when he sawed through the final pieces of bone but let his assistants hold the organ in place. When he was through, one of them lifted it out and placed it in a bowl on a table nearby.

Cane's brain was not heavy, weighing just over three pounds, but it was unable to maintain its shape and squashed out, leaking fluid. It didn't look like a cauliflower, as Howard had joked. It had a hard, smooth texture, a slight yellowish tinge on the surface, where the shiny, thin membrane covered the blood vessels, arteries, and veins. And the eyes, bulbous, obscene, hung at the ends of their connecting cords, white mainly—almost none of the pale blue of the irises to be seen.

For the first time since he was a child, Clive Lyle felt tears, and he brushed them away without anger. He stared through the glass at what had made David run, and fight, and love.

Lyle's cigarette flame had reached the filter, and the pain from the heat made him drop it on the floor and grind it with his foot. Wetness was on his cheeks.

Below, the second team were taking a break, but not leaving the operating room. The tension was palpable, despite Haydn.

The dollies were moved again, spread as far as their cords and tubes would allow, to give Howard and his assistants space to maneuver.

Ross's brain was lifted slowly up to fill the vacant space in the hollow left in Cane's skull. Gentle handling was vital. The slightest trauma and the brain would swell.

Howard and his assistants donned special binocular operating microscopes for the microsurgery needed to join the nerves, while others removed the thick padding at the base of the brain and let the cerebrospinal fluid drain into a metal vessel. The fluid would be reserved and returned later when the transplant was over, to do its work as a shock absorber, maintaining the delicate cells in an environment similar to that of a fetus in the womb.

The hours ticked past, with the neurosurgeons hunched over their painstaking work. Lyle could see nothing, so he concentrated on the second team packing Cane's brain into Ross's skull, replacing the bones, and sewing the scalp flaps. When they had finished, they bandaged the head neatly and lowered the body onto the table. The equipment was disconnected, the IV needles pulled out, the endotracheal tube retrieved, the sheet removed.

Martin Ross's body lay white, shrunken, still, looking older than its years. The mouth was slack and open. A pitiful shell of what had been a brave man. Lyle was glad when they lifted it onto a cart, covered it with a sheet, and wheeled it out of sight.

Time ceased to have meaning. One moment Lyle looked at his watch and it was late afternoon. The next it was 8 P.M. The tape cassette was back to Telemann again, and Lyle was on his second pack of cigarettes, the ashtray at his side and the floor around littered with ash and butts. Occasionally the surgeons straightened up to stretch or take a brief walk around the sterile zone of the operating room, but they never left their work for more than two or three minutes. Their muscles were becoming stiff and concentration more difficult, but they could not afford to stop for long.

The nerves were being joined through thin paddings of a furry, feltlike blanket, designed to match up the voltages between neurons on either side of the wound and coated with the nerve glue. In the few months before both glue and blanket began dissolving and became absorbed into the body, the millions of tiny neurons would have to make their own permanent links, pushing out radial glia in their new, artificial environment, forming parallel axons to touch their counterparts across the invisible electrical pathway mapped by the voltage blanket.

It was nearing midnight before the microsurgery had been completed in the neck, where the bones were set with pins to assist healing, and in the twelve pairs of cranial nerves that emerged through openings in the skull.

The team immediately turned their attention to attaching Ross's eye muscles into Cane's sockets.

Sixteen hours after the operation began, Jeremy Howard and his weary team were on the downward path, and the signs were continuing to be good. Ross's EEG remained satisfactory, and the perfusion system functioned without a hitch. Cane's body maintained a steady pulse and an adequate blood pressure.

The next crucial stage was to join the arteries of the brain to those of the body without interrupting the blood supply for too long. In some ways this was the most dangerous part of the transplant because it was being performed by men and women whose reactions were slowing and whose judgments were becoming uncertain. And the brain, preserved so far in good order, would not wait long for its nourishment.

Howard pushed a series of bypass shunts through each artery so that blood would still flow to the brain while he clamped the ends and stitched, neatly and quickly, drawing on his last reserves of energy.

Peter Barry opened the nitrous oxide tank and began piping anesthetic down the endotracheal tube into Cane's lungs, to be carried by the bloodstream to keep the new brain asleep.

At last, Howard straightened up. "Thank God," he said. "And thank you all. Let's get out of this guy's head. I think we need a drink."

He held his hand out for a scalpel, and with it cut a small slit in the dura so that when Ross's brain swelled, as it inevitably would, the taut membrane could allow this and heal by itself later on. He also slowly poured the reserved cerebrospinal fluid back into the dura, through a funnel inserted in the cut, allowing it to drain down through the hemispheres and the cerebellum to resume its role as a shock absorber. This took many minutes.

The heart in Ross's new body beat strongly.

The EEG leads were removed and the two large bone flaps, cut away the previous day, were taken out of their saline bath and held out to Howard, who used a rongeur, a large tool rather like a pair of pliers, to take bites out of one side of each flap—an extra precaution against swelling, permitting the brain to protrude through the bone if it needed further release from the buildup of pressure. Chunks fell to the floor. The flaps were again flushed with saline solution, while Peter Barry injected Decradron into the IV line to help soothe the brain and keep down swelling as much as possible.

Professor Howard fished sodden cotton pads out of the edges of the wound and placed them in a bloody heap in a bowl, while the scrub nurse made a careful count, ensuring that the same number were removed as had been inserted.

With the skull bones back in place, the scalp flaps were lifted over, the fishhooks taken out. Jeremy Howard saw that on both ends of each flap, Gordon had cut three small bisecting lines, matching similar cuts on the forehead and back of the neck. Thus, with the scalp properly lined up, he could begin stitching—a careful, neat job, like everything he had done through the long day and night.

It was over.

Howard's shoulders sagged, and he walked without a word from the operating room, stripping off his gloves, pulling away the green mask. In the gallery Lyle felt as drained as if he had been a member of the transplant team himself.

The assistants kept working, washing the skull, drying it, replacing EEG electrodes, covering the sutures with large gauze pads which would not stick to the wound, and winding a wide gauze strip around the entire head.

Peter Barry turned off the nitrous oxide supply and, as an experiment, disconnected the endotracheal tube from the automatic respirator.

Martin Ross's new body stopped breathing.

Barry reconnected it, and the chest rose and fell automatically as it had over the days when it was still inhabited by David Cane's destroyed cells. That part of Ross's brain, low at the back, which controlled breathing had yet to make the neural connections to take over the function. Perhaps, Barry thought, it never would, and their efforts would have been futile. But they would only know that later: days perhaps. Weeks, more likely.

The green linen masking sheet was pulled free, and Ross's new body was lowered from the sitting position.

Peter Barry began breathing for him, pressing the ventilation bag, releasing it. Ross was lifted onto a stretcher and pushed out, through the recovery room and down back to his old intensive care ward.

As they entered, Barry briefly noticed Elaine Ross frozen and white-faced by the window, but they were too busy getting Ross into bed, with the life-support system functioning, for him to pay immediate attention.

When it was done and the others had left, he turned to face her. They stared at each other. For a moment Barry in his green gown and cap, the mask pulled down around his neck, lacked the energy to speak.

Elaine walked quickly over to the EEG and studied the unfolding tracings. The mechanical writing pen squiggled along the graph paper, stronger as the level of anesthesia reduced. When she turned, she was laughing and crying, covering her face with her hands.

Barry had his second wind by then. "As you see," he said, "it's done. A long operation. Everything went well. Good EEG. Strong pulse. Now . . . we just wait. He can't breathe for himself yet. We have to let the neurons make their new connections, and that'll take a while. But it's looking good."

Elaine nodded, unable to speak, her mouth trembling.

Lyle walked into the room, face alight. "It looked . . . amazing. Unbelievable," he enthused.

"Your first brain operation?"

"Yes, and it was a doozy. But sad too."

"I know what you mean. Well, as far as we can tell, nothing went wrong, no hitches at all. That by itself is a miracle in a transplant of this magnitude. I thought at least someone would trip over a cord."

"Or drop the brain on the floor," Lyle offered.

"We don't even joke about that sort of thing," Barry said flatly. "Now I need some rest. You too, Mrs. Ross. Would you like me to prescribe a sleeping pill?"

"No thank you, Doctor. It's over, and I'm so tired I could sleep for a week."

"Well, I'll be in tomorrow morning to see how David's getting along." He turned away, but before he reached the door, the import of what he had said stopped him in his tracks, and he closed his eyes. Without turning around, he said, "I beg your pardon. I'll be in to see how Professor Ross is getting along."

FIRST, THERE WAS A HIGH-PITCHED singing like the wind, far off through taut electrical wires, and it continued for many minutes. When it ended there seemed to be a tense vacuum, a profound silence, with the expectation of something hovering on the fringes about to happen. A calm in the eye of the hurricane. He waited incuriously. Water was trapped somewhere, simultaneously sucked into the vacuum and pulled by gravity. It began to dribble, slipping free at the edges until there was a series of hollow poppings. The vacuum disappeared, leaving just silence.

After a time there were other noises in the distance. A cough, a throat being cleared. Silence.

Silence and darkness. Not an impenetrable black, because there seemed to be a lighter hue around the perimeter, and he stared at it without understanding what it was, or where he was. Gradually it seemed to brighten, perhaps because the single-mindedness of his gaze was bringing it into sharper focus.

Abruptly a searchlight blazed in with awful intensity, dimming after a few seconds.

Blackness.

A cover farther away was snatched up and then another searchlight, pitiless, fierce, dimming.

A voice, loud and distinct, making no sense. ". . . finished . . . eyes are . . . sleep."

A staccato popping, like an old motor mower starting up, running on one cylinder. Other sounds in the distance. Voices. He strained to overhear. A man and a woman, speaking quietly. This is a very strange dream, Martin Ross thought.

Silence, and an awareness of fluid, seeking its level still, then drifting into disturbed sleep. It seems you're having a problem hitting me, MISTER, so I'm gonna make it easy for you. I'll stand here and LET you punch. Now HIT! HIT, YOU FUCKER! Isn't there *any-thing* you remember? Strong hands held his head as he puked into the toilet. If I offended you in any way, I just want to say I'm sorry. Don't sit there pretending to be sorry. I saw your face man, and it looked like you'd found religion. That was the one thing I felt deep inside you might lack.

A searchlight again, dimly perceived, suddenly horribly bright and fading. A second searchlight. God, it's not a dream, Chersky's here, he wants the tape, he's hunting me. Ross began to panic, trying to escape, but was trapped like a butterfly pinned to a board. The Russian searchlight went off. They'd missed him by some miracle. He had to get away, but he knew he could not.

"Professor Ross." A voice—clear, American, not Russian. "This is Doctor Barry. The operation is over. I think you can hear me. Your pupil reflexes are good. Can you open your eyes? Try to open your eyes." Pause. "Try again." Pause. "All right, now relax. Listen carefully. The operation went well. It . . . went . . . well. What we have to do now is wait for the neurons to heal themselves. Don't worry about it. It'll take a few days before you start feeling anything. That's perfectly normal, so don't worry. Your wife is here with you. Just try to rest."

Silence.

Recall rushed in on Ross, unbearable and overwhelming, as if a dam had burst and a wall of water was engulfing him. *He had David's body.* He heard the cries of the girl in London .. . ooohhhhaaAAHHohGODGOD. I've got his body, oh, Christ, I've got his body and I can't even open my eyes. What did you do to me, David Cane? What did it feel like, sweetheart?

"David, my dear. It's Elaine. I'm with you. Right here. I won't go away. Try to rest, my dear."

The voice soothed him. He wanted to reach for her hand, but he had nothing to reach with, nothing he could summon to command.

The searchlight woke him, except now he knew it was a penlight testing the size and reaction of his pupils, and he could tell by the way the light quickly dimmed that the result was satisfactory.

"Professor Ross. This is Doctor Barry. The operation is over. Can you open your eyes? Try to open your eyes . . . try again . . . now relax. The operation went well. We have to wait for the neurons to heal themselves. Don't worry about it. It'll take a few days. Just try to rest."

A pain, starting dimly in the distance, just discernible as pain, without hurting particularly.

"Good morning, Martin." Clive Lyle. Thank God, Lyle had come. Good morning, he said in his mind. His eyelids were being opened, no penlight now, and Lyle's face was in front of him, relaxed, smiling. Lyle, the bringer of measles. Not yet. Too soon. "It's time to fight, Martin," Lyle said. "The transplant was fantastic. I watched it right through. Can you move your eyes?" He tried. Shit, he could! A fraction. A fraction to the left. Try to get them back to Lyle. Had he noticed? He had! He was grinning! "Not bad, you young bastard. Try it again." A fraction. Back. A face beyond Lyle's: Elaine, concerned, hopeful, trying to look cheerful. Good morning, my dear. "Now try it to the right."

Nothing.

"No good. Okay, look up."

Nothing.

"No good. Look down."

He did it, if anything, better than he could look to the left.

"Amazing. That's damn good for the first morning, Martin. Now I'm going to close your lids. Your eyes need a bit of lubrication."

Darkness. At least something was happening. He could hear, and see, and move his eyes a bit. He practiced with his lids closed so that next time he could surprise Lyle with how good he'd gotten, but it was difficult and when he gave up he wasn't sure there had been an improvement.

The pain was still there at the back. That's how pain should be, Ross thought. Remote. Just enough to let you know it's happening, not enough to be really sore.

He became aware of the rhythmic hissing beside him, and the beep of the cardiac monitor. Strange to listen, detached, to one's vital signs. The heart sounded strong and steady. The hissing would be the automatic respirator, which meant he couldn't breathe by himself. The neurons would be healing up, growing gradually toward each other, until axons touched at the synapses and—bang—connection.

Feeling would be restored, movement. He would become a man again. And not just a man, but David Cane. Ross lay, exhilarated. Time to fight, Lyle said. Make an inventory of things I can do.

Move eyes left? Not bad. Up? Nothing. Down? Good, very good. Right? Well, something there, a faint stirring. Try to open eyelids, concentrate on that. Nothing. Try to wiggle toes, move fingers. Nothing. Try, keep trying.

The drone of voices in the background: Lyle talking to Elaine? Difficult to tell. Now they knew he could hear, they were watching what they said.

Peter Barry came back and opened his lids. "Clive tells me you can move your eyes," he said. "That's very good. Let's have a demonstration."

Ross obliged as far as he could, managing to get them to notice a slight movement to the right this time.

"Excellent," Barry said. "Now let's work out a basic communications system. Look down for no, look left for yes. Okay?"

A pause. Ross looked to the left.

"Are you in any pain?"

Yes.

"Is it bad?"

No.

"Good. I don't want to prescribe pain-killers if I can help it because sometimes they mask symptoms we ought to know about. But if it gets really bad, let me know and I'll give you something."

The penlight shone into his pupils.

"Your reflexes are good. Do you have any feeling at all in your arms?"

No.

"In your legs?"

No.

"Anywhere on your body?"

No.

"Well, give it time. I'm just going to do a couple of tests in you."

Ross's eyelids were shut and he couldn't feel what Barry was doing, but the doctor kept up a running commentary. "I'm pulling back your blankets. Let's see if we've got any reflexes going in your body yet." Ross heard the faint sound of a fingernail snapping. "This is the Hoffman test. I'm snapping the nail of your middle finger to see if your thumb and other fingers bend. That tells me if there's a lesion in the CNS, the central nervous system. Of course, we know there is." Snap. "Mmmm. Something there, not much. Now I'm testing your knee-jerk reflex . . . nothing. Try the other knee. No. No luck there yet. Okay, last test is the Babinski. I'm stroking the edge of your foot with a smooth metal rod . . . No, nothing there either. I'll be making these tests regularly, or the nurses will, and we'll be able to chart your progress. We'll also be doing sensation tests on your skin to see if you can tell when something's touching you, and whether it's hot or cold. Meanwhile, practice the eye movements by yourself and try to concentrate on opening your eyelids. I'll see you later."

Ross could hear Peter Barry walking off, and Elaine with him, the distinctive sound of high heels. Then the drone of voices in the distance.

Elaine faced the doctor in the reception area just outside the ward. "How is he?"

"Pretty good. His vital signs are okay, strong heart, normal EEG, blood pressure fine. He can move his eyes because it's a muscular rather than a neural connection. There are sutures inside there which make movement difficult at the moment, but over the next few days the muscle will bond to the tissue and the stitches will start dissolving of their own accord, so it'll get better all the time. Let's wait and see how long it takes before he can open his eyes. That'll show the neurons are on the mend, and I'll begin testing to see if we can take him off the respirator."

"How long did it take with the dogs?" Elaine asked.

"I'm not absolutely sure, actually. I think a couple of weeks before they started showing real improvement. We've got to try to keep Martin's mind occupied as much as possible. Read to him whenever you can, let him listen to music on the hospital headphones, or bring in tapes of your own. Talk to him. Encourage him. Never fail to praise every advance he makes, however small it may be."

"I will, Doctor. Thank you."

She walked back to Ross's bedside and gently, uncertainly, opened his lids with her fingers. The brown eyes, the only familiar things in this strange body, looked out at her.

"My dear, would you like me to read to you?"

Yes.

She settled down and opened a book.

It was a bright, crisp morning. The leaves on the trees were a young, translucent green, and the sun warmed gently.

Maryann Cane walked along the road, her friends around her, behind the slow-marching military pallbearers. A little to one side was General Yardley, grim-faced. A little in back was Clive Lyle. She had a stab of conscience when she saw him at the entrance to Arlington. He was in the uniform of a major, the same rank as David. He saluted her formally, then put his arms around her and embraced her for a moment: the gesture of a friend, not a lover. Extraordinary how Lyle understood.

Boots crunched on gravel. They stepped onto the soft, springy grass, moving slowly to where the grave had been freshly dug. Bringing up the rear came an honor guard from West Point, rifles reversed. The officer in front carried a folded United States flag. David's cap rested on the coffin.

Maryann held herself as tall as she could, as if he was watching her, wanting her to be proud, dignified, and composed.

The priest halted and turned. The pallbearers lowered the coffin onto the grass. It was draped with the American flag, and the cap was again placed on it. Yardley himself stepped forward then, carrying David's medals, and set them out in front.

The priest opened his book. " 'The Lord is my shepherd, I shall not want . . .' "

Maryann stared fixedly at the covered coffin, imagining David inside, remembering him in life, letting the sad, familiar words wash over her.

" 'Then shall be brought to pass the saying that is written: Death is swallowed up in victory. O death, where is thy sting? O grave, where is thy victory?' "

Lyle caught Yardley's eye and held it.

" ' . . . and so we commit the body of thy servant, David, to the earth, ashes to ashes, dust to dust, in the sure and certain hope of the resurrection . . .' "

The coffin, cleared now of flag, medals, and cap, and held by guiding straps, was lifted, swung over the hole, lowered slowly. Maryann watched it until it rested on the bottom of the grave and the straps were pulled free and retrieved. Behind her, she heard the guard of honor come to attention, cocking their rifles. A trumpeter began to play "The Last Post." The rifles fired the final salute.

She dropped spring flowers onto the coffin, then bent and picked up a handful of earth, which she tried to sprinkle. The wet lumps landed hollowly on the lid. On the other side of the grave Yardley and Lyle stood at attention, saluting. Friends came to the edge, more flowers dropped in, more earth.

The clear trumpet notes died away. The United States flag, folded up, was formally presented to her by a young officer. He saluted. In the silence the guard formed up to march off.

Maryann turned to leave, to accept again the condolences of her friends. When she reached the gate, she looked back and in the distance she could see Lyle, still at the gravesite, watching the men with shovels throw in soil.

When it was done Lyle himself arranged the wreaths on the raw earth, completely covering the place where the body of Martin Ross and the brain of David Cane were laid to rest. On his own wreath he had written on the card: "There is no death."

Then he went back to the hospital.

16

COLONEL MIKHAIL ILICH MALIK relaxed into the seat and called an order. The lights dimmed. The large screen on the wall became gray as the start of the videotape was beamed onto it, then he saw the flat on Kutuzovsky Prospekt, where Filipp Ivanovich Levin was sitting on the edge of the bed, undressing Jean Buchanan, nuzzling his face into her abdomen. Without taking his eyes from the screen, Malik reached for a pack of cigarettes and lit up. The picture was good, the sound indistinct. They really ought to be able to do something about the sound on these things. There was always too much echo, too much hiss.

But beyond the extraneous noises, he could hear Levin murmuring, "Janni . . . my lovely Janni," and the girl made a sound somewhere between a sigh and a groan while her fingers stroked his neck. Levin was in his captain's uniform, and when she was naked, he stripped quickly, leaving his clothes in a heap on the carpet.

Malik enjoyed the once or twice weekly videos the couple provided, partly because they were young and looked good together, partly because their lovemaking was uninhibited. The girl had a supple, delicate body and an open, attractive face on which emotions registered clearly. She seemed hardly able to get enough of Levin

sometimes. Malik had seen films in which she walked into the apartment to meet him, and as they embraced just inside the door, her
hand immediately cupped the front of his trousers. Once Levin just
lifted her, still in that position, and carried her to the bedroom, and
it was forty minutes before they even got around to saying hello.
That made Malik laugh, a rare occurrence at the Second Chief Directorate.

Levin had a lean, hard body, an abdomen on which the muscles
were clearly outlined beneath its dark hair, contrasting with the
brownish blond of his head. His face often crinkled with amusement,
particularly around his eyes, which looked green on the video but
which Malik remembered as being brown. Perhaps they changed
color when he was aroused. Levin was well-proportioned, and at
thirty-two he had an appetite matching that of the American he now
called Janni.

Colonel Malik wondered why they hadn't spotted Levin before.
He was natural material for foreign women. Once Janni had served
her purpose, it would be interesting to assign Levin to someone else,
to see if he could overcome his sensibilities. Malik was confident that
he could.

He simply needed to be told that either he agreed to continue
working for the Directorate or he lost his privileges. Give him a little
time to get used to the idea, and Levin would find ways of overcom-
ing what scruples remained.

Malik stared at the captain and the girl on the giant bed, sideways
to the camera, and he saw Levin pause and reach out to turn off the
bedside lamp. Automatically the videotape switched to the infrared,
which made the colors all wrong, a predominance of washed-out
greens and blues. Malik cursed. He wished he could tell Levin to
leave the light alone. In the future when they understood each other
better, he would.

The couple changed position, Levin pulling the girl over until she
was sitting on top of him. A good view for the camera. The colonel's
tongue flicked around his lips. The sound track was mostly hiss
against a background of whispered endearments, hoarse responses,
breathing, the sound of damp flesh coming together, hard. A climax
for the girl, a change of position, Levin dominant. The sounds from
both getting louder, the captain straining, almost shouting in his passion, and Malik could tell from the way his body bucked that he was
coming, and so was she, digging her nails into his back until even the

video picked up the scratches. They relaxed, Levin murmuring unintelligibly into her ear.

"Stop! Run it back a minute or so."

The bodies pressed together froze on the screen. It went blank. A few seconds later Levin was again pulling the girl over on her back while he knelt, raised her hips onto the pillows, and began to thrust.

Malik watched it through to the end, and as their bodies went limp and Levin began murmuring, he called, "Can't you do anything to improve the sound, comrade?"

"No, comrade Colonel. This is the best."

Malik grunted and strained to hear, but apart from "Janni" and "love," there was nothing intelligible, and after several minutes they seemed to sleep, limbs sprawled across each other.

"Is that all? No more conversations?"

"No, comrade Colonel. You've seen the transcript of when the girl leaves."

"Yes. Very well, you can stop it now."

The screen went blank and the lights came up. Malik stood, acknowledged the salute of the man at the door, and returned to his own office.

It was going satisfactorily. Levin and Jean Buchanan had been sleeping together for just over two months. The liaison had proceeded smoothly without apparently arousing the suspicions of the Embassy. The girl seemed to realize instinctively that obstacles would be raised if it became known she was seeing a Soviet officer on a regular basis, so they met either at Kutuzovsky Prospekt, or in Gorkiy Park, or at another prearranged rendezvous. Apart from the one night at the beginning, Levin had not been into the foreigners' compound, and now did not go near it in his distinctive Volvo either.

If she left his apartment late at night, which she often did, he would walk her to the gates where the militia were on duty and watch from there as she went inside.

Levin had played the relationship very straight. He never questioned her closely about her work in the military attaché's office, or any other Embassy matter that might be sensitive. He was, however, insatiably curious about her own background, her family, her likes and dislikes.

They spent several hours during the weekends together, sometimes an entire night. Occasionally when there was a diplomatic function she had to attend, or if she felt she needed time with her American colleagues, she would turn up at midday on the Sunday, cook lunch, and go to bed with him in the afternoon. Once during the week, she would also arrive, usually on Wednesdays in the late afternoon. Levin had given her a key, and frequently she would be waiting, reading, listening to music, or chatting to Katya if the maid was around, when he got in from the Chief Artillery Directorate.

Colonel Malik watched their progress on videos and listened to monitoring transcripts when they were in the Volvo or out of the bedroom. For the first two or three weeks, he ordered every word transcribed and went carefully through them, but now he was simply sent a digest of anything of personal significance, particularly declarations of unusual affection, biographical details which had not been known before, anything professional—either Levin's remarks about CAD or his boss, the *General Polkovnik* Stupar, or hers about the military attaché's office—and anything political.

This meant there was still a lot to read, but the more the transcribers worked on the tapes, the quicker Malik was able to recognize repetition and discard it.

The declarations of affection were interesting. Jean Buchanan had progressed from calling him "Filipp Ivanovich," to plain "Filipp," then to "dear Filipp," "dearest," "my darling," and now finally "my love." But she had not yet said "I love you," although the captain had, many times. Miss Buchanan was clearly a woman who reserved these words for an occasion when she had no doubt she meant them. Malik couldn't help admiring her for that. It took great strength of mind. If someone close says, "I love you," it is very difficult to avoid replying, "I love you too." It is almost a ritual exchange. Yet one night, in the midst of making love, Levin said; "I love you, my Janni" with such gentleness and sincerity that Malik, watching the video, sat forward to hear the response he begged for, yet she only smiled in a strange, tender way and gave him a very long, loving kiss. Perhaps that was the reply. It was difficult to judge the point at which it would be right for Levin to begin turning on the pressure and start reaping some intelligence reward for their efforts. In many ways it would have been easier had they both been men: a KGB raid during a homosexual encounter, colored photographs by the dozen, the threat of prosecution, public exposure—these would probably be enough to ensure recruitment. But to burst into the apartment and pull Jean Buchanan naked out of Levin's bed had none of the same adverse implications. The older, simpler days when premarital relations were frowned upon had long gone, and the girl would feel little shame in telling the ambassador what she had done. It probably wouldn't even blight her career, although she would certainly be withdrawn from Moscow.

No, it was necessary to get the emotional commitment. The fact that she would not say the words "I love you" unless she meant them actually made Malik's job easier in the end. When the time came, the fish would be properly hooked.

An alternative Malik considered was to have Levin feed her more of Katya's marijuana cookies, or roll a joint. A drug raid was a more positive proposition. Levin and the girl could be accused of trafficking, an offense which carried the death penalty. But she, of course, had diplomatic immunity, and unless there was a strong emotional bond with Levin, she might be tempted to leave him to face the music rather than betray her own country, particularly if she suspected she had been set up.

Colonel Malik entered his office, and Filipp Ivanovich Levin rose to attention.

"Good morning, comrade Captain," Malik said, motioning him to sit, to make himself comfortable. "I am sorry I kept you waiting. Uavoidable business, I am afraid."

Levin resumed his seat, and Malik went behind his desk.

"Are you well, Captain?"

"Yes, thank you, Colonel."

"And how is Miss Buchanan?"

"She is well," Levin said formally. "You will have seen my latest report."

Malik sounded doubtful. "Ye . . . es," he said. He tapped a cigarette out of his pack and flicked his lighter. "I have been through all your reports again, and I find there is much they do not tell me."

Levin sat, silent. He had been careful to include any relevant item: everything that might be picked up by a bug was faithfully relayed. "I am sorry to hear that, Colonel," Levin said. "I am not aware of anything I have omitted."

Malik waved his cigarette dismissively, and through the smoke his black eyes regarded Levin without warmth. "Oh, you give me all the political stuff. Worthless. Gossip and rumors. I mean personal things. You and her. You understand?"

"We like each other very much. I say so in each report. We are lovers."

"Yes! That is more the sort of thing. Details. I want details."

Levin said stiffly: "I am afraid, comrade Colonel, I am not very good at writing the details of things like that."

"Well, you had better learn, comrade Captain," Malik replied shortly. "At the moment the state is providing you with a free luxurious apartment, all the foreign food and drink you want, a private car, and we are getting nothing in return."

Levin met his cold gaze, unflinching. "Perhaps, comrade, you had better tell me exactly what sort of *details* you require in my reports." He sat back calmly and waited.

Malik took a brown folder from his desk and extracted several sheets of handwritten paper. Levin saw they were his latest report. Malik brooded, flicking page after page. "Here we are," he said. "Listen to this. 'Miss Buchanan spent a total of six hours and twenty minutes at the apartment, during which sex took place.' That does not tell me much, does it, comrade Captain? Let me ask you some questions. The answers you give are the information I require. How many times did you make love yesterday?"

"Once."

"How many times did she climax?"

"Twice."

"How long did it take?"

Levin thought for a moment. "About an hour."

"Was she wet when you penetrated? Was she ready for you?"

Levin began to redden. "Yes, comrade," he said. "She was ready."

"Is she always ready, comrade Captain?"

"Yes."

"Does she always climax?"

"Yes."

"More than once?"

"Yes."

"And what about you? Can you keep it up longer than once?"

Quietly: "Sometimes."

"What does she say to you when she comes? What does she cry into your ear, Filipp Ivanovich?"

The muscles in Levin's face tightened. "May I ask, comrade Colonel, what interest the Second Chief Directorate has in things like this?"

Malik contemplated becoming angry and decided against it. "That is a fair question, comrade Captain," he replied equably. "Please do not think it is for my private amusement. Perhaps I should remind you what our purpose is. It is not to ensure the smooth continuance of your sex life. It is to recruit Miss Buchanan and get intelligence information from the military attaché's office. Your mission up till now has been to form a liaison with her. You have succeeded admirably. I asked you to get her into your bed, and you have become a champion stud. Congratulations. If there was a section in the Olympics for men like you, we would undoubtedly win a gold medal at the next Games. But that is as far as we have gone. What useful intelligence information have you produced, comrade Captain? What out of this"—he tossed the report onto the desk—"can I take before the Central Committee to justify the expenditure of the last two months?"

Levin had to admit it. "Not much, comrade."

"*Nothing*, comrade. Now, I am not blaming you. This was inevitable, and we have been very lucky. You are good-looking, personable, gentle, and a good lover. I think we will have use for you again." No harm in planting the idea, Malik thought. "But all we have done is the preparation. The question that faces me now is how do we take the next step and get Miss Buchanan working for us? To make that judgment, I need information. *You* are our only hold over her, Filipp Ivanovich. Does she like you? Does she *love* you? Is it your body she wants? Or anyone's body, so long as he can maintain an erection long enough for her to climax twice? What does she say when she comes that first time? What does she say when she comes the second time? 'I love you, Filipp'? 'I want your babies, Filipp'? 'I don't ever want to leave you, Filipp'? Or just 'Filipp, you've got a magnificent cock. Let's do it again'?"

Despite his blushes, Levin began to grin. Surprisingly, Malik smiled back. "Without this information, it is difficult for me to say to you, well, comrade Captain, it is time you got her talking about Washington's attitude to the next round of SALT talks. You see, I do not know how your relationship is progressing. I cannot judge if you need another month, another two months, because all I get is this." He picked up the report again. " 'Miss Buchanan spent a total of six hours and twenty minutes at the apartment, during which sex took place.' "

Levin said: "I see what you mean, comrade Colonel."

Malik's eyes went very soft, and with them, his voice. "You are an intelligent man, Filipp Ivanovich. We can work well together, you and I. You must give me the information I need to help you over the next hurdle. I have experience in this. It is a matter of timing and presentation; the right psychological moment, the right psychological approach. Shall I send the KGB into the apartment one evening to pull you off her, or her off you, and threaten to expose her to the Embassy?"

Levin shook his head emphatically. "Absolutely not, comrade Colonel."

"Well then, what? What do you suggest, comrade Captain?"

Levin sat in silence for a moment. "I will have to think about it, comrade."

"Do that. And meanwhile, I want you to write another report, in which you detail all the things we have been discussing now. A personal report. I want to know what she whispers to you. I want to know what you whisper to her. I want to know *everything*. Do not let it embarrass you. I deal with information like this every day of my life. It means nothing to me, it does not excite me. I am not disgusted or even envious." He smiled again and looked directly at Levin. "Well, perhaps sometimes I am a little envious. But they are facts, nothing more. Facts on which I shall base our next move. Today is Monday. You will probably see Miss Buchanan again around the middle of the week. She did not say when she would be in?"

"No, comrade."

"Well, she usually turns up in the middle of the week. When you are making love, pay attention to what she says to you. Remember what you say to her. Try to judge whether her words are genuine, whether they apply out of bed as well as in. And let me have the report by Friday evening."

"Forgive me, comrade Colonal. May I speak frankly?"

"Of course."

"You must have this information already. I know the KGB monitors conversations in the apartment."

Malik raised a quizzical eyebrow. "Oh? And how do you know that, may I ask?"

"I . . . well, I naturally assumed . . . and also watching, taking pictures . . ."

"Any two-way mirrors in your apartment, comrade Captain? If you find even one, I give you permission to smash it and arrest whoever is on the other side."

"Well, no, actually, but . . ."

"Have you any idea of the *manpower* that's involved in such surveillance? We do it, of course. But only when we have to. It is a most inefficient method of operation. The quality of the sound is poor. Teams of men and women work around the clock, monitoring, transcribing. Why should we bother in your case? *You* are our bug. *You* bring us the reports. Must I also deploy a team of twenty to thirty people to duplicate it? You are a captain in the Soviet Army, and surely that is a responsible enough position to allow you to operate without supervision." Malik's expression was bland. "Amateurs, and newcomers like yourself, often credit us with things we do not have the resources for."

Levin, remembering the transmitter in the heel of his shoe, nodded. "I see. Yes, I understand."

"So it is imperative you give me the information I require."

"I will write a full report as you wish."

"Good. Friday, then."

Levin stood up, saluted, and the escort outside Malik's office took him down to the "warehouse" loading platform, where a car was waiting to return him to the Chief Artillery Directorate.

The first phase was clearly drawing to a close. He and Janni could no longer simply enjoy each other's company and deal with the surprisingly infrequent messages from Michael Pitt and Levin's replies to them. Soon they would have to act out a new charade and do it cleverly. He felt he could rely on Pitt to provide suitable Embassy material, particularly as it had been clear right from the beginning that the Americans were prepared to do this. But it was the transition from a straightforward love affair to Janni's recruitment as a Soviet agent that would be difficult to arrange in a way that convinced Malik of its authenticity. It would be easier if he could get her alone, out of range of the eavesdroppers, to work out the details. As it was, they would have to go in virtually cold.

Levin decided to pass a note at their next meeting and take it from there: persuade Malik not to use heavy-handed blackmail tactics but let Levin maneuver Janni in such a way that he could appear to exert emotional pressure on her. He would have to think about how. He might even be able to stall the move for a few additional weeks —particularly as he was due to accompany the *General Polkovnik* to Kazakhstan in ten days' time for an underground nuclear test.

On Wednesday morning, undisturbed in his office—ironically, one of the few places he felt relatively safe from the KGB—he drafted a short note on a small piece of paper and tucked it in his pocket, hoping Janni would follow her usual pattern and be waiting for him when he got home. If she was he would suggest a drive in the Volvo and let her read it then. Afterward, they could go back to the apartment and to bed.

Levin was finding it an almost ideal life—as good as anyone could expect in the Soviet Union—and he could not remember being happier. The edge of danger remained, but only as spice. Michael Pitt's "imperative" questions had ceased, and Levin did not feel he was taking unusual risks any longer. The Minox camera which he kept hidden in the space behind the *General Polkovnik's* desk drawer was still there, a fact that worried him slightly. He had asked, in a note to Pitt, if he should dispose of it, but was told it might be necessary again later, and unless he knew of a specific cause for alarm, it was probably safer where it was.

When he got home after work, he could tell from the country and western music filtering through the door that she had come, and his heart lifted: not only because he could get rid of the note quickly, but the fact that he would be with her again.

He could tell from the way she kissed and touched him that Katya was not there, and he felt his desire rise, right on cue, but he whispered into her ear, "Shall we take a drive first? Clear the stale office air from my lungs?" She nodded.

He steered the Volvo through Mayakovsky Square, where the branched iron lampposts were hung with white globes, past Tchaikovsky Hall and into Gorkiy Street, talking about his day, its routine, some of the people he worked with. Never anything interesting or particularly informative, and certainly no secrets.

At a set of traffic lights, he pulled the small, folded square of paper from his pocket and pressed it into her hand. When the light changed to green, Levin headed for the southern outskirts and the road to Tula, chatting now about the Volvo and how well it performed, and how she could take a few days off and go with him to a *dacha* near the town of Babushkin. The *dacha* was owned by the Chief Artillery Directorate, which meant it was virtually *General Polkovnik* Stupar's property, but it had recently been offered to Levin for his occasional use. Now that spring had come, it would be pleasant to take advantage of it. Perhaps they could go when he returned from Kazakhstan?

After reading the note, Jean Buchanan seemed preoccupied. She chewed and swallowed the paper, letting him talk on while making few remarks herself. She said she wasn't sure she could get away. There was a lot of work to be done at the Embassy.

When they were free of Moscow, but still within the twenty-five-mile limit, Levin pulled off the road, and they walked through giant evergreens, mostly in silence, listening to the bird calls. The evenings were longer now but still cool, and after ten minutes they turned back. Whatever had been occupying Jean's mind had apparently been resolved because she spoke animatedly about her office and the other girls there. She said she suspected one of them had a crush on the military attaché, who had been seen drinking with her in the towered and turreted Hotel Ukraina, just off Kutuzovsky Prospekt.

Levin asked: "What's keeping you so busy that you can't take a few days off to come with me to Babushkin?"

"Reports," Jean said vaguely. "He's preparing some position papers. The usual things."

"When will it be over?"

"In a few weeks, I suppose. He keeps consulting with Washington and altering drafts. If he goes on like this, we might still be busy at Christmas."

"Perhaps the girl is taking his mind off his work."

"Do I take *your* mind off work, my darling?"

"All the time," Levin grinned. "So I know how your boss must feel."

He turned for Moscow, passing the KGB surveillance car parked just off the road a mile back, and noticed with humor that the two occupants studiously avoided looking at the Volvo. Usually they disguised themselves better than that—keeping out of sight, presumably a few hundred yards down some side lane.

In the apartment Levin poured them each a vodka, which they gulped, and beers which they sipped, listening to music, touching.

He paid attention, as Malik had asked, to what he said to her and what she said to him, particularly on the giant bed, the first, second, and—breakthrough—third time. Later they bathed and ate, then dressed, and he walked her back to the foreigners' compound just before midnight.

Levin was not tired. In fact, he felt keyed up and jubilant, so he poured himself a vodka and a Schlitz and began his report for the comrade Colonel: a crazy sensation of being a schoolboy again, writing something rude. If he and Janni had not be coconspirators, he might have felt ashamed and treacherous, but as it was, it was only a game, so he described what they had done, with all the detail Malik required, although for his own amusement he wrote it in a formal style, numbering the paragraphs in the officially approved way, using twenty words where two would do but being careful not to go too far so Malik would see he was being mocked. It was bureaucratic, except for the final paragraph, the part that made him feel so wonderful, so wide awake.

"After the third time, we were sweating," Levin wrote. "I put my mouth against the side of her neck and said, 'I love you, Janni. I wish I could marry you.' She made no reply, so I drew back to look at her face, and I saw that she was crying. I kissed her tears and said once more, 'I love you, Janni,' and she hugged my head and whispered, 'And I love you.' It was the first time she had said that."

Levin put down his pen, grinning foolishly at the recollection. The telephone rang suddenly, and he glanced at his watch as he went to pick it up. Three A.M. The comrade Colonel?

"Yes?"

"Did I wake you?" It was she.

He closed his eyes and smiled with pleasure. "I was awake," he said softly. "I can't sleep."

"Neither can I. I just wanted to say I meant it."

"So did I."

"Goodnight, my darling." She broke the connection.

If Colonel Malik had any doubt about the sincerity of Levin's feelings for the girl, they were dispelled when he watched the video on Thursday morning and saw the captain give a whoop of the sheerest joy, face alight, fists clenched, arms thrust high above his head, as if he were a football player who had just scored the winning touchdown.

Malik thought Levin would need careful handling if he were to be used again when Jean Buchanan had served her purpose. It might be a good plan to introduce him to other women, more attractive ones, when the recruitment had been accomplished, so he could get used to the idea of spreading himself more thinly.

He bided his time, however, waiting for Levin's report to reach his office on Friday morning and, first thing on Monday, watching the weekend videos, reading the transcripts.

It was clear the relationship had entered a new, serious phase. Jean Buchanan had made the emotional commitment, and as Malik anticipated, it was total. Some of the talk even involved whether Levin wanted children and how many.

He summoned the captain to the Second Chief Directorate to congratulate him on the successful accomplishment of his task and to discuss future tactics.

"Do you get the impression she would be prepared to live in the Soviet Union?" Malik asked.

"No, comrade, I do not think so. She seems too attached to the West."

"A pity. We might try to appeal to her on ideological grounds. New converts are very zealous."

"It is difficult lecturing on equality when one lives in Kutuzovsky Prospekt," Levin pointed out.

Malik smiled. "Perhaps. But people have a great capacity for self-deception. Consider the double standards prevailing in the West, Filipp Ivanovich."

"I still think it will not appeal to Miss Buchanan, comrade Colonel."

"What then? Would she like you to go with her to the West?"

Levin sat thoughtfully. That was exactly what they would both want: the answer to a dream. But he had to tread carefully. "It is too early to say with certainty, comrade, because we have not discussed it. But if she's unwilling to live in the Soviet Union, that leaves only the possibility of America. Perhaps she will want me to apply for an exit visa."

"Will you do that?"

"If necessary," Levin said, his voice neutral. "I will do whatever you instruct."

Malik exhaled a cloud of cigarette smoke and stubbed the butt out in an ashtray. "You love her, Filipp Ivanovich, do not lie to me."

Levin was startled. But he admitted: "I am very fond of her, yes. It may be love. It is too early to say."

"You are a cautious man?"

"In matters like this, very cautious."

"Well, comrade Captain, my advice to you is this: Don't let yourself get too involved. We are not going to send you to America with her. It's out of the question. Once the Embassy learns of your involvement, Miss Buchanan's security clearance will be withdrawn and she will be of no further use to us. What we will try to do is to keep *you* here and run her in the United States as an illegal. It would mean that she becomes the responsibility of the Third Directorate. But *you* are our hold on her, Captain, and we will not let you go. We might let her think we will, if she does good work for us—a final reward—but you, my dear Filipp Ivanovich, will have moved on to other things, other women. So do your job on Miss Buchanan, and keep your emotional distance. Remember, it is only a job. When she is gone, there will be others. I am not saying you will not be hurt by your first assignment for us: you are not a professional, not yet. But I am saying the next one will be easier, and the one after that easier still. You will forget, and you will do your duty for the motherland. And, incidentally, if you do, you keep the apartment, the car, and everything else. And you will get promoted. You will not be Captain Levin for much longer."

Levin's heart sank momentarily until he remembered Michael Pitt and the possibility of defection. He did have other alternatives. So he said: "I understand that, comrade Colonel."

Malik gave him a searching look, then said, "Good. So let us get back to our initial problem. How do we recruit Miss Buchanan?" He helped himself to another cigarette, and Levin watched while he lit it. Malik obviously had a plan, and it was just a case of waiting for him to reveal it.

"I have given this considerable thought over the weekend, and your latest excellent report persuades me that it is the correct approach. She has not yet begun putting pressure on you to come to the United States, but this must clearly be the next step. We do not want her confiding to anyone at the Embassy because that would get straight back to the CIA, so we must preempt it. You must tell her, Filipp Ivanovich, that you have discussed the possibility of emigration with someone in your department—perhaps Georgi Borisovich Stupar himself—and that he grew very angry. But later, after he had made some telephone calls, he said the only possibility would be if you were able to persuade the KGB you would be more useful to them in the United States. The KGB required tokens of your—and her—good faith. Tokens in the form of documents from the Embassy."

"And if she says that is impossible?"

"Then impress upon her the predicament you find yourself in. No one who wants to emigrate can retain his security clearance in the Soviet Union, or his job. You will, at the very least, be out of work. If you do not conform to the KGB requirements, your residence permit for Moscow will be revoked. You will have to return to Kiev. Perhaps you will even be required to undergo treatment for some personality defects which have become apparent in your decision to leave. I am sure you can persuade her that you have passed the point of no return, and that if she abandons you now, your life will be in ruins. Perhaps you will not even remain at liberty much longer."

Colonel Malik puffed at his cigarette. "Naturally this doesn't all have to be said at the one meeting," he went on. "It can be done over the course of a week or two—not longer than that. It may be necessary for the KGB to play some small role in the persuasion."

"Not breaking into the bedroom, I hope, comrade Colonel?"

Malik smiled. "No, Captain. I think we will leave you in peace there. It would be something outside the apartment to make it clear we mean business. Very basic. Nothing to worry about. But what it is, or whether it happens at all, will depend on how well you are able to put your case across when next you see Miss Buchanan. If she thinks you will be allowed to leave the Soviet Union providing she agrees to help, and that you will be penalized if she refuses, nothing else may be necessary. She is, after all, in love with you."

Levin nodded. It was a foregone conclusion anyway: He simply had to make the transition believable. "And you think I should do it at our next meeting? On Wednesday, or whenever it is?"

"Yes. There's no point in delaying. Particularly because of the risk she might talk to an American friend."

"Very well, comrade Colonel. I will do my best." Levin stood up.

"I have great faith in you, Filipp Ivanovich," Malik said. "I know you will not disappoint me."

Levin returned to his office, deep in thought, rehearsing the charade in his mind during that day and the next. On Wednesday morning Malik summoned him again, to ask whether he was prepared and to tell him what the initial document was that they required from Jean Buchanan—the position paper the military attaché had been drafting, which was almost certainly a preparation for the next round of Strategic Arms Limitation Talks. It might give some indications on how far Reagan could be pushed and would certainly show what the Americans knew of Soviet preparedness.

Levin thought personally they were aiming too high for a first shot, but Malik was adamant. That was what the Central Committee required, and they would have to get it if at all possible, he said. There was no point in wasting time on peripheral documents. The girl was well placed to help them, and it was his job to make sure she did.

Levin returned to his apartment in the evening, thankful that he really had no surprises to spring on Janni: Whatever he did, and however he phrased it, she would be prepared and would know how to continue the pretense.

What Levin was not prepared for were the three KGB men at the entrance to the building, or for the strength and brutality of the assault they launched against him there on the steps—two holding him while the third worked him over with hard, well-aimed fists.

Levin's mind remained totally clear during the attack, rationalizing, understanding what they were doing and why. That bastard Malik. It was over fairly quickly. The men walked to a waiting car and drove off at speed while Levin picked himself up off the sidewalk, feeling the tenderness of his cheek, tasting blood, knowing that one eye was closing.

The superintendent was nowhere to be seen: typical. He had obviously been tipped off. But nevertheless Levin was grateful there was no one in the foyer to see him in that state, and he rode up to the sixth floor, alone.

He unlocked the door, hearing the music inside, and went in, finding to his surprise that he was trembling but not at all angry. His costume—this blood, these bruises and cuts, the captain's uniform ripped at the sleeve where he had tried to pull away from those who held him—this was real. The shock he felt was real too, and the understanding of what they might actually do if he failed to carry off his performance. He had been given a taste of the reality awaiting him beyond the walls of the apartment and its transient luxury: something only hinted at inside, in that one painting of the wheatfield with the two men being taken away at gunpoint. He hadn't realized, even under marijuana, that it wasn't so much an artistic commentary as an official warning.

He closed the door behind him and leaned against it, seeing the shock on Janni's face. The play was on, and he hardly had to act.

17

THE PAIN CAME GRADUALLY, BUILD-
ing from a remote ache, not easily identified, to a giant squeezing
hand, gripping Ross's head with such intensity that sweat broke out
on his face, and if the endotracheal tube had not been in position,
Elaine and any others who happened to be in the room would surely
have heard him groan or cry out despite the paralysis. Instead his
face became damp, and behind his closed lids his eyes swung in desperation. Elaine continued reading aloud at the bedside, unaware of
his agony.

" 'Mr. Bloundell playfully took up a green wine-glass from the sup-
per-table, which had been destined to contain iced cup, but into
which he inserted something still more pernicious, namely a pair of
dice . . .' "

The pain was the most awful he had ever experienced, searing and
hammering his brain. He yearned to thrash around in an effort to
escape it, but his body lay passive and his brain endured the torture
in silence and alone.

" 'Mr. Bloundell, who had a good voice, began to troll out the
chorus from "Robert the Devil," an opera then in great vogue, in

which chorus many of the men joined, especially Pen, who was in very high spirits . . .' "

Ross could feel the skin on his face prickle and his eyeballs almost start out of his head. His body went rigid, arms flexed, legs extended, head thrown back, teeth biting hard on the endotracheal tube. His left cheek began to flutter, then to convulse in violent, contorting spasms. His right cheek twitched.

" 'Dice can be played of mornings as well as after dinner or supper,' " Elaine read. " 'Bloundell would come into Pen's rooms after breakfast and it was astonishing how . . .' Martin? Martin, are you all right? Oh my God! Nurse! Nurse!"

The convulsions were spreading now, his chest and arms, his legs thrashing. As he lost consciousness, he dimly heard voices.

Dr. Peter Barry did not often run, but when he got the call about Ross, he was out of his office in seconds and down the corridor, ignoring the elevator and taking the stairs three at a time.

Two nurses hovered over the bed. Elaine Ross stood at the end, her face registering shock. Barry went directly to the oscilloscope screen, checking the state of Ross's heart, then he studied the EEG tracings. The automatic pen had squiggled wildly, but was now flatter than its normal rhythm. Barry lifted Ross's eyelids and shone a penlight. There was no response.

"Your husband appears to have had an epileptic fit," he said, turning to face Elaine. "He's gone into a postepileptic coma. Can you describe to me what happened?"

"I was reading to him," she said, trying to control the trembling in her lower lip. "I looked up and saw he was sweating and his cheek was jerking. Suddenly his whole face changed. The muscles seemed to . . . crawl. I shouted for the nurse, and it spread down his body until he was just contorting in a really horrible way."

"He pulled out the IV line," one of the nurses observed.

"Okay, well you'd better reestablish it right away. Mrs. Ross, it looks as if he's had a Jacksonian fit. It's nothing to worry about particularly. There's no reason to believe he'll have another—or even if he does that it will become a pattern. We have a lot of drugs we can use to control epilepsy anyway, so I'm not too worried about it, and I suggest you don't worry either. It's a fairly common syndrome after certain types of neurosurgery."

"You said he was in a coma."

"That's right. Not like David Cane, though. It might last as little as a few minutes, or as long as several hours. When he recovers consciousness, he'll be confused for a while, but it'll pass. And there's a positive side to this too. The convulsions were over his entire body, which means the neurons are beginning to establish their connections. It might not have been pretty, but for the first time since the transplant, his body moved of its own accord." Barry's face broke into a smile. "It's good news, Mrs. Ross. I know how disturbing it must have seemed, but consider the implications. This was the first sign in almost a week that the transplant is taking. It's a big day for us."

Elaine looked doubtful. The fit had been so violent and terrifying it was difficult to view it as a hopeful indicator, but she could see what Peter Barry meant. "There might be other . . . attacks?"

"There might be. If there are, I'll prescribe some medication, but I'd rather be conservative in this if I can." He turned back to the bed and again tested the pupil responses in Ross's eyes. "I'll get back to my office now. Call me when he regains consciousness, please," he said. "I want him checked every ten minutes."

"Yes, Doctor."

When Barry left and the nurses returned to their stations in the reception area, Elaine Ross sat beside the bed and studied the motionless face which she was now coming to accept as her husband's. She felt increasingly restless and very isolated. Six days had passed since the transplant, and her only means of communication with Martin was by watching him signal yes or no with his eyes. Apart from the attack, nothing else had happened. Nothing at all. Clive Lyle spent an hour with them every morning, and looked in again in the evening before he went home, and she regularly saw Peter Barry and Professor Howard on their rounds. Yet there was no one she had *talked* to about herself, her feelings, and what was happening to her. She was simply an extension of Martin, and his helpless new body. Now after the crisis of the seizure, she badly needed to concentrate on herself for a while.

Geoffrey Howlett, the psychiatrist assigned to them, had visited the ward on several occasions, but she had not then felt inclined to discuss anything with him other than Martin's condition. Things were different now. She had changed her mind.

She went to the head of the bed and raised Martin's eyelids. "My dear, can you hear me?"

Nothing. He remained in a coma.

She walked to the reception area and used an internal phone to call Dr. Howlett, and was invited to come right up.

His caseload of patients had been lightened drastically in anticipation of the transplant, and by the time Martin Ross was moving about—if that ever happened—he and Elaine would take priority in a very slack schedule.

The psychiatric unit was painted in soothing colors and decorated in a bland, neutral style, so there was nothing one could say about it except it was antiseptic and unmemorable. It had neither the stamp of a bureaucracy nor of an individual. Howlett's office contained nothing personal that she could see: no photographs, calendars, diplomas, or diaries in sight. Just the man himself, in his late thirties, she guessed, quiet and confident, with the longest eyelashes she had ever seen.

He shook her hand and gestured to a seat in front of his desk. "What can I do for you, Mrs. Ross?"

She hesitated. Now that she was up here, she felt less certain than she had been in the ward. There was nothing specific she wanted other than attention. She was just aware of all the half-formed questions, the intangibles, which went around and around in her head, and of the loneliness of the vigil, which she didn't seem able to share with anyone.

"I guess I just wanted to talk," she admitted. "I'm probably wasting your time."

"Far from it. I'm delighted to see you. Even if you just want a cup of coffee, that's fine by me. My decks have been pretty well cleared for you and Professor Ross, so if *you* don't talk to me, just about no one does. I sit and twiddle my thumbs." He smiled charmingly. "Would you like some coffee?"

"I'd love some."

He picked up the phone and gave the order.

"How's Professor Ross?"

"He just had an epileptic fit. Terrible: his body convulsed in the most awful way. But Dr. Barry didn't seem worried. He said it wasn't unusual, and anyway it showed the nerves were starting to connect."

"Mmmmm. Peter's right. But epilepsy *is* awful to watch if you're not used to it and you don't know what's happening."

"It was as if his new body was turning into a monster. I know that sounds dramatic, but his head's covered in bandages, there's this tube coming out of his mouth, other tubes feeding him and draining him, and electrodes attached to his scalp, and he was jerking in the most horrible way. Sometimes I feel I'm getting used to the idea of Martin living in David's body, but at moments like that, both of them seem total strangers."

Howlett offered a pack of cigarettes. "Do you smoke?" She noticed his hands were long and slender like a surgeon's, with a mat of hair protruding from his cuffs.

"No thank you."

Howlett put away the cigarettes without taking one either and leaned back. "How do you feel about that?"

Elaine sighed. "I just don't know what to feel," she said. "The body, the skin. I try to touch it sometimes and I find I can't."

"Because it's young? Because it's different? Or because it's David Cane?"

She thought about that. "All three, I suppose. I liked David Cane. He was a very attractive young man. I liked his wife too, what little I saw of her, poor thing. She was . . . devastated by what happened. Do I now have to take over her husband's body? By rights, it should be hers. Look at me, Doctor. I'm in my fifties. I passed menopause six or seven years ago, and while there may be things to say in favor of the older woman and the younger man, I'm not at all sure they can be said about me."

"What about Martin's mind, Mrs. Ross? That's still there. And his eyes. David's were a very striking blue, if I remember. Martin's are brown. *That's* different. Even Mrs. Cane wouldn't be able to look at your husband once he recovered and say, 'There's David.' Heaven forbid that point will ever come, of course. The best she could do would be to say there was an uncanny resemblance—an almost identical twin. The eyes are the gates into the brain, after all. Martin's are a different color: an outward sign that the brain is different too."

"Yes, I see that. But even accepting your argument, it doesn't really help me come to terms with the new body. There are going to be changes. At the moment Martin's mind and David's body are still independent of each other except for the blood circulation. But that's not going to last, is it? At least, we all hope it isn't. Once the neural connections are made, the brain and body become one. David's glands and Martin's brain begin to interreact. Heaven knows what that will mean. Perhaps the mind is dominant, and Martin's responses will be much the same as they were in the past. Perhaps David's glands will dominate, and Martin will change as a person. He'll be more aggressive, more demanding."

"You're thinking of sex, I take it?"

"Among other things."

"I don't know the answer to that. No one does. The relationship between the glands and the brain is still obscure. What happens to your husband will give us a number of fascinating insights. That doesn't help you, of course. We'll have to wait and see. It'll be one of the adjustments you're going to have to make."

"Speaking frankly, Doctor, I'm not sure I will be able to make it.'

"May I ask you a personal question, Mrs. Ross?" Geoffrey Howlett said, picking up a pencil and tapping it lightly and noiselessly against the side of his index finger. "You don't have to answer, of course, but it would help me if you did."

"Go ahead. That's what psychiatrists are for, I suppose."

Howlett smiled gently. "Is Martin the only man you've ever slept with, Mrs. Ross? Or have there been others?"

Elaine sat quietly for several seconds, wondering whether to exercise her right of refusal. At last, she said: "I was a virgin when I married. I've been faithful to him since then."

"I see. Why was that? You're an attractive woman. You must have had any number of propositions."

"Not as many as you think," she said. "But it was out of the question. Martin gave me everything I wanted in a man."

Howlett had read the files. "Except children."

She looked at him sharply. "Yes," she agreed. "Except children. But we adjusted. We had each other and we were content."

"Were your marital relations satisfactory?"

"I think so."

"Frequent?"

They were getting into deep water now: deeper, Elaine felt, than she had intended. "Less frequent as we grew older."

"Once a week? Once a month?"

"About once a month." A little defiantly: "We have separate bedrooms."

"Many people do."

"Martin snores," she explained.

"Ah." David Cane, who shared a room with Ross at Fairfax for months, had not mentioned that on any report, and Howlett wondered if it was true. "Did he come to your room, or did you go to his?"

"Usually he came to mine. Isn't that how it's supposed to work?"

"It varies between individuals, but usually, yes."

"I'm glad to hear it."

"Please don't be defensive, Mrs. Ross. I certainly don't want to make you feel I'm prying in any way, although I suppose I am. That's my job. But there's nothing you have to answer, and if you prefer, we'll talk about something else. I just wanted to get the picture clear in my mind, and for you to get it clear in *your* mind, so it'll become easier to decide what to do when Martin is discharged from here. But it's not a decision that has to be made for weeks yet, months."

"Perhaps never."

"As you say, perhaps never," Howlett conceded readily. "If the transplant is not a success for any reason, he could still die. Or be so disabled that he never leaves the hospital. There's no reason to suspect that will be so, and we must work on the assumption that he'll regain his health and complete his mission."

The coffee came, and they fell silent while the receptionist served it and left, closing the door behind her.

"We might as well go on," Elaine said. "I suppose that's really what I came for. I don't have anyone else to talk to, apart from Clive Lyle, and there's absolutely no point in burying my head in the sand and pretending everything's going to be all right. It just isn't."

"Do you enjoy sex?"

"Not much, no," Elaine said frankly.

"Does your husband know that?"

"I guess he must. I almost never refuse him, but he's not a fool. I've often thought he must want to sleep with me more regularly."

"Is he gentle? Considerate?"

"Yes."

"And you fear with his new body, his new glands, that might not be so?"

She hadn't thought about that before, or not in those terms anyway, although it must have been at the back of her mind. "That's a possibility," she said. "But there are other factors too. He'll be young. I'm getting old. For God's sake, I'm old enough to be his mother. And how am I going to explain taking a handsome young man into my home?"

"What will the neighbors say?"

"Exactly. What the hell will they say? How do I pass him off? What do I tell them happened to Martin?"

"We're into a fairly knotty legal area here, Mrs. Ross. We haven't discussed it before, but since you raise it, it looks as if the time has come. According to our legal experts, your husband is still alive. You and he remain married. It becomes a can of worms at that point, because either of you could probably sue the other for divorce on the grounds of nonconsummation of the marriage in Martin's existing body, and the courts would have a hell of a job deciding that issue. But in practical terms, and certainly for security, Professor Martin Ross is dead. A death certificate has been made out. His body has been cremated. The man down there in the ward is someone completely new. When the time comes, the DIA will provide him with a background, a name, an identity."

Deep down, Elaine had known that all along, but hearing it spoken at last made her catch her breath. "And where does that leave me? Out in the cold?"

"No, not necessarily. You put your finger on the problem when you said you couldn't just bring a young man home to live with you without causing a scandal. So there are a number of propositions we can put to you for consideration. All of them start with the basic statement that Martin Ross is dead, and you are, to all intents and purposes, a widow. So what do we do? One, we've given him a new identity, so we'll give you one too. Relocate you somewhere different. You can choose a place. It doesn't matter to us where it is, and it doesn't have to be in the United States. Make a new start together, where no one knows who you are. The DIA will settle enough money on you, and a monthly salary for as long as you both live, so you can do pretty much as you please. You'll be free to make a new start. But you cut all your old ties, your friends and relatives.

"Two, you want to keep living in Princeton, in your home, with your friends and relatives, and you want to be together. Yet Martin is dead. So you take a bit of time. Meet him in his new persona. We could arrange for one of your mutual friends to introduce you without too much trouble. Strike up a friendship. Let it deepen. Get married. Okay, people will raise their eyebrows at the age difference, but you could probably live with that. And Martin—or whatever we call him then—will still be a computer expert, so you'll work side by side as you always did.

"Three, you live apart, making regular visits to each other. You don't share a bedroom anyway, so that shouldn't be too difficult. He comes to your house, or you go to his. The two of you know you're married, but no one else does. In Princeton, however, you're still thought of as a widow.

"Four, you live apart. No intimate relations. You see each other occasionally. But if you go for this option, Mrs. Ross, I have to warn you there's a pretty good chance your husband, in his new body, will need sexual and emotional outlets, so he may form bonds with others, either temporary or permanent. It wouldn't be necessary to get a divorce, because of his new identity, but that would be the net effect.

"Five is a hardened-up version of option four. You decide you want to split up. So you do. Martin goes his way, you go yours. You don't see each other again, ever. For you Martin is dead, and you've got a certificate to prove it." He paused. "Have you got any preliminary thoughts on any of those?"

She shook her head. "I have to think about them. It's too early to say. Of course, there's another option."

"What's that?"

"That the DIA give *me* a new, young body, and Martin and I start again as different people."

"You'd like that?" Howlett asked cautiously.

She smiled. "No," she said. "I'd hate it. This is me, Elaine Ross. I'm not immortal and I don't want to be. When my body dies, I'll die. It's the cycle of nature and I'm part of it. I don't have a mission to do for the United States, which puts me in a different category. No, it was a joke. I find the concept of brain transplants pretty disgusting actually."

"Why is that?"

"Because apart from Martin, it's going to be misused. Medical science is now effectively offering life everlasting, and once word gets out, there'll be a desperate rush. All the powerful people of the world, Soviet, American, British, French, and the rest of them, are going to want to keep on living. They'll be first in line for transplants, all mouthing platitudes about the national interest. And they'll want to choose their new bodies too. It won't be a case of a David Cane volunteering, sacrificing himself for the sake of the free world. In some countries it'll be a frightened dictator sending thugs out to locate likely victims. The new body snatchers. And as these things usually go, it's less likely to be the good, decent politicians who want to hang on beyond their natural time. It'll be the despots, the murderers, who fear the hereafter. Hitler would have loved the idea. The current Soviet politburo will go weak at the knees. Even some American senators, and maybe Presidents will want a new term of office. God, it'll be awful. I'm glad for all the quadriplegics, they'll be able to complete their allotted spans as whole men and women, and that's marvelous. But as for the rest of the can of worms it's going to open, this may be one of the worst, dehumanizing things that's ever happened to mankind."

Geoffrey Howlett sat deep in thought. Then he said: "Actually, I'm inclined to agree with you. If it does get out of hand. But perhaps the government will take steps to control its use. Or keep it secret."

"How?" Elaine asked. "Once it's known that brainstem-damaged cases are being cured, the implications are unavoidable. And if *we* can produce a nerve glue and all the rest of the parts that are needed for a brain transplant, so can other countries, even if we put our formulas under lock and key. Their scientists will stumble on the secrets. Or their operatives will steal them. Or they'll pressure us or blackmail us until we hand over the formula. Of course, everyone will swear on all that's holy and quite a few things that aren't that they'll act responsibly and humanely in the administration and use of the nerve glue. They might even agree to international safeguards, as if the stuff was plutonium or something. And none of it would make the slightest difference. How much value, Dr. Howlett, can you place on the word of a politician or of a nation? When it suits them, they're all liars, all of them, even ours. Naturally they pretend not to be, but the fact is when that amorphous, often questionable concept of 'national interest' is involved, there isn't a lie they won't tell or a dirty trick they won't play."

"That's a very cynical attitude, Mrs. Ross."

"Is it? 'Cynical' implies a disinclination to recognize goodness or selflessness. What I'm saying is there is precious little goodness or selflessness left in anyone who has fought his way to the top of the political tree, be he Republican, Democrat, or Stalinist. There might be a more gentlemanly progression in a democracy, not marked by actual corpses littering the ground, but the people who make it are there because they lust for power. They think that they alone have the answer to the problems of the nation. And just for that belief, you need an extraordinary amount of ambition and arrogance. You're a psychiatrist. What about that as a proposition?"

Howlett said: "Let's take specific cases then. Ronald Reagan. Ambitious? Sure. So's your husband. He's ambitious to get to Vologda."

"Ah, but that's selfless!"

"Maybe so's being President of the United States. Not entirely, and not to the same degree, but selflessness does enter into it. For example, it's a very dangerous job. Remember how close he came to being assassinated? Putting aside politically motivated killers, there's no shortage of emotional cripples with guns. And Reagan has no private life to speak of. He belongs to the nation, and so does his family. Privacy is a lot to give up. Any mistake, any misdemeanor, and millions of people know about it. It's cocktail party gossip throughout the nation. Selflessness in other things too. Reagan knows about Professor Ross's mission, and there's an election coming up which he badly wants to win. If he could get the word around that he's working on something secret and vital to the United States' security, and that it would be compromised if he wasn't given the extra term of office, he might swing a close contest."

"At the expense of that same national security," Elaine pointed out. "That would hardly be selfless."

"True. But Reagan's not going to do it. Vologda is a secret as far as you and your husband are concerned, and it's a secret to the President as well. And let's take your other point: arrogance. If you're seeing someone making a mess, whether it's organizing a billion-dollar computer system or running the United States, and you think, God, even I can do better than that, is that arrogance? Or does it mean the opposition are worse than you are?"

"Hmmm. I'm not convinced, Doctor. That might be the starting point for the political climb, but along the way the vestiges of humility and compassion get pretty dented, to say the least."

"I also wonder if you're not being unduly gloomy about the international effects of brain transplants," Howlett said. "There's nothing we can do about the march of science. As you point out, even if we kept the brain glue a secret, researchers elsewhere would stumble on it some day. Yet the world will survive. If Hitler's brain had been transplanted into some magnificent specimen of Nazi youth, he'd still have been Hitler, subject to the madness, hatreds, and pressures. He'd still have lost the war. If we'd captured him, he'd have been hanged in his splendid new body, that's all. He'd have bought time, but not life everlasting."

"I hope you're right."

"But I agree, it wouldn't be the sort of operation I'd like to have for myself. I'm not afraid of death."

"Neither am I. I am, however, a little afraid of life. Particularly now."

"Look at it this way," Howlett invited. "What's the absolutely worst thing that could happen?"

"Martin becomes a quadriplegic, trapped for fifty years."

"The second worst thing?"

"He recovers and we break up. He's young. I'm old."

"What would have happened if he hadn't had the transplant?"

"He'd have died, of course."

"And you'd have been alone."

"Yes."

"And if your second worst possibility comes to pass, you'll also be alone?"

"Yes."

"So, actually, there's no difference as far as you're concerned. Providing he's not paralyzed, you're no worse off, while there is a possibility you'll be a lot better off."

"Yes," she said slowly. "I guess you're right. It's just longer and more painful now, that's all. And different. I wasn't expecting it."

"No. And meanwhile, there's Vologda."

"Yes, there's that."

"Hang on to Vologda, Mrs. Ross. Keep it in your mind the whole time: the challenge, the stakes. Just remember that mushroom cloud over Hiroshima, and imagine what it would be like with an American city beneath. Then multiply that by ten thousand."

She stood up. "Thanks for the talk, Dr. Howlett. I appreciate it."

"Anytime. Just give me a call and come up. If you need me at night, ask one of the nurses and she'll have me bleeped. And if you ever feel you want to move beyond general discussions into actual therapy, say the word."

"Thank you. I will. And thanks for the coffee."

He saw her to the door, watched as she walked along the corridor to the elevator, and then returned to his office to make notes of the conversation. He was unhappy about her uncomplimentary attitude toward Western politicians. It showed a degree of alienation which could become a problem later. Mrs. Ross would have to be monitored carefully.

18

ROSS EMERGED FROM HIS POST-epileptic coma after six hours, disoriented and still in great pain; if anything, it was worse than it had been before. It had spread from being a great hand squeezing his brain and gone down into his neck, with below that, the agonies of stomach cancer. Nothing was worth such pain. Not Vologda, or life itself.

He opened his eyes to look for Lyle, to get his attention and remind him of their deal. The raw ends of nerves screamed for release. Elaine was in a corner of the ward talking to a nurse. No sign of Clive.

Ross couldn't get his eyelids to open properly, nor could he move his head. He stared at his wife, half-turned away from him, willing her to notice him, but after two or three minutes, the two women went out. Ross closed his eyes in exhaustion and bleak impotence.

Although the pain remained constant, with it came the realization of two new facts: He was regaining the ability to open his eyes, an indication that the nerve glue was working, and there was no reason for him to have pain in his stomach—there was no cancer in David Cane's body. His mind was playing a grim trick on him, in the same way that causes amputees to scream with the agony of a limb long since severed and disposed of.

Ross tried to confront the treacherous pain centers of his brain, order them to stop the pretense, to make it clear that he was on to them and that he'd tolerate the torture no longer, but they had independent life and paid no heed either to threats or entreaties.

He opened his eyes again. It was good to be able to do that at least, even if the view was dulled and reddened by suffering. He was able to move his eyes almost at will now, and he was aware that the function of his right lid was somewhat better than the lazy, drooping left one. It was something more to practice, to distract his attention.

Elaine was coming back into the ward, a nurse behind her. Time to demonstrate his new trick, and try to communicate to them about the pain so he could be given something to relieve it.

"Martin! Martin, you've got your eyes open! My dear, that's wonderful!"

"Well, Professor Ross. Welcome back," said the nurse. "Let's have a look at you." She shone a penlight into his pupils to check their reaction. "That's very good," she congratulated him. "Close your eyes."

He did so.

"Now open them."

He stared at her.

"Excellent. Try just the left eyelid by itself . . . mmmm, a little lazy that one; now the right by itself . . . much better. Well, that's coming along fine. Dr. Barry will be very pleased. Try to rest now."

He looked at her intently, his eyes imploring her to ask how he felt.

"You had a little seizure a few hours ago and you were in a coma for a while," she explained, misinterpreting the look.

His eyes begged.

"But you're fine now. Nothing to worry about at all. In fact, Dr. Barry said it showed how well the neurons were healing up."

Please, nurse, please.

"So just keep practicing using your eyes, doing those exercises we showed you, and pretty soon there'll be other things for you to practice. Okay, Professor?"

Jesus, ask how I feel! You're a nurse. Ask. The hand squeezed his brain, sending waves of agony beating down behind his eyes.

"I'm just going to tell Dr. Barry you're awake at last. He'll probably want to see you."

Thank God. Peter Barry would know what to do.

Elaine said: "Would you like to listen to some music, my dear?"

No.

"Shall I read to you then?"

No.

"Well, just lie quietly. I'm here if you need me."

Ross closed his eyes in exhaustion and defeat. Time to fight, Clive Lyle had said, but Lyle wasn't suffering and probably never had at any point of his life. It was easy to preach and encourage from the sidelines. If he could communicate with Lyle, he would say, Clive, you and I have a deal. You gave me your word, we shook on it. If I've had enough and I want to quit, then you'll respect my decision. Well, I've made up my mind. If they can't relieve this pain, I want out. Do it now, Clive, because I can't go on. This pain is driving me crazy.

What was taking Peter Barry so long? Ross looked around the ward, catching Elaine's eye and holding it beseechingly. For God's sake, understand, he urged her silently. I want to tell you something. Don't just smile at me. I'm in agony.

Lyle! Thank God, Lyle was coming in. Thank you.

"Hello, Mrs. Ross. How's Martin?"

"Better now. You heard about the seizure?"

"Yeah."

"Well, he's conscious again and—you won't believe it—he can open his eyes by himself."

"Well, I'll be . . ."

Ross fixed his stare on the agent. Help me, Clive. Lyle was grinning.

"Jesus, you young bastard! Let me see how it works."

Ross blinked for him. Help me, Clive.

"How are you feeling?" At last.

No.

"Not feeling good?"

No. No. No.

"A lot of pain?"

Yes. Yes. Yes.

"Okay, friend, leave it to me. I'll get Peter Barry down here to take a look." Lyle ran for the door. Ross could almost feel himself sag with relief.

Perhaps Barry had already been on his way, or maybe Lyle put the fear of God into him, because the familiar, immaculate figure arrived at the bedside sooner even than Ross expected.

"Hello, Martin. Clive tells me you're in a lot of pain."

Yes.

"Very bad?"

Yes.

"Does it feel like a giant hand squeezing your brain?"

Yes. Yes.

"Is there pain anywhere else?"

Yes.

"Neck?"

Yes.

"Anywhere else?"

Yes.

"In your body?"

Yes.

"Chest?"

No.

"Arms?"

No.

"Stomach?"

Yes. Yes.

"Like cancer again?"

Yes.

"Anything else?"

No.

"Okay, I think I understand, and I can give you something for it. The pain in your head is normal. Patients always have it after neuro-surgery, although not usually so late. Your brain has swollen because it's been handled and pressure is building up inside. I'm going to increase your dose of steroids to bring it down, and I'll prescribe an analgesic to help the pain. Now, it's probably not going to eliminate it entirely. You'll have to put up with some, but I'll try to make it bearable. The thing is, if we give you very strong analgesics, you won't know if the pressure buildup gets too great, and we won't be able to find out either until it's too late. Anyway, let me give you what I can, and we'll talk again after that."

Barry gave an order to the nurse, who went to the drug-supply closet and returned with an ampule, which he injected into the rubber IV connector.

"Okay, that's done," he said. "It'll take a few minutes to work. Now, the other pain you're complaining about, in your stomach, is probably psychological. I'll just make a check to be sure." Barry pulled back the sheets and prodded and probed around his abdomen. "Are you feeling anything?"

No.

"Well, there's no sign of swelling or anything unusual down here, so it looks as if your mind is playing tricks on you. You probably worked that out for yourself. Did you?"

Yes.

"Not that it hurts any less for knowing. Anyway, the injection will control the ghost just as easily as it does the reality. You had an epileptic fit earlier today. The fit was pretty normal in neurological cases, and it isn't anything to worry about. It probably won't happen again. The good news is that it demonstrated your body was beginning to respond. The neurons are connecting. And your eyelids—that shows the first cranial nerves have already matched up. Try to wrinkle your forehead."

Ross made the effort, without success.

"Smile."

No luck.

"Well, it's pretty good so far. I think we should start seeing improvements every day from now on."

Imperceptibly the pain-killer began to take effect, and the assault on his brain diminished in intensity until he could live with it rather than trying to cringe away. Thank God for Lyle. He always seemed to be on top. He was the one who first noticed Ross could move his eyes slightly the day after the operation. He was the man who discovered—quickly—that he was in pain.

Clive Lyle was like David, in the ways that counted. He was intuitive, sensitive, trustworthy, and the reverse too, of course—a killer, not to be trusted at all unless you were of no consequence to his mission and not in his way. Lyle was two people, existing side by side. Ross felt they'd get along well once they got to Fairfax.

But if suddenly finding he was able to blink was the first real step toward that goal, Ross waited with growing impatience over the succeeding days for more progress to be made. In some ways there was progress. The swelling in his brain subsided, and with it most of the pain. His skull and neck were still sore as the bones and muscles began to knit.

But in other, more important ways, there was nothing to report. His left eyelid continued to be lazy. He still couldn't breathe for himself, although each day Peter Barry disconnected the endotracheal tube from the respirator to check whether his brain was ready to resume this automatic function.

He couldn't smile or wrinkle his forehead, feel heat or cold, or even touch, beyond a vague sensation of pressure on his cheeks. His legs wouldn't move. The knee-jerk-reflex was absent, and none of the other tests Barry and the nurses gave him regularly showed anything. Everyone remained cheerful and supportive, encouraging him, telling him it took time. Professor Jeremy Howard visited daily, checking progress, or the lack of it, and eventually ordered a brain scan.

It took place on a Tuesday morning, three weeks after the transplant, and showed that the neurons in Ross's skull and severed spinal chord had small smudges around them, indicating that axons had been pushed out. But there was still a gap. They had not linked up through the microvolt blanket.

Seven days later, when no further improvement had been noted, an additional brain scan was made. The smudges remained unchanged. The axons on each side of the severed nerves were separated by a distance of less than a centimeter, but it might have been a million miles. Until they touched and formed synapses, Ross would be what he had feared most of all: a quadriplegic, trapped in David Cane's body.

Apart from Clive Lyle, with whom he had a pact, Ross felt alone and increasingly desolate, particularly as he realized that both Barry and Professor Howard were holding back on the implications of the results. Ross yearned to be able to talk with them, to ask questions and demand answers instead of trying to convey what he felt and feared through his eyes, hoping to prompt a truthful explanation.

Ross fell into deep and hopeless depressions. More than a month passed.

He remembered Jeremy Howard's words on that morning near Chesapeake Bay, when he first learned about the transplant. *You should have some function fairly shortly after regaining consciousness, and the rest will return gradually after that. In three months you ought to have full function. Add another three for general rehabilitation, and after that you're off and—literally—running.*

It was stupid. Something had gone wrong, and no one had the guts to say what it was. Lyle was his only hope: the only straightforward man among them.

Ross took to staring beseechingly at Lyle, sometimes refusing to answer questions that did not deal with what he wanted to communicate—his condition and his death. He kept his eyes steadily fixed on

Lyle's, and as he hoped, it didn't take long for the agent to understand.

Clive Lyle waited until Elaine Ross had taken a break and gone out of the hospital for lunch. He pulled up a chair beside the bed.

"So, old friend," he said, "you want to talk."

Yes.

"About the transplant?"

Yes.

"About our deal?"

Yes.

Lyle sighed. "I thought you would. They haven't told you what the brain scans showed, I suppose?"

No.

"Well, the news isn't good. There's some sign of growth of the nerves, but not enough. They haven't connected. And they seem to have stopped trying."

That was it. At last, he knew. Ross reacted in the only way available to him, by closing his eyes.

"And now you want to die."

Ross's eyes opened.

Yes.

"You don't think it's worth hanging on a while longer, so we can see what happens? Give it a bit more time?"

Ross held his eyes steady. Maybe. As long as Lyle and he still had their understanding, and his escape route remained open, there wasn't any harm in waiting a bit longer.

Yes.

"Yes, we wait a little?"

Yes.

"Okay, my friend, but you've got to keep fighting in there. If there's any change in the prognosis, I'll come back and tell you. If the mission's off, I'll tell you that too. Then we can think again. But it's been, what, six weeks? Not very long. Give it another couple of months and see how you feel. Meanwhile, I think we should work out a better eye code. Let's see you roll your eyes in a circle . . . that's pretty good. In the future that's going to mean you want something. If you're in pain, look left-right-left. If you want to speak to me alone, it's down-up-down. Got it?"

Yes.

"Okay, we'll stick to those signals for a while and add to them when we have to. Anything else?"

No.

Lyle left the ward and went up to see Peter Barry, but apparently neither he nor Professor Howard could explain why the axons had suddenly stopped growing. It had not happened with the dogs or the macaque monkeys. Jeremy Howard theorized that the human body might metabolize the brain glue more quickly and that therefore they should have either used more of it or a different, stronger version. No one offered much hope that the axons were only pausing before making the final connection.

The weeks stretched out, marked by the final easing of pain and a third brain scan, which showed no change. An atmosphere of depression settled on the ward, despite the professionally cheerful neutrality of Barry, Howard, and the nurses. Everyone knew it wasn't working, including Ross, thanks to Clive Lyle. The consensus among the others was that, on this occasion, the patient should be told as little as possible in order to keep his morale high. Lyle thought that was stupid. Martin Ross was far too intelligent a man to be deceived, and he hated the neutering that was implicit in the decision.

Ten weeks after the transplant, Martin Ross spent an entire, virtually unbroken day exercising the pitifully few parts of his body that responded to commands, and willing the others to show some flicker of response. After all, David's body had convulsed during the fit: There must have been axons touching somewhere for that to have happened. Perhaps they were still in place, a fraction distant from their connections, and if just one or two could send an electrical signal down to a limb, that would be enough to give him hope.

When nothing happened, Ross lay quietly and reached a decision. He slept on it overnight, and by the time Clive Lyle made his regular morning appearance, he was ready. He caught the agent's eye and looked down-up-down. I want to speak to you alone.

Lyle suggested that Elaine take a break, go for a walk, and she readily agreed. She hardly left the hospital now, and it was particularly welcome to be able to get away from what was clearly turning into a nightmare—what Geoffrey Howlett had identified as her worst fear: Martin, a quadriplegic, living on for fifty years.

Lyle sat next to the bed. "You wanted to talk to me."

Yes.

"About our deal?"

Yes.

"You want the latest prognosis?"

Yes.

"Well, there's nothing much to say. I get the feeling they don't know what the hell to do. The transplant seemed to go fine. Your recovery has been okay as far as brain swelling and the healing of the wound are concerned. Those damn nerves just won't join through and that's the mystery. You're stuck on a plateau."

Ross rolled his eyes in a circle. I want something.

"You want out?"

Yes.

"You know what you're asking? You want me to kill you?"

Yes.

"It'll be the end of Vologda. You know that."

Yes.

"Oh Christ, I suppose it's the best thing to do. You're not getting any better, are you? No tinglings in the nerve endings?"

No.

"And you're absolutely sure?"

Yes.

"You don't want another couple of days to think?"

No.

"When do you want to do it? As soon as possible?"

Yes.

"Okay. I'll fix it. Maybe this afternoon. We'll have another talk before I do, in case you change your mind."

Ross stared levelly at Lyle. He wasn't going to change his mind.

"Is there anything else you want?"

No.

"All right, old friend. I'll see you later." Lyle walked from the ward, feeling sick and disturbed. Were they being too hasty? Should he insist that Ross wait longer? Lyle wondered briefly whether he should have a word with General Yardley and tell him what they planned, but he knew that Yardley, who no longer had anything to lose, would demand that Ross be kept alive at all cost and would probably ban Lyle from seeing him again. Ross was really the only man left with something to lose: and that was his right to choose death.

Lyle's mood changed from morose to savage. It was such a waste. David Cane had died for nothing. A stupid, futile gesture, and Vologda was as far from being cracked as it had ever been. He went down to the gym to work off his aggression, but didn't feel noticeably better when he had finished.

He drove to his apartment and collected from the safe in his bedroom the sealed, sterilized syringe and needle which he would push carefully into a vein in Martin Ross's useless new body and pump in enough air to stop his heart. With any luck the nurses would fail to resuscitate him. If they succeeded Lyle would try again later with something else. An injection of potassium probably, which would be almost impossible to pick up in a postmortem. But he would have to get that. He didn't have a supply on hand.

He hadn't told Ross that it might not work the first time. Medical help was too close at hand, and the life-support system was connected to a computer that would alert the nurses the minute he showed signs of cardiac distress. And that would give Lyle only enough time to get rid of the syringe. Jesus, it was all such a mess.

With the small, flat package in his pocket, Lyle returned to the DIA headquarters to complete administrative work until the slack time came in the ward routine when he would be more likely to get a few minutes alone with Martin.

At four o'clock he went to the intensive care ward. Ross was waiting for him, eyes fixing on him as soon as he entered and watching his every move. But Elaine was also there, back from her break.

Lyle drew up a chair and tried to make conversation, finding it difficult with Ross staring at him in that intense, private way. He wondered if Elaine noticed.

The minutes stretched into an hour, then nearer two. Lyle asked Elaine if she wanted more time off. He would stay with Martin.

"No thanks, Clive. I had a good walk this morning. It did me a lot of good. I'm fine now."

Lyle glanced at Ross and raised an eyebrow. *We'll have to wait.* Ross stared back, unflinching.

Perhaps Elaine would go to the bathroom and give them their chance. But after two and a half hours, when the nurses were again making their rounds, it became obvious it was too late.

Lyle contemplated coming back later, although he knew it would look suspicious as hell if Ross's heart faltered moments after an unusual late-night visit from him. Yardley would know immediately what had happened, and he wouldn't be pleased.

"I'll call in tomorrow morning, Martin," he said. "Try to get a good night's sleep. 'Bye, Mrs. Ross."

Ross watched him all the way out.

Lyle slept badly, dreaming about David Cane and their fight in the gym, which ended with Lyle killing his opponent twice: the first time by accident, the second in a frenzy because he had come alive again and Lyle desperately wanted him dead.

In the morning Lyle kept to his usual schedule, getting to the DIA shortly after eight and attending to the normal chores which confronted him at base when an operation had stalled or he was waiting for an assignment.

At ten he took the sealed needle and syringe and walked over to the hospital.

Ross's room was empty.

Lyle wheeled round and stared at the nurse on duty. "What's going on?"

"Oh, Professor Ross's up in the operating room."

"Since when?"

"Eight o'clock. He should be back quite soon if you'd like to wait."

"No thanks. I'll go and take a look."

Lyle hurried along the corridor to the elevator. He presumed they'd have him back in the large operating room where the transplant had taken place, but that was empty. He tried the viewing gallery in the next one, along another corridor, knowing immediately that this one was right because of the armed DIA guards outside the door. Lyle showed his pass and was allowed in.

General Yardley looked around. "Oh, hi, Clive."

"Morning, General. What's happening?"

"Jeremy Howard decided there must have been something wrong with the glue. It started working, then gave up. They've just been injecting more into the area around the wounds to see if it makes any difference. If you ask me, they should have done that a long time ago. Nothing left to lose."

"You've given up hope?"

"Unless something comes out of this, yes. I'd say we had a vegetable on our hands."

Lyle was glad to hear his own opinion confirmed. He settled into a seat and took in the scene in the room below, the green-gowned, capped, and masked surgeons, the scrub nurse, the circulator, the assistants. Ross was sitting upright, covered except for the skull with its livid red scars, the hair again shaved, and his eyes, open, looking out.

"Shit, there's no anesthetic!"

"No point, Clive. He doesn't feel anything, so why bother?"

"But his brain's okay. And it looks like Howard's been drilling holes again."

"Yeah. He did it before I got in. But I don't think the brain itself feels anything, Clive. If it did they'd knock him out."

"I hope to God you're right."

"Well, he hasn't been moving around."

"He can't though, can he? You don't know what that guy's feeling unless he tells you with his eyes. And I can't see them properly from here."

"Consider the probabilities, Clive. No neurosurgeon is going to operate on a person who's conscious if it's going to hurt too much, is he? He'd come out the other end with a crazy man on his hands."

Lyle reached for his cigarettes and settled back to watch. "How much longer to go?"

"I think they're just about done," Yardley said.

"When do we know if it works?"

The general shrugged. "Your guess is as good as mine. We're in effect back at the beginning of the transplant again—maybe a little more advanced than that because the neurons had started to grow. But give it a month, six weeks, I guess."

It became clear that the team working below were clearing up. Howard stitched new sutures around small scalp flaps where burr holes had been drilled to allow the brain glue to be injected around the cranial nerves of the skull. The wound in the spinal cord had received its extra dose through a series of injections.

Ross was cleaned up, bandaged, and lowered to a lying position on the operating table. Professor Jeremy Howard went around to talk to him.

"We're finished now, Martin. I've pumped in a lot more glue, which ought to revitalize those axons. Did you feel anything during the operation?"

Ross's eyes obviously signaled yes.

"Oh, was it painful?"

No.

"Just a strange feeling of poking around?"

Yes.

"Well, it's over now. We'll get you back to bed."

They lifted him onto a stretcher, with an orderly pressing the ventilation bag, and the procession left the operating room.

In the viewing gallery Lyle and Yardley rose.

"So, General," Lyle said. "Our last chance."

"It looks that way. Keep your fingers crossed."

Lyle went down to the ward. Ross had again been hooked up to the life-support equipment, and the operating room staff were leaving. Elaine was nowhere to be seen. She'd obviously taken a break

and hadn't expected Martin back so quickly, not after the whole day
and night the transplant had taken.

Lyle stood over him. "Martin."

Yes.

Something to get cleared up first. "I didn't know about the operation today," Lyle said. "Not until I arrived this morning and you
were gone."

Yes.

"I've been speaking to Yardley. This is our last chance. He agrees.
If the nerve glue doesn't work this time, that's it. I guess you could
catch measles with his full blessing. But it means we need to wait a
bit longer. You don't mind?"

No.

"We've still got hope. A fighting chance. So you've got to keep
fighting, you hear?"

Yes.

"Are you in pain?"

Yes.

Lyle reached out and put the palm of his hand against Ross's
cheek. "I'll stick by you, guy," he promised. "If it doesn't work out,
I'll make sure you get free."

There were tears in Ross's eyes, and the professor's gaze was on
him fiercely, but Lyle didn't understand the significance just then.

It was the first time Ross's ducts had worked to the extent of producing tears. And the reason they did was when Lyle touched his
face, Ross felt not only the slight pressure but also the sensation of
warmth and skin. He was starting to come alive.

The following morning Ross wept again when the orderly shaved
his beard, and he could feel the abrasive buzz of the electric razor. By
the end of the week, he could wrinkle his forehead and smile, or try
to smile, around the protruberance of the endotracheal tube.

Also, Peter Barry experimented turning off the artificial respirator,
and Martin Ross's brain automatically took over the task of breathing. The hissing machine fell silent for the last time.

They left the endotracheal tube in place in case of an emergency,
but the following morning Peter Barry slid out the nine inches of
slightly curved plastic, and Ross felt an overwhelming relief. He lay
in bed, breathing experimentally and feeling a pins-and-needles sensation in his right hand. Elaine and Clive Lyle watched anxiously.

Ross was exhausted and jubilant. At last, it was working, really
working. The pain in his head from the burr holes was bad, but he

didn't care much about that now. He, who had twice faced up to the prospect of imminent death, was again getting used to the idea of survival.

He was conscious of his own breathing, and sensations were beginning to crowd in on his mind. He smiled and tried to move his head, managing to turn it a fraction.

He tried to talk: difficult. His vocal chords were dry and unused. He swung his eyes around in a circle. I want something. Lyle came close.

"What is it, Martin? You want to talk?"

No.

"You in pain?"

No. He made his mouth move, trying to form the word. Water.

Lyle looked pleased enough to be a new father, if that had been his sort of thing.

He held the glass to Ross's lips, and the liquid dribbled down his chin. But he managed to swallow.

Ross made a sound, a sort of grateful croak.

A few hours later he was ready to try his first words. Lyle was still there. Things were happening fast now, and he didn't want to move from the ward.

"Clive," he said hoarsely, "I'm glad you didn't get your chance."

As he spoke, he heard himself—a stranger—and at the end when he stopped, he was embarrassed and discomfited. The sound had been rough: the tongue and mouth were not yet functioning freely. Yet his confusion was caused by something he had given no thought to. With the body and vocal chords of David Cane, he had also inherited the voice, deeper than his own, although the accent was different.

He looked quickly at Elaine, and while she seemed pleased at the latest breakthrough, he could see something else on her face too: shock. She recognized the voice and had expected it no more than he.

Only Lyle was unreservedly jubilant. His job, after all, was to re-create David, only better, and once Ross got used to the new sound, it would be a useful training aid. *You look like Cane, you sound like Cane, now you'd damn well better act like Cane.*

In three weeks Martin Ross was learning to walk again, leaning on Lyle for support.

19

FILIPP IVANOVICH LEVIN WAS DIS-
appointed in Helsinki: a drab city, different from Moscow only because it promised freedom, which Levin, surrounded as he was by
the KGB and other delegation members, was not able to taste. If he
had wanted to break and run, he could have done so, although he
detected beneath the official joviality of their Finnish hosts a nervousness and a determination not to offend. The Russian bear remained a
potent threat. Levin realized that any would-be defector would have
a hard time breaking out if the Finns got to know of his intentions
first, or Moscow had the opportunity of exerting pressure. The
Americans and the British would probably be more helpful if a
defector managed to reach the havens of their embassies, and yet
Levin couldn't shake the feeling that he would have to be a very
important person, or carry vital secrets, before the West would be
encouraged to offend Helsinki by taking him in.

Would the Americans accept Levin if he disobeyed Michael Pitt's
orders and made a run for it? It was hard to say. Levin liked to think
they would, because he hoped they were different from the Soviets,
more trustworthy, truly concerned with individual freedoms. Nonetheless, he did not seriously consider taking the risk.

There were certain truths and self-interests common to all sides, broadly defined by the elastic term "national interest." Until he knew more about what the American national interest was currently conceived to be, it was unwise to gamble. Michael Pitt, his window into Washington, had ordered him to remain a defector in place.

Levin concentrated on the formal meetings and receptions, on doing his job for the *General Polkovnik* as efficiently as ever. Only once was he sent out by himself.

Although it was his first time abroad, Levin knew that the Soviets normally moved at least in pairs and that he would certainly be followed, at least by one man, perhaps by several.

He tried to keep a discreet watch, and once thought he saw the same face twice in the space of half an hour, but it was difficult to be sure. He made no attempt to throw them off. This was obviously a test: The KGB were giving him rope, to see if he hanged himself.

He browsed through stores, quickly choosing for Janni a silk scarf he knew she would like, but taking longer over a gift for Stupar's formidable wife. He wished he had seen the sort of things the *General Polkovnik* had bought on earlier trips, and which she had spurned. Would she like perfume? It was a very individual thing, so he decided to play it safe. Levin looked through displays of garments and rejected them, too, mainly because he wasn't sure of her size.

He paused at a counter to inspect a display of intricately carved music boxes. They were the sort of thing his mother would like, and he could buy a piece of jewelry to put inside. He decided to get one each for his mother and Yelena Yakovlevna, and chose almost identical brooches from another store.

A pair of American jeans and stockings for each of his sisters completed his shopping, and Levin returned to the hotel.

Apart from the store assistants, he had spoken to no one. The surveillance squad would have nothing to report.

Dawn at Fairfax. Lyle standing over the bed, looking at David Cane's relaxed, sleeping face, stung by the poignancy of the moment. The fair hair was getting long now, covering the scars on the scalp. The eyebrows had almost grown back. The breathing was deep and even. The scars down the front side of the ears were still livid, but would fade in a couple of months.

Lyle shook his shoulder. "Martin!" he urged. "Wake up, you lazy bastard!"

The eyes flickered open—brown, not blue—focused on Lyle, moved around the room.

"Come on, Martin. On your feet! Time to get moving!"

A groan. "God, Clive, have a heart."

"Up! Up!"

Ross swung his feet out of bed and stood. Lyle looked him over. The months spent in the hospital, mainly not moving, had done Cane's body no good. Its weight was down by thirty pounds, and strong muscles had atrophied or slackened. It would be a hard road back.

"Dress," Lyle ordered. As Ross pulled on a track suit, Lyle continued, "Okay, this is day one. Your body's a mess. We've got to build up slowly. Don't expect it to be easy. Don't try too much at once."

Ross, lacing up his Nikes, felt a strong sense of déjà vu. Once, a hundred years ago, he had brought an aging, out-of-condition body to this same room and had heard almost the same words of caution. But he was different now. People looked smaller. When he saw Elaine, he had to look down at her, not level into her eyes. He was more assertive too. The new voice helped. When he spoke he remembered how Cane used to be, and he mimicked that.

They walked out into the cool morning air and began jogging slowly down toward the trees. Ross trotted behind Lyle, trying to keep his breathing even but feeling the weakness of the muscles in his legs and stomach, the pain in his back. There was no cramp as there had been on that other first day, but there were exhaustion and pouring sweat. And this time Ross didn't make it back into the gym before stopping to throw up. He did it at the side of the field a few hundred yards short when his mouth, which had been bone dry, suddenly flooded with saliva.

Lyle was quickly beside him, arms around his shoulders as he heaved, his voice encouraging. It felt right. Ross knew he was home.

On the long drive out to the *dacha* at Babushkin, Jean Buchanan suggested they stop and stretch their legs. Levin knew what this meant.

She passed the note as soon as the Volvo had halted at the side, and kept up a monologue while he read.

FROM NOW ON, NEED ADVANCE WARNING OF ALL VISITORS TO VOLOGDA BASE, INCLUDING NAMES, RANKS, PURPOSE OF VISIT,

AND DATES. ALSO NEED KNOW YOUR OWN PLANS FOR VISITING
VOLOGDA. HOW OFTEN DO YOU GO? FOR HOW LONG? WHEN IS
NEXT TRIP DUE? YOU'RE DOING VERY WELL. KEEP IT UP.
MICHAEL.

Levin blew air through his lips. Pitt was back to Vologda again.
He knew the lull had been too good to last. He would have to tell
them it was impossible for him to learn the names of everyone going
to the underground citadel. Some did cross his desk, but only those
whose tasks were connected with the Chief Artillery Directorate, or
whose visits were organized by Stupar. His own next trip to Vologda
had not yet been finalized: In fact, it was not even under discussion
as far as he knew.

However, as Stupar made at least one visit there a year, and it was
seven months since the last, it was reasonable to assume it would take
place in autumn or winter.

He tore the small note in half and chewed it.

"Come on," he said. "Let's go for a walk."

Levin locked the Volvo and, taking Jean's hand, headed into the
trees. The constant surveillance was beginning to irritate him. He
wanted to take off his shoes, leave them somewhere, and talk freely
to her.

But then the bug might as easily be a button on his shirt or be con-
cealed in some other item of clothing. He would only be sure if he
was naked.

As soon as that thought crossed his mind, he cheered up and
looked around.

They were entering a forest of spruces and evergreens, and there
was no sign of anyone else. They walked for half an hour, talking of
inconsequential things. Levin picked up the sound of water and led
her toward it. The coolness of the forest gave way to a hot sunny day
on the banks of the small river. Levin dipped his fingers into the
water.

"What's it like?" Jean asked.

"Cold. Nice for a quick swim. Do you want one?"

"I didn't bring a bathing suit."

Levin grinned. "Neither did I."

"Is it safe?" she asked cautiously.

Levin threw his hands wide. "Have we seen one single person since
we left the car?"

"No."

"Then it's safe. I'll protect you." He began stripping off his clothes, folding them into a neat pile over the shoes, which he was sure still contained the microphone and transmitter, and waited while Jean undressed.

The river wasn't deep enough to do more than splash around, and they played like children.

Afterward Levin chose a mossy spot protected by rocks from the view of anyone who might casually pass that way but still in the sun, and pulled Jean toward him.

"I don't know what do do," he murmured. "Make love to you, or talk."

She laughed softly. "Better talk. We've got other chances to make love."

They lay together and whispered, far enough away from their clothes to be undetectable by any microphones.

Levin went straight to the heart of what was worrying him most. "When can I go to America?"

"Not yet, my darling. There's something coming up. I can't tell you what it is yet. I don't know myself. But something big."

"Vologda?"

"I think so."

"Are they going to attack it?"

She chuckled. "Good God, no."

"What then?"

"I don't know." She nibbled his earlobe, and he felt his body stirring.

"When will you know?"

"A few months, I think. When are you going to Vologda?"

"It's not settled. By the end of the year, I suppose."

"As soon as you know, you must tell me. It's very important. How are things going for you, my darling? Is it difficult?"

"No. They're happy with the information you bring. I don't think they suspect."

"Good."

"How about you?"

"It's going like a dream. I'm doing my job and I've got you."

Levin kissed her deeply. "I do love you, my Janni," he said simply. "I want to marry you. When this is all over, will you marry me?"

"You know I will."

In the forest, a short distance away, a twig snapped, and its report carried to them like a pistol shot.

Jean whispered: "We'd better get back to our clothes. I don't think they like the break in transmission."

Levin began to laugh and rose immediately to fetch their things. Although he could see no one, he knew they were being watched.

Lyle's mood changed. He hectored Ross and shouted at him every day, through all their working sessions. There was a grimness about him there had never been with David Cane, and it slackened only slightly when they ate together or had a beer in the evenings.

Ross began to think he really didn't know the first thing about Clive Lyle and what made him tick, and that it was impossible to get close to the man.

Weeks had gone by, and physically he had passed the point where, in his old body, he had peaked. They routinely ran the cross-country course over the hill twice without pause and then went into the gym to begin the formal workout. Ross still found it extraordinarily difficult, and the muscles in his back, arms, and legs ached. Lyle kept pushing, piling on the pressure, but at least he was doing everything himself as well, not just standing around shouting orders while someone else sweated.

There was constant progress. Ross could see it when he looked into the mirror, sometimes still with disbelieving pride, at the man he had become and saw how his body was filling out. Not as good as David yet, although coming close.

Ross wrote to Elaine even more regularly than he had earlier, in a handwriting which was different from his own. The old neat script had gone, partly because the hand that held the pen was larger. But the more assertive style was also a reflection of what was happening to him mentally.

Clive Lyle, however, did nothing but criticize. He was a thorough teacher, painstaking and good, but the standards he demanded were always beyond Ross's reach.

One morning Lyle ran with him down to the assault course. It was in a part of Fairfax he hadn't been to before, at the eastern end of the woods.

It consisted of an eight-foot-high wall to scale, a long, low area of barbed wire to crawl under, a narrow pipe to squirm through, rough, rocky ground to run across, a muddy ditch to jump, more barbed wire, a sixteen-foot climb to a narrow piece of wood, which had to be traversed over a filthy, slimy pool, a rope to catch and swing across another pool, and a hundred-yard dash to the finish.

Lyle handed him the stopwatch.

"Time me," he said.

Ross positioned himself a little up the course and shouted, "Go!"

Lyle was up and over the wall as if it was no challenge at all, then he flung himself on his stomach and kept low, crawling under the wire so none of the barbs snagged his clothes. He really knew what he was doing, and he made everything seem easy. His only slight mistake was falling a fraction short on the first ditch, his heels sending up a muddy splash as he landed. But Lyle never paused or looked back. Ross jogged along beside him as the second hand moved around. When Lyle got to the end, he clicked the button. Four minutes flat. David's record.

If Lyle was pleased with his performance, he gave no sign.

"That's what you've got to do," he said, his breath coming hard. "And that's how quickly you've got to do it."

They jogged back to the start. Lyle never let up, not even on himself.

"GO!"

Ross got over the wall without trouble, but once under the wire, the barbs snagged the back of his shirt, and when he stopped to free himself, Lyle screamed, "Don't stop! Go! Go!" The material tore and he crawled on. Jesus, it was a long way. "Get your head down! Keep your backside down! Move! Move!"

Free, and running for the pipe. His gasping breath echoed metallically back at him as he crawled through it, then he dashed over the rocky ground, tiring quickly, but the ditch was coming up ahead. Ross picked up speed and jumped. As he took off, he knew he would fall short. The water was not deep, but when he landed his feet slipped and he sprawled forward. He heard screaming close to him, "Move! Move!" and he pushed on, feeling dispirited and humiliated. Jesus, Lyle had done it so easily.

More barbed wire, then the climb. He pulled himself up the wooden ladder, and when he reached the top it seemed so impossibly high, and the plank he had to cross was so narrow, that he hesitated.

"MOVE! MOVE!"

Ross stepped gingerly onto the wood and felt it shift. Shit, it wasn't even secured!

"MOVE, YOU BASTARD!"

One careful foot in front of another. Halfway, and his knees began to buckle. Ross knew he was falling. Even Lyle's furious shouts couldn't stop him. Sixteen feet, into a deep pool into which whatever bastard designed the course had shoved everything stinking and slimy he could lay hands on. The mud was more like a rotten ooze which, when disturbed, gave off a disgusting smell. It was in Ross's nose, his mouth. He could feel slime against his skin, and something in the water brushed coldly across his arm.

Ross gave a roar of horror and stumbled for the side.

He had never seen Lyle so angry. Veins stood out on the man's forehead and in his neck. "YOU FUCKING CUNT! GET BACK UP THERE! MOVE! MOVE!"

Without thinking, Ross climbed the wooden ladder for a second time. The filth from the water covered him, and the odor made him want to puke. He was becoming confused.

Sixteen feet up to the narrow, unsecured plank. And below, the slimy, noxious water.

"MOVE!"

Ross ran. If the plank had been three feet longer, he would have fallen again, but he just made it and he felt a surge of relief.

The next pool had to be crossed by swinging on a rope and letting go just as it reached the top of its arc so the momentum could carry him the final couple of feet to the safety of the bank, but he misjudged and was in the water again.

At least this time it was fairly clean and helped wash some of the mud and slime off him. But Ross thought Lyle would go beserk. He cursed and screamed as if the most unthinkable sin in the world had been committed before his eyes, and Ross, whose mind was at last beginning to function clearly, made sure there was no misjudgment next time.

He put his heart into running the final hundred yards.

Lyle, already at the finish, clicked off the stopwatch.

"Twelve minutes, fourteen seconds," he said drily. "A new Fairfax record. Okay, you fucker, get back to the beginning and do it again. Properly this time."

Ross looked at him in disbelief. "Now?" he panted. "Shit, Clive, let me have a break."

"You've been having a goddam break for the last twelve minutes and fourteen fucking seconds," Lyle said savagely. "Now you're going to do some work for a change."

They jogged to the start, Ross gritting his teeth with anger at the unfairness of it. Shit, what did Lyle expect?

"GO!"

The wall was more difficult the second time around. Fatigue was sapping Ross's strength. He felt a barb snag his shirt again and dig deep into his back. He shouted a curse.

He could hardly believe what happened next. There was an explosion nearby, a puff of dust in front of his face where a bullet struck, and Lyle was screaming, "MOVE, YOU FUCKER, OR I'LL KILL YOU!"

Lyle was firing at him—really shooting—shots falling just behind his legs. He was crazy. Ross gave a strangled cry and began to crawl forward, heart pounding.

While he was in the metal pipe, a bullet ricocheted off the side, and the vibration and the metallic clang echoed until he was out the other end. Bullets puffed in the dust near his feet as he ran and vaulted over the rocks, and one passed very near as he began to climb the wooden ladder, singing past his ears like a bee, a high-pitched, deadly bzzzzzz. Ross didn't even remember crossing the narrow plank, and he never saw the water below. He was running blindly, hearing the sobbing in his throat, and he jumped down the ladder, sixteen feet, landing hard, but was off again before Lyle could shoot.

He got his feet wet on the rope swing, but not enough to slow him much, then he was on the final dash, conscious of Lyle running beside him.

At the finish line he fell to the ground, breath heaving. Lyle could shoot now, and he wouldn't move. He was exhausted and could go no farther. The stink of the mud invaded his nostrils. Jesus, he had to get showered and changed.

Lyle said: "Five minutes, twenty seconds. Cut one minute twenty off that and you'll pass." No congratulations, no praise for a good effort. "Get on your feet."

Ross obeyed. Lyle had put the pistol away—back in his belt, Ross supposed, he hadn't noticed it at all earlier—and without waiting, began running off. Ross fell in behind him. After the assault course, running was easy.

They went to the gym, but Lyle wouldn't let him shower and change, even though the smell must have been every bit as offensive to him in the confines of that room. And Ross could see himself in the full-length mirrors that covered one wall. His face was caked with mud and sweat. There was a strip of slime in his hair and his clothes were filthy. His feet squelched in his Nikes when he moved through the exercises Lyle ordered him to do.

When Lyle finally called a five-minute break, Ross ran for the showers. That fucking Lyle, he thought, as the water hit against his skin. Fucking sonofabitch.

Levin kept a close watch on every document or piece of paper that mentioned Vologda. There were missiles in place around the citadel as defense, and for this reason the Chief Artillery Directorate maintained a close interest. When they visited the area, they stayed in the underground complex because that was where a man like Georgi Borisovich Stupar could be accommodated and entertained in a fitting manner.

Anyone below Stupar's rank was usually quartered in the army camp at Sverdlovsk because of the problems involved in arranging security clearance for those not directly concerned with work at the citadel.

Levin hardly ever came across notifications of visits to Vologda by members of other departments or directorates, although he suspected a fuller record would be kept in the complete file in the central registry. Yet he could not bring himself to go down and draw the file; not without a valid reason already worked out.

No notifications of visits crossed his desk, and so he had nothing to report.

Lyle and Ross, in karate uniforms, faced each other in the gym. Ross's body was back to its old weight, and the muscles were hardening.

Lyle was playing with him, goading, sneering. Lunging with a punch, which pulled short so it was painful but not disabling, then shouting because Ross hadn't blocked it, lashing out with the side of his foot before Ross could get clear.

Ross was starting to seethe. He could see why people hated Lyle, but what he couldn't understand was how, at the end, David Cane had decided he liked the man.

Ross rammed his rigid hand, fingers bent, at Lyle's stomach, but the blow was easily deflected with a focused block, and Lyle half-turned, sending his elbow chopping down into Ross's abdomen, really hurting. Ross grunted and fell to the floor.

Lyle stood over him, shouting: "Fucking bullshit! A goddam sheep in wolf's clothing!" Then after a pause: "You'd better shower and get dressed. You make me sick."

His words stung, more than anything that had happened in their months together at Fairfax. Ross got up slowly. Lyle was nowhere to be seen, but from the showers came the sound of running water.

Ross inspected himself in the mirror. He had become everything he wanted to be and it wasn't enough. A sheep in wolf's clothing. He really hated Lyle. First because he had said it, and second because Ross thought it was true.

And he *was* trying. He never stopped trying. But he hadn't made the grade: not once. And there was another problem he hadn't mentioned to anyone, but which was beginning to dominate his thoughts. He had not managed an erection, not once, in his new body. Not in months. It would be just his luck if that was the one set of nerves that didn't glue together. A sheep in wolf's clothing. Jesus.

He wished he could talk about it to someone, but Lyle and he seemed to have grown apart, and the hostility that was generated during training carried over into their leisure periods. He still saw the DIA psychiatrist, Geoffrey Howlett, three times a week but could never bring himself to broach the subject. It was a personal failure somehow. Admitting it would, in some indefinable way, be letting David down.

And maybe his potency would come back. It might just need time.

Ross walked through to the showers and stripped. He stood under the cold water for several minutes before soaping himself. Lyle was taking his time. The atmosphere could be cut with a knife.

They walked together out of the gym and down the corridor to the exit.

Clive Lyle came at Ross without warning, suddenly whirling, right hand rigid, fingers extended, edge of his palm slicing toward the professor's larynx. In a moment Ross realized what was happening. It was a replay of the scene when Cane had attacked him and Ross ended up punching him in the balls. Instinctively he blocked the blow with his forearm and waited calmly, properly balanced, for Lyle to cross the line of confrontation again. Ross was suddenly very angry.

Lyle lashed out with the side of his foot, and Ross jumped away.

Then, because Lyle was becoming complacent about his adversary and didn't snap back his foot and slide it forward to resume his proper stance, Ross saw his opening and kicked sideways at Lyle's leg, sweeping him off his balance and onto the floor.

Ross was on to him at once, kicking down at every vulnerable point that presented itself, while Lyle struggled to regain his feet, and when Lyle was halfway up he chopped a fist hard into his groin.

Lyle gave a shout of agony and fell, clutching himself.

Ross stood watching silently. Then he said: "Get up."

Lyle rolled over. His face was pale and sweating. Ross pulled him to his feet with surprising ease.

Lyle said softly: "I'm gonna be sick."

Ross took him back into the gym, through to the bathroom and stood in the doorway of the stall, watching Lyle heave.

He didn't say he was sorry, and he wasn't.

General Yardley received the video the following morning at DIA headquarters in Washington and laughed so much he almost fell off his chair. He ran it through three times. Then he sent a message to Moscow telling them to get their fingers out.

They needed information on Vologda, and they had to have it soon. Ross was almost ready.

Michael Pitt's message was terse, and the order was unmistakable. If there was any way at all Levin could find out about visitors to the citadel, he was to do it. They had to have the information.

Levin bided his time until the *General Polkovnik* had left for a conference at the Ministry of Defense, then went down to the central registry and asked for the Vologda file. There was a lengthy delay while they checked his credentials. He tried to wait with calm indifference. People drew files all the time. That was what the registry was for, after all, and Levin's security clearance was adequate. But the palms of his hands grew damp.

Finally, the clerk came back and made him sign for it.

The file was bulky. Levin locked it in a briefcase and carried it back to his office.

He flicked quickly through it. There was much that the Americans would have liked, but it would take too long to photograph it all. He found a schedule of visitors to Vologda, and noticed that the *General Polkovnik* was due to make the trip on November 1 to 3. So he could answer all Michael Pitt's questions with one picture.

He carried the file to Stupar's office and opened the bottom drawer, fishing around at the back for the Minox and a film. He placed the file in the center of the desk, as if it was awaiting the attention of the general himself, while he threaded the film and wound it on.

The telephone began ringing in the next room. Levin, taken by surprise, forgot to put the camera and film back into the recess behind the drawer, but ran to the phone, leaving them on the desk.

"Captain Levin?" He recognized the voice: It was one of the KGB security officers assigned to CAD. And the camera . . . on Stupar's desk, beside the file! If anyone should walk in . . .

"Yes, comrade Major."

"You have taken the Vologda file from Central Registry?"

Levin licked his lips. "Yes, comrade."

"For what reason?"

Levin heard himself saying: "The *General Polkovnik* is visiting there in November. It is necessary to acquaint ourselves with any changes made since the last trip and to decide if further recommendations are necessary."

There was a pause. "I see. Very well, comrade Captain. When will the file be returned?"

"I shall bring it down in about an hour."

The connection was broken. Levin replaced the receiver, noticing that the plastic was wet with sweat, and he was trembling. He was out of practice.

Levin went back to Stupar's office and started again. When the camera was loaded and properly adjusted, he photographed the list of names. Then with relief, he removed the film, returned the camera to the drawer and locked it, and put the cassette in the old hiding place among his files.

That done, Levin settled behind his desk to read the Vologda file in earnest. He had to find something to show Stupar to justify him drawing it.

After an hour he felt calmer. He pulled a typewriter toward him and began:

"Vologda base. Recommendations for missile security."

October 10, David Cane's birthday. Ross stared into the mirror. Happy birthday, David Cane, thirty-one years old today. Also fifty-nine, but we won't think about that. Sorry you can't get it up anymore. You used to be able to, no trouble. Remember the Australian woman? Oh hell.

It was not yet dawn. Lyle was still sleeping in the next room.

What had happened to Cane's wife? And his kid?

Cane had come increasingly to dominate Ross's consciousness, second only to his own perceived sexual failure. It wasn't that Ross had tried to sleep with someone since the transplant and had failed. It was that he felt no desire, and expected he would fail if he tried.

On his infrequent weekend passes, he went to Washington and

Elaine came down to see him there. They had separate hotel rooms. He registered as David Ross, the name he had insisted on adopting, and everyone assumed he was Elaine's son.

They treated each other with diffidence and avoided touching. Ross found this suited him. He was conscious that young women looked at him, and he was disturbed by it but not excited. He felt he was a great advertisement, with nothing to sell.

Ross dressed quickly; not in his track suit for the morning work-out but in slacks and blazer. He wasn't going to run around any track with Clive Lyle. Not today.

He signed himself out with the guard at the gate and hitched a ride into town on a truck. He waited until an Avis office opened and rented a car. The DIA had provided him with a complete new set of documents. David Ross. Color of hair: fair. Color of eyes: brown.

He drove fast toward Washington, not really sure what he would do when he got there. He reached the capital in the afternoon and headed automatically through the city for the suburbs. He parked on a tree-lined street and sat quietly behind the wheel. He waited like that for more than an hour. Finally, he got out and began walking.

He knew where he was going. God knows, he had looked at it often enough on the map. Today, his birthday, he just wanted to see what it was really like.

The street was quiet and suburban. The lawns were well-mowed, and the flower beds neatly tended, although at this late time of year there was little to show.

The house was set back off the road, similar to a dozen others. The name on the mailbox said Cane.

Ross's pace slowed and he stared at the house. He was so engrossed he did not notice a small boy detach himself from a group by a hedge at the side and start toward him, uncertainly at first, but picking up speed and finally giving a scream of delight: "Dad! Dad!"

Ross turned in horror and saw the child coming toward him.

Ross ran.

The child faltered and stopped, then turned and raced for the house: "Mom! Mom! My dad's come back! My dad's come back!"

Tears blinded Ross's eyes. God, what had he done? His feet pounded on the sidewalk.

He was conscious of a car braking sharply a few yards ahead and a door opening.

"Get in!"

Lyle.

Ross threw himself weeping into the seat, and the MGB accelerated away.

Lyle's face was a mask of anger. Real anger, not the phony stuff he showed in training when he wanted to push a man beyond his normal limits.

Ross took deep breaths to control himself and slumped down, emotionally drained.

"What the hell were you doing?" Lyle asked grimly.

"I'm sorry, Clive. It was stupid."

"It was unforgivable. It could have compromised Vologda."

"Sorry."

Lyle pulled the car into a lane and stopped. He lit a cigarette.

"Okay," he invited. "Talk. Why did you do it?"

Ross, too exhausted to pretend any longer, confessed his sexual problem and his sense of failure. He hadn't been able to have a child of his own because of his sterility, and now, in his new body, he couldn't even sleep with anyone because of his impotence. He had failed Cane.

Lyle listened in silence, and his anger evaporated.

"It's my fault," he said at last. "If I hadn't been pushing you so hard, I could have been more of a buddy. I might have found out about this earlier and done something to fix it."

"There's nothing you can do," Ross said, defeated.

"Bullshit. You don't have a physical problem, you've got a psychological block. I'm not trained, so I can't pinpoint exactly what it is, but Geoffrey Howlett can, and we're going to see him now."

Ross started to protest, but Lyle silenced him. "I don't want to hear any more about it. You're gonna have a talk with Howlett, and then you and I are going to go on the town and get you straightened out. Seeing you've given yourself a vacation, we might as well take one: tonight anyway. There's not much time."

"Why? What's happened?"

"Vologda," said Lyle. "Word's come through. You leave in four days."

Marine sergeant thomas apple-ton, a couple of corporals, and three diplomats beginning their tours of duty in Moscow passed without trouble through Sheremetyevo Airport immigration and were met routinely by Embassy officers. Routinely the KGB photographed them with cameras in fixed, hidden positions.

Appleton's picture was attached to his dossier, along with the color portrait which, three months earlier, had accompanied his visa application. The dossier had nothing particular to say about Appleton. He was a big man, like a lot of marines. His hair was black, his eyes brown. He was single.

From time to time during his stay in Moscow as an Embassy guard, the KGB would take a special look at him to see if perhaps he was material for recruitment. Otherwise he would be subject to routine surveillance. Russians who worked in and around the marines' quarters would inform on him. At some point when the opportunity arose, a Russian girl might make herself available to him. If he turned her down, a few months later a Russian man would try his luck. Occasionally one of these tactics worked, and the KGB would move in for a closer look.

For six days Sergeant Appleton undertook routine duties. He was invited to three parties. He met and slept with an Embassy secretary, who became the envy of her friends. In the small foreign community, bachelors were scarce, and Appleton was considered quite a catch.

On the seventh day, Appleton was called to the office of Michael Pitt, the Second Secretary, Information. A recording of cocktail party conversation came at them from four speakers, and they sat close to each other, talking in low voices.

"Welcome, Mr. Ross," Pitt said. "You've settled in okay?"

"Yes, thanks."

"Any problems?"

"No."

"Well, we're about ready to go. You have to be in Vologda on November first and out by the third. That's how long your second is going to be there. His name by the way is Captain Filipp Ivanovich Levin, and he's special assistant to Stupar, the boss of the Chief Artillery Directorate. Stupar's going on a tour of inspection of the defensive missile sites, but he's quartered in the citadel. Now you've been given your identity for the mission, haven't you?"

Ross nodded. "Otto Petrovich Suslov, captain, computer department, Ministry of Defense. Married. Three kids—four, two, and eight months old. Etcetera, etcetera. We're sure Suslov hasn't been to Vologda before?"

"Ninety percent sure."

"And none of his friends are going to be waiting there with a big hello?"

"Not as far as we're aware. His record shows he was in Leningrad for a long time. That's where he was trained. He's only been in Moscow over the last year, so he shouldn't have met any of the guys in the citadel. You know how the mafia operates. You've also seen the dossiers on his associates at the Ministry of Defense?"

"Yeah. I've got all that. Suslov isn't GRU, is he?"

"Not as far as we know."

"Or KGB?"

Pitt shook his head. "Don't think so."

"Hope you're right. Okay, tell me about Levin."

"A nice guy. Very Western in some ways. We had a look at him when he was at the Second Kiev Artillery School. He comes from a middle-class background. Grandfather was a White Russian who fought against the Bolsheviks. The family fell on hard times after that, but they kept their standards, if you know what I mean. Made sure the kids knew English and French. Taught them there was a world outside Kiev, and even beyond Moscow. Levin looked like obvious material, but we kept our distance. He was working hard in the system, getting good grades. Then he was sent to the Frunze Academy, and he fell out with the KGB."

"How so?"

"They ran a detailed check on him. Obviously had him marked out for bigger things. His grandfather came to light, and they didn't like that one bit. I was never sure what upset them more: the fact that he had a blood relative who fought in the White Army, or that Levin had managed to hold out on them for so long. I guess it was a combination of the two. Anyway, they laid it on him and told him he was virtually washed up. His career was up shit creek. Levin took it hard. So we moved in and offered an alternative."

Michael Pitt explained about Levin's one lucky break with his patron, Stupar, and his subsequent slow rise up the ladder, then about the arrangement with Jean Buchanan.

"It's going okay, so far. He seems to be a hell of a stud, from what Jean tells me. But we'll be glad when it's finished. Frankly, we're having to hand over a lot of good stuff to the Russians."

"Why not feed them garbage?"

"That was the obvious alternative," Pitt agreed, "but we didn't want to take the chance. A lot of it they can check, and of course we never know whether they've got another mole at any point in our structure who's feeding them genuine stuff. If they found Jean was giving them garbage, they'd terminate the arrangement. At first, we needed Levin for basic information about Vologda, but we need him badly for himself."

"Does he know what he's got to do?"

"No."

"When are we going to tell him?"

"Jean will give him a message before he leaves. He'll be instructed to link up with you in Vologda and follow your orders."

"Will he do it?"

Pitt smiled wryly. "He'd goddam better do it. But I think so, yes."

"If he doesn't, you know the deal's off."

"Yeah, I know. You need two guys working simultaneously."

"That's right. It's Levin, or no Vologda. You haven't got a fallback for me in the citadel?"

Pitt shook his head. "Not really. You know about our contact in the security, of course?"

"Yeah. But he doesn't go underground."

"Not much. He's quartered in Sverdlovsk. I don't think we could rely on him for anything more. Try him in an emergency if you have to. And if you can find him."

"Well, we'd better pray Levin comes through."

"He should. I wouldn't worry too much."

Ross crossed his long legs and sat thoughtfully for a moment. Then he asked: "What's in it for Levin?"

"Defection. I'll tell him that if he cooperates with you, we'll get him out as soon as we can."

"Will we?"

In the silence Michael Pitt grinned wryly. "What the hell do you think, Mr. Ross?"

Ross grimaced. This was Lyle territory and he hated it. They spoke for another few minutes, Ross going in detail over the equipment and documents he would need. Pitt seemed to have everything under control.

Ross was surprised at how calm he felt. It helped that he knew Moscow well and there were no adjustments for him, but even so he was going alone into uncharted waters. If he was captured, Peter Barry had provided him with the means to take his own life, and Yardley had issued the order that he should do so without hesitation.

Ross returned to his duties and, later that night, to the Embassy secretary who cooked him dinner, and then moaned and cried out beneath him just as women had done for Cane, and who made him feel complete.

The last days of October passed.

It is infinitely more difficult for Western intelligence to operate in the Soviet Union than it is for the KGB or GRU *rezidenturas* based in free societies, where they can rent houses and move about at will. It is not, however, impossible, and concerted efforts are saved for special occasions.

The apparatus of a police state can even be turned to advantage. Soviet citizens expect to be spied on, and they assume that anyone with a sufficiently authoritative manner must be obeyed.

If Captain Otto Petrovich Suslov noticed that his movements were being watched in the early winter days, he would have assumed the KGB were making a routine check. If he had anything to be nervous about, he might have suffered mentally. If he did not, he would have paid little attention. Occasional surveillance was such a fact of life as to be unworthy of special mention.

Jean Buchanan passed the final note to Levin in the Volvo three days before he was due to leave for Sverdlovsk, and she could see by his face he didn't like what he read. Before he could destroy the paper, she reached for it and scrawled in pencil: *Don't worry, my darling. After this, you're free.*

And Levin wrote: *If it wasn't for you, I'd refuse.*

He ate the paper while she stroked the inside of his thigh. Gradually Levin's reservations evaporated. Soon he would be in America and they would be married. He loved her, really loved her in a way he'd never imagined possible. When they were apart, he thought of her so much it became a dull ache. When they were together, he couldn't get enough of her company. He was eager, devoted, loving, and very happy.

He drove her home, and they made love on the king-size bed, while from inside the television set a few feet away, the video camera recorded the scene for Colonel Malik and the archives of the KGB's Second Chief Directorate.

Janni seemed preoccupied. She went through the motions of love without conviction, and it occurred to Levin that she was faking her orgasm. But he loved her for that too: To him it was another sign of how much she cared. And when he gripped her fiercely to thrust and cry out, she buried her face against his neck, and he could feel the wetness of tears.

Levin understood. She was worried lest there be danger for him at Vologda. He wanted to reassure her, tell her he would be careful and that he could look after himself, but who knew where the microphones were? He contented himself by whispering, over and over, "It's all right, my darling; it's all right, my love."

He did not see her again before leaving.

On the last night of October, Ross, with the help of Jean Buchanan, washed the black coloring from his hair and eyebrows. Most of it came off easily, but after several soapings it had still not returned to its original fair shade, so she used a blond dye.

Ross packed his suitcases carefully. He checked his identification cards and security credentials. As far as he could tell, they seemed in order.

He was ready shortly after midnight and caught four hours' sleep. Michael Pitt woke him, rapping at the door.

Ross was shaved and dressed in ten minutes, while a tape cassette played nearby, and Pitt gave a final run-through of what they would do. They synchronized their watches.

The night was very black and cold. Ross locked his suitcase in the back of the car and climbed into the passenger seat beside Pitt. He wore a coat over his Russian army uniform. Their breath came in clouds of vapor.

"Good luck," said Pitt.

"You too."

They drove out past the militia guards. The car number would certainly be taken and a check would be made, but they had prepared for that.

At a point between the foreigners' compound and the ambassador's residence, Pitt pulled into the side, behind a black Russian limousine which was waiting, engine running.

Ross transferred his suitcase to the Soviet car, which he and Pitt would take to the apartment building where Captain Suslov was already preparing for departure for Sverdlovsk. The changeover was completed swiftly and without words.

The American car continued to the ambassador's house, with a new driver and passenger.

Pitt and Ross drove quickly through the deserted streets. Suslov's apartment was on the second floor of a block indistinguishable from a dozen others in the area.

Ross led the way. Their footsteps echoed on the stairs, but no one was about. At the top of the second landing, Ross fumbled along the wall for a light switch, and when he could not locate it, Pitt produced a cigarette lighter, and the low yellow flame illuminated a corner of the darkness.

Ross walked briskly along the corridor to the apartment and knocked. Pitt hung back.

After a few moments, there was the sound of a bolt being withdrawn, and the door opened a crack.

"Captain Suslov?" Ross flashed a KGB card and withdrew it before the young officer had time to read it: Not that he would have found anything wrong, but that was the way of the secret police. "KGB. Open up."

The door swung wide. Suslov was blond, about the same age as Ross. He was probably an inch or two shorter, but there the similarities ended. Two suitcases waited nearby.

"Comrade. Is anything wrong?" Suslov looked anxious.

"A routine matter. Some questions. We must ask you to come with us. Bring your cases."

"But I am supposed to go to Sverdlovsk on the early flight," Suslov protested. "A matter of great importance."

"We are aware of that, Captain. The plane will wait for you. Your ticket, please."

Suslov fumbled in his pocket and handed it over. Ross took it and stood aside. Reluctantly, Suslov stepped into the corridor. Pitt led the way down, Suslov after him. Ross stayed long enough to make sure the door remained ajar, then followed.

Ross ordered Suslov into the back of the car before removing his own suitcase from the baggage compartment and replacing it—after a quick inspection of the contents—with the one containing Suslov's personal belongings. The second smaller case was filled with booklets on the IBM 7090 computer, together with the tools necessary for working on the operator's console. Ross kept that back. He checked his watch and felt his heart jolt. Jesus, they were cutting it close.

Inside the car Suslov was watching with ghastly fascination as Pitt prepared an injection ampule, ignoring the stuttered questions from his passenger.

Ross climbed into the back seat behind him. "Do not be alarmed, comrade Captain," he said. "This is only to make our questioning quick and efficient. It will not harm you. You are going for the first time to Vologda base, and these precautions are necessary."

He gripped Suslov's unresisting wrist while Pitt plunged the needle into a vein, and when it was done, Ross got out and shut the door. The car pulled away, with Suslov rigid in the back, wondering if it was all a nightmare, before he slowly slipped sideways.

Ross picked up his own case and Suslov's computer kit and went back up the stairs to the apartment. His feet were loud and echoing, and he felt for the first time completely alone.

He entered the apartment and closed the door. It was very quiet. Ross glanced around Suslov's small, neat living room. The shelves were filled with officially approved volumes, and there were several framed photographs of the captain and his family. Ross inspected them. His wife was a thin, pretty girl with deep clefts around her smiling mouth and dark, merry eyes. The children looked carefree and healthy, and the new baby was fat. Too bad, Ross thought abstractedly.

He was glad Suslov's wife was still asleep. It saved an extra complication.

There was a knock at the door, and Ross opened it immediately. A uniformed Ministry of Defense driver stood in the corridor.

"Captain Suslov?"

"Yes, comrade, good morning. You are in good time, I see."

"You are ready, comrade?"

"I am ready." Ross picked up the smaller case while the driver took the larger one, and they went down to the street.

The car reached the airport in under thirty minutes. There was still no sign of dawn.

According to Levin's information, the only others officially aboard the Sverdlovsk flight were himself and *General Polkovnik* Stupar, neither of whom had met Suslov before. Ross hoped to God he was right.

Ross presented the ticket at the Aeroflot desk, together with his identity papers. They were accepted without question. He checked in the cases and looked around to see if he could identify Levin or Stupar, but it did not seem as if they had arrived yet. A man like Stupar would probably turn up only at the last minute anyway.

Ross went across to a bank of seats and waited for the flight to be called.

He spotted Stupar immediately when he entered Sheremetyevo Airport and quickly picked out Levin too. Stupar seemed amiable, although Ross had no doubt there was steel beneath. Levin was young and good-looking, with an air of quiet authority. He reminded Ross slightly of Clive Lyle. He felt a wave of relief. It wouldn't be too bad working with Levin after all, if first impressions were anything to go by. He looked competent. He didn't seem like a man who lost his nerve easily.

Ross waited while Levin checked in for himself and Stupar and followed them through security and into the departure lounge. Again his papers were accepted without demur.

The flight would be called in ten minutes: enough time to make the initial contact. Stupar was sitting reading an early edition of *Pravda*, and Levin walked to the bathroom, Ross after him.

Two other men were already inside, but it made no difference. "Filipp Ivanovich?" Ross began as soon as Levin had turned away from the urinal.

"Yes."

"Forgive me. I am Otto Petrovich Suslov."

There was a momentary flash of apprehension on Levin's face but it was gone so quickly, Ross wondered whether he had imagined it.

Levin smiled and held out his hand. "Well, comrade, I didn't expect to make your acquaintance so early. You are on the flight to Sverdlovsk?"

"Yes."

They stared, sizing each other up as their hands gripped.

"Things are well with you, Otto Petrovich?"

"Very well. And you?"

"Of course."

Levin liked what he saw. There was something about the American agent, his size perhaps or his self-assured calm, that made him feel better about taking his orders at Vologda. He was a man who could be relied upon. And his Russian seemed excellent. If Levin hadn't been told about him in advance, he would never have guessed.

They walked toward the door together. Outside in the lounge, Levin asked, "How are you getting to the base?"

"I imagine someone will meet me at Sverdlovsk."

"Do you anticipate . . . difficulties?"

Ross looked at him squarely. "No."

"Then I shall no doubt see you at a later time."

"Yes. Until then, Filipp Ivanovich."

The Captain went to rejoin Stupar.

"Who was that you were talking to?" the *General Polkovnik* asked, still reading his paper. He didn't miss much.

Levin explained.

"Do you know him, Filipp Ivanovich?"

"Slightly, comrade General. He seems very agreeable."

"What's he doing at Vologda?"

"I understand he is to install some new computer equipment. I don't know the details."

"Ah." Stupar turned his attention to the sports columns.

The flight to Sverdlovsk left on time, and they climbed east into the dawn. Ross ate breakfast and dozed for an hour, dreaming about how he had become David Cane. If he was careful, thoughtful, and calm, he could crack Vologda as David would have done. This operation would be the memorial for his incredible sacrifice, and while Ross had breath in him, he would try to make it succeed.

The Ilyushin throttled back and its nose dipped toward Sverdlovsk. Snow lay on the Urals, and somewhere down below, among those icy and inhospitable mountains, were the citadel and the key to Western security.

Twenty minutes later the tires screeched briefly against the runway, and the plane settled.

The passengers were held back while Stupar and Levin deplaned, and Ross watched from the window as the *General Polkovnik* saluted and shook hands with a welcoming committee at the foot of the stairs and stepped into a car.

By the time Ross left the aircraft, they were on the other side of the apron, getting into a Sikorsky helicopter for the shuttle to Vologda. Their baggage, retrieved from the hold, was being taken across.

Ross watched, feeling a pang of nervousness. That was the way to do it: eased through security by a formal reception, not going in cold as he was.

He walked to the terminal building, hunching his shoulders against the freezing wind.

"Your papers, comrade." The KGB man in the arrivals lounge was bulky and unsmiling. He took his time inspecting the documents. "So. Captain Suslov." His eyes flickered from the photograph up to Ross's face. Ross looked back, unblinking. The man returned the papers. "Collect your luggage, comrade Captain," he said shortly. "Transport is outside."

"Thank you, comrade." Ross turned away and put distance between himself and the KGB guard. There was no sign of the baggage. They had gotten Stupar's and Levin's out of the hold within minutes, but were taking their time about those that mattered less.

The terminal building was overheated and there was steam on the windows. With a determined effort, Ross stopped himself from pacing anxiously. At last, the conveyor belt clanked into operation and the first suitcases arrived.

When Ross had collected his, he walked out into the icy morning where an old military bus waited.

"Your papers, comrade." Ross produced them again and was motioned aboard. Half a dozen men in uniform were scattered among the hard upholstered seats. The engine was running, sending vibrations down the length of the passenger section. Outside, porters packed luggage into the hold. No one paid any attention to Ross, and he took a seat at the back.

They waited for forty-five minutes until the bus was three-quarters full and it was clear there were no other passengers. Then, with a grinding of gears, they moved off.

They followed the road through Sverdlovsk, past the bleak army barracks, and up into the Urals, winding slowly in first gear, or in second if they were lucky, toward the snowline.

Ross rubbed clear a patch on the window and gazed at the first white dusting on the rocks and bushes, which soon gave way to deep drifts. The sound of the engine drowned out much of the talking, but occasionally laughter carried through to the back.

They drove for nearly four hours before, in response to loud requests from the soldiers, the driver pulled in to the side, and a line of men dismounted to relieve themselves into the snow. Ross joined them.

It was bitterly cold, and steam came from their mouths and rose in wisps where the streams of warm urine drove holes into the thick white snow.

"How long until we reach Vologda?" Ross inquired of the young officer next to him.

There was a shrug. "Another hour, perhaps. Perhaps two."

"Have you made the trip many times?"

"Too often, comrade Captain. This is your first?"

"Yes."

"Well, I'll tell you. It is a pig getting there. It is a pig going through security. It is a pig when you're down, and it is a pig getting out."

Ross laughed. "Is there nothing good underground?"

"Nothing, comrade. Unless you play cards. There's a film twice a week."

Ross zipped his fly and buttoned his coat. He returned to the bus. It was two o'clock. They were clearly going to miss lunch, but should be there in good time for dinner. Ross wondered when he'd get his first chance at the computer. Obviously he wanted to work as quickly as possible, get it over with as soon as he could. But there was also the matter of linking up with Levin and that mightn't be as easy as it sounded. A man like Stupar would be kept away from the lower-ranking officers, and Levin would be by his side. Except at night. The memory maps of Vologda which he and David had studied at Fairfax showed the officers' quarters grouped together in one section of the citadel, and it was most likely he would only be able to make contact with Levin in the early hours of the morning. Providing he could find the right room. He hoped Levin was able to do without sleep.

The bus jerked into motion again, winding on up the narrow road. The view was splendid, but Ross soon grew tired and hungry.

The journey seemed to take forever. Another two hours passed and there was still no sign of the increased security which would indicate they were approaching the citadel.

But at last they hit a roadblock. Four armed soldiers boarded the bus, checking everyone's papers and authorizations to visit the area. They paid no more attention to Ross's than to the other passengers', and he began to relax about his documentation. The DIA seemed as good as they cracked themselves up to be.

His thoughts turned idly back to Washington and Fairfax. His final briefings. He particularly liked Clive Lyle's explanation of what he had to say if he was captured and for some reason was not able to kill himself. "If they torture you and you've got to talk," Lyle urged, "blame it on the CIA. They'll believe that, for sure. Never shit on home base. We'll look after Langley; see they take their medicine like men."

Ross grinned to himself. That goddam Lyle. He was something else.

The armed soldiers left the bus, and the checkpoint barrier was raised to let them through. Ross paid attention to the security precautions and how many men were on duty. Even if he cracked the computer, the DIA would still want to know stuff like that. Intelligence agencies, like nymphomaniacs, had insatiable appetites.

But Ross saw nothing of interest until they reached the second checkpoint, a mile farther on, where another four armed soldiers repeated the document inspection.

In the distance Ross noticed what appeared to be the tops of missile silos and a few bunkers. Occasionally dark figures moved against a dirty gray slush of trampled snow.

Two miles farther on, and the engine died. Vologda. After a moment of silence, boots shuffled on the metal floor as everyone prepared to disembark. Through the window Ross could see armed men but not much else. Yet deep underneath them was the citadel.

They were made to wait in the cold until their luggage had been unloaded. Ross looked around, pretending idle curiosity. They were in a valley, with the snow-covered mountains around. There was a road which disappeared behind a rise. A hundred yards away was an unimpressive concrete blockhouse, covered with snow camouflage to break up its stark outlines. And that was all.

Was this Vologda? If Ross had driven past by himself, he would not have spared the blockhouse ten seconds' thought.

The passengers identified and collected their luggage, and then, under armed guard, began marching toward the entrance: officers and men, it made no difference. Everyone who came on the bus was treated with identical suspicion, presumably until security procedures had been completed.

The line of men began disappearing into the blockhouse, with guards behind every half dozen.

As soon as he entered, Ross found there was a black metal handrail, icy to the touch, and steep stairs down twenty or thirty feet to a well-lit, sparsely furnished room. The walls were reinforced concrete, and there were chairs along the sides. At one end KGB security men sat behind bulletproof glass in enclosed offices, almost as if they were immigration officers who feared contamination from some foreign virus. Lines formed at each of the three windows.

The men placed their security passes, identifications, and authorizations on one side of a metal carrousel, which swung around, taking the documents into the offices and presenting them instead with a numbered disk. Each man then found a seat. It was obviously going to be a long wait.

The armed guards positioned themselves near the security door, which gave access deeper into Vologda, and also beside the entrance stairs to prevent unauthorized departures. Ross noticed that they were alert for trouble.

The men, who had talked almost continuously during the bus journey, now sat silent and morose. Most lit cigarettes, and Ross noticed the smoke was quickly sucked into air vents so none would escape up the stairs to the blockhouse entrance.

After twenty minutes voices began calling over loudspeakers: "Seventeen!" "Twenty-two!"

The men whose disks corresponded with these numbers surrendered them at the windows and recovered their documents and a gate pass. The electronic door clicked open, and they vanished from sight.

The anteroom slowly emptied. Ross waited expectantly for his number to be called.

"Twelve!" "Forty-five!"

Ross's hands were becoming damp. The remaining men sat, smoking.

"Five!" "Thirty-three!"

An hour passed. There were only four of them left. The guards remained alert, treating them as potentially hostile. Ross cleared his throat. Even if the guards hadn't been there, it would be pointless trying to get away. He was committed, and there was no going back. Jesus, imagine getting right to the very gate of Vologda and crapping out!

"Nine!"

Three left. Ross could feel the stares of the guards, wondering why it was taking so long to get their authorizations.

"Thirty-nine!"

Two. Ross looked wryly at the corporal in the chair opposite who was studying his fingernails with detachment, and tried to catch his eye. The man pretended indifference.

"Seven!"

Just me, Ross thought. Jesus, just me. One solitary American agent, unarmed, with orders to fuck up the computer below. Surreptitiously he wiped his hands on his trouser legs and hoped the guards weren't watching. They were, of course. There was nothing else to look at. He wondered if he should engage them in conversation, make a joke to break the tension. But he sat silent, while the minutes stretched out.

At last: "Forty!"

Christ! It was him! Ross was out of his seat like a shot. He placed the metal disk on the carrousel and a pile of papers came back to him.

"Thank you, comrade," he said, scooping them up. His gate pass was on top.

"Comrade captain!" The metallic voice calling him back.

Ross turned. "Yes, comrade?"

"Your suitcases. You've left them behind."

Ross felt the color rise in his face. Shit, what a fool. "Oh! Oh, of course! Thank you, comrade." He collected them. The electronic door clicked open, and Ross walked through.

He was in a second anteroom, almost identical to the first except this was the customs shed. The last stragglers from the bus had unpacked their suitcases and duffel bags, and KGB men were going through everything.

Ross put his suitcases on the counter, and four inspectors came up immediately.

"Open, comrade Captain."

Ross obliged.

"What are these?"

"Tools, comrade. For the computer. I've come to fit new terminals. And instruction manuals."

The men flicked through the books and inspected every implement individually. They left Ross to repack and turned their attention to his personal gear.

He hoped the DIA had made as good a job of supplying genuine Soviet goods and uniforms as they had with the documentation.

Finally, he was given a thorough personal search.

One of the men signed his gate pass and stamped it.

"Thank you, comrade." Ross carried his cases to the next electronic door.

Christ! It still wasn't over. He was in a third anteroom. Almost everyone from the bus had collected there. There was some conversation now and fewer armed guards. Those there were seemed more relaxed.

How long did this security go on? Ross wondered. It was unbelievable. One by one, the men disappeared into a room at the side and did not reappear. It was a long time before Ross's turn came.

There was a desk, a camera, and piles of forms.

"Stand by the wall, comrade Captain." The flash blinded him briefly. A few seconds later two photographs were ejected from the camera. The KGB official cut them up and pasted one on a piece of colored printed cardboard. He wrote beneath it: CAPTAIN O. P. SUSLOV.

"Sign here."

Ross did so, conscious of how dry his mouth had become. The cardboard was placed in a laminating machine, and a Vologda I.D., valid for three days, was handed to him.

Ross studied it. Printed across the top were the magic words: COMPUTER ACCESS.

Ross grinned with relief. "Thank you, comrade," he said. He pinned the badge to his coat, picked up his luggage, and went to the final electronic door.

It clicked open.

He'd done it. He was through.

Immediately ahead was a heavy steel door, which, in the event of a nuclear attack would swing closed to provide the first of several seals against the possibility of a direct hit. Beyond the doors were stairs going down at least twenty feet before opening out into a tiled tunnel. Ross could see there were moving walkways in each direction, and that the tunnel sloped gently farther down into the earth. There was also a central road, which Ross knew from DIA intelligence was used by electric cars, although he could see none in operation.

He stepped onto a walkway and was carried smoothly toward an open concourse perhaps half a mile distant.

As an engineering achievement, Vologda was extraordinary. It must have cost hundreds of billions of rubles, and have taken years to gouge out of solid rock, but it would withstand any weapon the human mind could imagine being invented for the next century. Sixty feet underground would have served well enough for protection in the 1980s, yet Ross must be at that depth already, and he hadn't even reached the elevators, which would carry him 500 feet down. He wondered if the Soviets had discovered a massive natural cavern at that depth in which to construct their citadel. There had to be something to justify the enormous expenditure. But perhaps it was just Moscow planning well ahead.

He was approaching the concourse. There were very few people around, which surprised him. He could see half a dozen armed guards stationed near the elevators, and two men from the bus were waiting for the doors to open. Apart from that, no one.

Three elevators serviced the citadel, and when the first arrived, Ross was surprised at its capacity. It could take thirty men with ease.

They entered with their baggage. The operator pressed a button and the doors closed noiselessly. There was a pause before the elevator began its descent, picking up speed. After a few seconds Ross felt his ears close up, and he swallowed to clear them. Almost immediately they popped again. He was no longer conscious of the rate at which they were falling, but it must have been very fast because when the car slowed down, he felt his knees buckle slightly.

The doors opened. It was almost as if they were stepping into a hotel lobby. It was not luxurious, but plain, functional, and clean. There was a reception desk ahead and somewhat more comfortable seating than had been installed above for those who arrived in busy periods and had to wait.

The desk was staffed by the KGB. Ross was first out of the elevator and first to reach them. He passed over his papers.

"Good evening, comrade Captain."

"Good evening, comrade," Ross replied.

"You have been allocated quarters in Green Block, room Six. I will have you shown to your room."

"Thank you. Is there a key?"

"There are no personal keys here, comrade. Your quarters will remain open at all times. If you have any valuables, or sensitive documents, you are to deposit them at this desk."

"Oh, I see. Of course." He hesitated, wondering whether to push his luck. "I have a friend who arrived today with *General Polkovnik* Stupar. Captain Levin. I wonder if you could tell me how I might locate him?"

The KGB man consulted a list behind the desk. "The comrade Captain is in Red Block, room Eighteen."

It was as easy as that. "Thank you, comrade."

The KGB man signaled for a guide, and Ross carried his cases along several corridors, noting arrows pointing to the Officers' Mess, the movie theater, and one marked "Computers."

Ross's room was small and sparsely furnished, with a bed, a small table, and a chest of drawers. There was also a telephone.

"Where is the bathroom?" Ross asked.

"Turn left out of the door. It's at the end of the corridor on the right."

Ross nodded his thanks. When the man left, he lay on the bed and looked idly around. He had to assume that this room, as well as everywhere in the citadel, was bugged. Levin himself certainly was, but there were ways of taking care of that.

Ross looked at his watch. It was after nine. He hadn't eaten since breakfast on the Ilyushin, and he was very hungry.

He went in search of the Officers' Mess.

There were groups at a few tables who glanced up when he entered, but paid no attention otherwise. The food was substantial in portions, although indifferent in quality, and even Ross, as hungry as he was, could see that it would quickly pall. Still, he felt better when he had finished.

Then he went to locate the computer room. Vologda was meticulously signposted and there was little difficulty. Ross was able to check the visible security as he walked down a long corridor leading to it. There was a sign warning unauthorized personnel that it was a forbidden area, and there was a guardroom. Beyond that was a door and beside it, a window of what was probably bulletproof glass, looking into the room itself.

Ross debated whether to turn back until he saw two armed men observing his approach. He *was* authorized, and to retreat now might rouse their suspicions.

Ross presented himself to them. One checked his badge carefully while the other stood behind him with a Kalashnikov. He was told to empty his pockets. Apart from his identity papers and some money, he had nothing. He put them on a table.

"Spread your legs. Hold out your arms."

Ross did so, and the man gave him a thorough frisking.

"You may enter, comrade Captain."

The KGB guards stood back to watch. This was the final test: whether he knew the code for the security buttons on the entrance door. He would get no help from them. If he made a mistake, an alarm would ring, and the captain would be taken off under guard for an additional security check.

Ross stared at the buttons for a moment. Then he began to stab at them. Five. One. Five. One. Six. Two.

The lock clicked. Thank God for Vladimir Petrovich Metkin and the Pentovar.

Ross stepped into the room. It was air conditioned a couple of degrees lower than the rest of the citadel, with the clean, filtered air that computers require.

The IBM, comfortingly familiar to Ross, was arranged pretty much as he and David had imagined, although the two operators' consoles were farther away from each other.

Three men were on duty, and they stared at the stranger.

"Good evening, comrades," Ross said. "I am Captain Suslov."

They rose as he came over and shook his hand, murmuring introductions. The first was a stocky lieutenant in his mid-twenties, the second, a taller, slender man with glasses. The third was Major Metkin.

It took a second for Ross to recognize him, to make the mental leap from the sleeping face in a hotel bedroom to the alert one watching him now.

But before Metkin said his name, the realization had hit Ross. It was the thickening on the bridge of the nose which gave the first clue —the boxing injury—and then everything else fell instantly into place. The graying hair, the aristocratic, even features. Christ! And Standish Smith!

Ross wondered if he had shown a fleeting second of surprise and confusion because Metkin was looking at him quizzically.

"I have come from Moscow to install the new terminals," Ross explained. "I take it the equipment is ready?"

"Yes, Captain," Metkin replied. "It is in storage here, but we will have it brought in whenever you require it."

"In that case, perhaps I can start in the morning. I am only here for two nights, and I will need all tomorrow for the task."

"Will eight o'clock suit you, comrade Captain?"

"Yes, comrade Major. It will suit me perfectly." Ross gestured to the IBM. "Are you having any problems with the computer?" he asked.

"None," Metkin said. "It was simply decided to update the operators' consoles."

"I see. Well, there should be no difficulty." He wondered if he should mention he would be bringing in an assistant—Levin—at some point, but decided against it. Metkin was senior enough to know that this had not been agreed and would start asking questions which could torpedo everything. He was after all an officer in the GRU. Better simply wait until he was not around, and just walk Levin in.

Metkin was looking at him strangely again, as if he expected Ross to say something. Ross met his eye briefly but glanced away.

And Metkin thought suddenly: *I know this man from somewhere. We have met before.* He puzzled over it while Ivan Ilich Aristov and Igor Viktorovich Mikoyan engaged the visitor in general talk about Moscow and computers. Metkin only half-heard what they had to say, although he listened intently to the big captain's voice, a sound which also seemed familiar.

Metkin checked his watch. It was 2300 and time for him to go to bed. Aristov and Mikoyan would remain on duty until 0600.

Captain Suslov was preparing to take his leave. He would walk with him awhile. Perhaps invite him to his quarters and offer him a vodka? Try to discover where it had been that they first saw each other.

When Ross realized Metkin was planning to go out with him, he felt a faint surge of alarm, but he suppressed it as being ridiculous. The whole point about Pentovar was that the patient remembered nothing when he woke up. He'd tested that out himself.

So when after they passed through the door into the passage and were searched again by the guards, Metkin suggested that the captain join him for a vodka, Ross readily agreed. There was nothing to be lost in trying to establish good relations with the major.

Because of his senior rank, Metkin's room was larger and more comfortable than Ross's, with its own bathroom.

"Sit down, comrade Captain," Metkin invited, pointing to an easy chair.

"Thank you." Ross regarded his host with a frank stare. He was beginning to relax, and the irony of the situation amused him. *The last time I was in your bedroom, comrade Major, you were talking in your sleep about Vologda. Now here I am again, and you're pouring me a vodka. You wouldn't believe me if I told you what had occurred between these two events.*

Ross accepted the tumbler.

"To a successful visit, comrade Captain," Metkin said, raising his glass.

Ross smiled self-consciously at him. "Thank you," he said, and drank. Metkin poured another.

"This is your first time in Vologda, Captain?"

"Yes, comrade Major. It is a remarkable place."

"Better for visitors than for those of us who live here. I myself prefer big cities. Moscow. Leningrad. London. Have you ever been to the West, comrade?"

Ross couldn't remember if Suslov ever had. It wasn't mentioned in any of the briefing papers, so that probably meant not. "I haven't even traveled widely in the motherland," Ross said, "so I do not think I am yet ready to spend my vacations in the West."

"Even if you were permitted to do so," Metkin said flatly.

Ross looked at him curiously. He was getting onto dangerous ground. "Yes," he agreed. "Even if I was permitted."

"The reason I ask is that I *know* I've met you somewhere before, comrade Captain."

Fear prickled down Ross's spine.

"As soon as you walked into the computer room, I said to myself: I know that man. But I couldn't place where it was. I have been thinking, and suddenly I wondered: Perhaps it was in London."

Ross said stiffly: "As I say, I have not been abroad." He swallowed his drink. "Have you traveled much, comrade Major?"

"Not widely. I have visited London several times. I lived there for some years when I was younger."

"Did you like it?"

"Very much."

Ross remembered Standish Smith and the girl he shared with Metkin. Metkin, and whoever else the Russians provided. "Did you find it easy to make friends there, comrade?"

The major looked at him levelly. "Very easy," he said. Then abruptly: "Tell me about yourself, Captain Suslov. Let me see if I can work out where we met."

Ross rehearsed Suslov's history, suggesting perhaps that the comrade Major might have been in Leningrad during part of his training. Metkin ruled that out.

When they parted at about midnight, the major's curiosity had not been satisfied. He lay in bed, conjuring up Ross's face and voice and wondering why it haunted him so. And why there was an unpleasant connotation to the memory which he couldn't pinpoint. He was still thinking about it when he fell asleep.

Back in his quarters, Ross scribbled a note to Levin, saying that he would call for him around midnight the next evening. Then he followed the signs to Red Block. The door to room 18 was closed, and he knocked. There was no reply.

Ross opened it cautiously and looked in. The spill of light from the corridor showed the bed empty. Ross cursed silently and returned to his room. He tried again an hour later. Still no sign of Levin.

Christ, if it was going to be like this tomorrow, it would be a complication. Ross would have to contrive to keep working through the night, so he could justify going out well after midnight to bring in an assistant.

But at 2 A.M., Levin was there. He sat bolt upright when Ross closed the door softly behind him and switched on the light.

"Oh, it's you."

Ross said nothing, merely passed over the scrap of paper. Levin read it and after a second, nodded. Automatically he put it in his mouth and began to chew. Ross grinned. Levin was obviously welltrained.

He gave him the thumbs-up sign and went back to his own room to get some sleep. Tomorrow was the big day.

In his dream Metkin was aware of something in the air. Nothing that smelled, but instead prickled and tasted at the back of the throat. A memory of hospitals. Doctors. Then he heard Suslov's voice: *Vladimir Petrovich!* And the sound of flesh being struck. Captain Suslov was hitting him. It was not at all painful, but the action was unmistakable. *Vladimir Petrovich, can you hear me?* The KGB gorilla, Chersky, undressed for bed, stinking up the hot hotel room with his filthy sweat. He stood naked in front of the mirror, ostentatiously flexing his muscles, while Metkin tried to ignore him, and thought instead of the different smells produced by himself and Standish Smith and the girl. Standish Smith was saying apologetically: "Old boy, I couldn't do that." And he replied softly: "My dear friend, lie beside me. All things are possible among friends." *Com rade Major!* Slap. Another voice: *Not so loud, David.* Speaking English. *Can you hear me?* Speaking Russian. Old boy, I couldn't do that. Do you like it when I do this to you, my dear friend? Standish Smith groaned with pleasure near to pain. Suslov said: *There are some questions you must answer.* He was indignant. Why should I answer your questions? You're only a captain. Slap! *Comrade Major!* Chersky turned to him, scratching his matted chest hair. Perhaps your friend would like me to service the girl instead of you. *Not so loud, David.* Perhaps he would like to see me service you as well. Metkin heard himself saying: "Those who are not dogs are pigs," and Chersky laughed. Two men stared at him: Suslov and an older man. They looked at each other, and Suslov grinned. A special grin: a private joke. The older man spoke: "Vladimir Petrovich, I want you to tell me, precisely and in every detail, the procedure for . . . the procedure for . . ." what? "Old boy, I couldn't do that," said Standish Smith, and the dream dissolved.

Metkin woke, with the nagging feeling of something very wrong. He flicked on his bedroom light and checked the time: 0600. In the citadel there was no sense of day or night, weather or seasons, only of shifts going on duty and coming off at eight hourly intervals, and of weeks measured by movie shows.

While he showered and dressed, he tried to recall his dream. There was a clue in it somewhere, of that he was certain. He concentrated hard, trying to summon it back, but like a mirage it disappeared as he approached. He sighed with frustration.

Metkin, as a senior supervisor, set his own hours, usually much longer than the required shift, and today he was determined to stay around as much as possible. Until he had satisfied himself, he would be Suslov's shadow.

Metkin toyed with the idea of asking the KGB to get further details on the visitor, but that required explaining to them he was acting on a suspicion he could not even pinpoint. If there had been an official GRU presence in the citadel, Metkin would not have hesitated, but he was loath to go to the KGB. They would mock and deride him if there was nothing, and claim full credit if by chance there was a real reason for alarm. Metkin felt it was better if he worked by himself and presented them, if it came to that, with a watertight case.

He picked up his telephone and dialed the reception desk to check the number of Suslov's room. Green Block was a hundred yards away.

Metkin went out into the corridor. Because of the 0600 shift change, there were people about, making their way to their quarters to sleep. He hoped their voices and the noise of their footsteps had not disturbed Suslov.

The door to room 6 was closed. Metkin paused outside it listening, then slowly turned the handle. As the door opened, the wedge-shaped spill of light from the corridor broadened into Ross's room until it touched his sleeping face.

Metkin stared, uncertain. The face *was* familiar: relaxed and at peace now, yet even as he looked at it he felt uneasy.

Metkin closed the door quietly and went for breakfast. Suslov had said he would start work at eight, so he ought to wake within the hour. By that time Metkin would have eaten and be in the computer room. He would watch the comrade Captain with unwavering attention for all of this day, until the installation was completed. Tomorrow Suslov would return to Moscow.

Metkin made arrangements for the new equipment to be brought to the computer room immediately, so there would be no delay when Suslov arrived, and by 0745 the cartons were stacked neatly at the side.

The captain arrived promptly at eight, bringing with him a black case of IBM manuals and tools.

Suslov was surprised to see Metkin. "Good morning, comrade Major. I didn't expect you'd be up this early."

"The same hours as you, Captain."

Suslov smiled in response. He seemed so totally at ease, Metkin wondered if he was not being ridiculous about his suspicions.

The captain checked the cartons of equipment and began unpacking them. He worked slowly but was obviously familiar with the IBM. Methodically he removed the plastic bags and the cardboard and polyurethane packing, and laid the relevant pieces in the correct order for assembly. He did not consult the instruction booklet or the computer manuals.

Metkin sat on the other side of the room, watching. Occasionally Suslov would catch his eye. The first few times the captain either smiled or glanced away, but eventually the scrutiny began to wear him down, and once when their eyes met, it looked as if the color was rising in his face. *Where have I seen you, comrade,* Metkin mused, observing the man work, *and why does it worry me so much?*

The major studied everything Suslov did. He was certainly competent, but it was almost as if he was deliberately stretching the job out. At last, Metkin called over: "You don't seem to be making very good progress, comrade Captain. How long will it take to complete the installation?"

Suslov looked up. "I prefer the slow and sure method, comrade," he replied evenly. "I check every part before I install it. That way there are no mistakes. I shall be in Moscow tomorrow evening, and everything will be working and tested to my satisfaction before I go." He paused. "I am not interfering with your work, am I?"

"No," Metkin conceded reluctantly.

"I will make sure the computer is disconnected for as little time as possible. The more preparation I do now, the shorter that will be."

But Ross, for all the firmness with which he stuck by his position, felt a growing unease which he could not control. He noticed that when he touched a piece of equipment, he now left a damp patch.

That goddam Pentovar. Something had been retained. He and David ought to have been warned when Metkin's eyes opened in the hotel room. They hadn't seemed to focus, but how the hell could anyone tell? Obviously Metkin had seen something, and warning bells were ringing in his head. Would memory return to him in a sudden burst? Would he look at Ross with dawning realization and rise to denounce him, to order his arrest?

Death was so near. It had almost touched him twice already, but he had been snatched away at the last moment, once by David Cane's sacrifice, once because Elaine refused Lyle's offer to take a break. The first was a deliberate act, the other a roll of the dice. Perhaps today would be the third and final confrontation. There would be no escape. If he was discovered, there was a small tooth implanted in the side of his mouth which would snap if he pushed it hard enough. After that, he simply had to swallow it. The capsule it contained would dissolve on contact with gastric juices, and he would die. Peter Barry promised it would be swift and relatively painless. Relative to what? he wondered, conscious of Metkin's eyes on him. Relative to being tortured by the KGB?

He tried to put the thoughts from his mind. He was living on borrowed time anyway, for this specific moment. So much was riding on it, he dared not fail. Dear God, he prayed, look after me this day.

In Moscow the informers who work among the foreigners, and who had something of interest to impart, made their first duty reports by noon. Much was routine and useful only because it helped build up dossiers of political convictions or personal or sexual preferences. In the routine category came the information that Marine Sergeant Appleton, a newcomer to Moscow, had not spent the night in his quarters with the other marines.

The information went to the First Department of the Second Chief Directorate, where a junior officer considered it. He already knew Appleton was having sex with a secretary in the Consular section, so he leafed idly through the papers to see if he had stayed with her. But there was no report on this. The officer put the information on Appleton into a pending tray. The matter would probably be resolved in an hour or two. If not, he would send a man to mobilize the staff involved. Sometimes they were slack and needed to be reminded of their duty.

Ross had lunch before he began connecting the first console. Metkin followed him to the Officers' Mess, not joining him at the table, but sitting on the other side of the room where he could watch. Ross began feeling spooked. His appetite had gone and it was difficult to eat.

Metkin made no pretense about what he was doing. There was nothing surreptitious about his actions. He just observed, casually and openly.

Ross wondered whether in fact Metkin already knew and was just playing a cat-and-mouse game, waiting to see how he proposed reprogramming the computer. The mission could be over already, with just a charade to play out before the KGB moved in and death intervened.

He forced himself to eat most of what was on his plate, but it sat uneasily on his stomach. After a few minutes, Ross pushed back his chair abruptly and walked out of the mess, heading for the bathroom. He locked himself in a stall and threw up his lunch. Cold sweat broke out on his face. After several minutes he flushed the bowl and left the cubicle.

Metkin stood at the basin, pretending to wash his hands. How long had he been there? Jesus, Ross thought savagely, this is too much.

"Are you all right, comrade Captain?" Metkin asked.

"Perfectly, thank you, comrade Major." Ross splashed his face and took a drink of water from the cooler. He could see in the mirror how pale he had become. *Get a grip on yourself. David Cane wouldn't act like this.*

He tossed the paper cup into the bin and walked out, back to the computer room. Behind him he could hear the door open and close, and Metkin's footsteps, following.

The woman who cleaned the apartment of the Consular department secretary was indignant at the suggestion that she had failed to report the overnight presence of Marine Sergeant Appleton. As far as she could tell, she said, the man had not been there at all. As evidence, she cited the contents of the garbage can. Where were the beer cans? she asked rhetorically. Did the sergeant drink Coca-Cola? And where was he in the morning when she arrived? The girl was there, sitting down for breakfast, yes, but she was by herself. The maid opened the apartment and took the KGB man through to the bedroom. She wrenched back the covers, exposing the sheets. They had been put on fresh the night before, she said. See, they were wrinkled. They had been slept in. But could the comrade point out any stains? He could not because there were none. Yet if he had seen the sheets she had taken to the laundry the day before, ah, that was a different matter indeed. Or the ones before that. But not last night, not Sergeant Appleton.

The KGB man reported back to the junior officer. It was becoming puzzling. Had Appleton found another girl? Had he been working?

The officer made contact with an Embassy informant who had access to staff rosters. Appleton had not been on duty the previous night, but he was down for duty that day.

It was still a mystery. The officer ran one final check. He called in a colleague whose American accent was very good and had him phone the Embassy to speak to Appleton. The colleague did so, giving his name as Jim Clark. He was passed between four departments. Finally, they said Appleton was not available.

The junior officer collected what documents he had and went to knock on the door of Colonel Malik, head of the First Department. It was becoming a matter for more senior men, perhaps another section of the KGB.

It took Ross the whole afternoon to connect and test the first console. Metkin never moved. He went to the bathroom when Ross went and took tea when Ross did. He sat and watched.

Halfway through the afternoon, Ross called over, "Do you remember when it was we met, comrade Major?"

Metkin replied flatly: "No."

Ross said: "I think you have made a mistake. You are remembering someone else."

"Perhaps."

At 6 P.M. Ross decided to take a break. He went back to his room and lay on the bed. He felt exhausted. It was a nightmare. The constant presence of Metkin, the unwavering stare—not hostile exactly, just watching, alert—was wearing him down. Ross's palms had stopped sweating, but he felt detached and very alone.

He turned off the light and the room went black. That was one good thing about life 500 feet underground. It was night whenever you decided it was night. He closed his eyes and tried to relax. Just as he felt himself drifting into sleep, Ross heard a sound at the door. His eyes opened, but he lay motionless. A wedge of light from the corridor spread into the room, a silhouette at the entrance.

Metkin.

Ross said quietly: "Come in, comrade Major."

The door closed and the room was again dark. Ross wasn't sure whether Metkin was in or out until he felt the man's weight on the edge of the bed. He moved over to make room.

Metkin pulled a pack of cigarettes from his pocket. "Do you smoke?" he asked.

"No thank you, comrade."

A match flared, and Ross studied Metkin's face by it. He wished he knew what the hell was going on and what he ought to do. He could always kill Metkin: It would be easy enough.

But what about the body? And how to avoid suspicion falling on him and his work on the computer?

Ross lay relaxed, waiting for Metkin to make whatever move he wanted. The flame of the cigarette glowed in the darkness.

"Are you married, comrade Captain?" Metkin asked at last.

"Yes, comrade."

"You have children?"

"Yes, three. And you?"

"No. I am not married."

Was that it? Was Metkin making a pass? Ross said nothing. The silence grew, neither companionable nor hostile. Just a silence.

When the major finished his cigarette, he dropped it on the floor and stood on it. He left the room without a word.

Ross stayed where he was, not wanting to sleep any longer. He stared into the darkness. What would Cane have done in a case like that? Or Lyle? What had Lyle told him in the briefings? There was a lot he didn't know and probably never would learn.

He turned on the light and waited until his eyes had adjusted. Time to get back to work, he thought.

He presented himself to the armed guards outside the computer room and was searched as thoroughly as ever.

Through the bulletproof glass, he could see Metkin, waiting.

Colonel Malik ordered the word be sent to every KGB employee in Moscow to look out for Sergeant Appleton. He didn't like Americans disappearing. Copies of his photograph were run off and circulated. No one was to apprehend the sergeant, merely to report where he was.

A telephone call was made to the marines—Jim Clark wanting to talk to Tom Appleton—but he was not there. Jim said he'd call back later, and no, he didn't want to leave a message.

Malik's eyes were cold and his expression impenetrable.

Every vehicle that entered the foreigners' compound was stopped and its occupants scrutinized. Taxis were ordered to pull to the side of the road, and policemen and soldiers peered in. One Scandinavian who looked vaguely like Appleton was asked to produce his papers, and was then waved on brusquely.

Word passed quickly around the foreign community that something was up.

Michael Pitt was stopped as he entered the compound. He rolled down the window and asked, "Are you looking for someone? Can I help at all?"

But there was no reply, and he was waved on.

As he locked his car and took the elevator to his apartment, Pitt decided to look on the bright side of things. If the KGB were hunting for Ross in Moscow, that could only mean they hadn't found him at Vologda.

Ross connected the second console and was finished before ten o'clock. He reached a decision. Ignoring Metkin wasn't serving to send him away. Perhaps if he tried to be friendly, it would do the trick. There wasn't anything to lose.

"Would you care to join me for dinner, comrade Major?" Ross asked.

Metkin raised an eyebrow. "Yes, comrade Captain. Thank you."

Metkin waited while Ross was searched by the guard, and Ross loitered until the major had been cleared. They strolled together to the Officers' Mess.

Ross did his best to be charming and encourage Metkin to talk, but through it all there was the feeling of time running out. The computer had to be cracked tonight, the first and last chance. Ross could never return to Vologda.

Metkin spoke about his youth in Moscow and the changes there had been in the city. Ross questioned him about his military training, and whether his broken nose was a boxing injury. Cane had been right. Metkin had once been the middle-weight champion at the Leningrad Artillery Academy.

They spoke until 10:30, and it seemed as if the barriers were being lowered. Metkin invited him to his room for a vodka, but Ross, anxious to keep his head clear for later, said he would prefer going to bed.

Metkin walked with him right to his door.

"Good night, comrade Major," Ross said, offering his hand.

"Good night, comrade Captain."

Ross went and lay on his bed with the light out. Levin would probably not be back in his room for another two hours at least, but although there was time for a short sleep, there was too much adrenaline pumping around Ross's body for him to relax. He stared into the blackness, rehearsing the computer program, stage by stage, and the point at which he would have to call a password to Levin so the Russian could punch in the appropriate authorization code on the other terminal within the required ten seconds, to prevent the alarm sounding. Even though Levin had never operated a computer keyboard before, there ought to be no problem, providing he kept his head.

A sound at his door again. The handle turned. Jesus, it was unbelievable. Metkin again! Ross cursed himself for not getting undressed and under the sheets. At least he would have been able to pretend he was asleep! Now Metkin would know he was lying there, waiting for something.

The door closed again, and after a few seconds, he felt the weight of the other man on the edge of the bed and an arm brushed his chest.

"You are not undressed," Metkin observed.

"No."

"Why is this?"

"I was lying, thinking."

"I see. Is the installation complete?"

"Yes, I need only to make a final test."

"When will you do that?" Metkin lit a cigarette.

"I haven't decided. Tomorrow morning, perhaps." There was a long pause. Finally, Ross asked: "May I speak frankly, comrade Major?"

"Yes, of course."

"Why are you in my room again? Do you want to come to bed with me?"

There was a long silence. Metkin drew on his cigarette, and the glow illuminated his face. "No," he said at last. "That is not why I am here. I am drawn . . . I don't know by what. I know you, Captain Suslov. We have met. I can't tell you where, or under what circumstances, but I think they were not pleasant. I thought perhaps you would tell me."

"No, comrade. You are mistaken. We have not met before. I should have remembered. You are thinking of someone else."

"Yes, perhaps." Metkin did not sound convinced. He stood up. "I will let you sleep."

"Yes," Ross said.

"Good night."

"Good night, comrade."

Two hours passed.

Ross rose from his bed and, without turning on the light, walked to the door and opened it cautiously. He almost expected Metkin to be waiting on the other side. If he was he would have to kill him. But the corridor was deserted.

Ross made his way to Red Block and pushed open the door to room 18 without knocking. Levin was awake, fully clothed on the bed. Ross put his index finger to his lips for silence and returned quickly to his own room. From his suitcase he collected a pair of shoes and a complete change of clothes for Levin. He carefully ripped the lining of the jacket along a seam of the shoulder and extracted a laminated I.D. card for Vologda. He compared it with his own: It was an excellent job. The words COMPUTER ACCESS were printed across the top. Levin's face stared seriously from the photograph.

Ross carried the bundle to Red Block. As soon as he saw the clothes, Levin began to strip. Not a word passed between the men. It would not be safe to talk until every item which might contain a bug had been discarded.

The uniform fitted perfectly, and the shoes seemed fine. Michael Pitt had done a great job. Ross wondered if he'd ever get the chance to tell him.

When Levin was ready, he led him to the Officers' Mess to discuss what was required this night.

Ross judged that while the bedrooms might be monitored, it would be more difficult picking up conversations in the mess, where conspirators would scarcely be expected to gather.

He and Levin ordered tea and chose a table as far away as possible from the handful of other officers present. Ross outlined what Levin was to do, stressing the need for accuracy and speed. On the signal "I'm almost ready," Levin was to press three carriage returns, eight space bars, and three carriage returns. It had to be completed within ten seconds. He made Levin tap it out on the tabletop, to get used to the rhythm and the speed necessary. No need to rush, he said, just be deliberate and there would be no problem. But be sure. If Levin's finger touched a wrong key, the alarm would be triggered and they would both die.

Levin understood. When they finished their tea, Ross took him through the plan once more.

He rose. "Shall we go?"

Levin nodded. They went to Ross's quarters to collect the small suitcase and headed for the computer room.

As they turned into the final corridor leading to the entrance, Ross faltered and stopped, a sickness in his throat.

Standing at the door, his back to them, was Metkin, arms outstretched, being searched. Ross turned and walked back, Levin behind him. Ross cursed under his breath. Goddam Metkin. Goddam fucking Metkin. He should have killed him earlier when he had the chance.

But was Metkin being searched going in or coming out? Ross stopped at the end of the next corridor and waited to see.

Levin asked quietly: "What's the matter?"

"Trouble," he said. "Someone's there. Go to my room. I'll join you in a couple of minutes."

Levin's footsteps faded into the distance. Ross waited, positioning himself at a corner so that if Metkin emerged, he could step back and, with luck, avoid being seen.

One minute passed, two. If Metkin was coming out, the search would be over by now. Ross forced himself to wait another sixty seconds, then he walked along the passage which bisected the corridor leading to the computers. As he crossed the junction, he glanced left toward the guardhouse.

Metkin had gone. He was inside the computer room.

Ross felt tears of anger and frustration sting his eyes, and his fists were clenched so tight the knuckles showed white. It was nearly 3 A.M. He couldn't afford to wait much longer. And he couldn't do anything while Metkin was inside. There was no way he could bring in Levin, and if he didn't have Levin, he wouldn't be able to cross the fail-safe obstacle and get to a point in the program where he could give new instructions. It was like a game of chess, with his king hemmed in on all sides. Checkmate. The end of Vologda. Sorry, David, it was all for nothing. Oh Jesus! Sorry, David. So very, very sorry.

Ross walked down the corridors. There was sweat on his face and hands. He told himself: Calm down, for Christ's sake, calm down. Try to think. Try to plan. First problem: how to get Metkin out of the way. Lure him out. Get him into your bedroom. Shit, you weren't able to *keep* him out earlier. Kill him. Take Levin in to the computer room and do the job.

But what about the body? The questions, investigations? The interrogation? Once he swallowed Peter Barry's suicide capsule, they would know he was an enemy agent, and they would also know he'd been working on the computer. No, Metkin had to live.

Problem: how to lure Metkin from the computer room and keep him out of the way while Levin and Ross did their work. Hit him on the head? No, when he recovered, he'd know what had happened. Hell, he was a GRU major. The end result would be the same: interrogation, death, discovery.

Lure Metkin away and keep him clear by setting up a diversion? Yes, but what sort of diversion, and set by whom? Levin could do something. Light a fire. Jesus, yes! Light a fire in Metkin's goddam room! That would keep him occupied. Long enough to give them a chance to reprogram? Ross estimated he would need twenty minutes. But then Levin would be outside the computer room. Would he have time to get back in? Would he remember the combination of the security door at the entrance?

Ross stopped and leaned against a wall. If only he didn't need Levin to overcome the fail-safe. If only he could use those other two men on duty, Aristov and Mikoyan, without them knowing what was going on . . . but that was impossible. They'd routinely be watching him work. Basic security. There was always someone to keep an eye on the man at the computer keyboard. On the other hand, he would have disconnected the visual display unit, so there'd be nothing for them to see on the screen. But he couldn't say, "Listen, when I say GO, I want you to punch three carriage returns, eight space bars, and three carriage returns, and you've got to do it in ten seconds."

He had to use Levin.

But . . . Christ, of course! Although there was a ten-second deadline for the fail-safe code, there was no time limit on any of the other stages! So if Ross, on the operator's keyboard, punched in everything except, say, the final digit *before* the fail-safe stage, and then went across to the supervisor's keyboard, it would only be necessary for one of the others to press that single digit and he'd be in position to punch in the code himself! He didn't even need Levin!

Ross expelled lungfuls of air in relief. That's what they'd do. Levin wouldn't come into the computer room at all. He would just stage the diversion, get a decent fire going, and head back for his room. Ross would phone word to the computer room that would bring Metkin rushing to see what had happened.

Ross walked quickly back to his room. Levin was sitting on the edge of the bed. He seemed calm and composed; Ross hadn't been wrong about him. He took back the forged ID card and motioned him into the corridor. They walked up and down while the new plan was explained. Levin didn't like it much, but if he got clear as soon as the fire was going, there ought to be no particular danger. The corridors were virtually deserted. They agreed on the timing and synchronized watches.

The two men stared at each other. Ross held out his hand, and Levin grasped it.

"Good luck, my friend," Ross said.

Levin nodded and turned on his heel. Ross watched him until he rounded the corner, out of sight.

Dear God, we need a break. Help us tonight.

Levin bought a box of matches in the Officers' Mess and scooped up old copies of *Pravda* and *Izvestiya* from one of the tables. He walked toward Metkin's room.

He knocked cautiously on the door. When there was no reply, he opened it. Empty. He turned on the light and looked around.

Metkin was a smoker. There were butts and ashes in the ceramic ashtray. At least that was in their favor. The major could easily have left a cigarette burning there, a carelessly placed newspaper, just touching the edge—and . . . fire.

Levin selected one of the longer butts and smoothed it straight. That would have to do. And on the floor he spotted some cellophane from the wrapping! Just the sort of thing to flare up. It was getting better and better.

He checked his watch. In four minutes he would have to start the fire. In six Suslov would phone the computer room and tell them. That gave him one minute to make sure the fire was burning well, and at least one minute to get clear.

Levin began to construct his fire: the cellophane next to the edge of *Pravda,* then other pages crumpled and bunched around to provide a good air supply for the flames. He became engrossed in his task.

Major Metkin also looked at his watch. It was ridiculous. He was tired. He couldn't remember where he had met Suslov, and it didn't seem important anymore. Aristov and Mikoyan were on duty in the computer room, the KGB were outside. Nothing could happen. Suslov would probably make his final check in the morning, and if he snatched a few hours' sleep now, he could be back on duty to oversee it.

Metkin rose. "I'm going to my room," he announced. "Call me there if you need me."

"Yes, comrade Major."

"Good night, comrade Major."

Metkin let himself out and wearily submitted to the routine search.

Aristov glanced wryly at his friend. "What's the matter with Metkin?"

Mikoyan shrugged. "He's having trouble sleeping. So am I. He needs a woman. So do I."

Aristov laughed. "You wouldn't know what to do with a woman."

Metkin walked slowly down the corridor to his room. Should he look in on Suslov? No, it was becoming absurd.

He thought he smelled smoke. A pipe perhaps, or a cigar. He stopped at his door and turned the handle. The light was on, the air was hazy. And the shocked face of an officer stared at him, lit by the spreading flames from burning newspapers.

Metkin drew a startled, disbelieving breath: Huh? And the next moment the man charged into him, knocking him sideways so that he cracked his head on the doorway, and raced up the corridor.

Metkin began to shout. "Help!" His voice echoed through the deserted passageways. He ran indecisively a few yards forward, then back. What should he do? Try to catch the arsonist or put out the fire? The man had reached the end and darted out of sight.

"HELP! FIRE!"

Doors opened. Men emerged, half-asleep and bewildered. Footsteps ran toward him. Distant commands were yelled.

The noise carried easily into Green Block. Ross heard it with a sinking, sickening sensation. But he had to go on. He couldn't stop.

He picked up the phone to call the computer room. The exchange did not answer.

Ross threw the receiver impatiently back onto the cradle and took a deep breath.

He headed for the computer.

Filipp Ivanovich Levin ran in panic, not sure whether he was being followed. He had been seen! He would be identified! Blindly he took the wrong turn. The room that should have been his was occupied by someone else, a young man, who jerked upright in bed and stared dumbly at the white-faced, panting officer standing over him. Levin turned and fled.

He could hear the echoes of shouting behind him. He was no longer sure where he was. He turned right, and right again, around a corner, until suddenly he smashed head on into a guard coming in the other direction. The breath grunted from Levin's body, and his skull cracked painfully against the other man's head, and they both fell to the floor.

Levin touched metal. His hand closed. He struggled to his feet, a little ahead of the guard. He was hardly aware that each had a grip on a Kalashnikov. The guard cursed through clenched teeth. Levin saw the rifle and knew he had to get it away. If he ran he would be shot. He pulled and the guard resisted. They tussled briefly. Levin tried to twist the Kalashnikov from the man's grasp, and he saw the guard's fingers buckle.

The world seemed to explode. His head jerked back at the noise and his ears were deafened. And then the guard was no longer trying to take the rifle, but went limp and began toppling to the floor with open, uncomprehending eyes. Blood poured down his face.

Levin heard himself sob. He wrenched the rifle away and began to run. Run, but where?

Men were stepping into the corridor, naked, unarmed, wearing pajamas. He raced past them. Others were shouting, coming after him. He turned left.

He heard a cry of anguish without realizing he was making it. He was in a dead end.

He ran as far as he could, whirling around, his back to the wall. At the other end of the corridor, a group had paused, staring at him, uncertain what to do. Then they ducked away out of sight.

Levin looked frantically around. A bathroom! He raced to the door and almost fell inside.

It was empty, clean, white-tiled, and cool. Water bubbled down the urinals.

Levin caught sight of his reflection in the mirror. His face was wild with desperation.

He walked to the far end of the bathroom and sat with his back to the cool tiles. He waited, breath heaving.

The guards weren't interested in letting Ross into the computer room, not with the shouts and the burst of rifle fire echoing through the corridors. Ross became very angry until reluctantly they searched him. He punched the buttons on the security lock and passed through.

"What's happening, Captain?" Aristov asked.

Ross shrugged. "Sounds like someone had too much to drink. Where's the comrade Major?"

"Gone to bed."

"Oh, I see. Well, I'm back to Moscow in the morning. I thought I'd run a final check on the terminals before I went."

"It's a bit late for that, isn't it?"

"Not really," Ross said calmly. "I worked until I couldn't concentrate properly anymore. You know what swine these things can be sometimes? I thought I'd get a few hours' sleep and come back with a clear head."

Ross went across to the operator's console and began removing the cover. He disconnected the VDU so that the screen would remain blank.

He tinkered with a screwdriver for a couple of minutes until Aristov and Mikoyan had settled back in their seats and were paying scant attention. As far as they were concerned, the console was out of action.

Ross pressed the button to bring the computer on-line. He visualized the display. The computer would print a question mark.

?

Who are you?

Ross typed in an operator's name: Mikoyan/I.V. and his number: 2876/44.

The computer would demand:—PASSWORD.

Ross typed VOSTOK.

Again the computer would ask:—PASSWORD.

Ross typed SPECIAL COLLECTION.

On the screen in his mind, the IBM cleared him into the system, printing up the date and time.

Ross's mouth went dry. He left the keyboard and crouched below, apparently concerned with wiring.

After a moment he began again, slowly, cautiously. The computer language was FORTRAN. He punched the codes.

He crouched again, glancing back to see what Aristov and Mikoyan were doing, whether they were suspicious, but only Mikoyan was watching him idly. Aristov was reading a magazine.

Ross stood up. Now ALGOL, right through to that critical point where the fail-safe mechanism operated. Ross knew the program was being displayed automatically on the supervisor's VDU, but that screen faced away from the view of the men.

His fingers punched through the program.

He reached the last line: 87.955.020. One digit to go: a five.

Ross's stomach had knotted to the point of nausea. He strained to hear what was happening outside, but now there was silence. Had Levin gotten away? Had he been captured? Was he telling the KGB everything he knew because four of them were holding him down while someone twisted and squeezed his balls?

I mustn't think of that, Ross told himself. Levin's gotten clear. No one suspects. Just do your job. Don't worry about anything else.

He walked over to the supervisor's console. There was the program, looking good.

He removed the cover and disconnected the VDU, just in case one of the men came to see what he was doing. And yes, here came Mikoyan, strolling over to check.

Ross pretended to study the wiring.

Now was the moment.

He said: "Comrade, would you do me a favor?"

"Certainly, comrade Captain."

"Go over to the other keyboard and punch the figure five. Just punch it once, that's all. It's a routine check."

"Just five?"

"Yes. If you wouldn't mind."

Ross prayed: nothing else, please, comrade. Just the five, and just do it once. Or I'm dead.

Mikoyan adjusted his glasses and walked to the other console.

"Tell me when you've done it," Ross called.

He stood and watched Mikoyan approach the keyboard and glance down at it, an unfamiliar sight without its covering, the wires, rods, and levers exposed. Mikoyan's finger went out.

"Just once," Ross reminded him. "The figure five."

Mikoyan pressed. "I've done it."

Ross's hand darted down. Three carriage returns, one . . . two . . . three, eight space bars, one . . . two . . . three . . . four . . . five . . . six . . . seven . . . eight, three carriage returns, one . . . two . . . three.

Ross froze, waiting for the shrill of the alarm and the guards to burst in with orders to kill anyone who hadn't thrown himself face down on the floor.

Silence.

He heard Mikoyan say: "Is that all?"

Ross found it difficult to speak. He tried but the only sound he made was a croak. He nodded and smiled. Finally, he said: "Thank you, that's fine. Just a test."

He returned to the operator's console, and Mikoyan made way for him. Ross pretended to study the wiring.

"You've really got to know what you're doing with this thing," Mikoyan said.

Ross grinned weakly and waited for him to return to his seat. Mikoyan was in no hurry, but at last he went back.

Ross punched the final code. Then it was time to insert the new instructions. He had rehearsed it so often, it was almost second nature.

He instructed the computer to keep secret the new section except to those who, at this point in the program, punched in the password, a series of ten zeroes.

Then Ross inserted the new section. Translated into layman's language, it ordered all the land-based missiles of the Soviet Union to deviate from their targets one minute after launching and to assume an upward trajectory for an additional three minutes before self-destructing.

For this instruction to be overridden, the operator at his console had to punch in the words DAVID CANE R.I.P.

Ross pressed a button. In a microsecond the onboard computers of every Russian missile connected to Vologda received, and accepted, the new program.

Ross glanced round and noticed Mikoyan staring. He was spending too much time at the keyboard. He crouched again to toy with the wiring. Three minutes passed.

One final thing: another instruction, ensuring that every other missile that came under the Vologda computer in the future would automatically receive the abort program. When the target coordinates were fed in, it would slip in simultaneously.

And it was done.

Ross logged himself out.

BYE, he typed.

BYE, replied the computer and went off-line.

Ross rewired the VDU and replaced the cover. He did the same on the supervisor's console.

He felt drained and elated and terrified. What had happened to Levin? Even though he had completed his task, everything could still end in discovery and disaster.

"I've finished now, comrades," Ross said. "Everything seems to be working well. Would you like to check it yourselves?"

He waited while Mikoyan and Aristov tested the consoles. It took five minutes.

He shook their hands and left. Both of them noticed how wet his palms were.

The guards checked Ross one final time, and he walked away to Red Block to find out what had happened. Levin's room was empty.

A small knot of dread formed in the pit of Ross's stomach. He didn't know what to do. He ought to go past Metkin's room and see what had happened there. Perhaps Levin had been shot and killed. It was inevitable anyway. If the Russians didn't kill him, the Americans would. Levin knew too much. His dream of defection was nothing more than that: a dream. Ross had to concede the force of Michael Pitt's argument that it was impossible to allow a Russian, whose own family would be vitally threatened, to possess the knowledge that an American agent had doctored the Vologda computer. The information might be safe for a while, but what if Levin had a second change of heart? What if he was haunted by thoughts that his own family, abandoned in the Soviet Union, would die in a nuclear holocaust? What if he decided to restore the status quo?

Ross returned to his room and dropped off the small suitcase. If

Metkin saw him it would be better he did not know he had been at the computer again.

The door to Metkin's room was closed, and there were no signs of damage or bloodstains to indicate someone had been shot. A few people were still around.

Ross asked: "What's happening, comrade?"

"Someone's gone mad. He's got a gun in one of the bathrooms."

Jesus. Levin. It had to be Levin. God knew where he had got the weapon.

"Who is he?" Ross asked.

"I don't know."

"Which bathroom?"

The man pointed along a corridor. Ross began walking. Soon he could hear the sound of voices, and as he rounded a corner he saw armed KGB guards looking down a corridor. There were senior officers with them. One was the *General Polkovnik* Stupar, gray-faced and worried.

"Get back, comrade Captain. This isn't a circus," a KGB officer snapped at him.

Ross stood his ground. "What's happening? Who is he?"

"A man called Levin. Get back to your room."

"Levin!" Ross let his voice rise, playing for time. "I know a Levin."

He could see other officers looking around, and he heard Stupar say, "I think that man is a friend of his."

Ross plunged on: "I can't believe it. Has he gone mad?"

"He killed a guard."

Ross's eyes widened. Jesus, that was what the shooting was about. "Oh no," he said softly.

Stupar called him over. "You're a friend of Levin's?"

"Not a friend exactly, comrade General. We know each other slightly."

"You spoke to him at the airport in Moscow, didn't you? How did he seem to you? Unbalanced?"

Ross shook his head emphatically. "No, comrade. He seemed perfectly normal."

"That's what I thought. Levin was caught trying to start a fire in the citadel, and then he shot a guard."

"That is . . . terrible. Where is he?"

"In the bathroom at the end. He is armed with an Kalishnikov."

Ross took a breath. "With your permission, comrade General, may

I approach him? If he recognizes me, perhaps I can persuade him to give himself up. He needs treatment."

A KGB officer snapped: "He needs to be shot."

Stupar looked at him speculatively. "You don't understand, comrade Captain," he said. "Levin is dangerous."

"I could speak to him through the door," Ross suggested. "If it was unsafe, I would not go in."

"He might take you hostage."

"I can't believe he would," Ross said. "We know each other. This is a tragic situation. I'm sure it can be resolved without further violence. Let me at least try, comrade General."

Stupar glanced at the KGB officers around him. Then he said: "Let him try."

"Thank you," Ross said simply.

He began walking down the corridor. He could feel their eyes on him.

When he reached the end, he stopped and called out: "Filipp Ivanovich! This is your friend, Otto Petrovich Suslov! Don't shoot! I'm coming in!"

Ross pushed open the door.

At the end of the corridor, the KGB waited for the explosion of rifle fire, but there was silence.

Levin sat against the far wall of the bathroom, the Kalashnikov across his lap. His face was exhausted, and even from that distance, Ross could see his mouth trembling.

Ross squatted near the door and stared at him with compassion. For several seconds the men looked at each other wordlessly.

Then Levin said simply: "It is over."

Ross nodded. "Yes."

"For you too?"

"No. Not for me."

"For me."

"Yes."

Levin lifted a hand to rub his eyes, and Ross could see how badly it shook. There was a long silence.

"You are a brave man, Filipp Ivanovich," Ross said. "I salute you."

Levin tried to grin. Then he asked. "What will happen?"

"That depends on you." Ross paused. "The KGB will come in here in a few minutes. If they capture you, they will torture you and afterward they will kill you. When you talk—as you will—they will torture me and kill me also."

Levin said distractedly: "Metkin came back early. He walked in and saw me."

Ross said nothing, wishing Levin's terrible trembling would stop.

Levin said: "I am a dead man."

"Yes."

Levin began to weep. "Tell Janni . . . you must speak to her. I love her. You must tell her that."

"I will tell her. I will tell her you died bravely. A soldier of freedom."

Outside in the corridor, Ross heard a noise. The KGB were closing in.

He whispered urgently: "There is not much time, Filipp Ivanovich! They are coming! They are outside!"

Levin tried to pull himself together. His movements were slow, as if he was forcing his body, with enormous effort, into action. He turned the Kalashnikov toward himself, staring at it as if it was a strange, inexplicable instrument and he was trying to work out how to use it.

Another noise from the corridor.

"Quickly!" Ross hissed. He opened his mouth and indicated with his fingers that Levin should put the muzzle into it. Levin's eyes met his, pleading, but after a second his face bent forward until his lips covered the black metal. Slowly his hands slipped down the barrel to the stock. His fingers fumbled for the trigger. Their eyes met, Ross's lips moved. *God bless you.*

The explosion was deafening in the echoing bathroom. Blood gushed back onto the white tiles. Ross jerked with shock at the noise, and when he looked again, the life had gone out of Levin's eyes and he was toppling sideways.

The bathroom door burst open, and a KGB squad poured in. Ross squatted where he was, eyes closed in exhaustion. He felt hands lift him up.

Ross mumbled: "I tried to stop him. He wouldn't listen. I tried to stop him."

Stupar's voice: "You did well, comrade Captain. And bravely. I congratulate you."

Ross looked at him. "The poor man. His mind . . . it had gone."

"What did he say to you, comrade?"

"He didn't make much sense. He was speaking about a girl, over and over again. He wanted to marry her, but he could not. I don't know who she was. He did not explain."

After a pause, Stupar nodded. "I know who," he said.

The KGB gathered around the fallen body of Filipp Ivanovich Levin, searching the pockets, while the blood spread over the tiled floor.

Ross was routinely questioned about his acquaintance with Levin, but it was accepted the man must have had a nervous breakdown. There could be no other explanation. Later Stupar offered Ross a ride to Sverdlovsk Airport in the VIP helicopter shuttle. There was a spare seat.

As the helicopter rose from the pad near the camouflaged bunker, Ross looked down on the seemingly innocent stretch of snow-covered valley, and soon they were flying over the white peaks of the Urals.

Ross was also invited to sit with the *General Polkovnik* on the Iluyshin which took them to Moscow. He felt exhausted and numb, and there was an unpleasant taste in his mouth.

It wasn't as it had been at the end of the London assignment, when he and Cane were pumping adrenaline and there were euphoria and a sense of accomplishment. Perhaps those would come later when he had rested. Perhaps he didn't believe he would still be able to get out of Russia. Perhaps he felt he didn't have much longer to live.

He thought wearily: *We did it, David, you and I. It was not without bloodshed as we planned, but it is done.*

The wheels thumped onto the runway at Sheremetyevo Airport.

Stupar insisted on dropping Ross back at the apartment building where Captain Suslov's wife would be awaiting her husband's return. Darkness had fallen. He saluted the *General Polkovnik* and shook his hand, then turned and walked into the entrance of the apartment building where he waited until the limousine had moved away and turned the corner.

A man watched him curiously, but he paid no attention.

Ross picked up his suitcases and walked toward a Metro. In the concourse he stood in line for a telephone and dialed a number. After three rings he replaced the receiver. He dialed another number. He hung up after three rings.

He took the Metro for two stops. Outside on the street, he had to wait no more than five minutes before the car halted in front of him. He loaded the suitcases into the trunk and climbed in the back.

The car sped off.

There was a large box beside him. He opened it and found it contained a pair of Western trousers and a Western coat. He put these on and folded the military clothes into the box together with his hat. He raised the collar of the jacket to cover his army shirt.

The car pulled over to the side of the road. Ross got out and fetched from the trunk the suitcase containing his clothes. He left the other behind.

He walked fifty yards around a corner, where Michael Pitt's Chevy was waiting. Three men got out—Captain Suslov and two escorts—and moved toward him. They passed without a word and rounded the corner to enter the Soviet car. Suslov looked pale and dazed, an automaton.

Ross climbed in beside Pitt, who pulled away immediately, heading for the foreigners' compound.

"There's a flap on about you," Pitt said tersely. "The KGB have put out an alert. We're going to say you were ill and our doctors suspected something infectious, so they kept you in quarantine for a couple of days. Is that okay?"

"Yes."

"But you're clear and feeling fine." Pitt glanced at him. "How did it go?" he asked cautiously.

"Levin's dead."

A silence. "KGB?"

"No. He shot himself."

"I don't understand. What about the computer?"

"It's done," said Ross. "All fixed. Finished."

Pitt stared at him in disbelief. "Really?" His face began to break into a smile. "You really did it?"

"I really did it."

Pitt gave a whoop of glee, and his left hand smacked hard onto Ross's thigh. Pitt roared with laughter and triumph. He sang: "Fuck me! Fuck me! I can't believe it! That's fucking fantastic! Oh my God!"

"Shit! Watch where you're driving, Michael!"

With difficulty Pitt switched his concentration to the road, still grinning fit to split his mouth. "Jesus, you incredible sonofabitch! I never thought you'd get away with it! I thought you were a goner, for sure!"

They drove past the militia guard and went up to Jean Buchanan's apartment.

Ross told them what had happened, how Levin had died, and what he had said in the bathroom at Vologda. Ross felt surprised and a little cheated when Jean didn't cry. She listened seriously, in silence, and then she nodded.

Later she dyed his hair and eyebrows for him so that Marine Sergeant Thomas Appleton could reappear.

She did not mention Levin again.

Captain Suslov, in his dazed state, saw that he was being taken home. He recognized the streets, the apartments. Once he even saw a friend crossing the road.

For two days he had been kept in a bare, windowless room. He was asked questions, stupid, basic questions that the KGB should have known. The food was good, although he was not hungry. And now he was being taken home. He had missed going to Vologda. It was all so senseless.

The car pulled in beside his apartment building. He started to get out, but they pulled him back. He couldn't understand that. One of them fetched his suitcases from the trunk and put them on the sidewalk.

The man got back into the car, took his arm, and jerked up his sleeve. Suslov tried to wrench away. Another injection! What was going on!

The needle pierced his skin, entered a vein. He stared at the syringe. It was dark, and he couldn't see much. The man pushed the plunger. It hurt as the air bubbled in.

The door opened. He was pushed out.

"I don't understand," Suslov protested, standing on the sidewalk.

The door slammed and the car moved away. Suslov picked up his suitcases, feeling the pain in his arm. He walked into the building.

The air reached his heart and stopped it before he got to the second floor. His fingers raked his chest in agony as he tumbled down onto the landing.

ROSS TOOK A SUITE IN THE WASHING-
ton Hilton, had a long, hot bath, and changed his clothes. He phoned
Clive Lyle and told him where he was.

Lyle was jubilant, but couldn't understand why Ross hadn't been
on the plane he was scheduled to catch. He said he'd be along in
twenty minutes.

Ross opened the door to him, feeling calm and totally in control.

Lyle punched him on the arm and hugged him. "You magnificent
bastard!" he cried. "It was terrific. I couldn't have done it better
myself."

But Ross did not respond. At last, Lyle stepped back and looked at
him, puzzled. "What's up, Martin?"

"The name's David."

"Sorry. What's up?"

"Take a seat." Lyle sat on a plush sofa, Ross in an armchair. "We
had a deal once, you and I."

"Yeah. That's right." Lyle became serious.

"We had it because I felt I could trust you. You wouldn't bullshit
me. You'd keep your word."

Lyle nodded. "So?"

"So, I've been thinking. I went into the Vologda operation partly because I was told it would be bloodless. Things changed. David Cane died. Levin died. Suslov died. We'll leave Cane out of this. But if Levin hadn't killed himself, we'd have done it for him. We killed Suslov. Both of them knew too much for Vologda to stay secure. And that leaves me."

He reached into his pocket and brought out a flat package. He tossed it onto the coffee table between them. Lyle knew immediately what it was: a sterilized syringe.

Ross undid his shirt cuff and pulled up the sleeve.

"I've been doing a lot of thinking," he said. "I know the sort of shits you are because I know the sort of shit you tried to make me. And I think the word's out to kill me. That way, Vologda stays in the family. There's no security risk."

Lyle listened quietly.

"Now, I'm not criticizing you. I understand the thinking behind that," Ross said. "It makes sense. But I don't want to wait around for you, Clive, or someone like you, to come along in your own time and do it. I want to go like a man, when I choose. So, what I'm saying is, here I am, Clive. And there's the needle. I'm asking you to do it now. As a favor for a friend."

He held out his arm.

Clive Lyle took a breath. He neither denied nor protested. He merely said: "I have no orders at this stage. I can't do it."

Ross replied: "Then go and get your orders, Clive. Go and see Yardley now. I'll wait for you to get back."

Lyle left without a word. Ross stared out of the window at the buildings of Washington and the traffic below.

An hour passed, two. Ross didn't mind. It was all the same to him now. He'd cheated death twice, he'd cracked Vologda—the most important thing a man could ever do for his country—and he wasn't afraid.

There was a knock on the door. He let Lyle in.

"Sit down, David," Lyle said.

Ross sat.

"I saw Yardley. I told him what you said. We discussed it at length. No decision had been made on sanctioning you, but Yardley agreed the idea had merit. He called it a noble offer."

Ross shrugged. "Then do it, Clive."

Lyle pulled a pack of cigarettes from his pocket and took his time lighting one. "He turned it down."

Ross looked at him in surprise. "What do you mean?"

"We don't want you dead, David. We want you alive. There's a risk, sure. But it's the same risk with me, with Michael Pitt, with your wife, for Christ's sake, and with a couple of dozen others. We're all DIA people except you and Elaine. We could sanction her, and we could sanction you. But as Yardley said, what would that make us? We don't have any doubts about either of your loyalties. We'd be no better than the fucking Russians, and goddam it, we are better. But I am authorized to make you an offer. There's a place with us if you want it. Cane left a gap. You can fill it. You're only half-trained, but we can fix that easy enough. If you'd like to join, the job's yours. The money's not great, but it's not bad."

"And if I refuse?"

Lyle exhaled a cloud of smoke. "It's a free country. You can help us fight to keep it free, or you can go and do your own thing. Naturally we'll keep a pretty close watch on what you do, who you see, but we will anyway, whatever happens. It's up to you."

Ross thought about it. It would be the final commitment. He'd have to become like Clive Lyle: a killer, amoral, untrustworthy. But like David Cane as well.

"What do you say?" Lyle asked.

Ross rolled down his sleeve and buttoned his cuff.

Acknowledgments

I should like to thank Dr. Harold Hillman, Reader in Physiology at the University of Surrey, England, for his help and advice, and for introducing me to the pioneering work in brain transplantation done by Dr. Robert J. White, Dr. Maurice S. Albin, and others at the Department of Neurosurgery, Cleveland Metropolitan General Hospital, Ohio.

I am grateful too for the advice of Anthony Tucker, Science Editor of *The Guardian,* London.

Any errors are my own.

Nerve glue does not yet exist. But Dr. Geoffrey Raisman at the National Institute for Medical Research, Mill Hill, London, is heading a team studying whether the environment of the neural pathway is the factor determining if damaged nerve cells regenerate. There are strong suggestions that this is so.

Thanks also to Marcia Gauger, the New Delhi bureau chief of *Time* magazine, for putting me right on a number of things, and to colleagues and acquaintances whom I pumped for information, often without them knowing why.

And to my wife, Nonie, who read the manuscript and gave me many helpful and constructive editing suggestions.

New Delhi
March, 1981